WiZKiT

An Adventure Overdue

Tanya J. Scott

atheneum

ATHENEUM BOOKS FOR YOUNG READERS

NEW YORK   LONDON   TORONTO   SYDNEY   NEW DELHI

ATHENEUM BOOKS FOR YOUNG READERS

An imprint of Simon & Schuster Children's Publishing Division

1230 Avenue of the Americas, New York, New York 10020

For information about special discounts for bulk purchases, please contact Simon &
Schuster Special Sales at 1-866-506-1949 or business@simonandschuster.com.

The Simon & Schuster Speakers Bureau can bring authors to your live event. For more
information or to book an event, contact the Simon & Schuster Speakers Bureau at
1-866-248-3049 or visit our website at www.simonspeakers.com.

The text for this book was set in Little Boy Blue.

The illustrations for this book were rendered digitally.

Manufactured in China

1122 SCP

First Edition

10 9 8 7 6 5 4 3 2 1

Library of Congress Cataloging-in-Publication Data

Names: Scott, Tanya J, author.

Title: Wizkit / Tanya J. Scott.

Description: First edition. | New York : Atheneum Books for Young Readers, [2023] |
Audience: Ages 8–12. | Audience: Grades 4–6. | Summary: Wizkit, a one-eyed cat
who is the Wizard's apprentice, does not like exploring, but when an overdue library
book cries out to be returned, Wizkit sets off with the annoyingly optimistic Book
on an adventure back to the library.

Identifiers: LCCN 2022008527 | ISBN 9781665900829 (paperback) |
ISBN 9781665900836 (hardcover) | ISBN 9781665900843 (ebook)

Subjects: CYAC: Graphic novels. | Cats—Fiction. | Magic—Fiction. | Adventure and
adventurers—Fiction. | Books—Fiction. | LCGFT: Graphic novels.

Classification: LCC PZ7.3.S4135 Wi 2023 | DDC 741.5/973—
dc23/eng/20220729

LC record available at https://lccn.loc.gov/2022008527

For my mum, dad, and sister
(plus Belle, Teasel, and Kalia—our family cats)

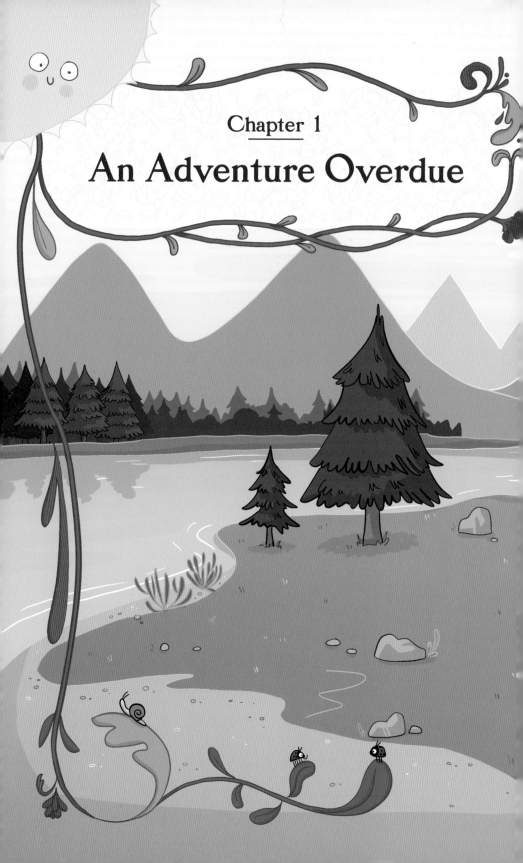

Chapter 1

An Adventure Overdue

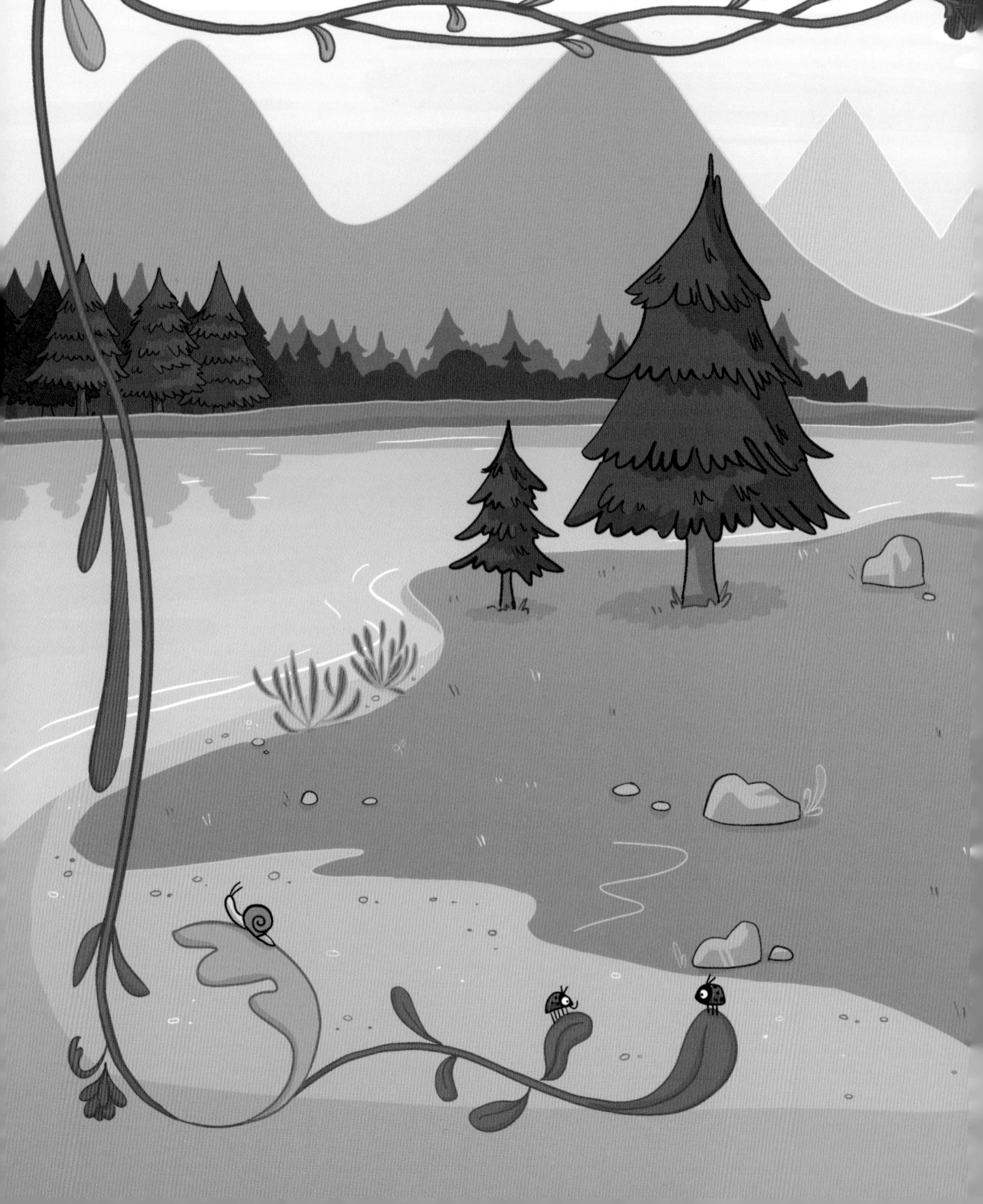

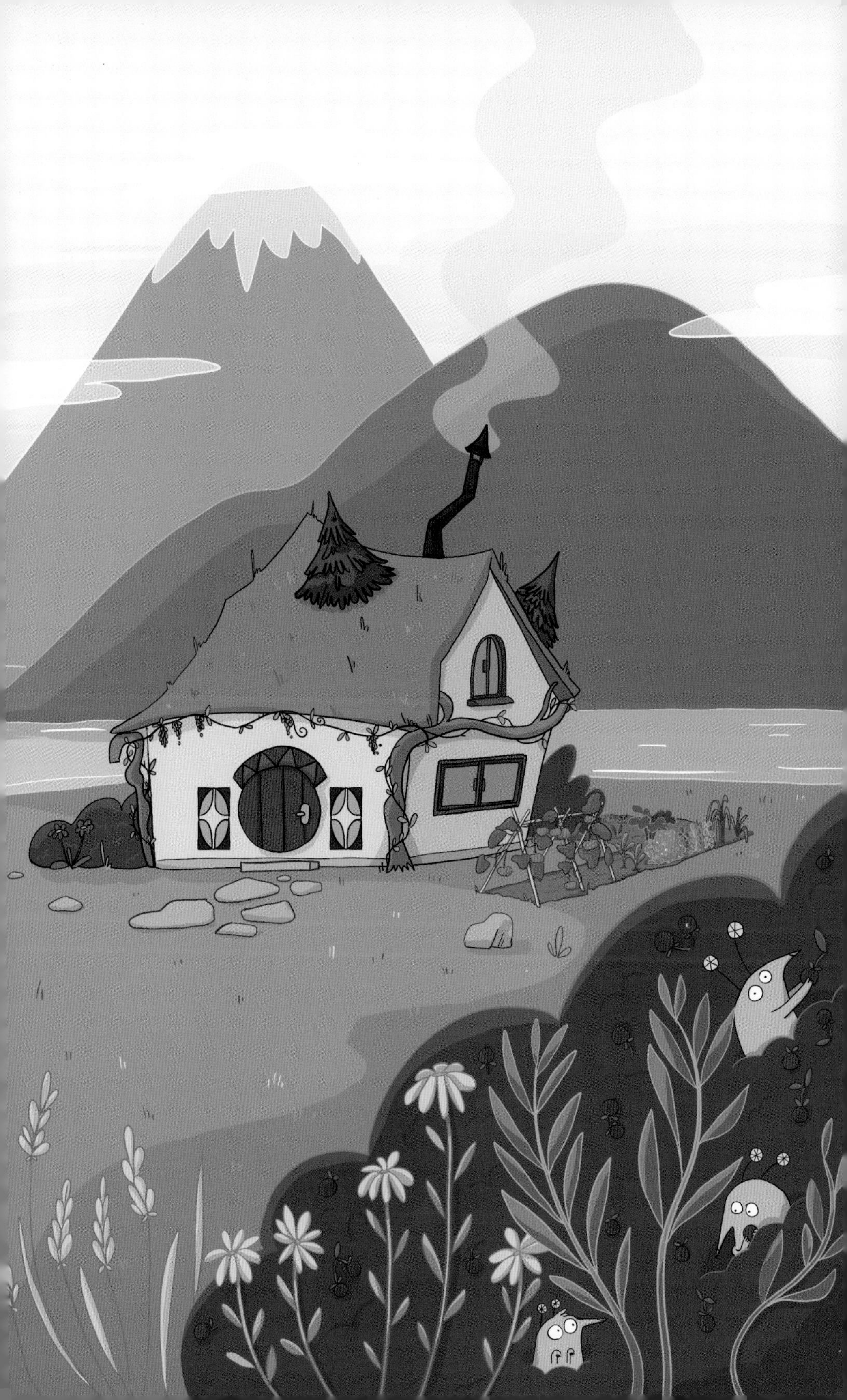

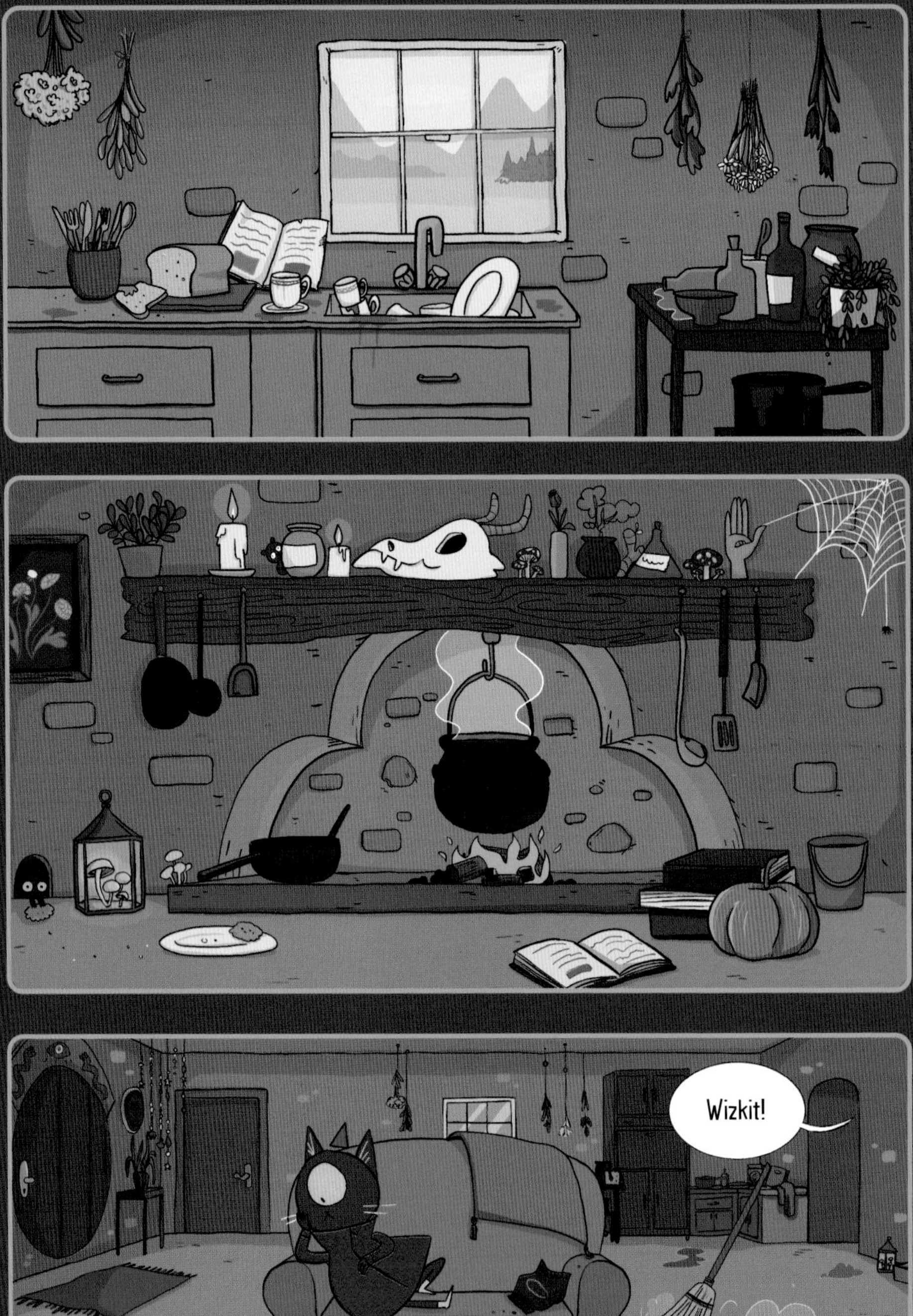
Wizkit!

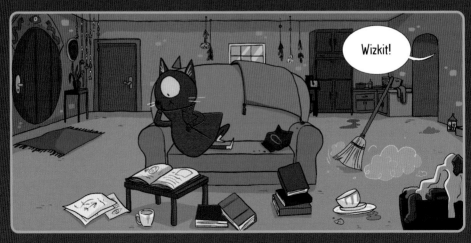

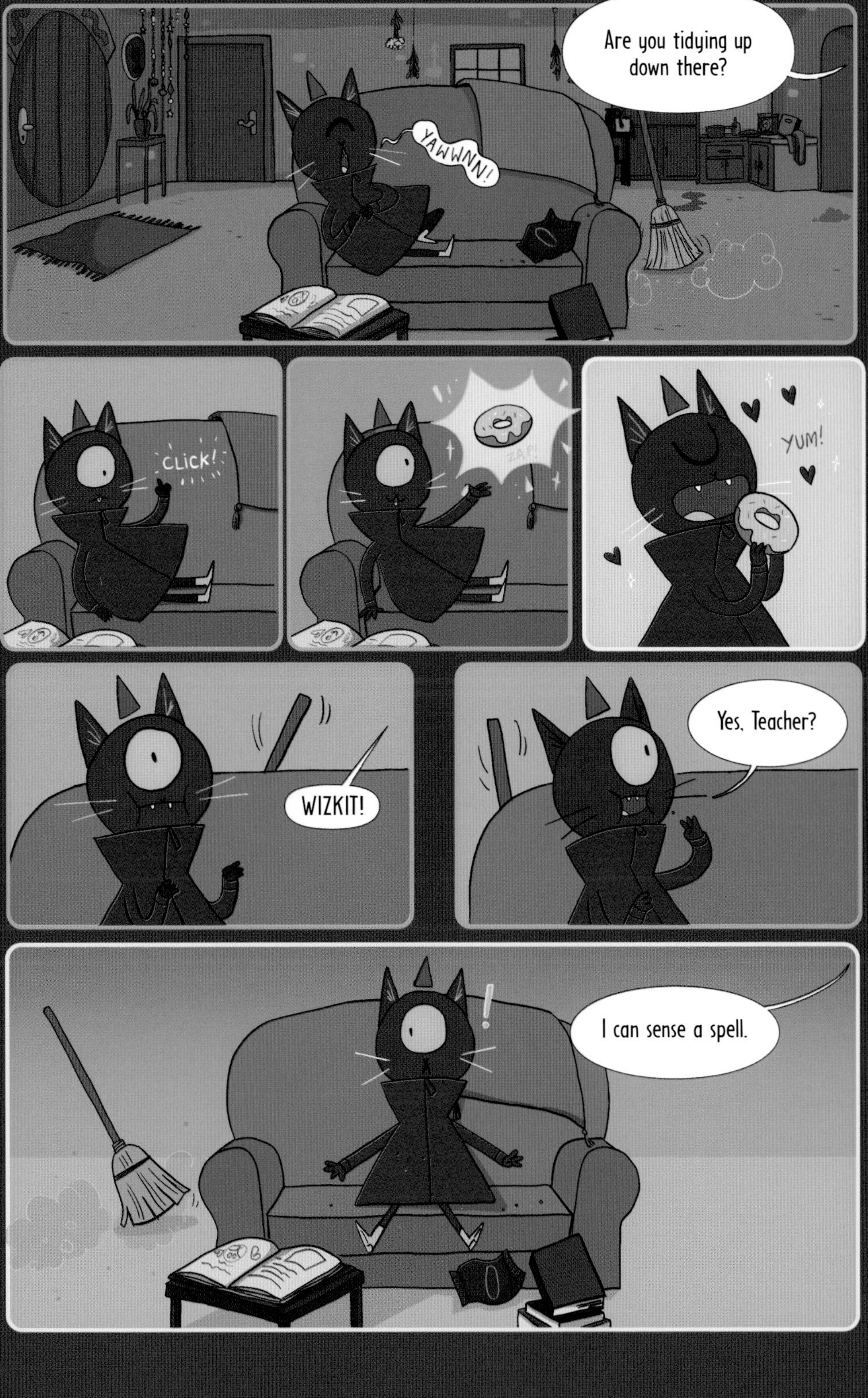
Are you tidying up down there?
YAWWNN!
CLICK!
YUM!
WIZKIT!
Yes, Teacher?
I can sense a spell.

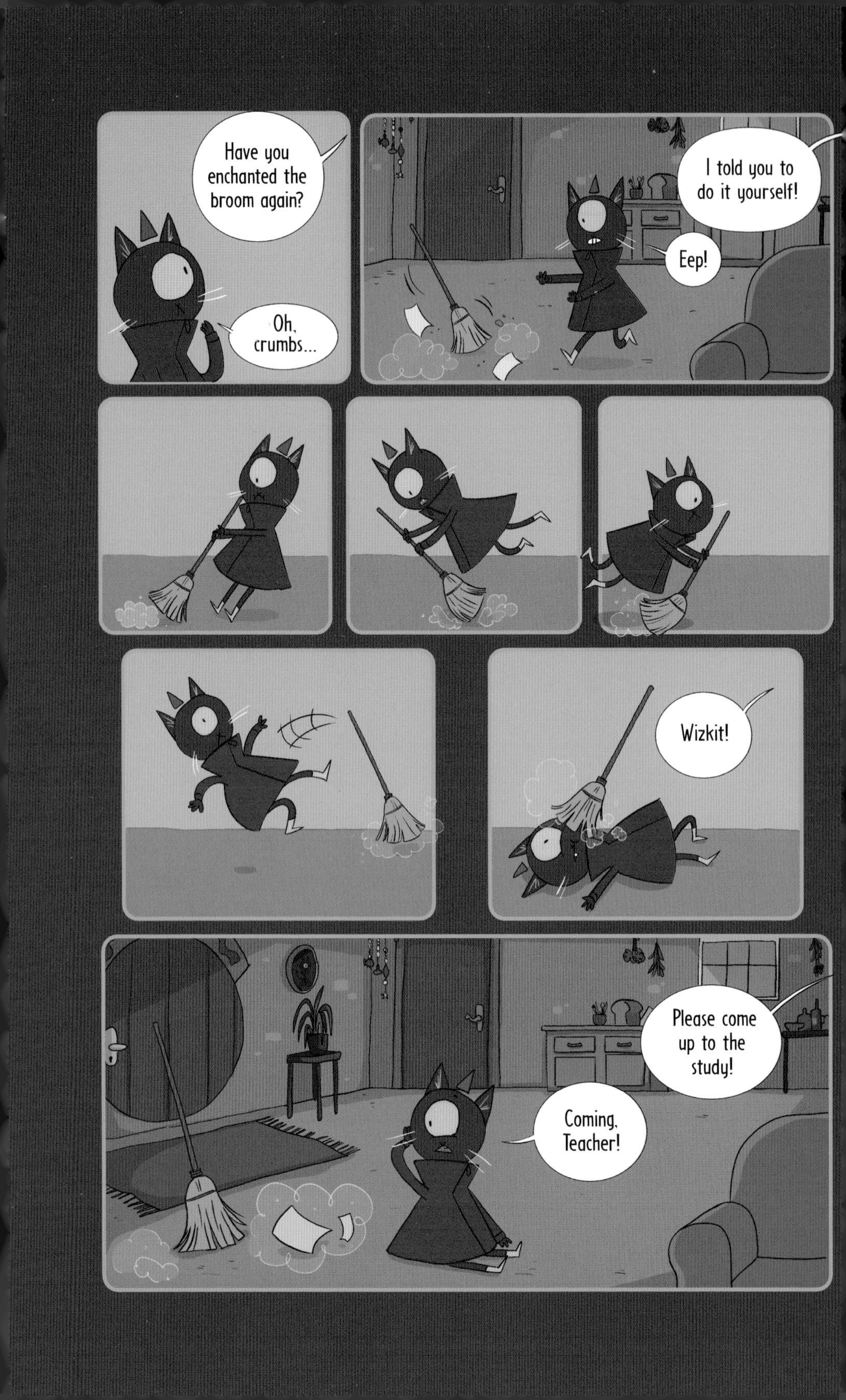

Have you enchanted the broom again?
Oh, crumbs...
I told you to do it yourself!
Eep!
Wizkit!
Please come up to the study!
Coming, Teacher!

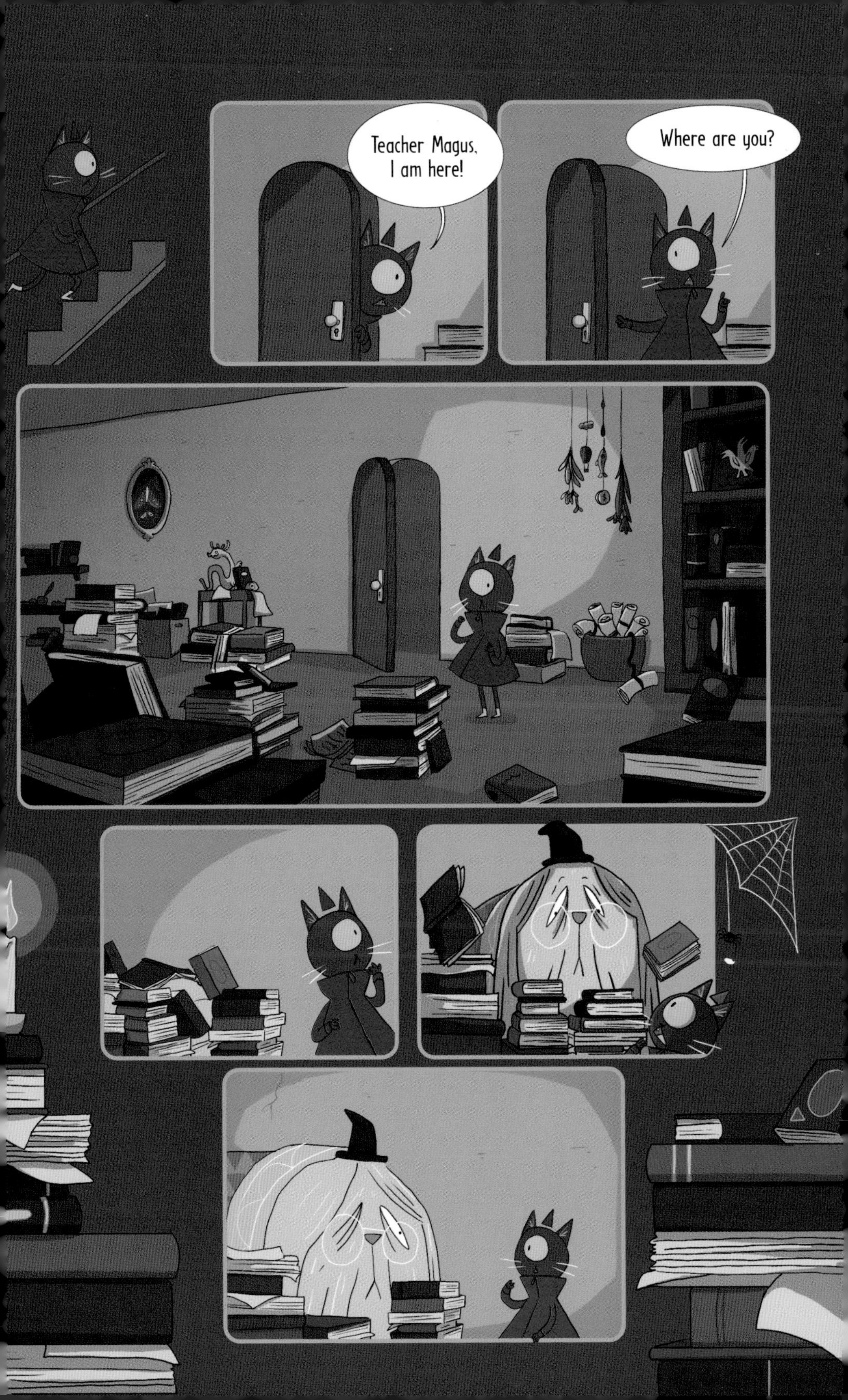
Teacher Magus,
I am here!
Where are you?

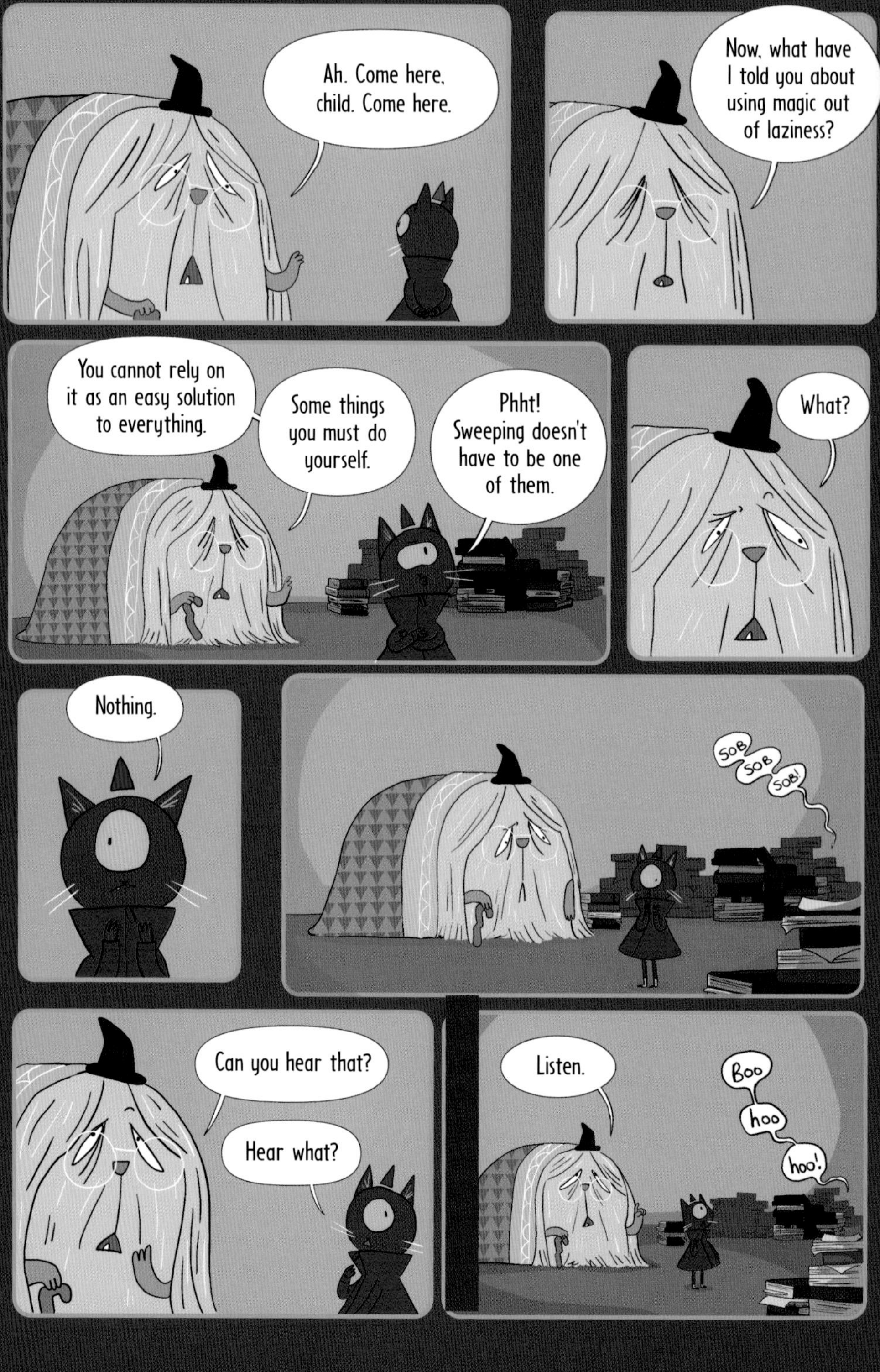

Ah. Come here, child. Come here.
Now, what have I told you about using magic out of laziness?
You cannot rely on it as an easy solution to everything.
Some things you must do yourself.
Phht! Sweeping doesn't have to be one of them.
What?
Nothing.
SOB SOB SOB!
Can you hear that?
Hear what?
Listen.
Boo hoo hoo!

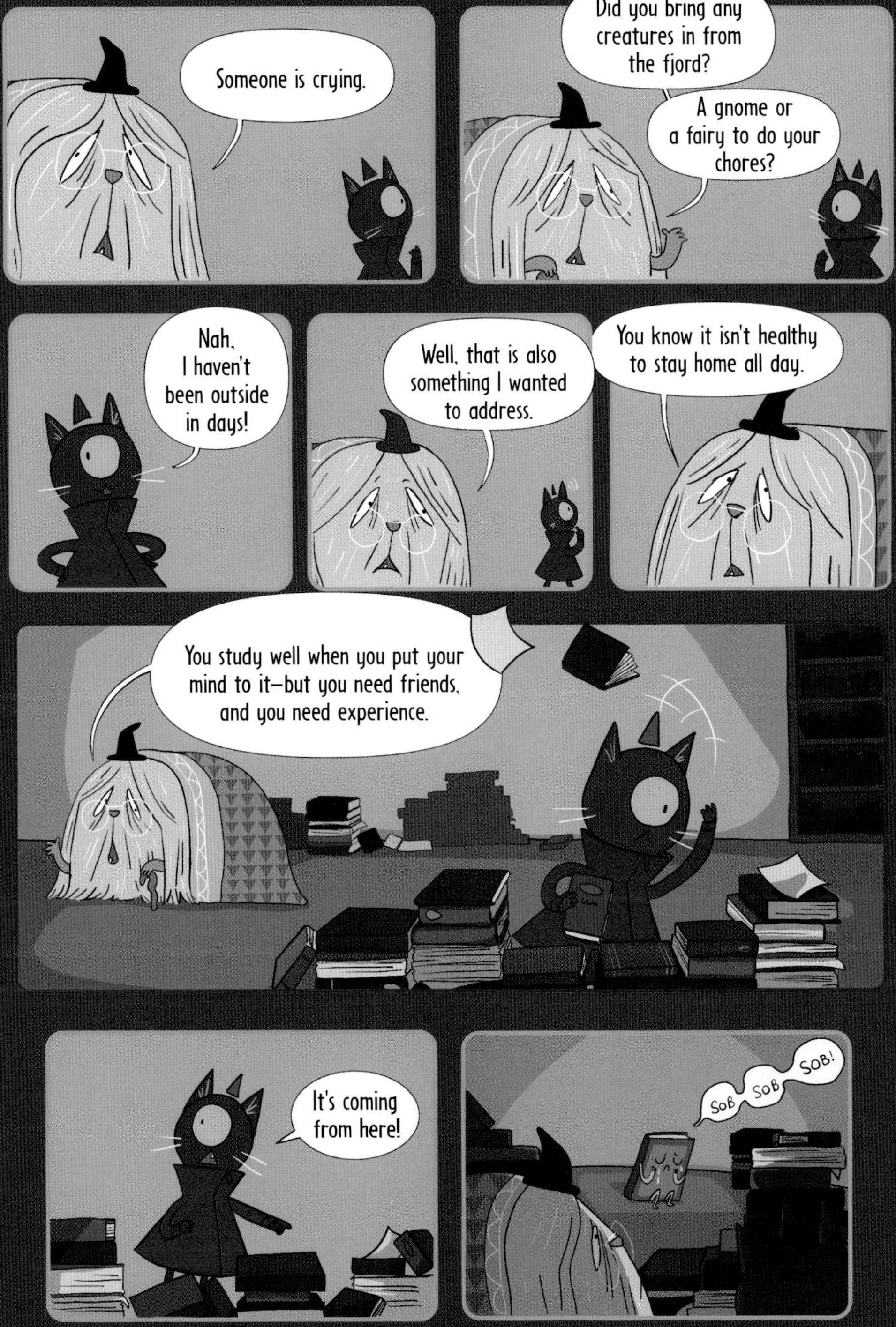
Someone is crying.
Did you bring any creatures in from the fjord?
A gnome or a fairy to do your chores?
Nah, I haven't been outside in days!
Well, that is also something I wanted to address.
You know it isn't healthy to stay home all day.
You study well when you put your mind to it—but you need friends, and you need experience.
It's coming from here!
SOB SOB SOB!

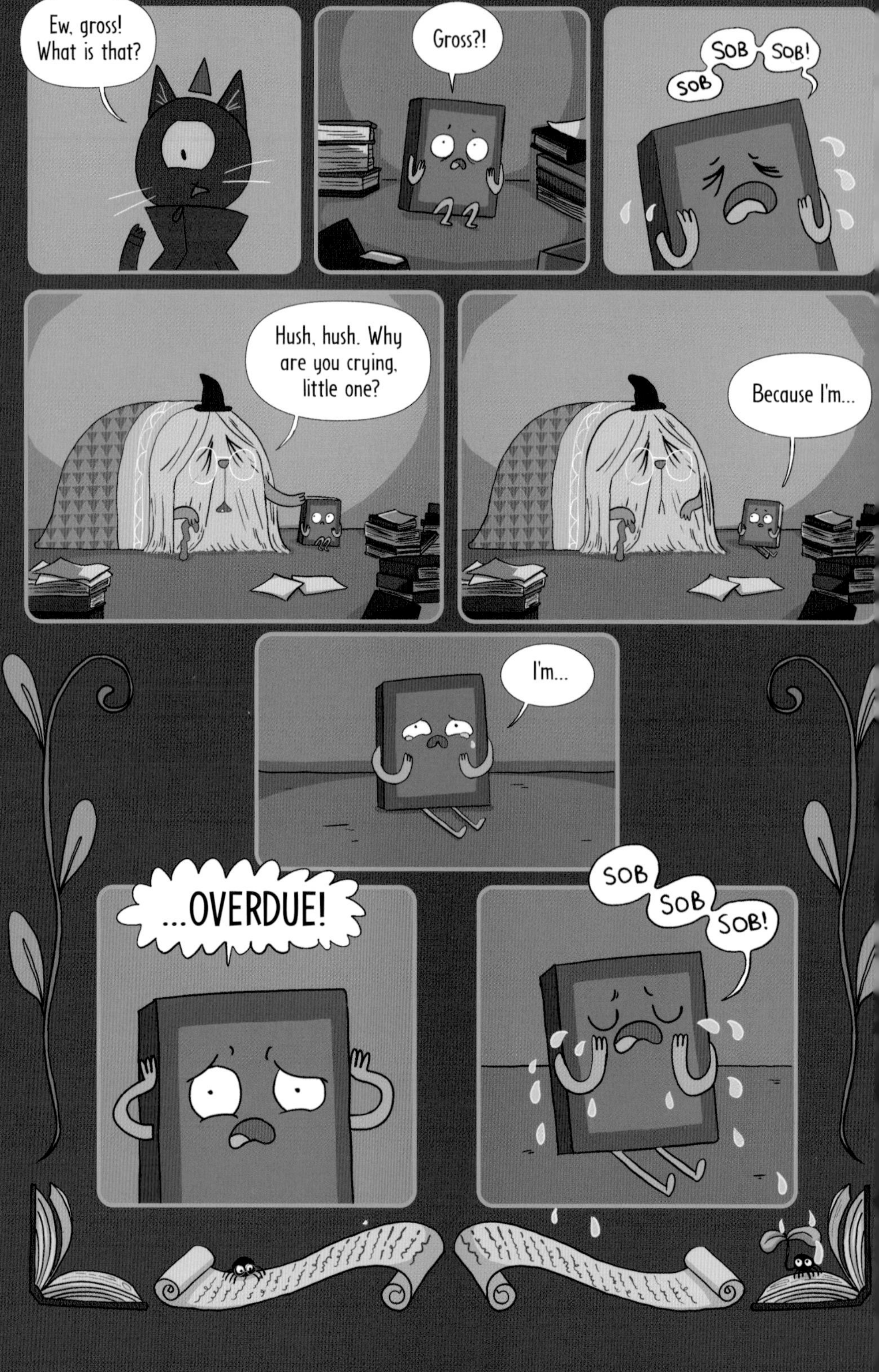
Ew, gross! What is that?
Gross?!
SOB
SOB
SOB!
Hush, hush. Why are you crying, little one?
Because I'm...
I'm...
...OVERDUE!
SOB
SOB
SOB!

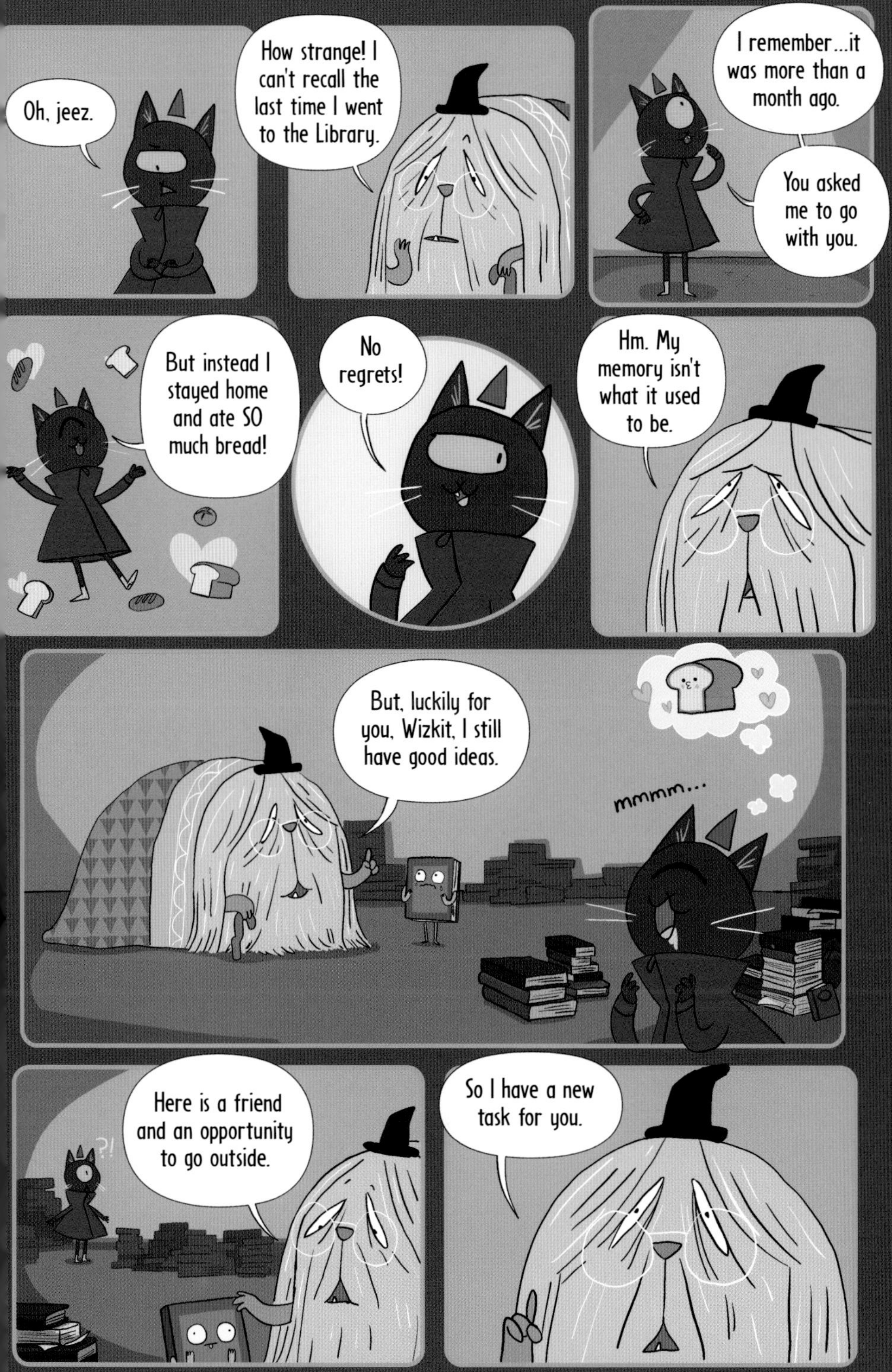
Oh, jeez.
How strange! I can't recall the last time I went to the Library.
I remember...it was more than a month ago.
You asked me to go with you.
But instead I stayed home and ate SO much bread!
No regrets!
Hm. My memory isn't what it used to be.
But, luckily for you, Wizkit, I still have good ideas.
mmmm...
?!
Here is a friend and an opportunity to go outside.
So I have a new task for you.

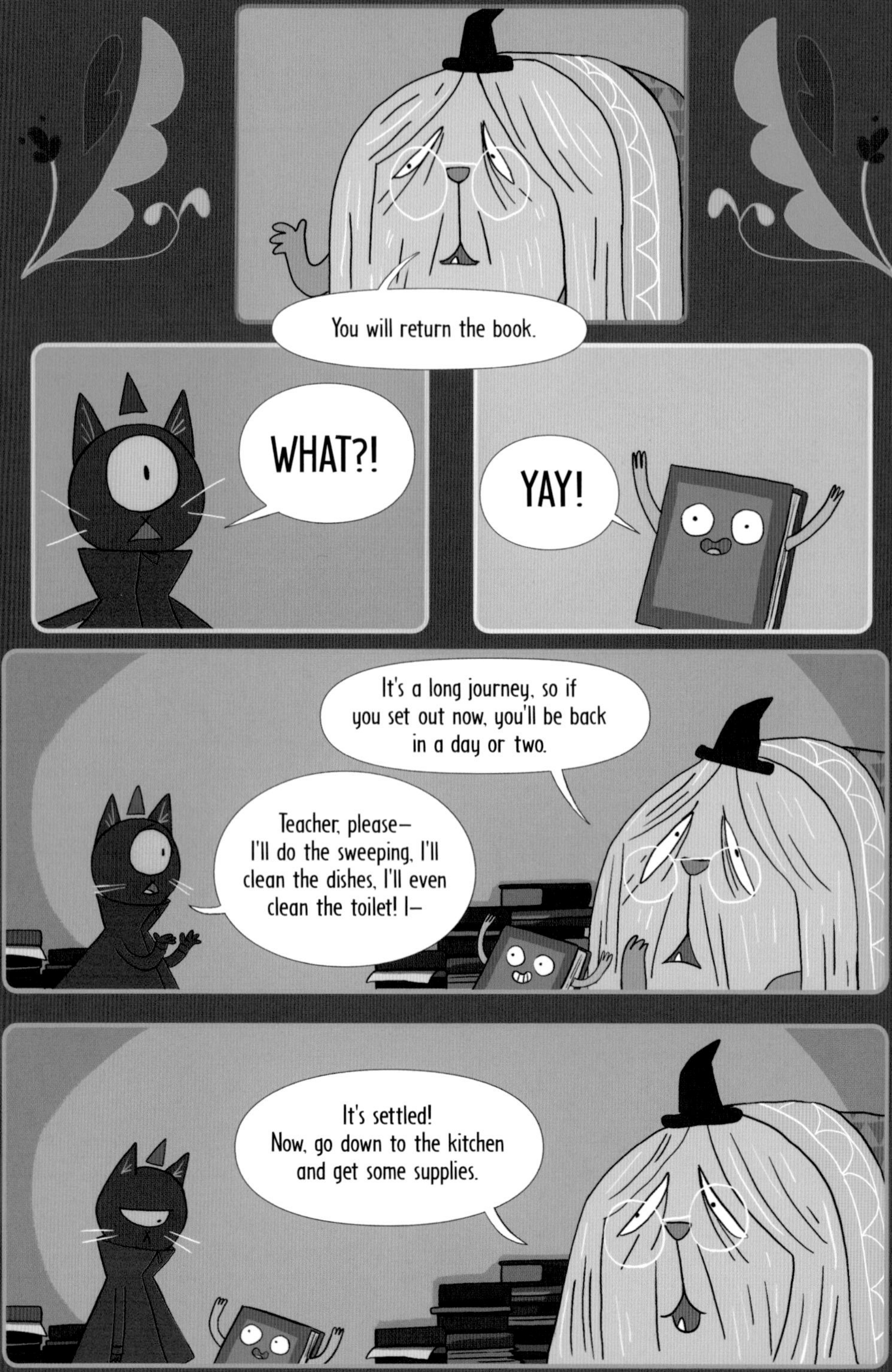
You will return the book.
WHAT?!
YAY!
It's a long journey, so if you set out now, you'll be back in a day or two.
Teacher, please— I'll do the sweeping, I'll clean the dishes, I'll even clean the toilet! I—
It's settled! Now, go down to the kitchen and get some supplies.

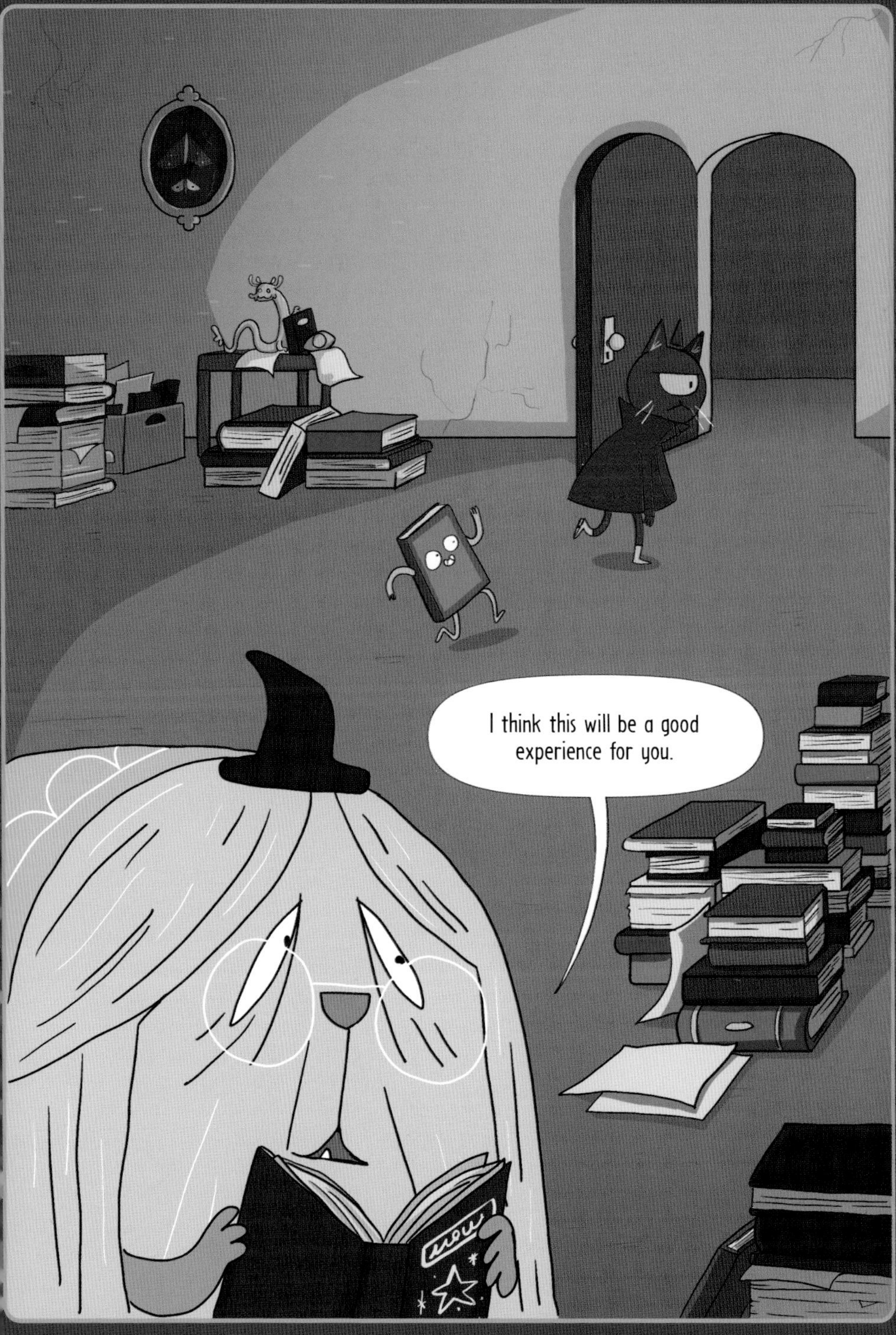
I think this will be a good experience for you.

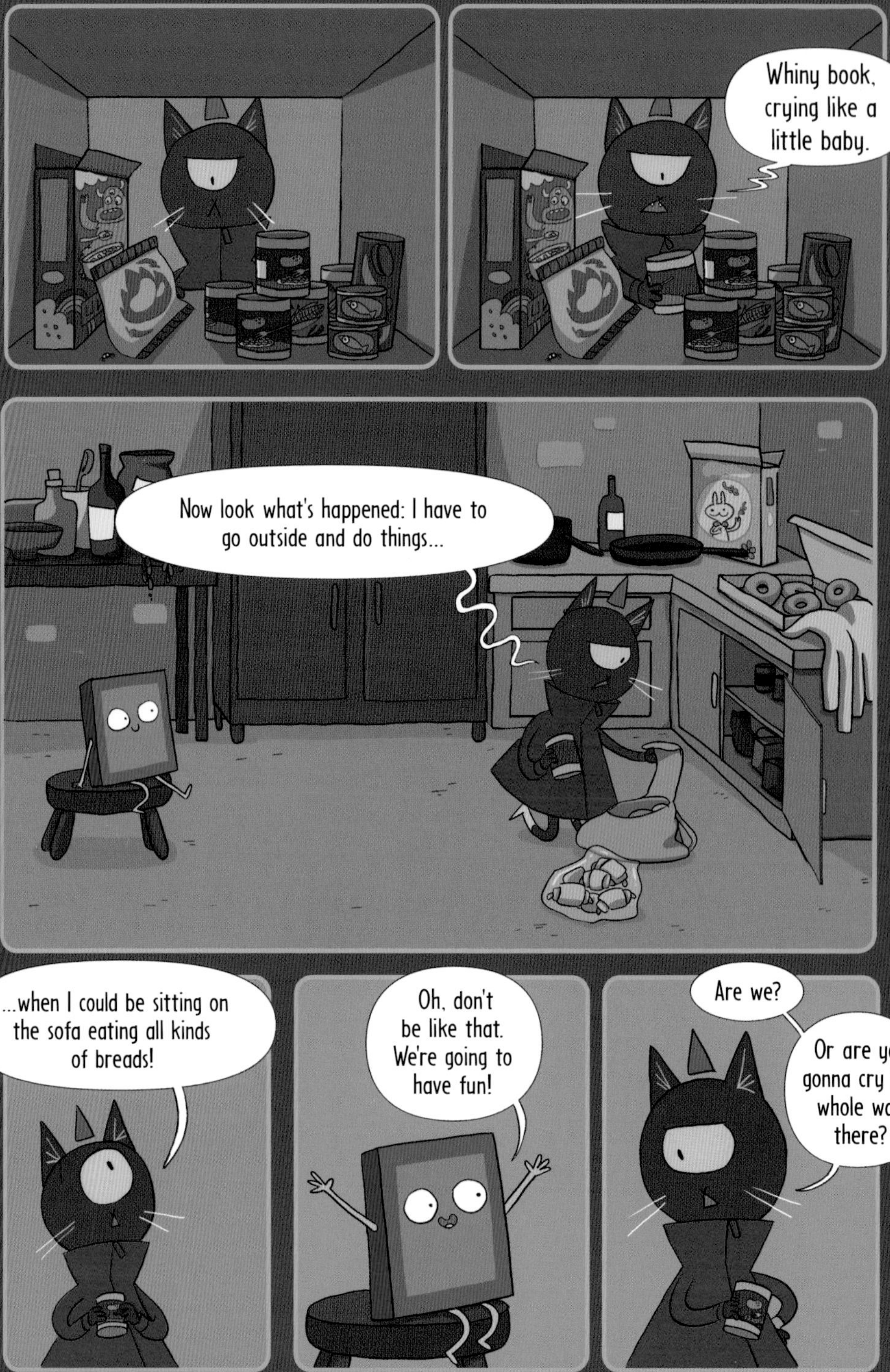
Whiny book, crying like a little baby.
Now look what's happened: I have to go outside and do things...
...when I could be sitting on the sofa eating all kinds of breads!
Oh, don't be like that. We're going to have fun!
Are we?
Or are you gonna cry th whole way there?

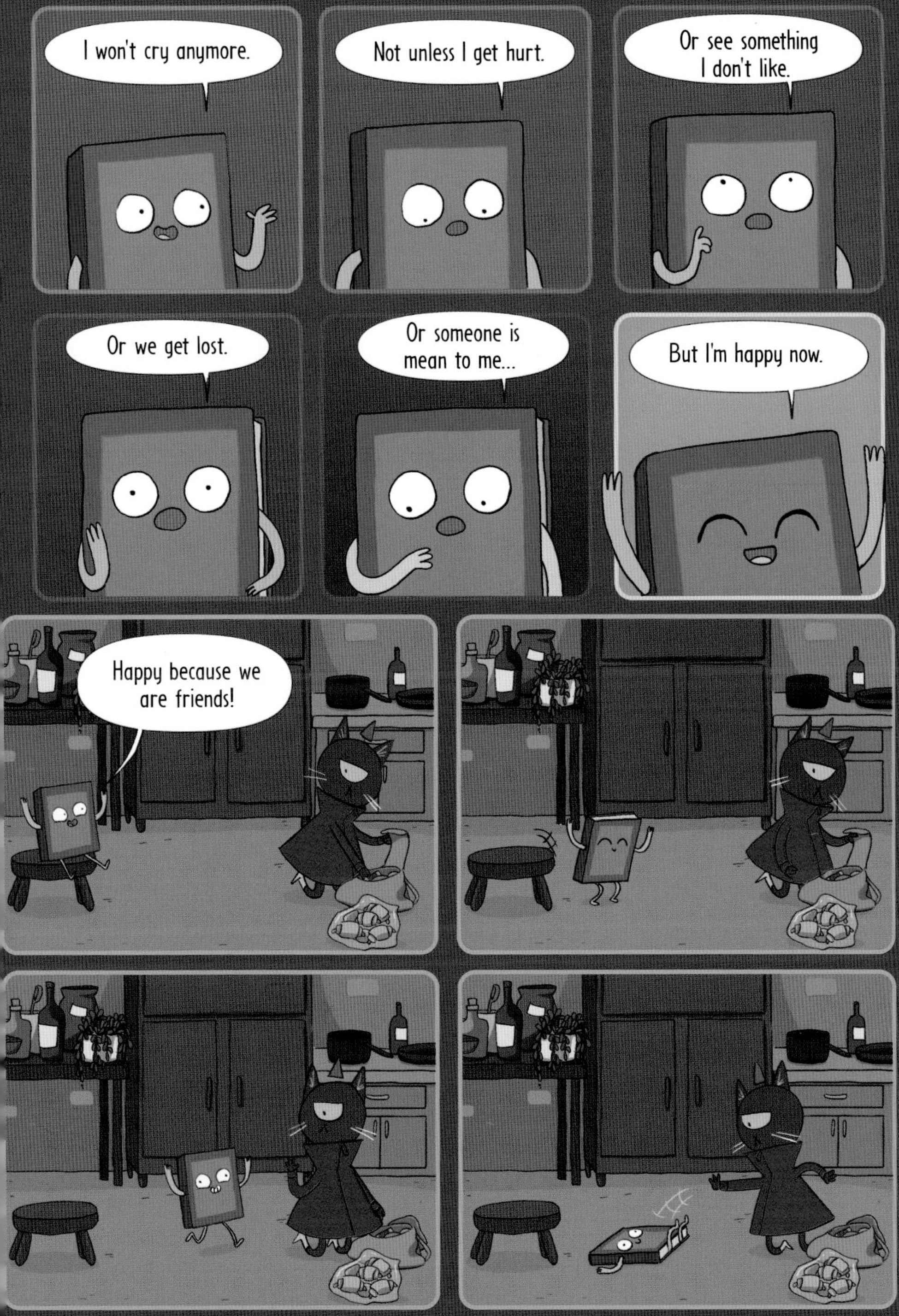
I won't cry anymore.
Not unless I get hurt.
Or see something I don't like.
Or we get lost.
Or someone is mean to me...
But I'm happy now.
Happy because we are friends!

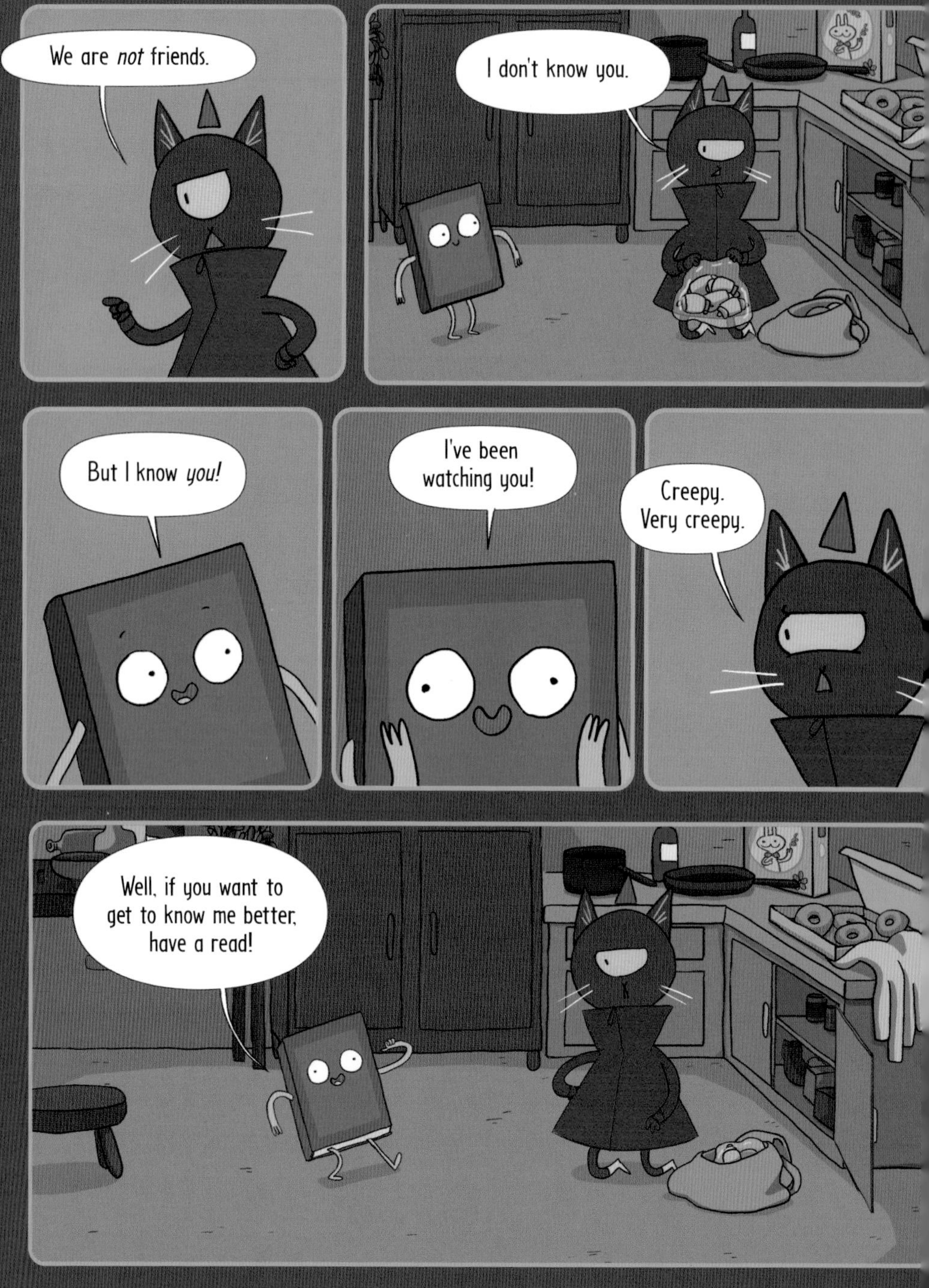
We are *not* friends.
I don't know you.
But I know *you!*
I've been watching you!
Creepy. Very creepy.
Well, if you want to get to know me better, have a read!

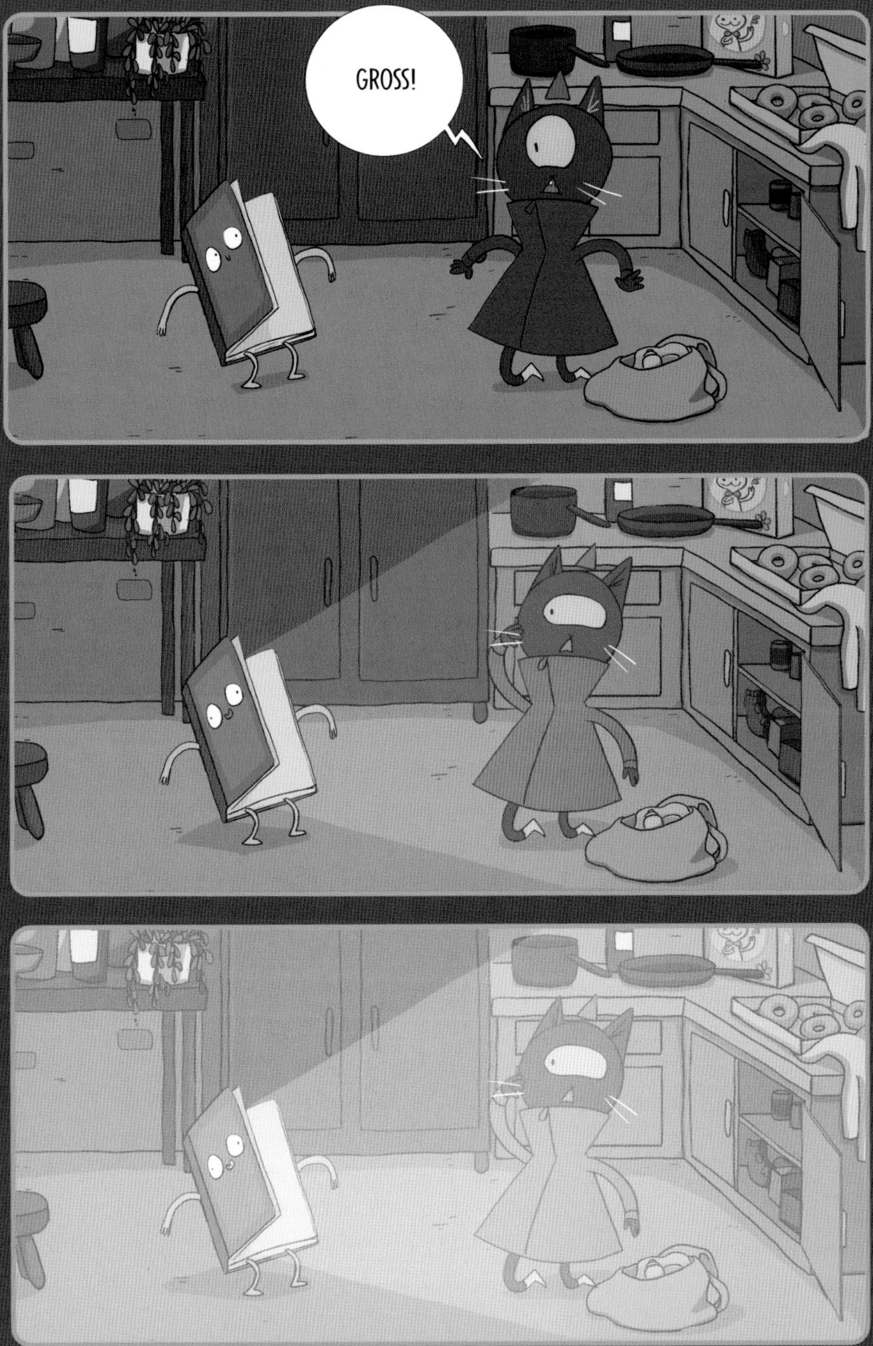
GROSS!

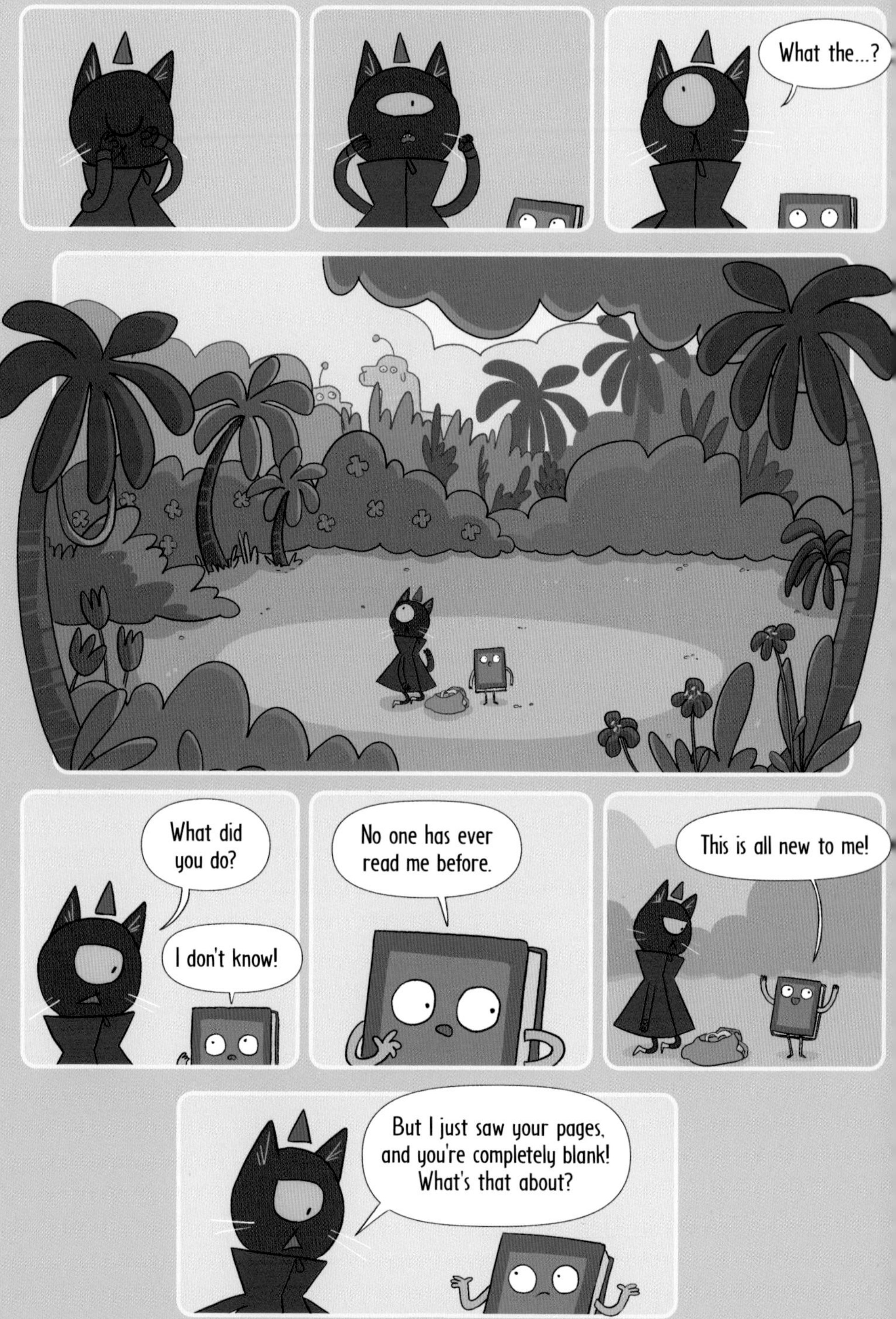
What the...?
What did you do?
I don't know!
No one has ever read me before.
This is all new to me!
But I just saw your pages, and you're completely blank! What's that about?

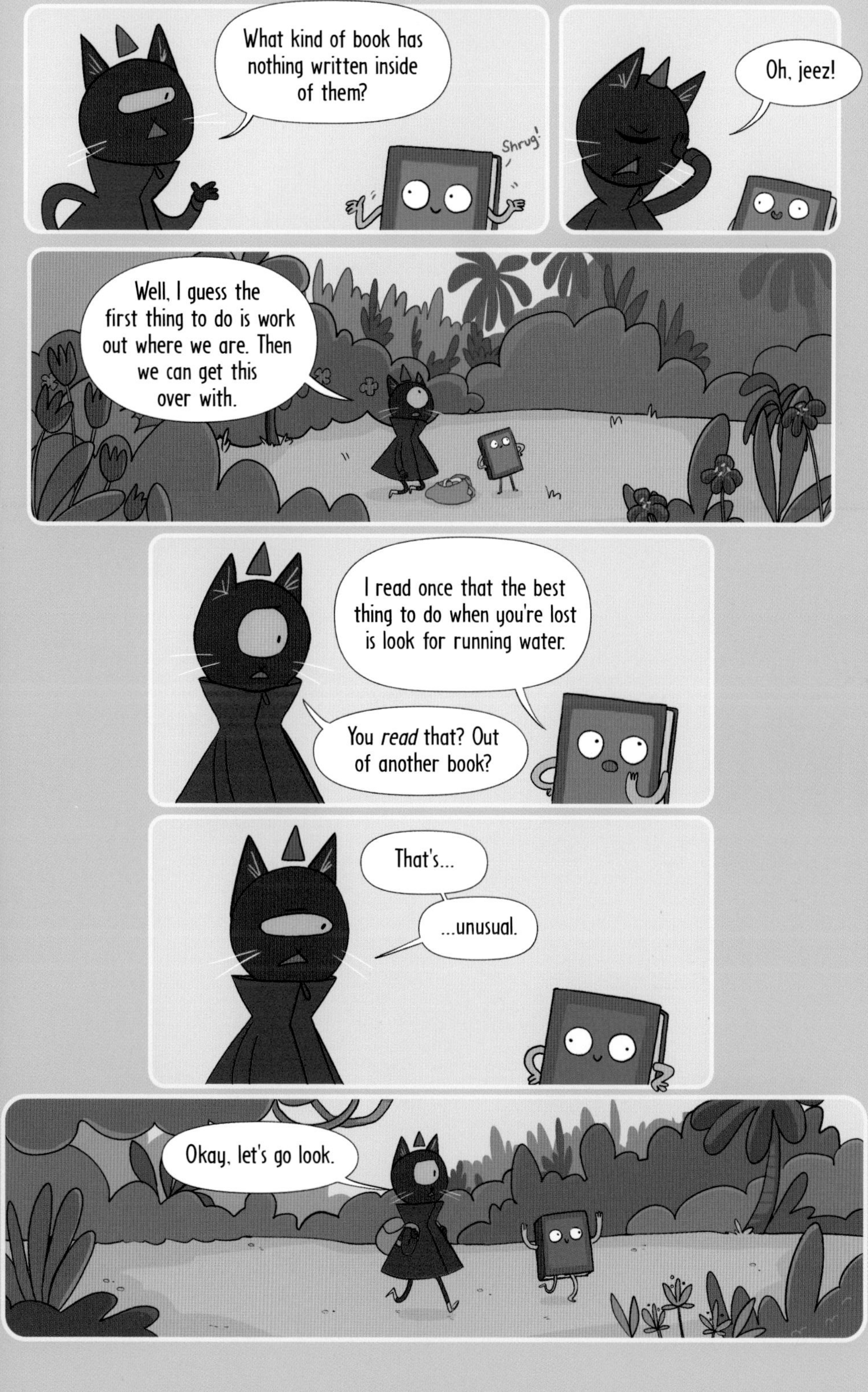
What kind of book has nothing written inside of them?
Shrug!
Oh, jeez!
Well, I guess the first thing to do is work out where we are. Then we can get this over with.
I read once that the best thing to do when you're lost is look for running water.
You *read* that? Out of another book?
That's...
...unusual.
Okay, let's go look.

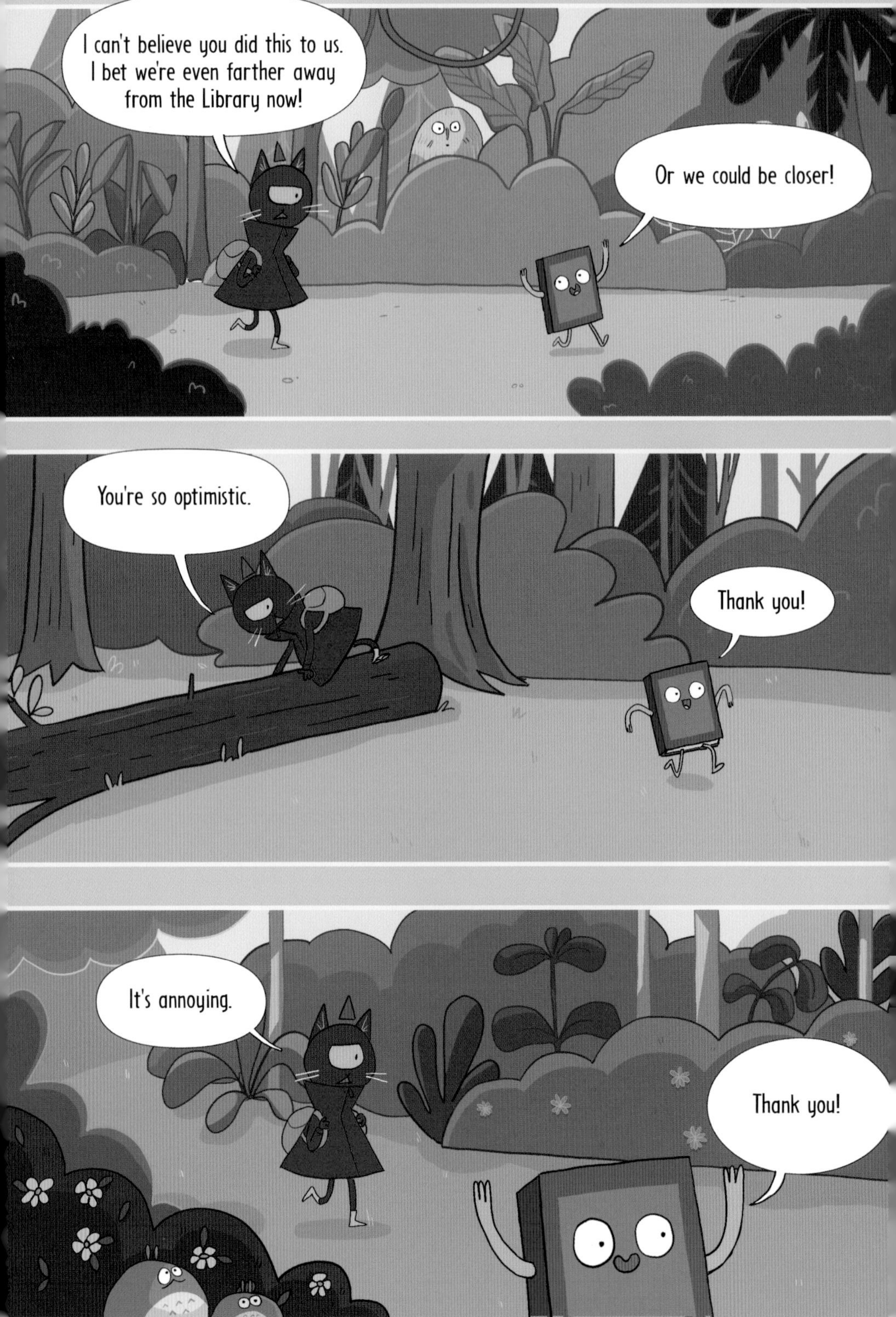
I can't believe you did this to us. I bet we're even farther away from the Library now!
Or we could be closer!
You're so optimistic.
Thank you!
It's annoying.
Thank you!

Chapter 2

Fishy Business

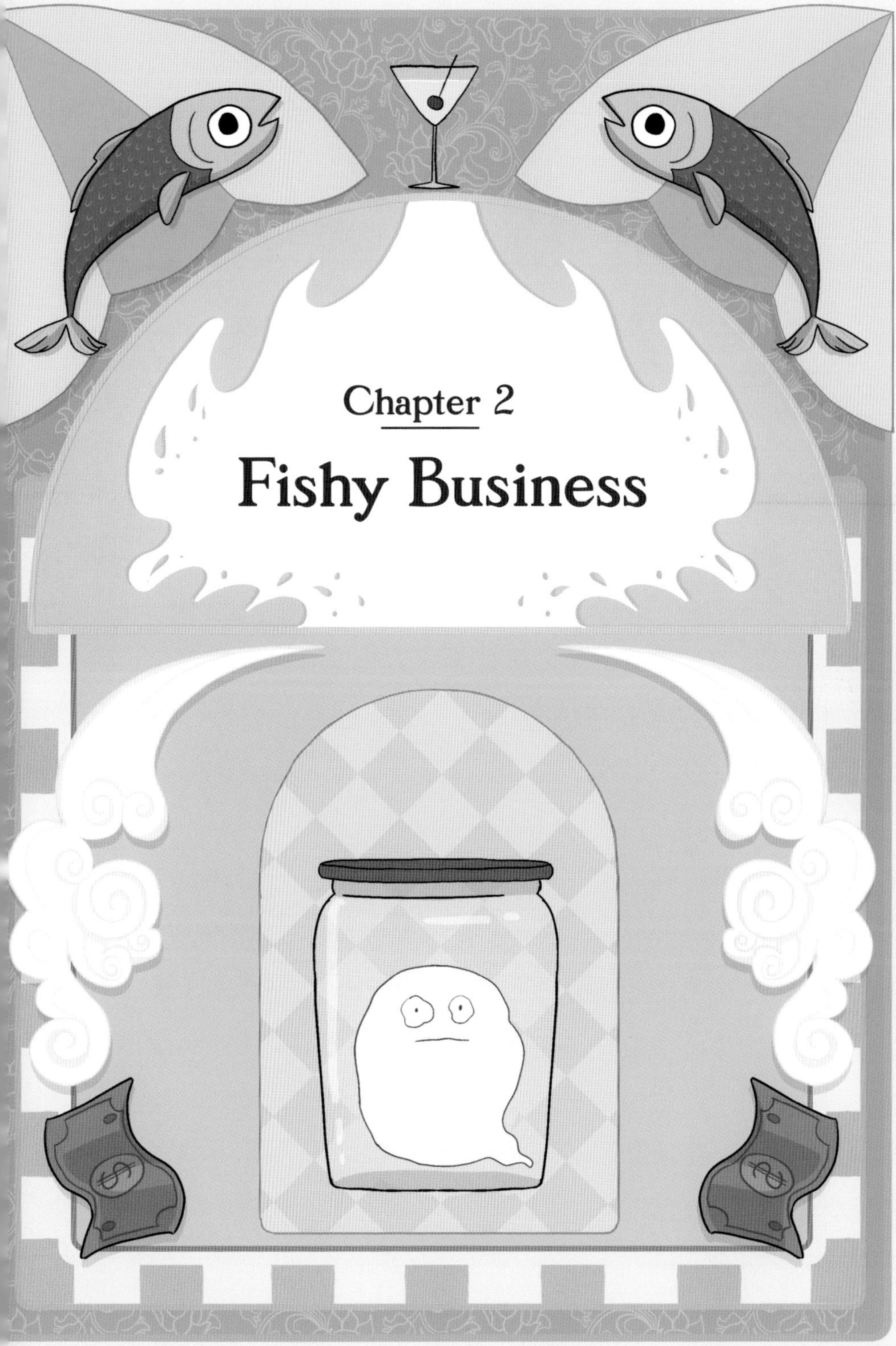

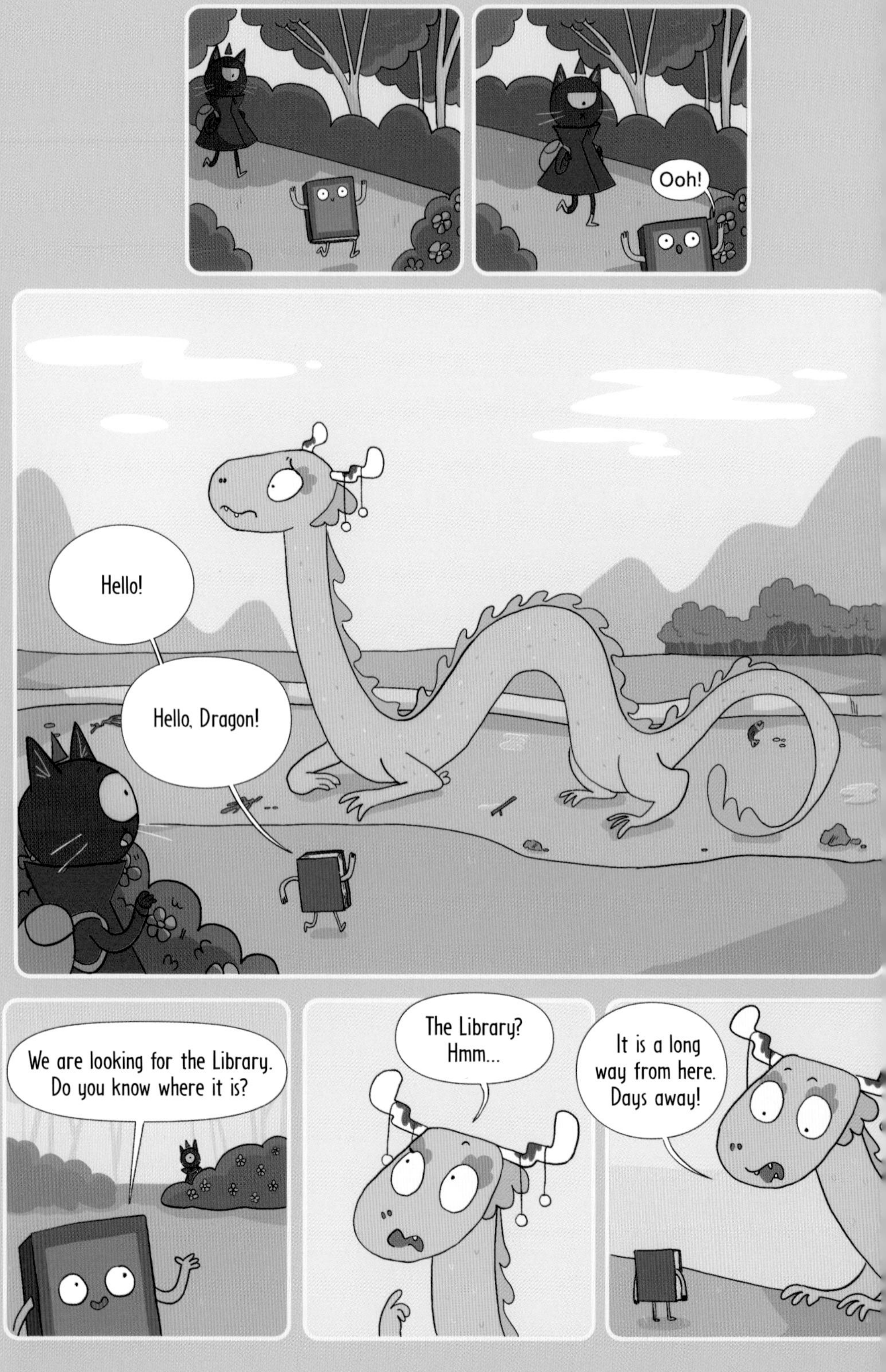
Ooh!
Hello!
Hello, Dragon!
We are looking for the Library. Do you know where it is?
The Library? Hmm...
It is a long way from here. Days away!

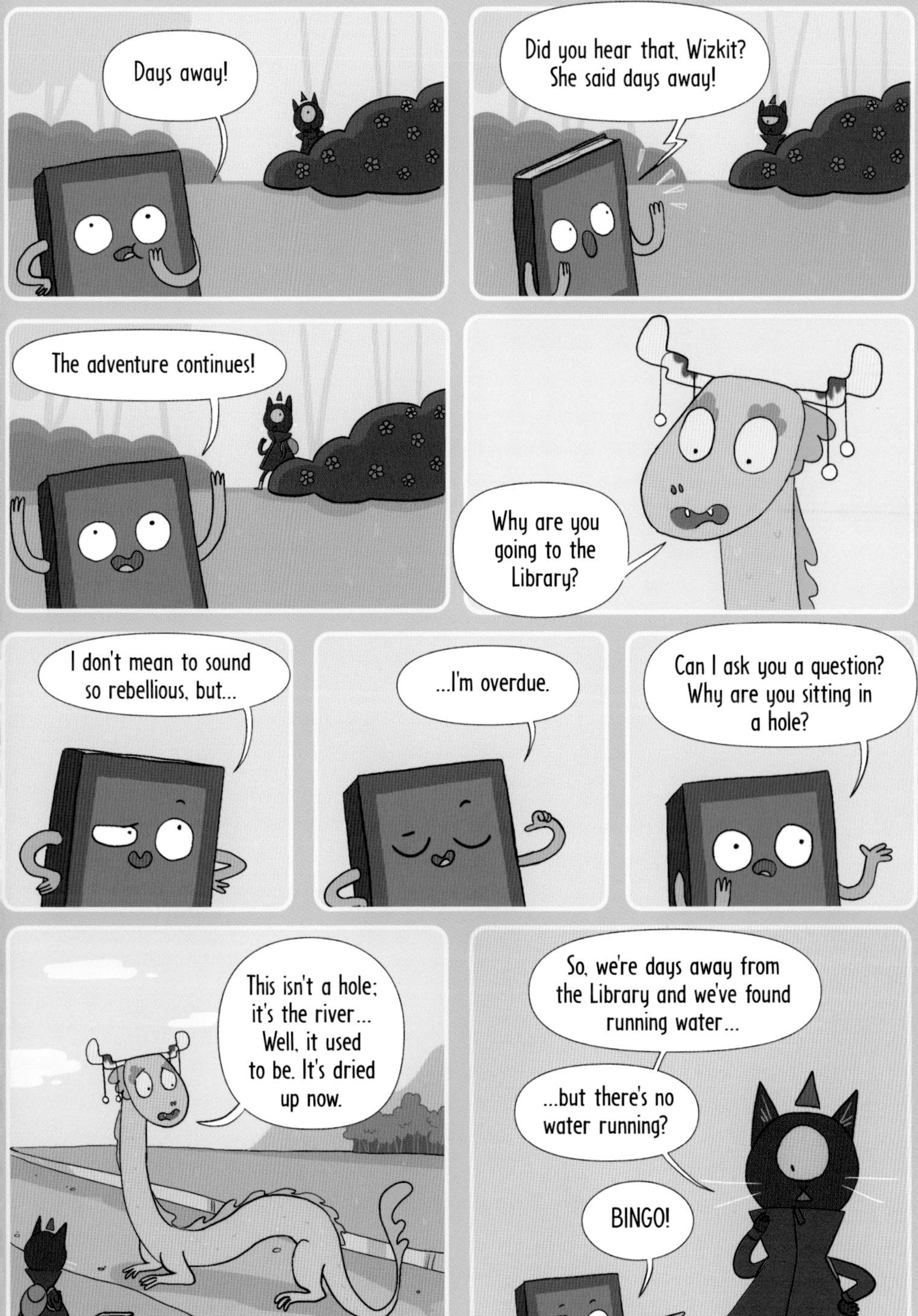
Days away!
Did you hear that, Wizkit? She said days away!
The adventure continues!
Why are you going to the Library?
I don't mean to sound so rebellious, but...
...I'm overdue.
Can I ask you a question? Why are you sitting in a hole?
This isn't a hole; it's the river... Well, it used to be. It's dried up now.
So, we're days away from the Library and we've found running water...
...but there's no water running?
BINGO!

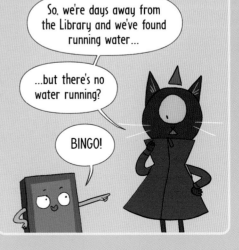

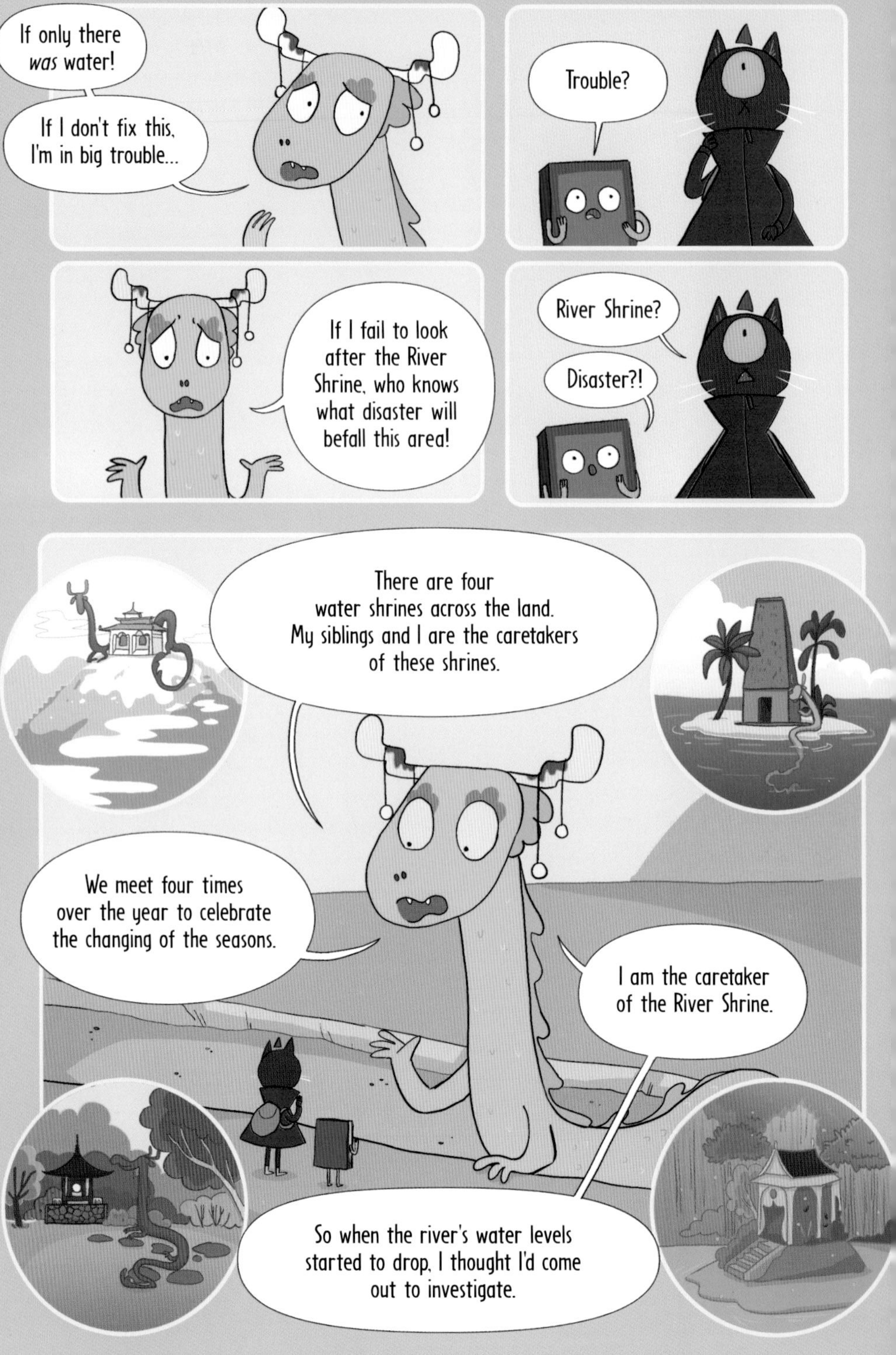

If only there *was* water!
If I don't fix this, I'm in big trouble...
Trouble?
If I fail to look after the River Shrine, who knows what disaster will befall this area!
River Shrine?
Disaster?!
There are four water shrines across the land. My siblings and I are the caretakers of these shrines.
We meet four times over the year to celebrate the changing of the seasons.
I am the caretaker of the River Shrine.
So when the river's water levels started to drop, I thought I'd come out to investigate.

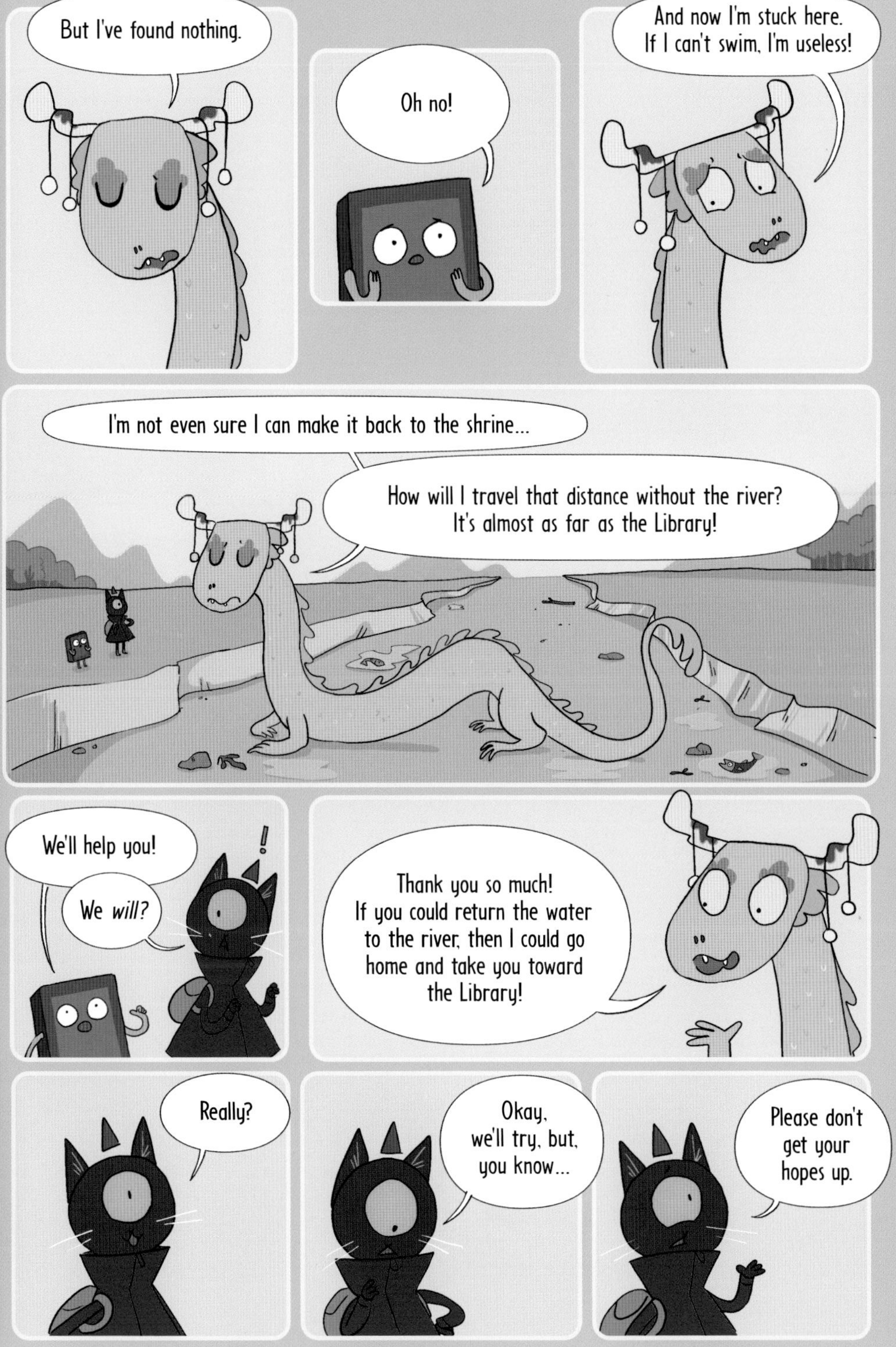
But I've found nothing.
Oh no!
And now I'm stuck here.
If I can't swim, I'm useless!
I'm not even sure I can make it back to the shrine...
How will I travel that distance without the river?
It's almost as far as the Library!
We'll help you!
!
We *will?*
Thank you so much!
If you could return the water to the river, then I could go home and take you toward the Library!
Really?
Okay, we'll try, but, you know...
Please don't get your hopes up.

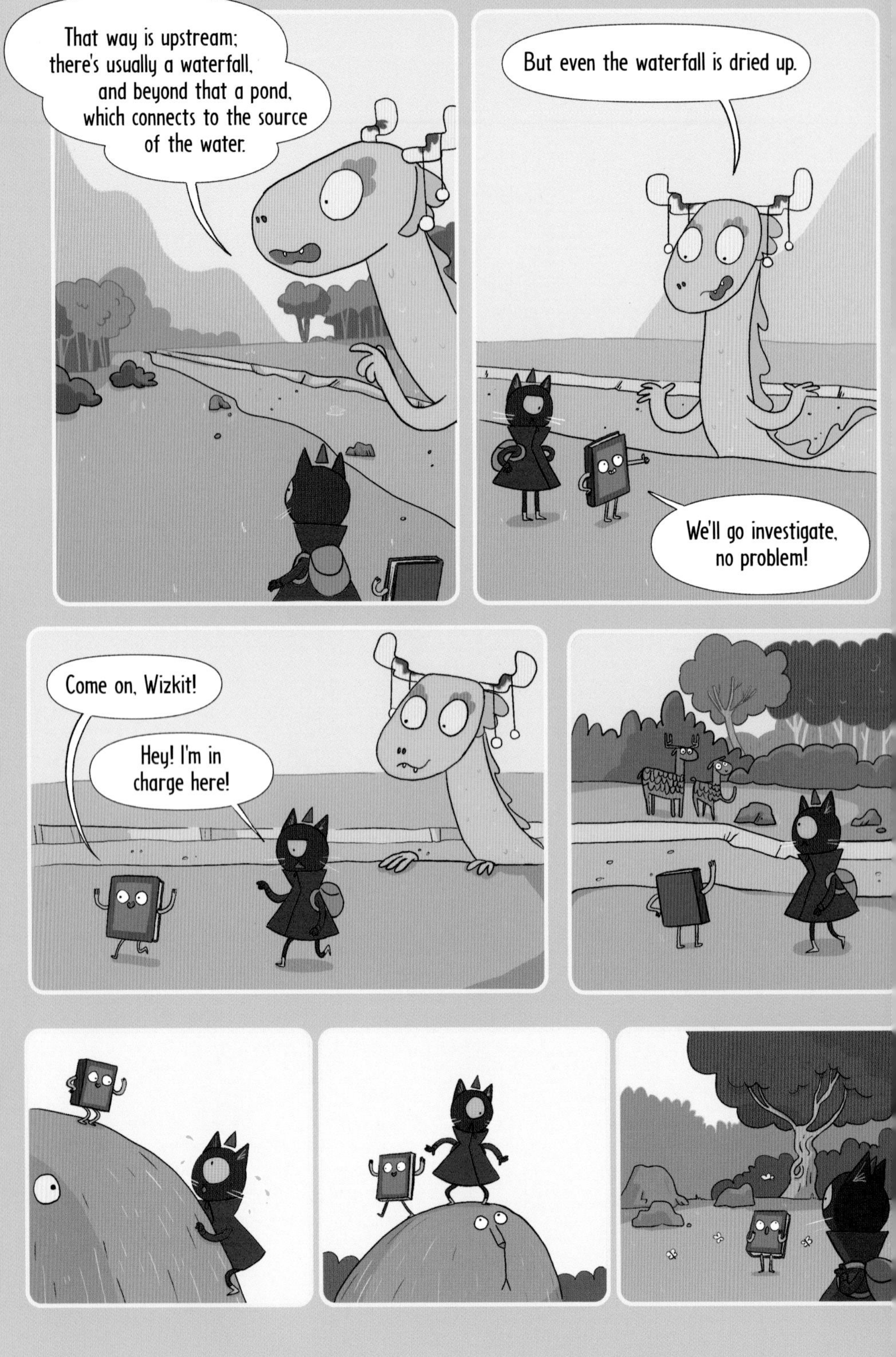
That way is upstream; there's usually a waterfall, and beyond that a pond, which connects to the source of the water.
But even the waterfall is dried up.
We'll go investigate, no problem!
Come on, Wizkit!
Hey! I'm in charge here!

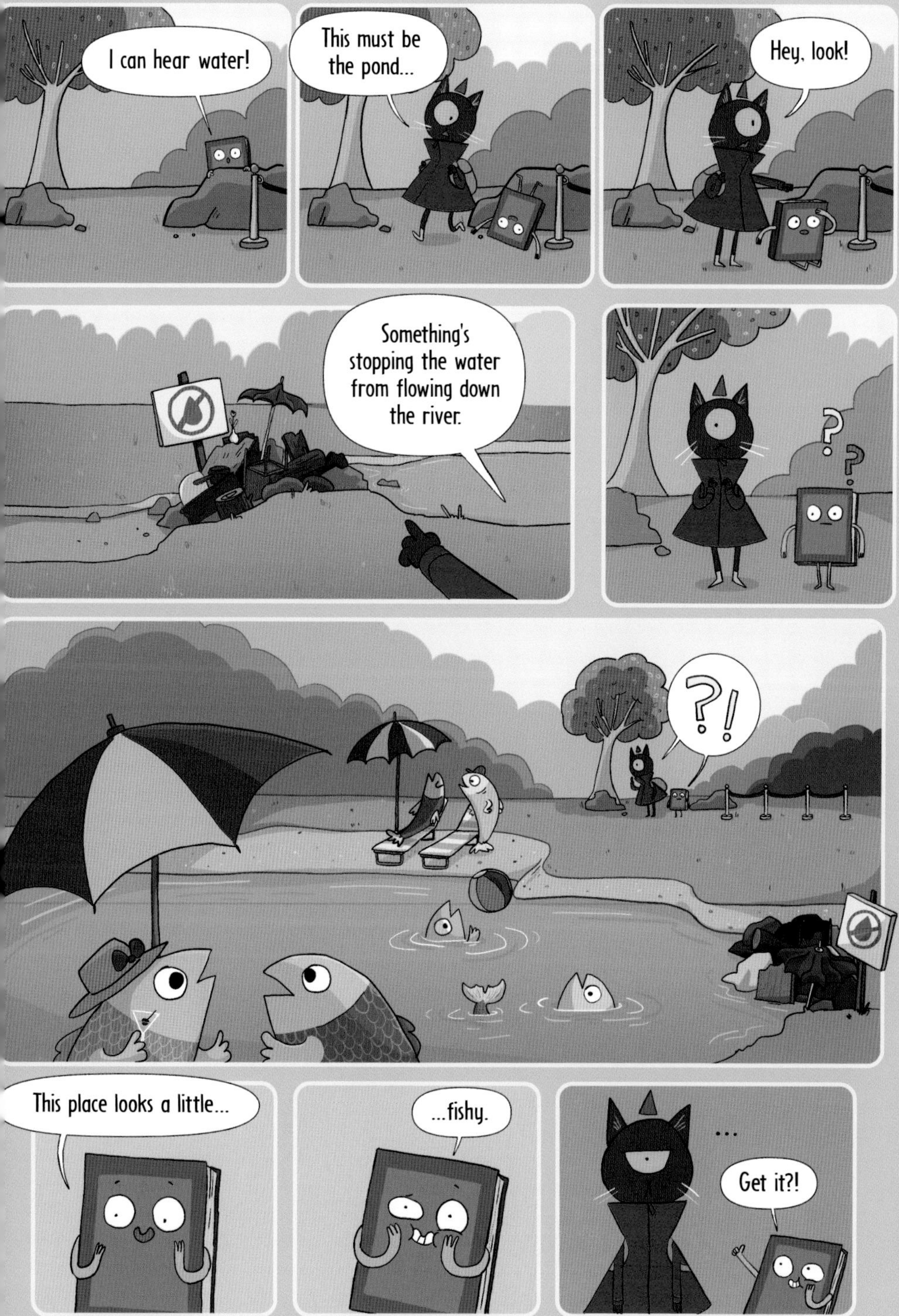
I can hear water!
This must be the pond...
Hey, look!
Something's stopping the water from flowing down the river.
?
?
?!
This place looks a little...
...fishy.
...
Get it?!

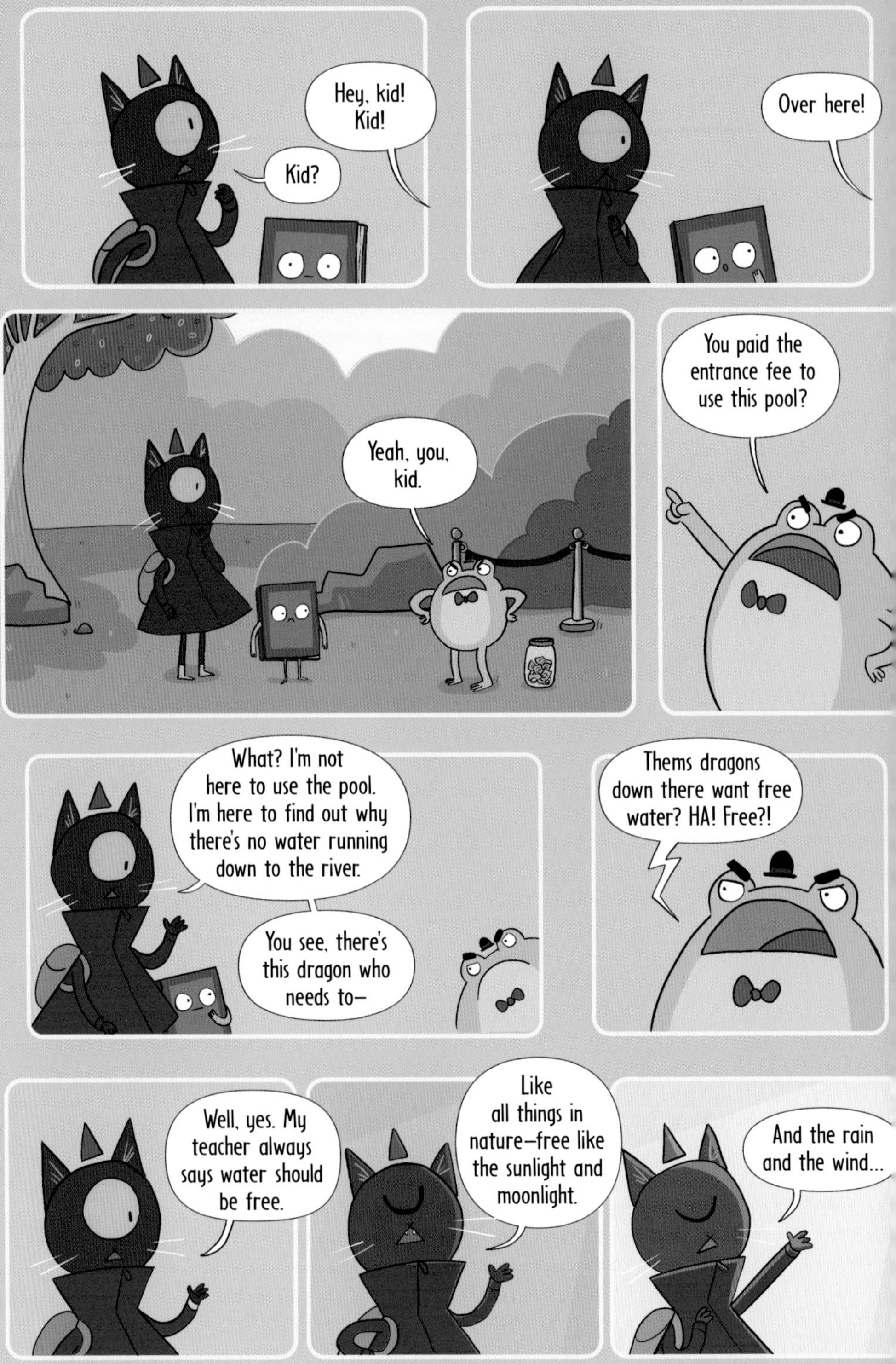
Hey, kid! Kid!
Kid?
Over here!
Yeah, you, kid.
You paid the entrance fee to use this pool?
What? I'm not here to use the pool. I'm here to find out why there's no water running down to the river.
You see, there's this dragon who needs to–
Thems dragons down there want free water? HA! Free?!
Well, yes. My teacher always says water should be free.
Like all things in nature–free like the sunlight and moonlight.
And the rain and the wind...

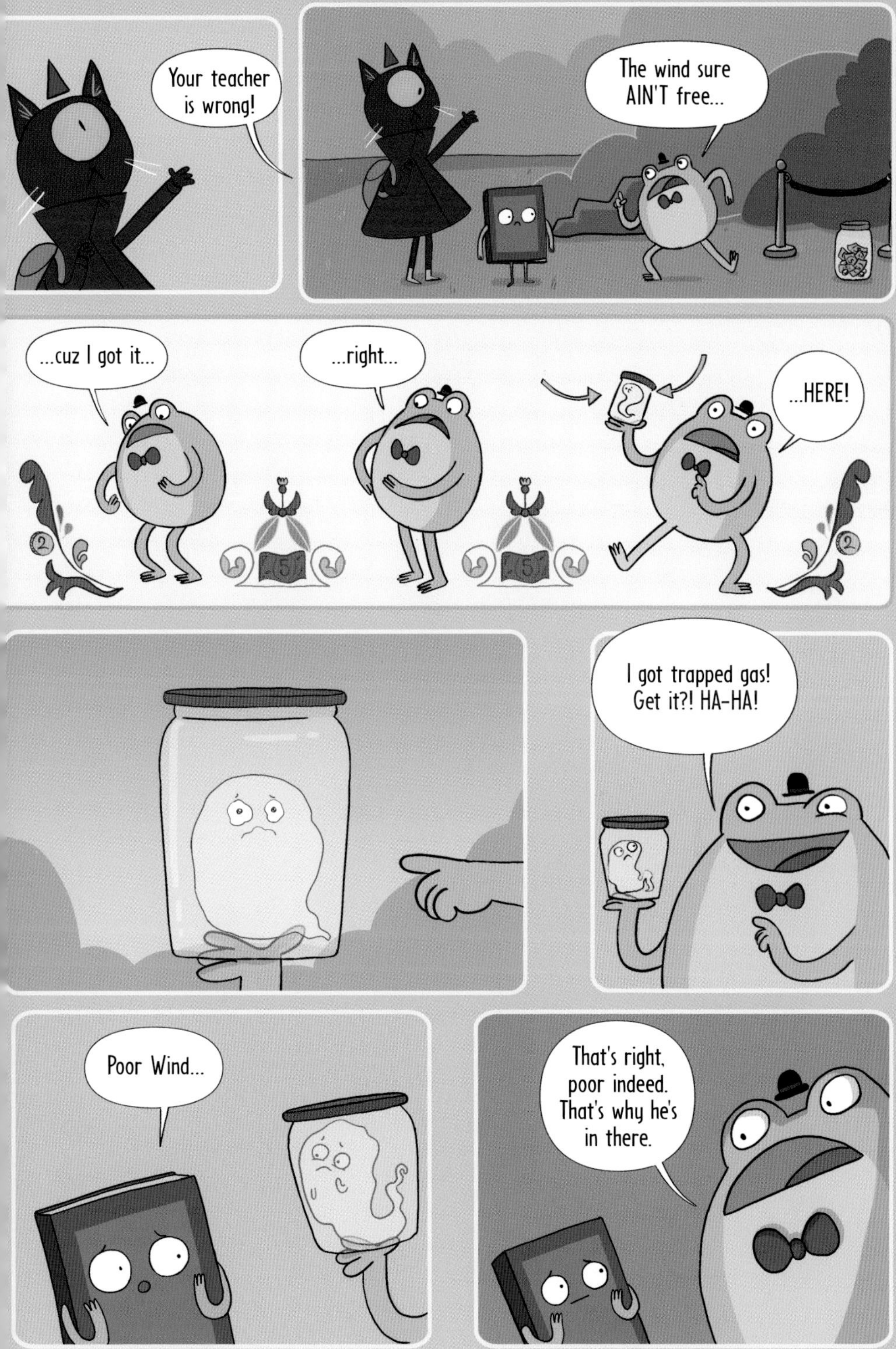
Your teacher is wrong!
The wind sure AIN'T free...
...cuz I got it...
...right...
...HERE!
I got trapped gas! Get it?! HA-HA!
Poor Wind...
That's right, poor indeed. That's why he's in there.

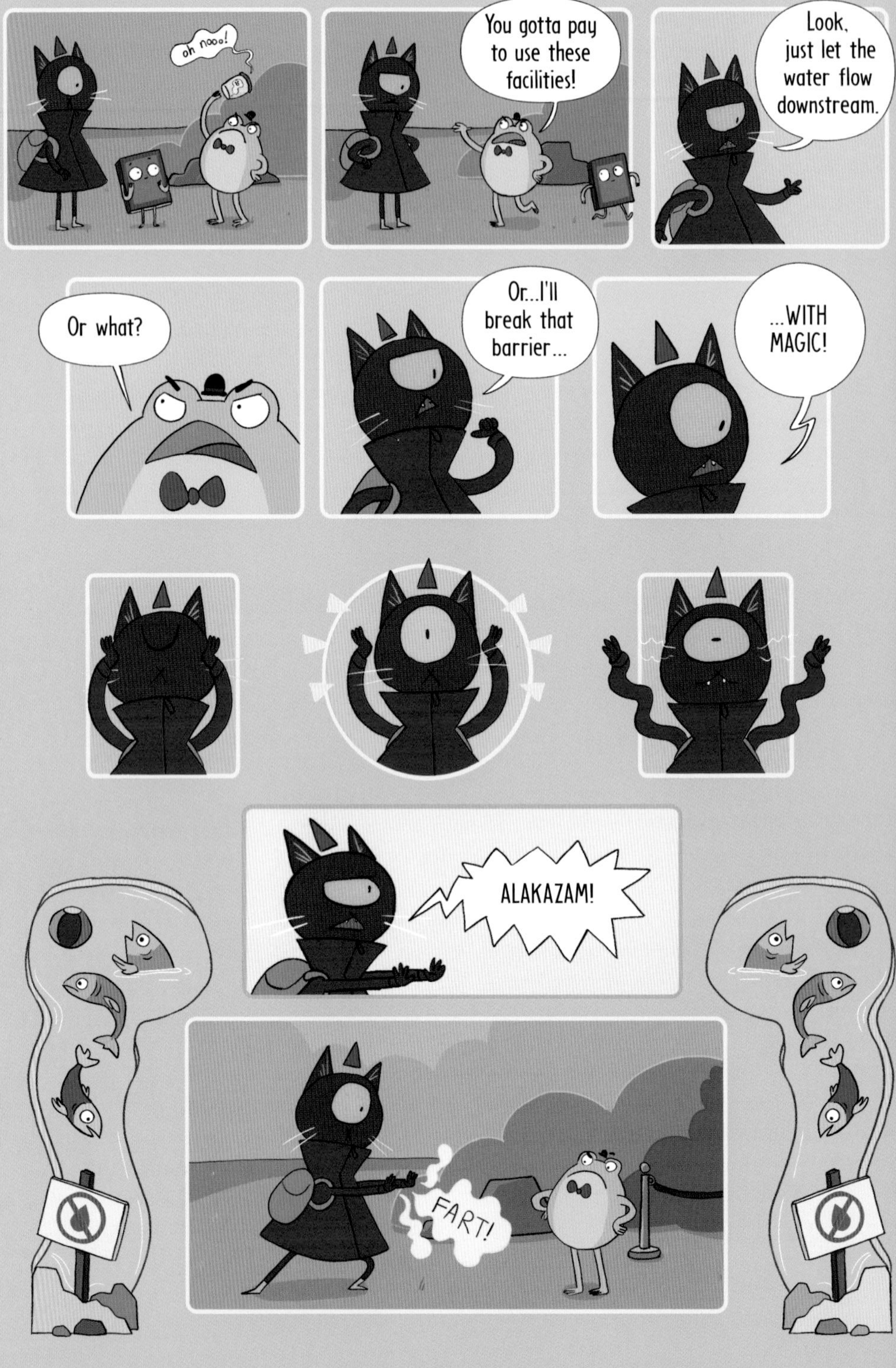
oh nooo!
You gotta pay to use these facilities!
Look, just let the water flow downstream.
Or what?
Or...I'll break that barrier...
...WITH MAGIC!
ALAKAZAM!
FART!

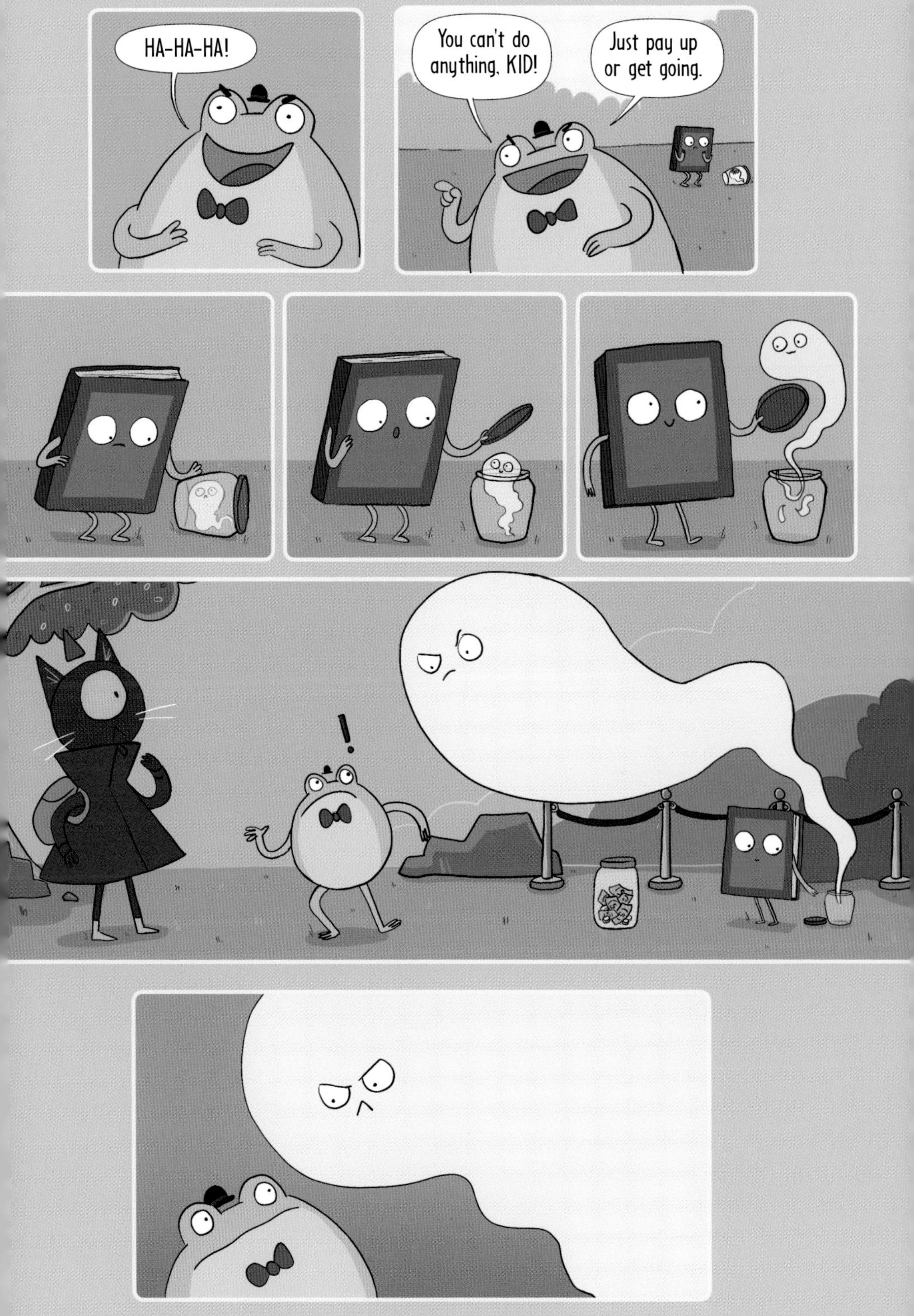
HA-HA-HA!
You can't do anything, KID!
Just pay up or get going.
!

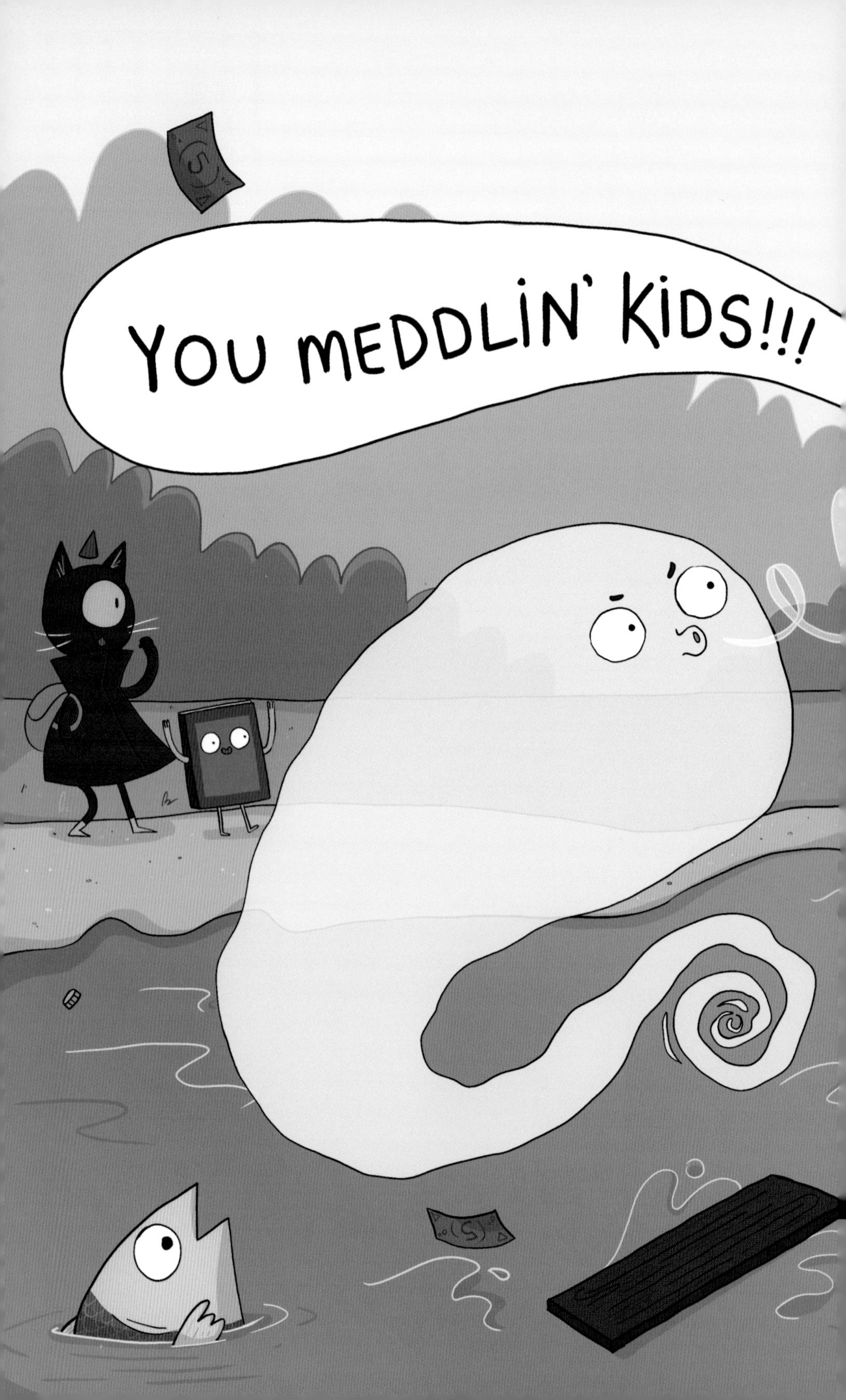
YOU MEDDLIN' KIDS!!!

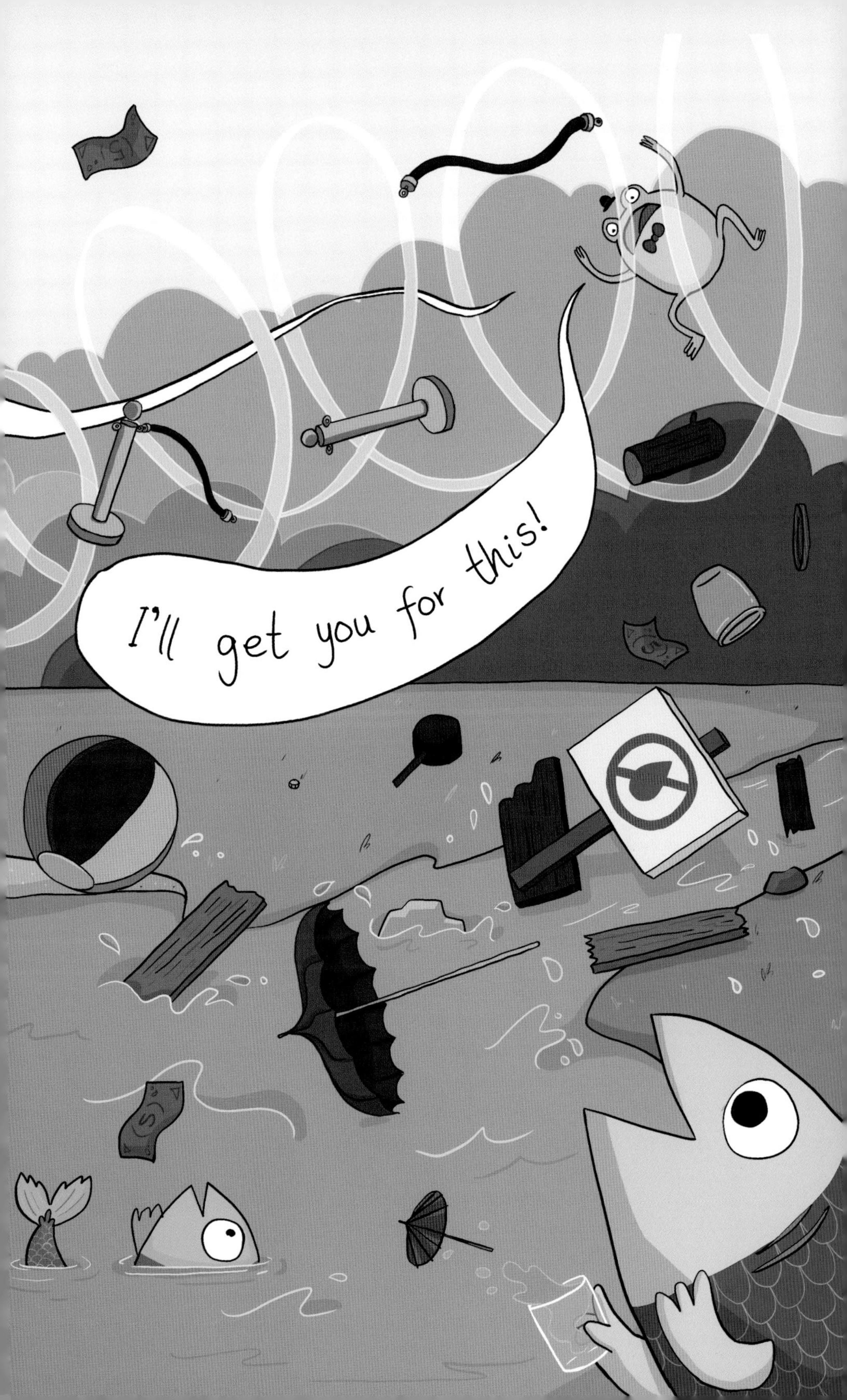
I'll get you for this!

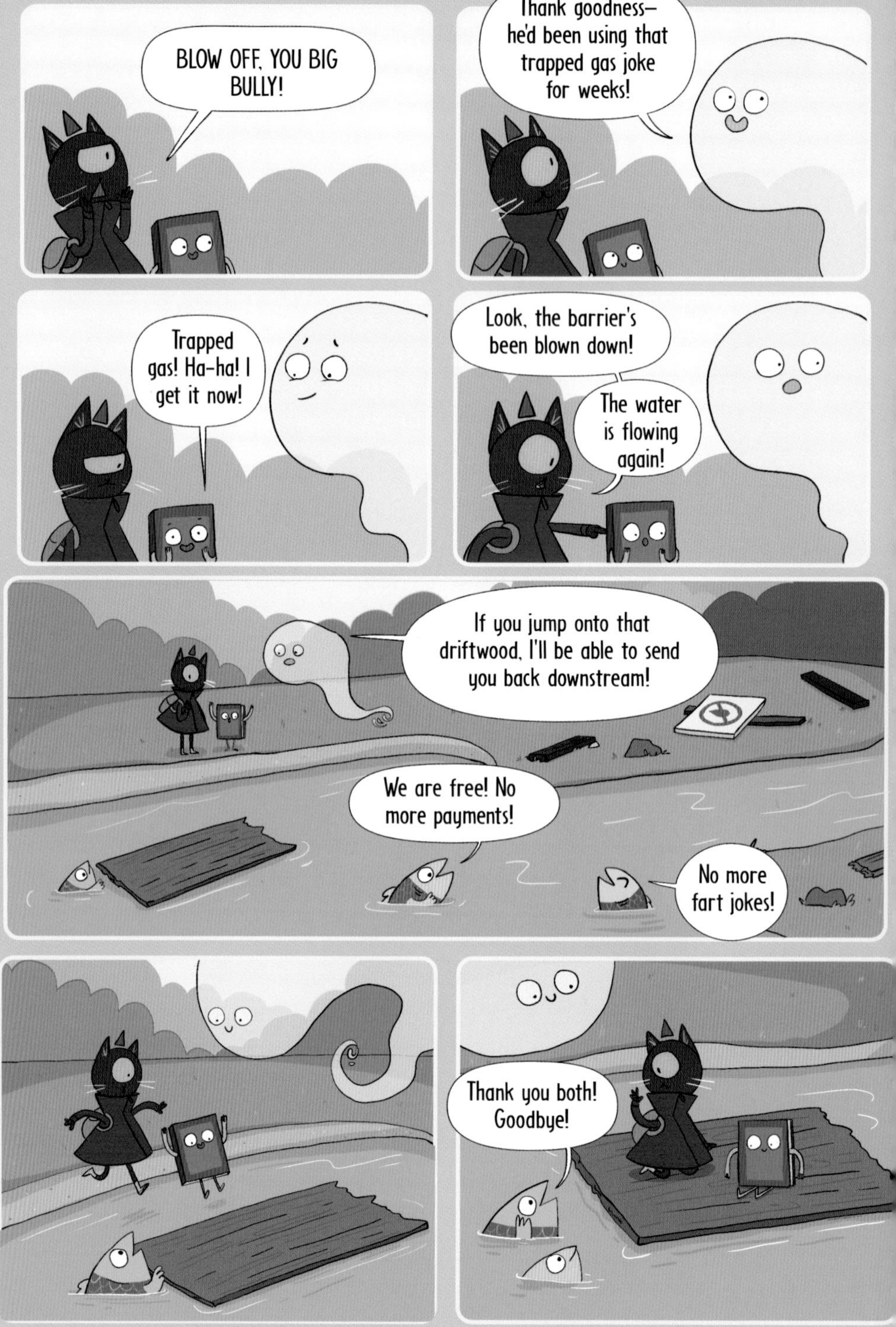

BLOW OFF, YOU BIG BULLY!
Thank goodness— he'd been using that trapped gas joke for weeks!
Trapped gas! Ha-ha! I get it now!
Look, the barrier's been blown down!
The water is flowing again!
If you jump onto that driftwood, I'll be able to send you back downstream!
We are free! No more payments!
No more fart jokes!
Thank you both! Goodbye!

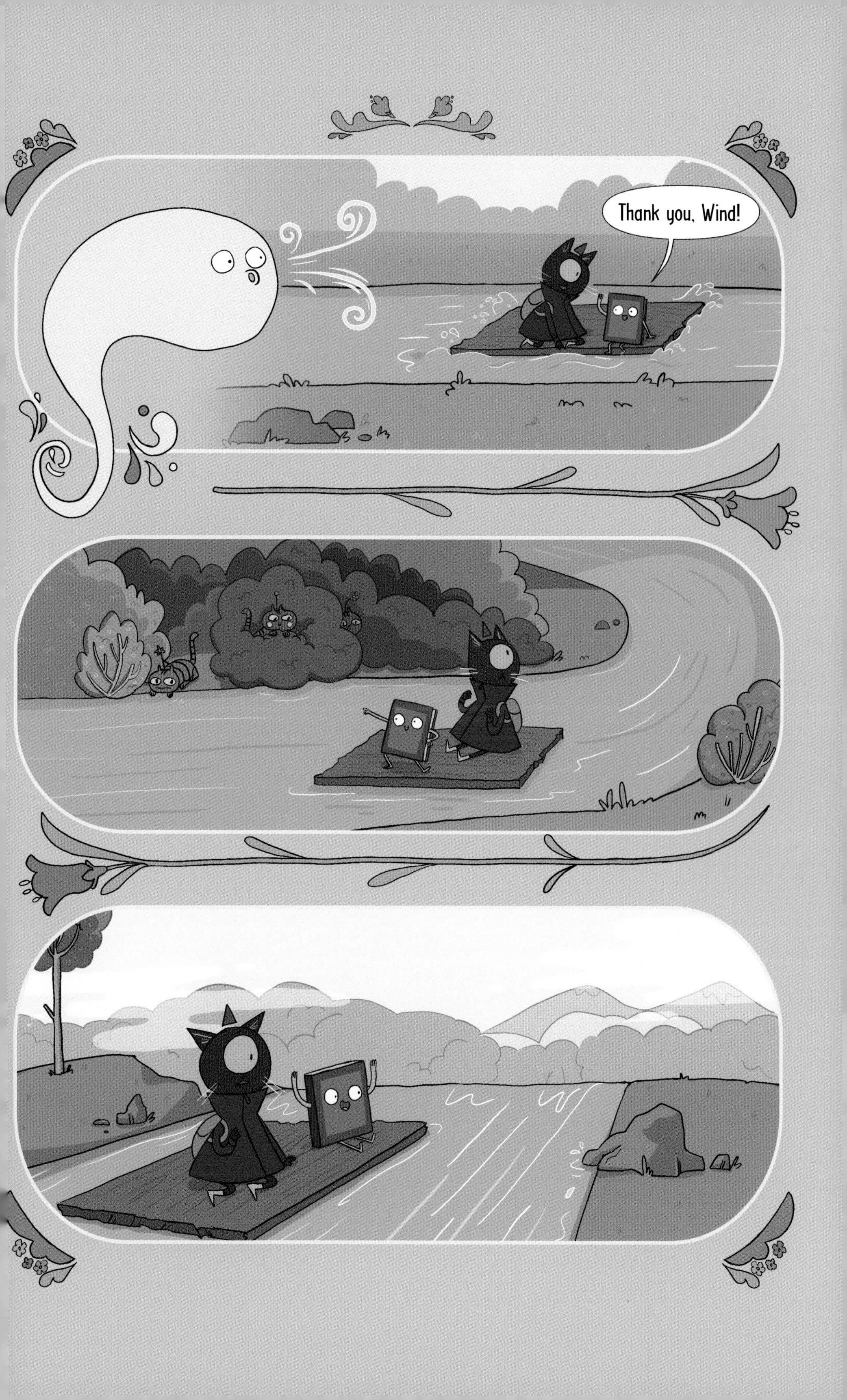
Thank you, Wind!

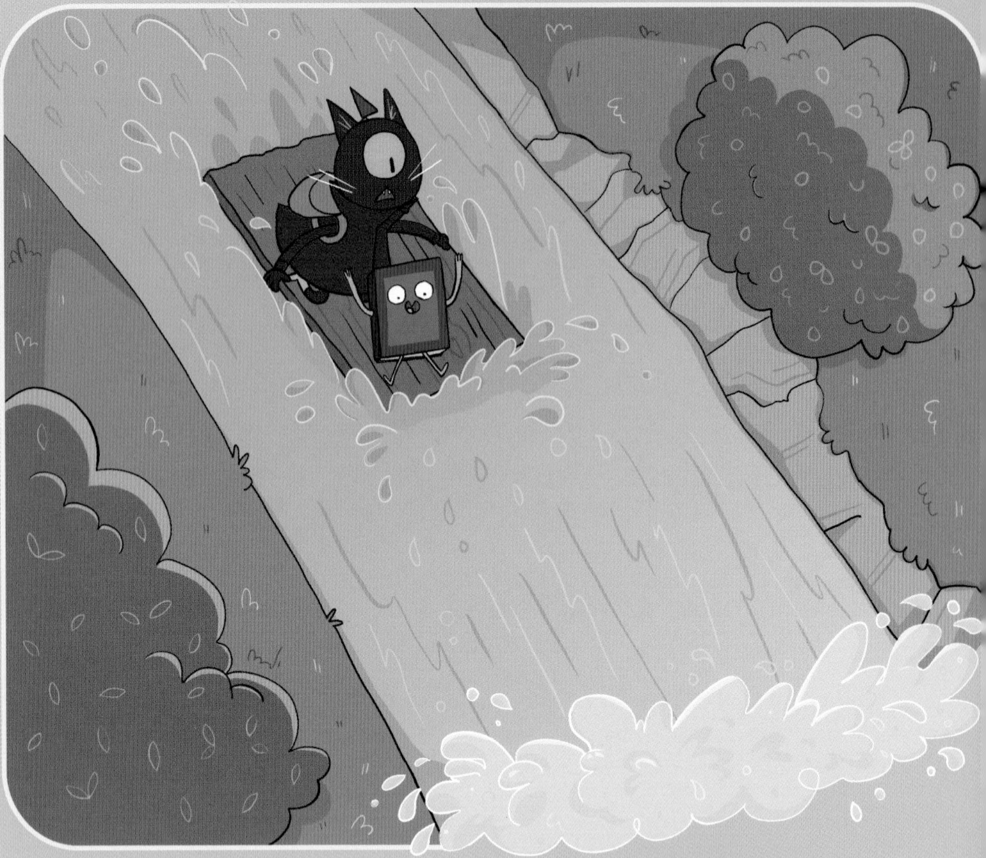

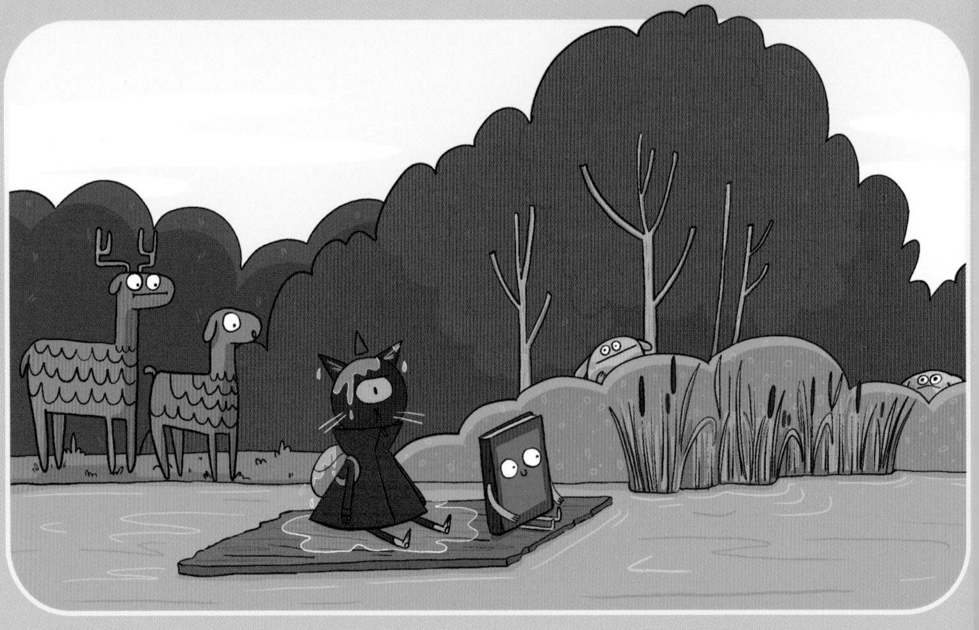

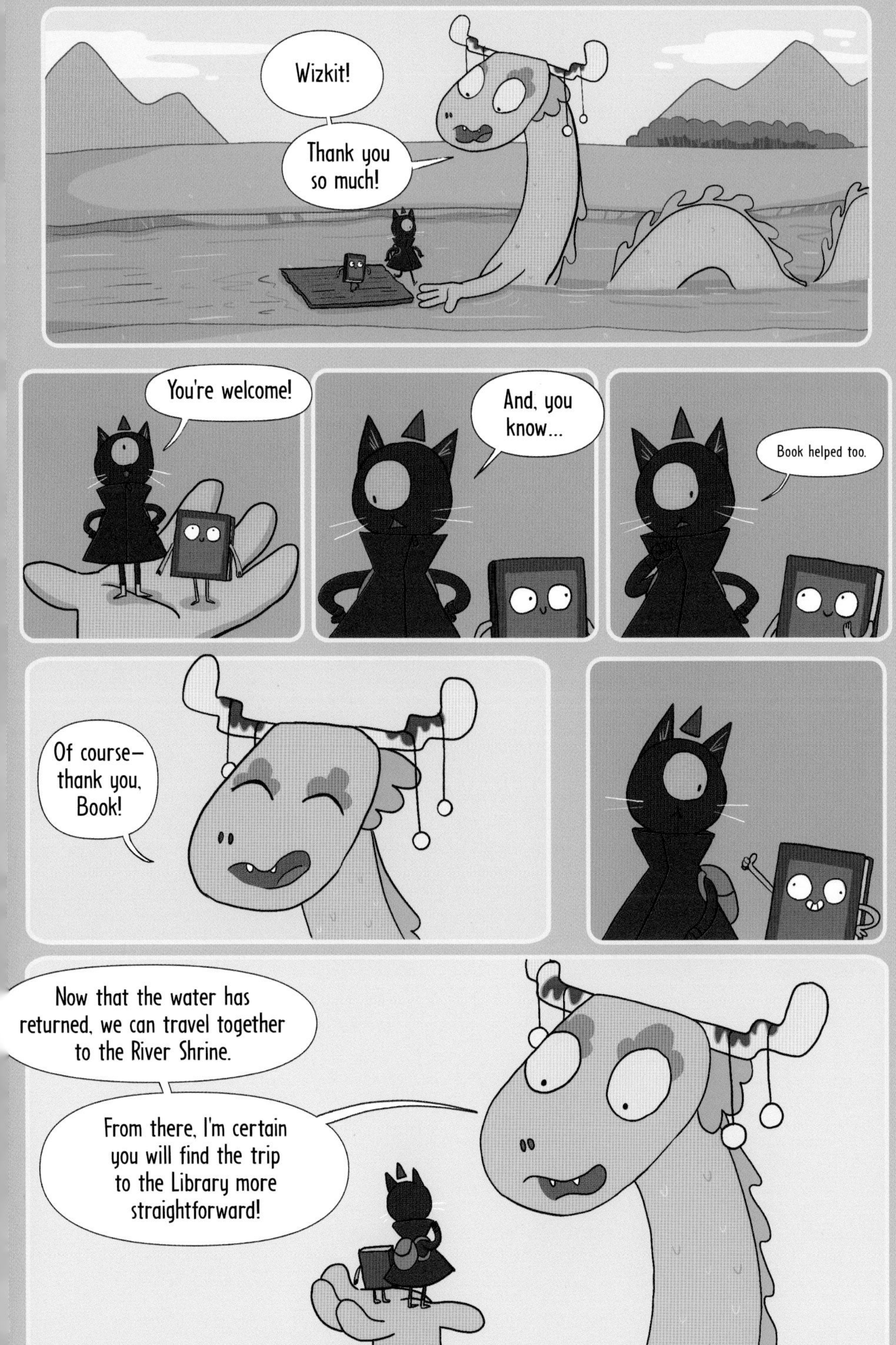

Wizkit!
Thank you so much!
You're welcome!
And, you know...
Book helped too.
Of course—thank you, Book!
Now that the water has returned, we can travel together to the River Shrine.
From there, I'm certain you will find the trip to the Library more straightforward!

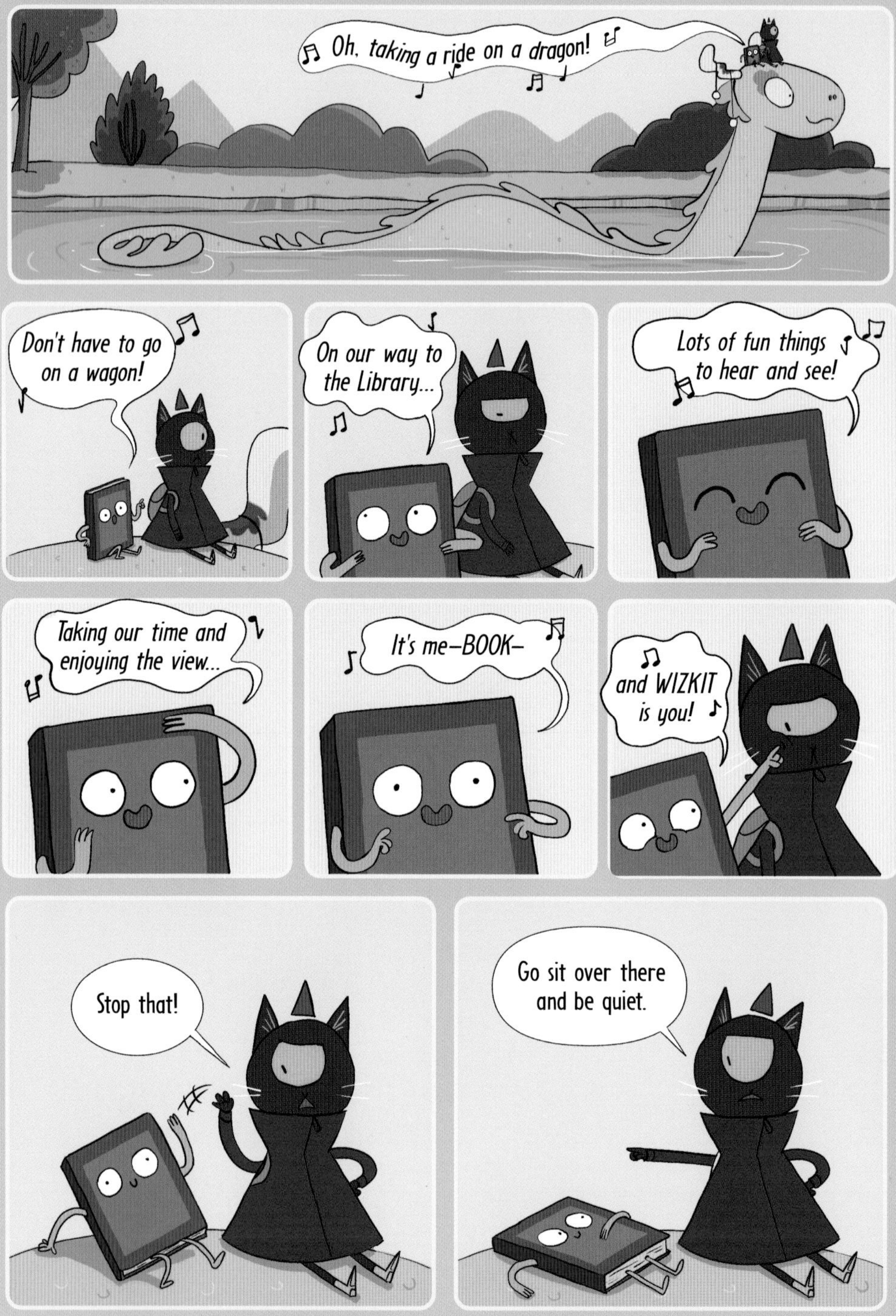

Oh, taking a ride on a dragon!
Don't have to go on a wagon!
On our way to the Library...
Lots of fun things to hear and see!
Taking our time and enjoying the view...
It's me—BOOK—
and WIZKIT is you!
Stop that!
Go sit over there and be quiet.

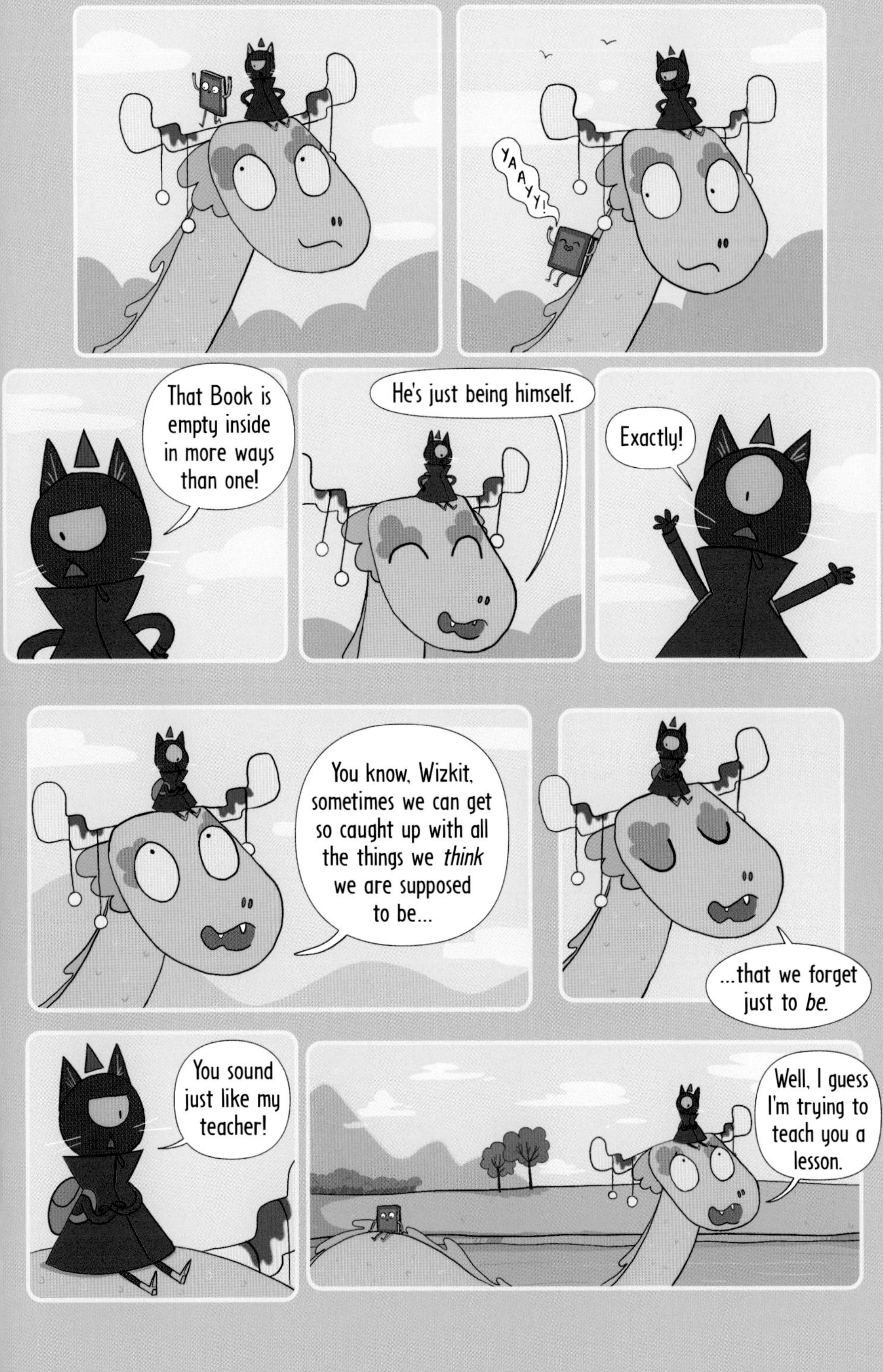
YAAYY!
That Book is empty inside in more ways than one!
He's just being himself.
Exactly!
You know, Wizkit, sometimes we can get so caught up with all the things we *think* we are supposed to be...
...that we forget just to *be*.
You sound just like my teacher!
Well, I guess I'm trying to teach you a lesson.

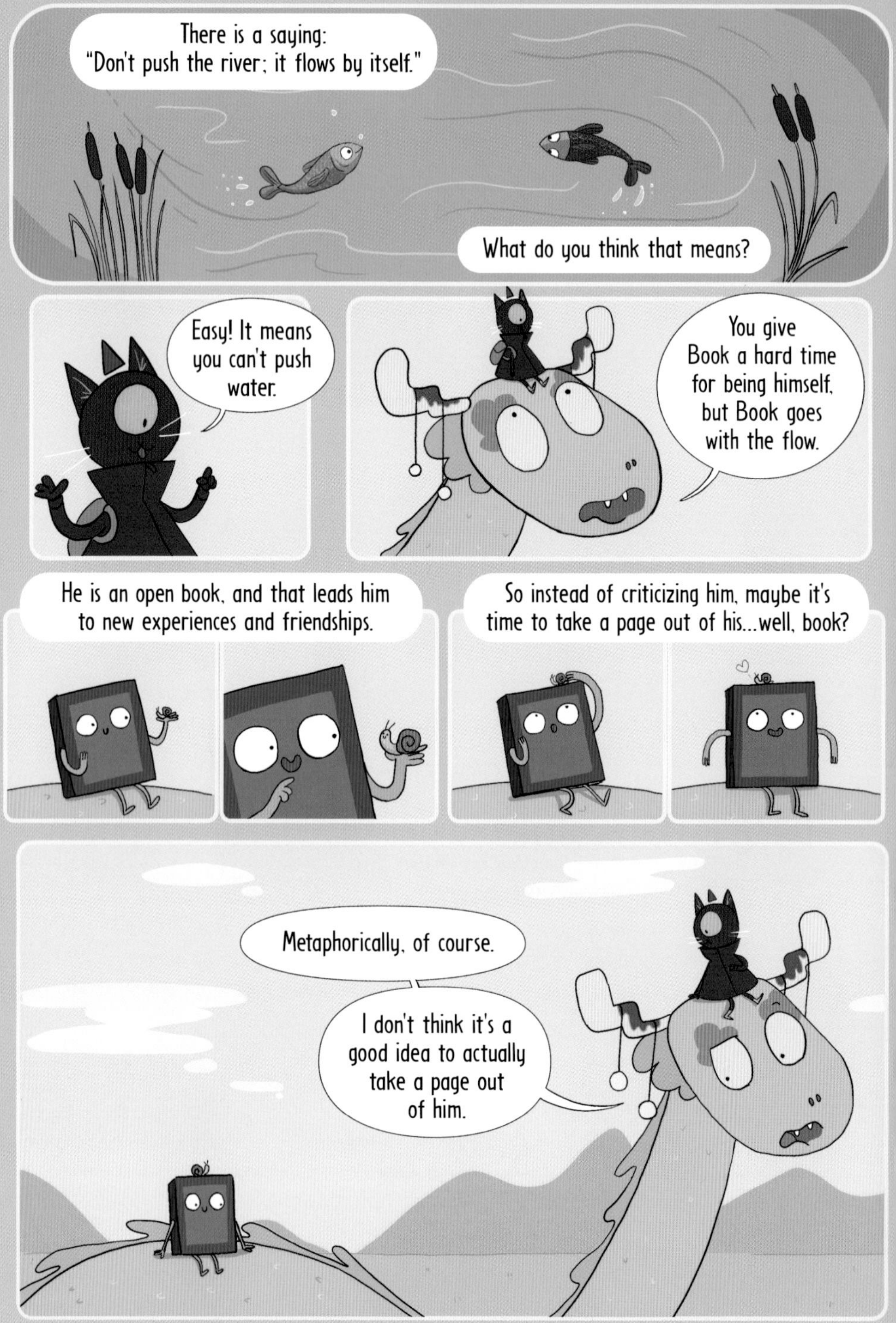
There is a saying: "Don't push the river; it flows by itself."
What do you think that means?
Easy! It means you can't push water.
You give Book a hard time for being himself, but Book goes with the flow.
He is an open book, and that leads him to new experiences and friendships.
So instead of criticizing him, maybe it's time to take a page out of his...well, book?
Metaphorically, of course.
I don't think it's a good idea to actually take a page out of him.

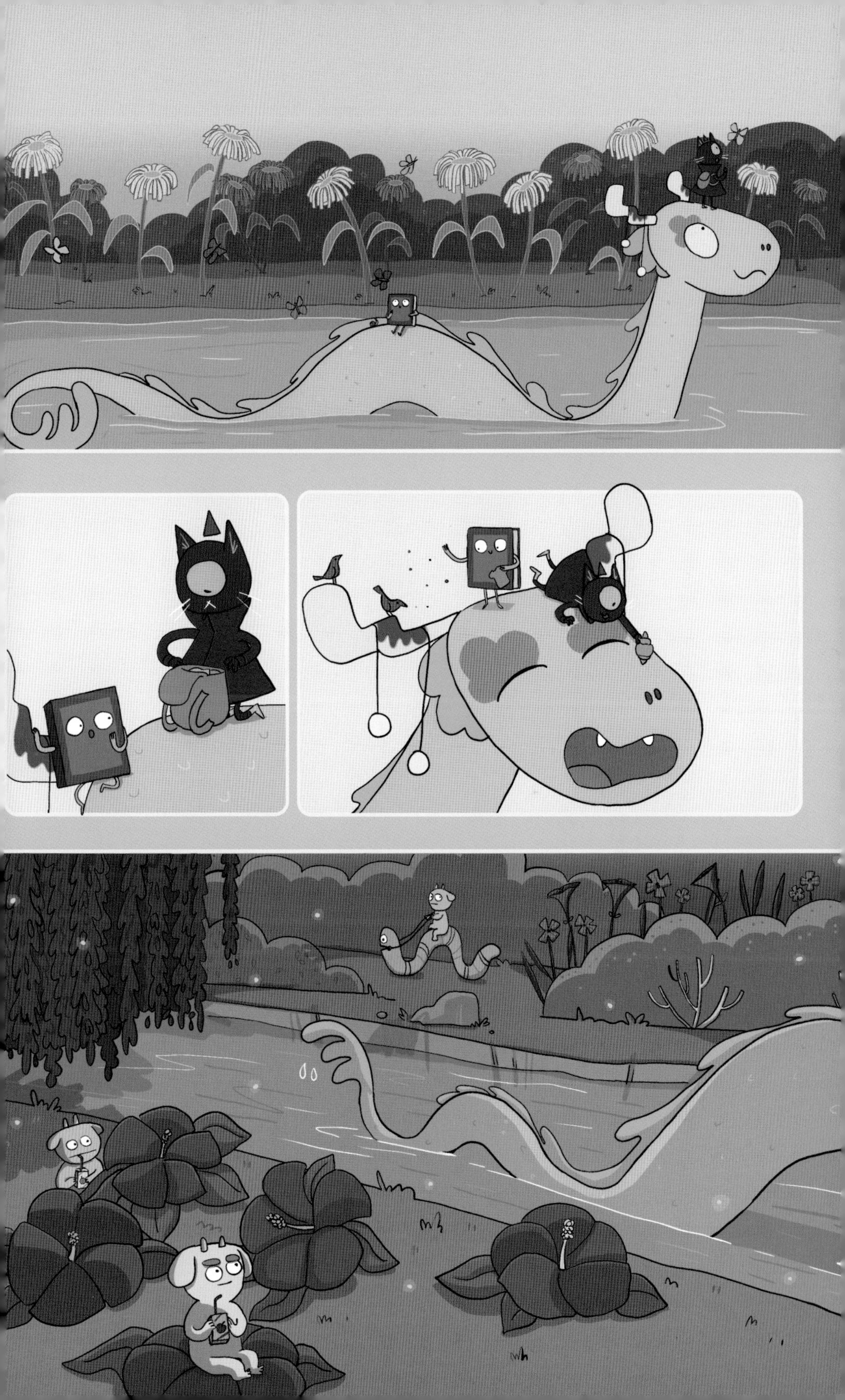

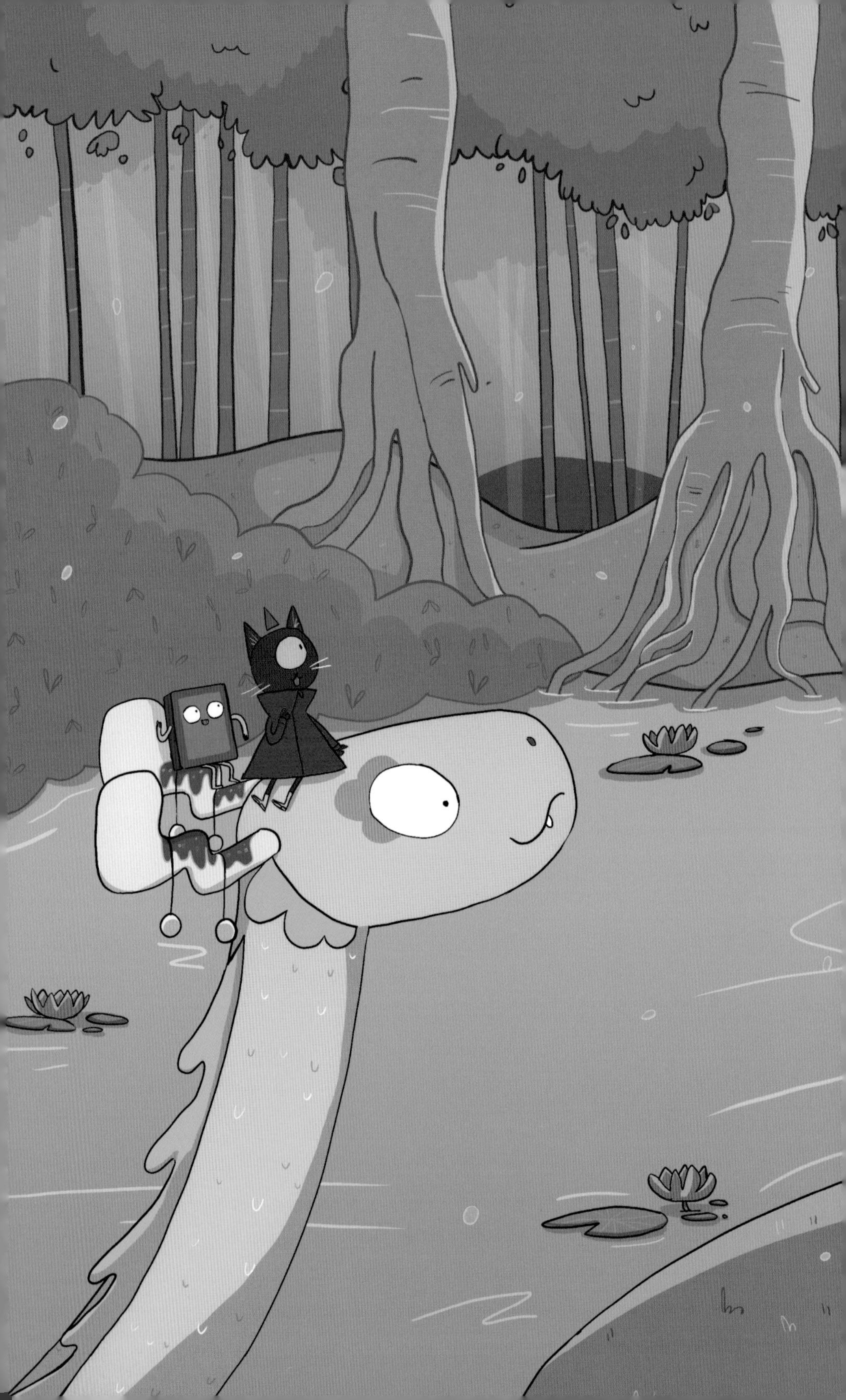

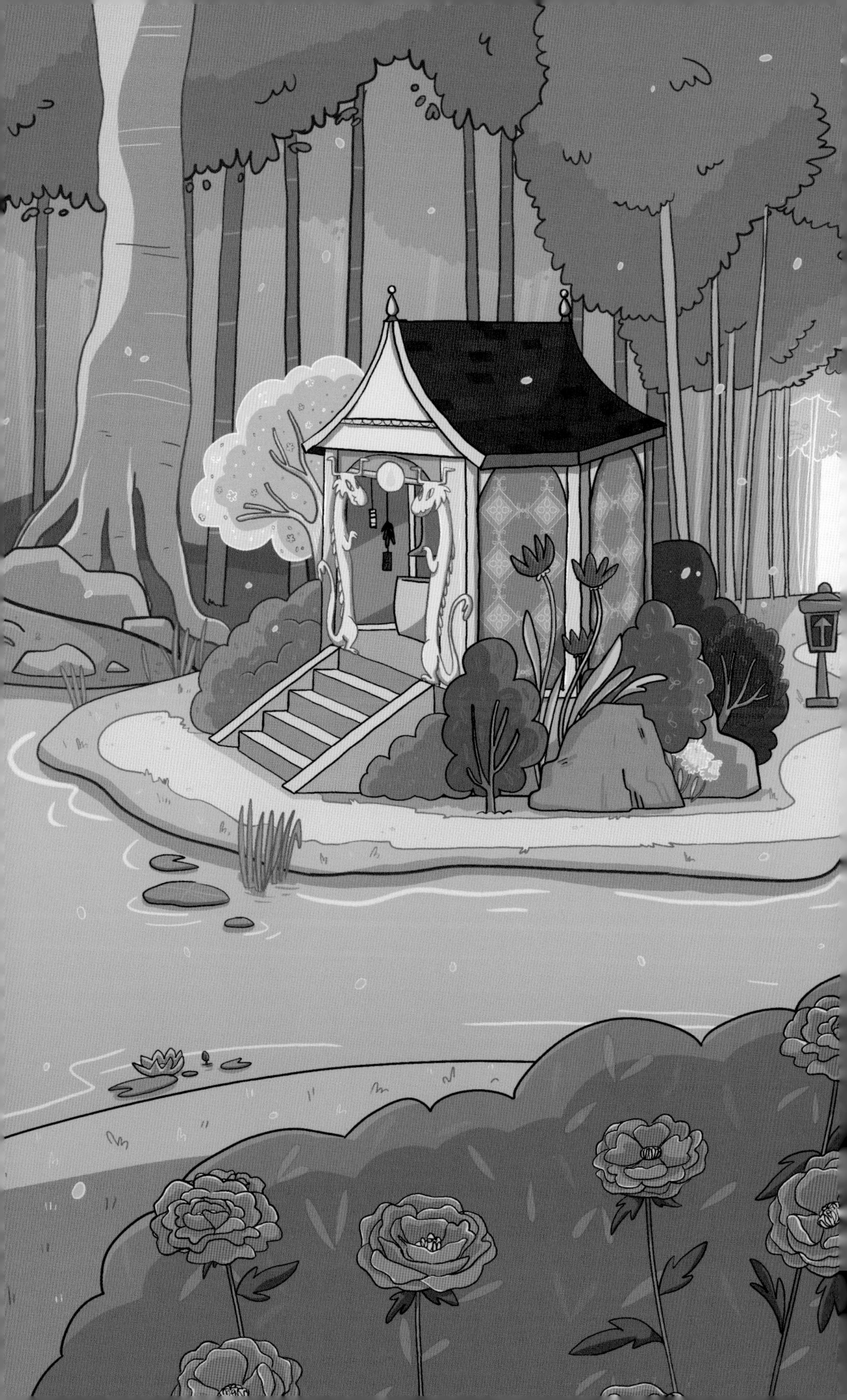

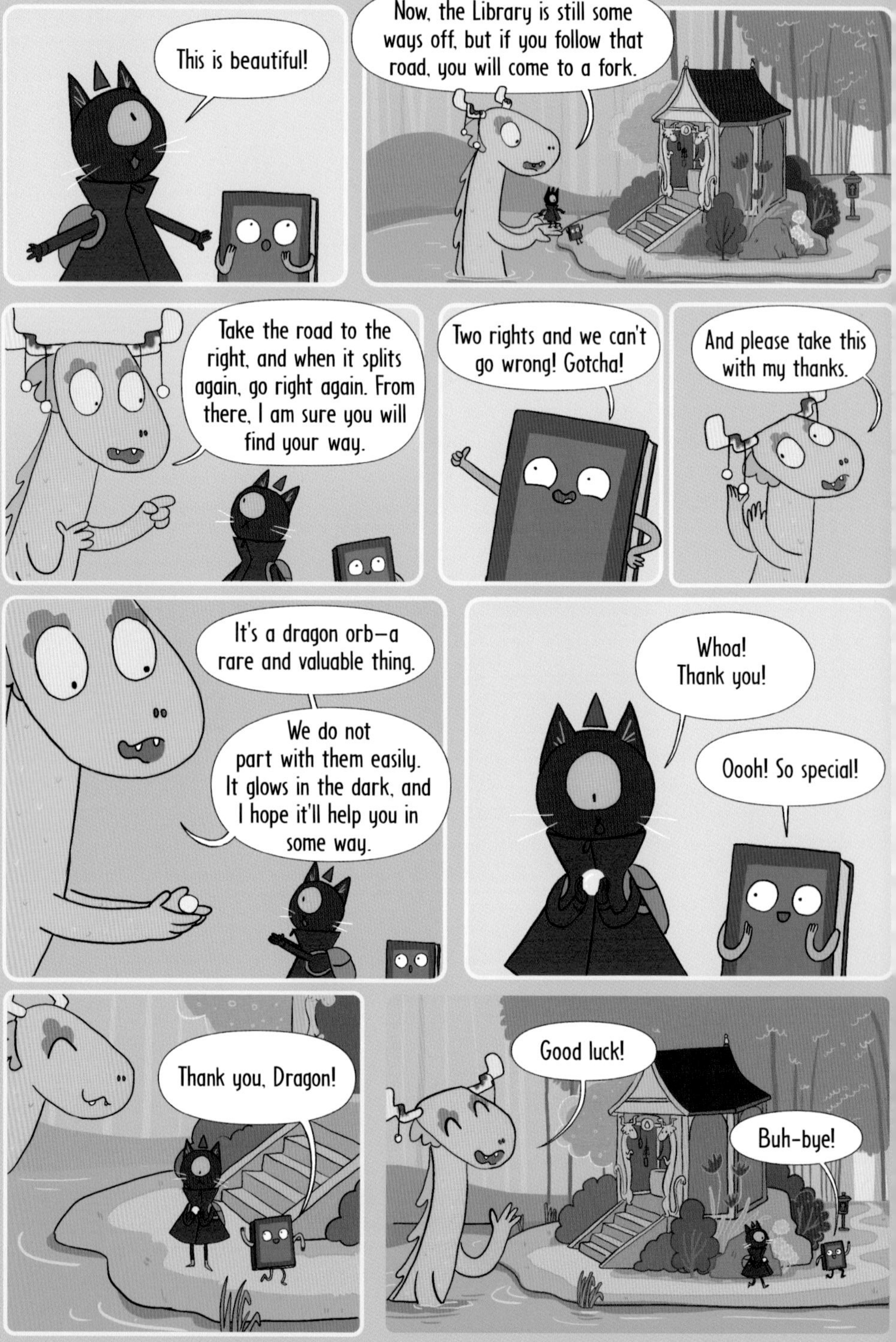
This is beautiful!
Now, the Library is still some ways off, but if you follow that road, you will come to a fork.
Take the road to the right, and when it splits again, go right again. From there, I am sure you will find your way.
Two rights and we can't go wrong! Gotcha!
And please take this with my thanks.
It's a dragon orb—a rare and valuable thing.
We do not part with them easily. It glows in the dark, and I hope it'll help you in some way.
Whoa! Thank you!
Oooh! So special!
Thank you, Dragon!
Good luck!
Buh-bye!

Chapter 3

A Friendship Kindled

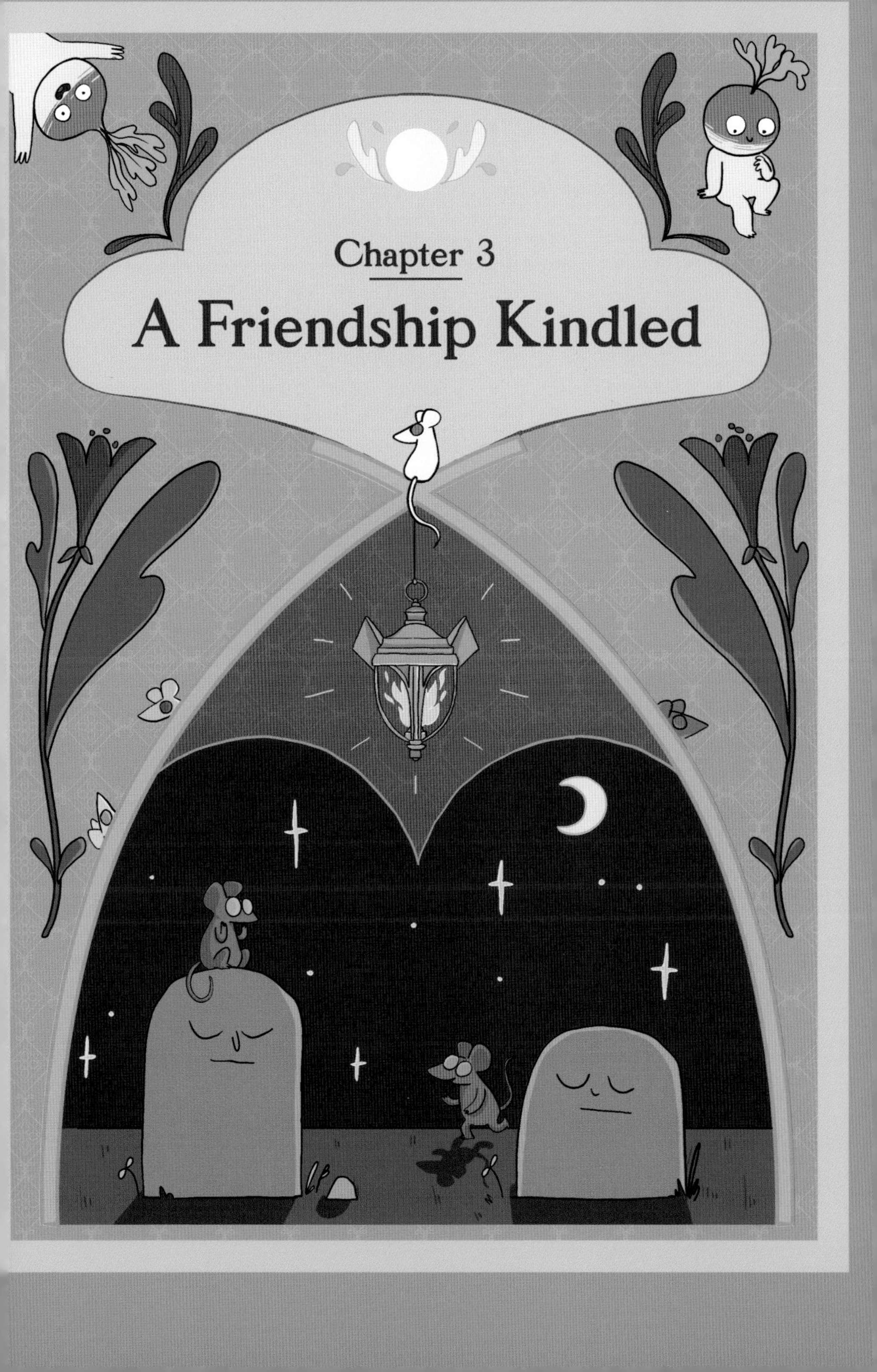

Well, hello, little cuties.
Whatcha doin'?

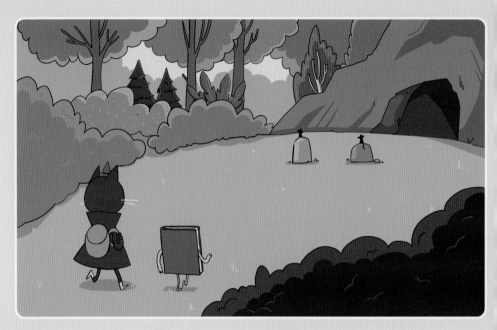

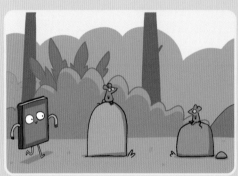

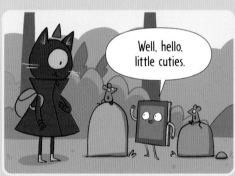

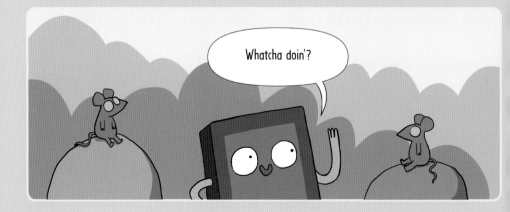

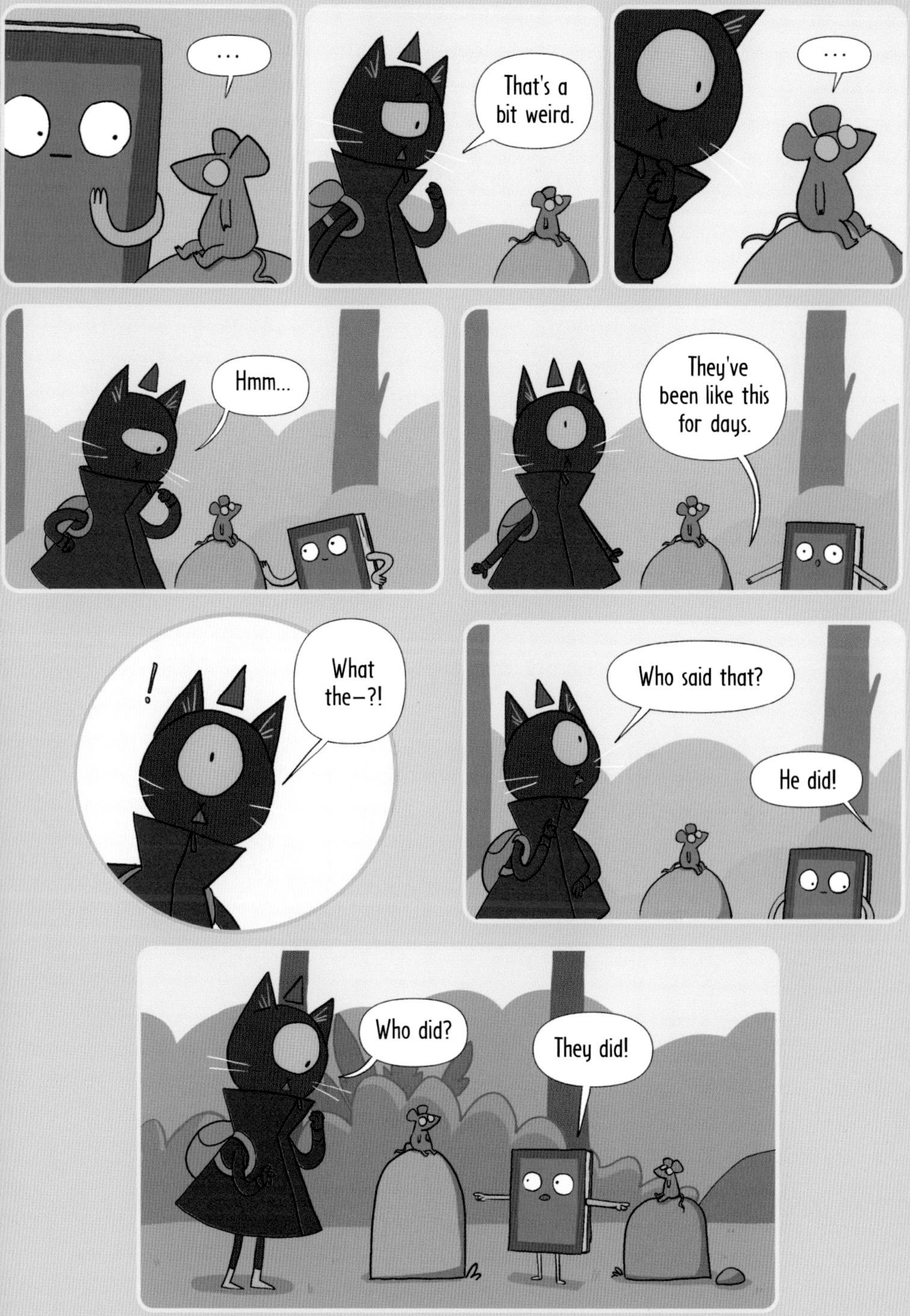
...
That's a bit weird.
...
Hmm...
They've been like this for days.
!
What the–?!
Who said that?
He did!
Who did?
They did!

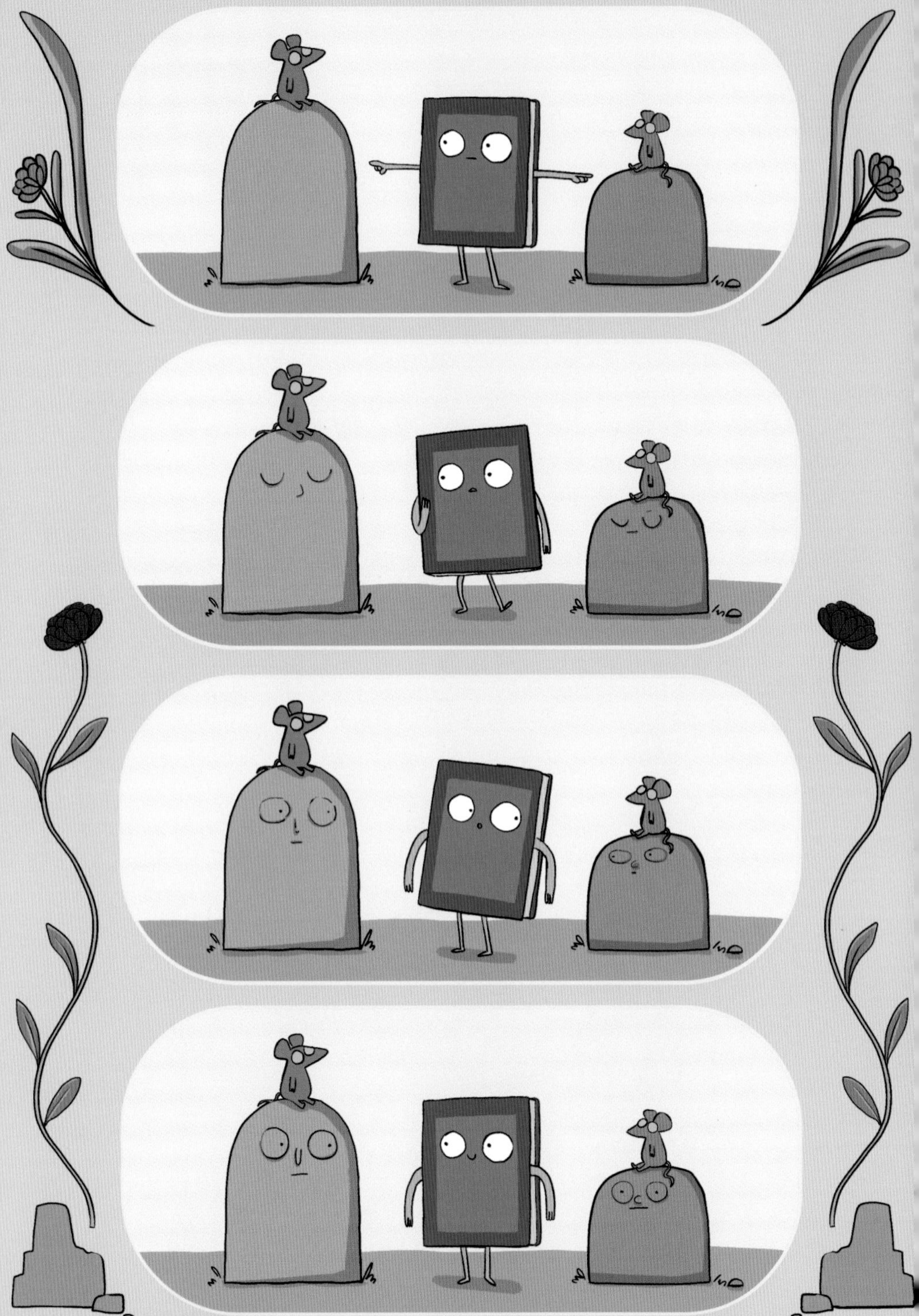

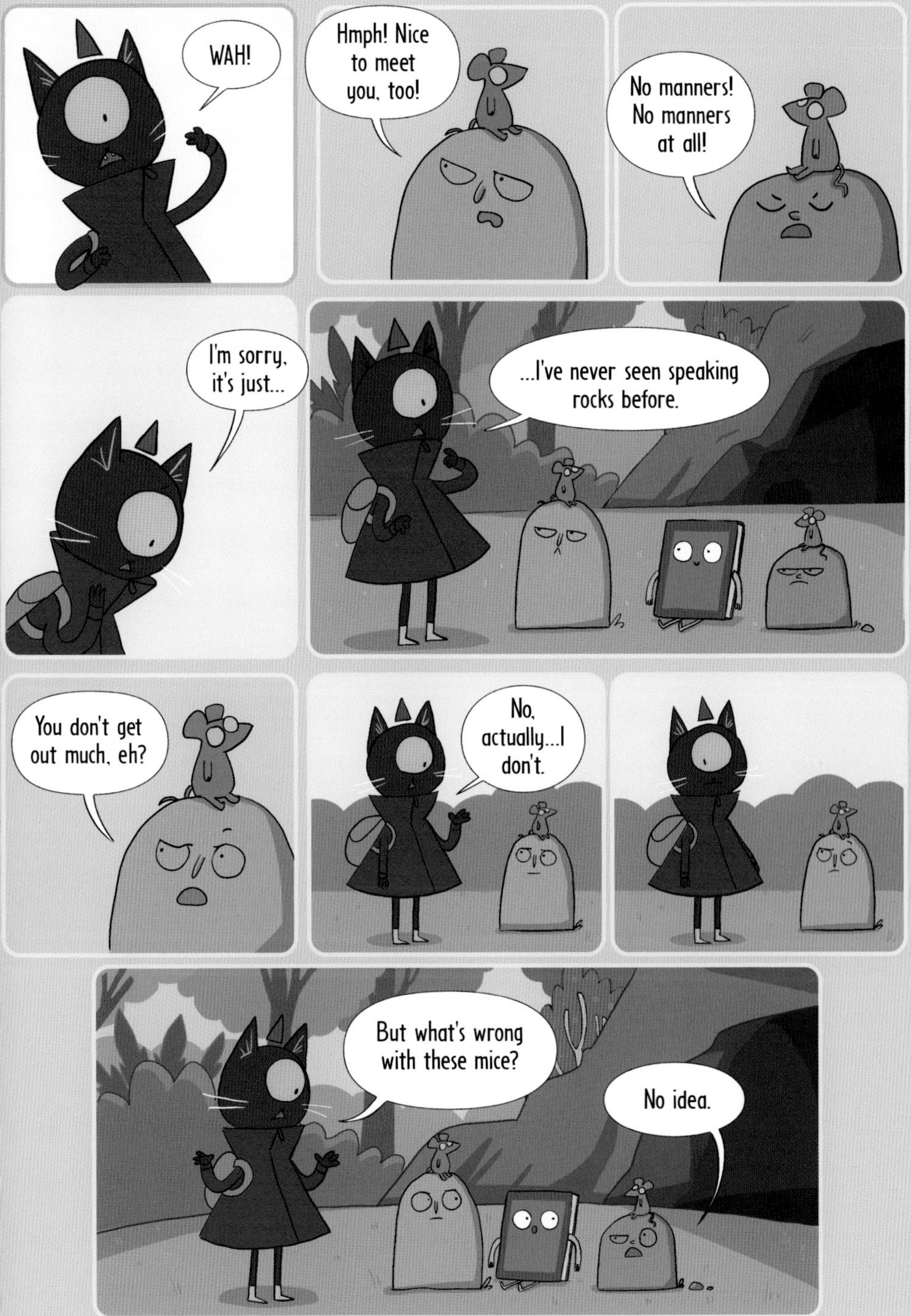
WAH!
Hmph! Nice to meet you, too!
No manners! No manners at all!
I'm sorry, it's just...
...I've never seen speaking rocks before.
You don't get out much, eh?
No, actually...I don't.
But what's wrong with these mice?
No idea.

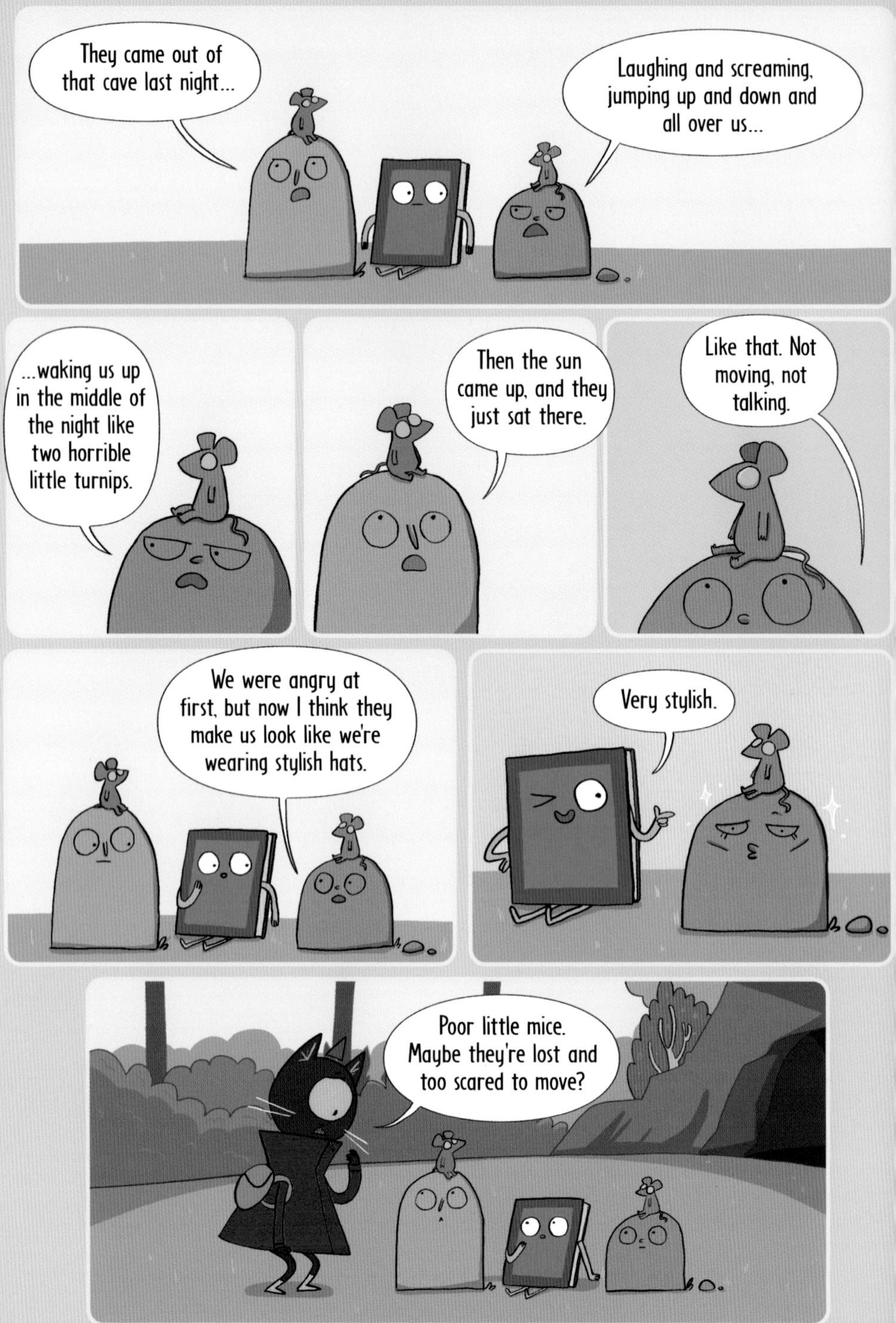
They came out of that cave last night...
Laughing and screaming, jumping up and down and all over us...
...waking us up in the middle of the night like two horrible little turnips.
Then the sun came up, and they just sat there.
Like that. Not moving, not talking.
We were angry at first, but now I think they make us look like we're wearing stylish hats.
Very stylish.
Poor little mice. Maybe they're lost and too scared to move?

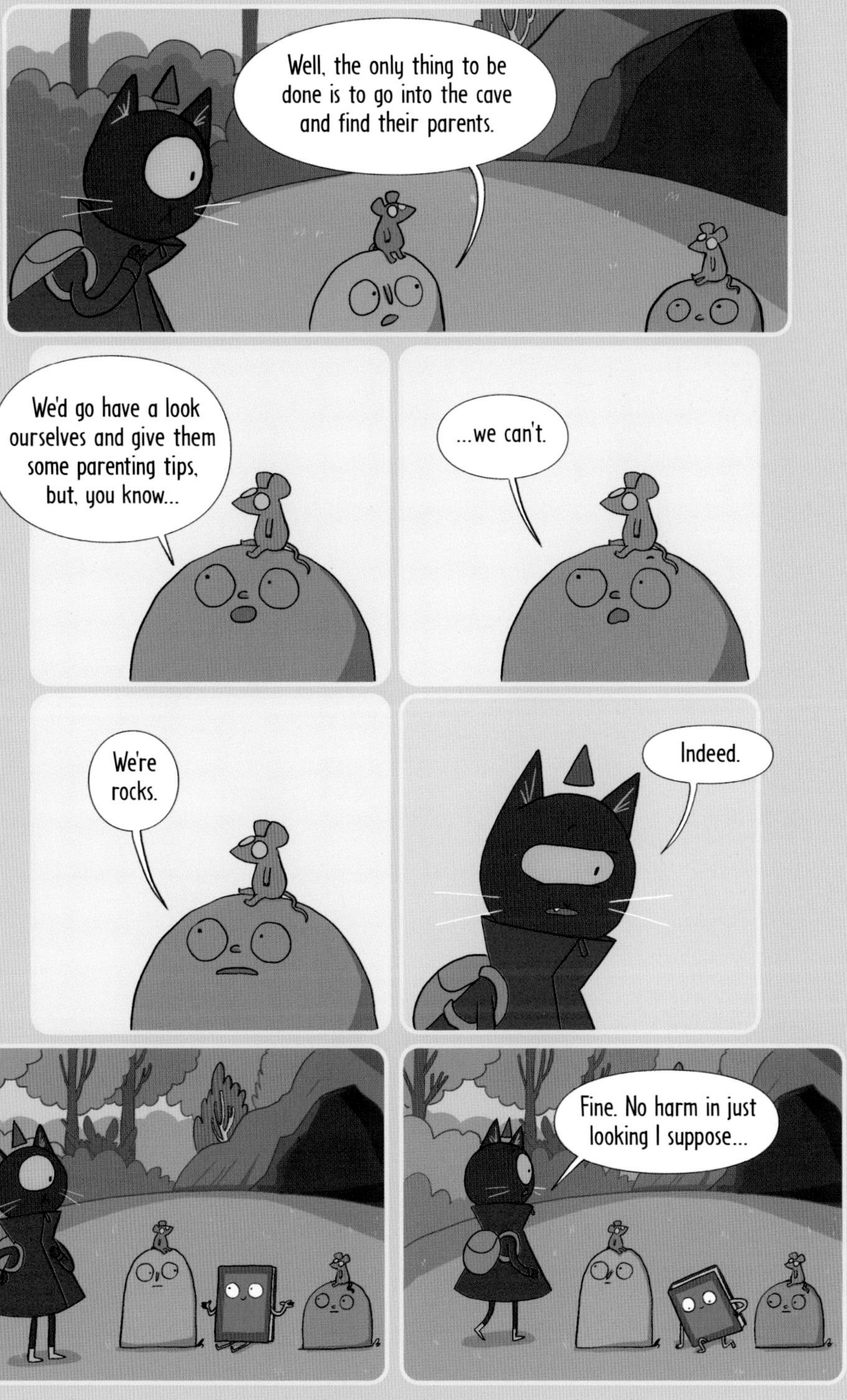
Well, the only thing to be done is to go into the cave and find their parents.
We'd go have a look ourselves and give them some parenting tips, but, you know...
...we can't.
We're rocks.
Indeed.
Fine. No harm in just looking I suppose...

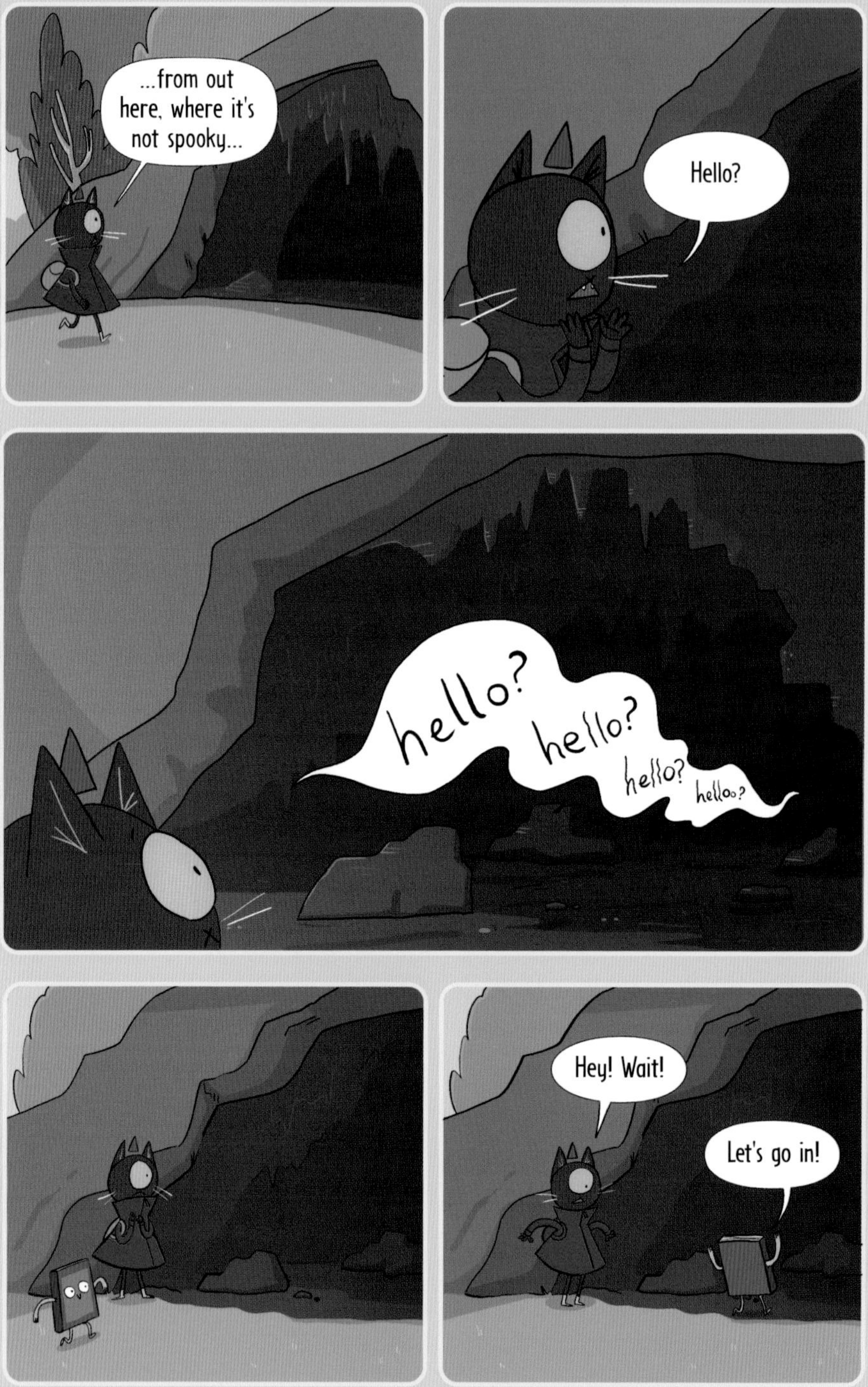
...from out here, where it's not spooky...
Hello?
hello? hello? hello? helloo?
Hey! Wait!
Let's go in!

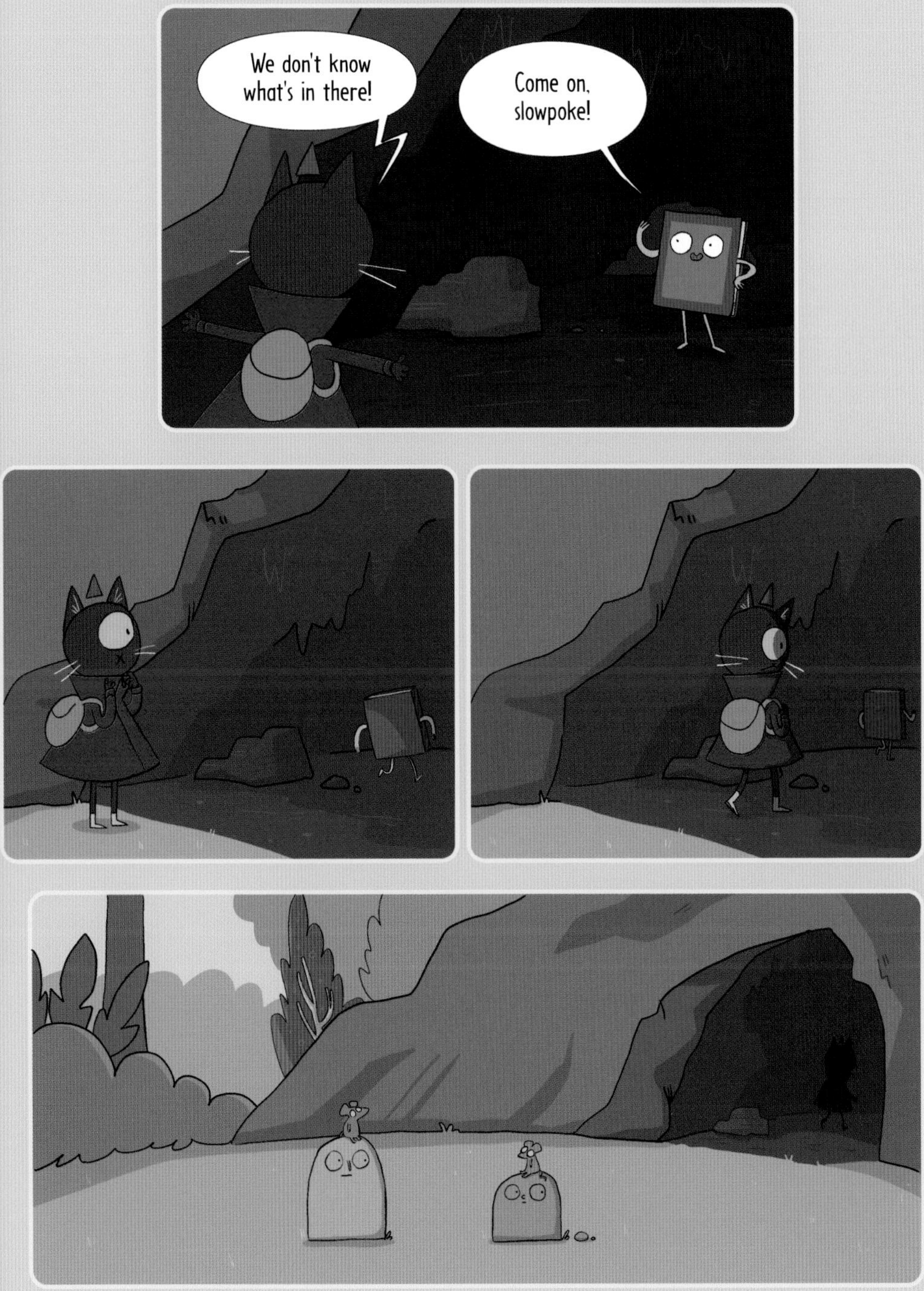
We don't know what's in there!
Come on, slowpoke!

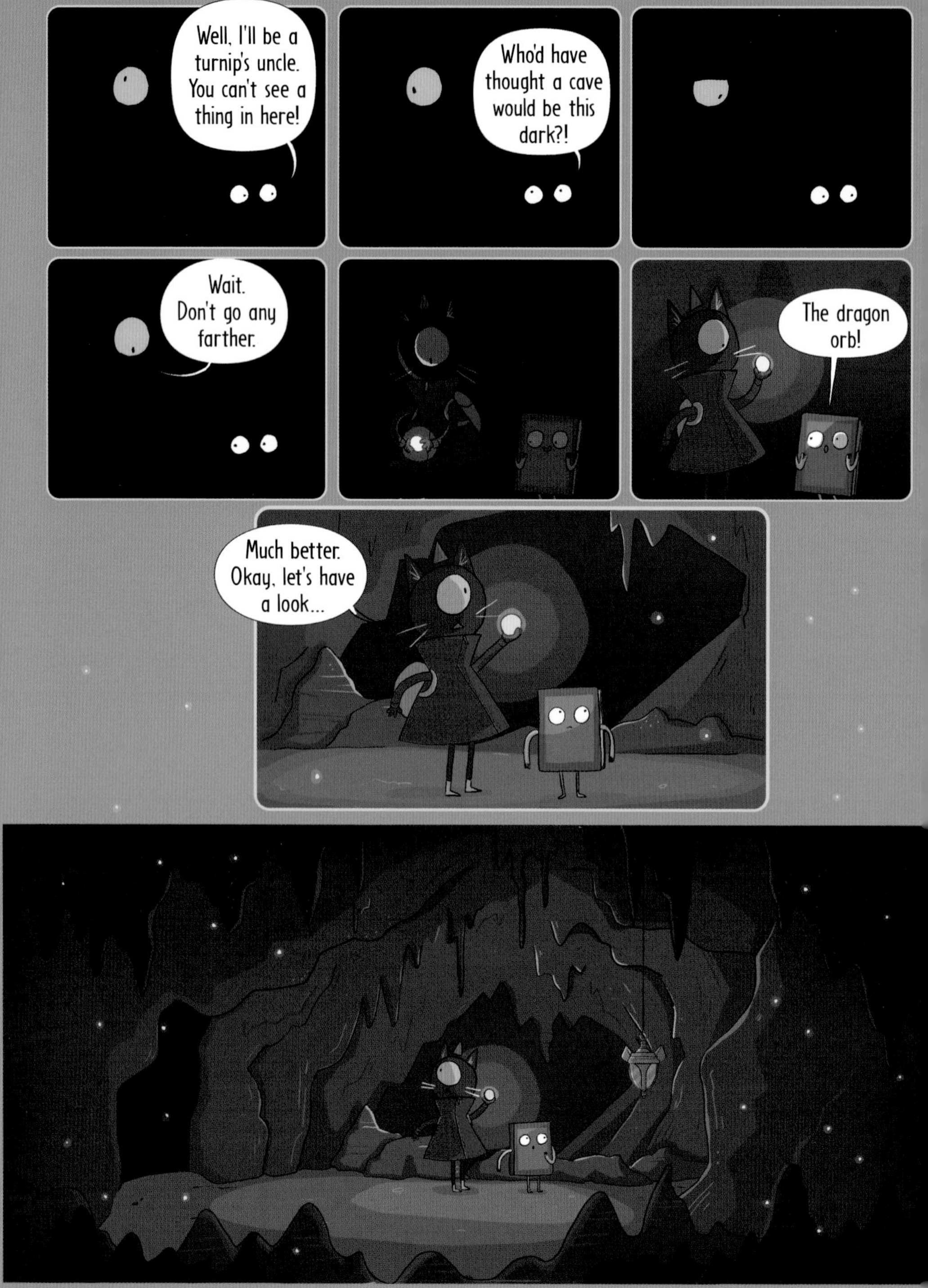
Well, I'll be a turnip's uncle. You can't see a thing in here!
Who'd have thought a cave would be this dark?!
Wait. Don't go any farther.
The dragon orb!
Much better. Okay, let's have a look...

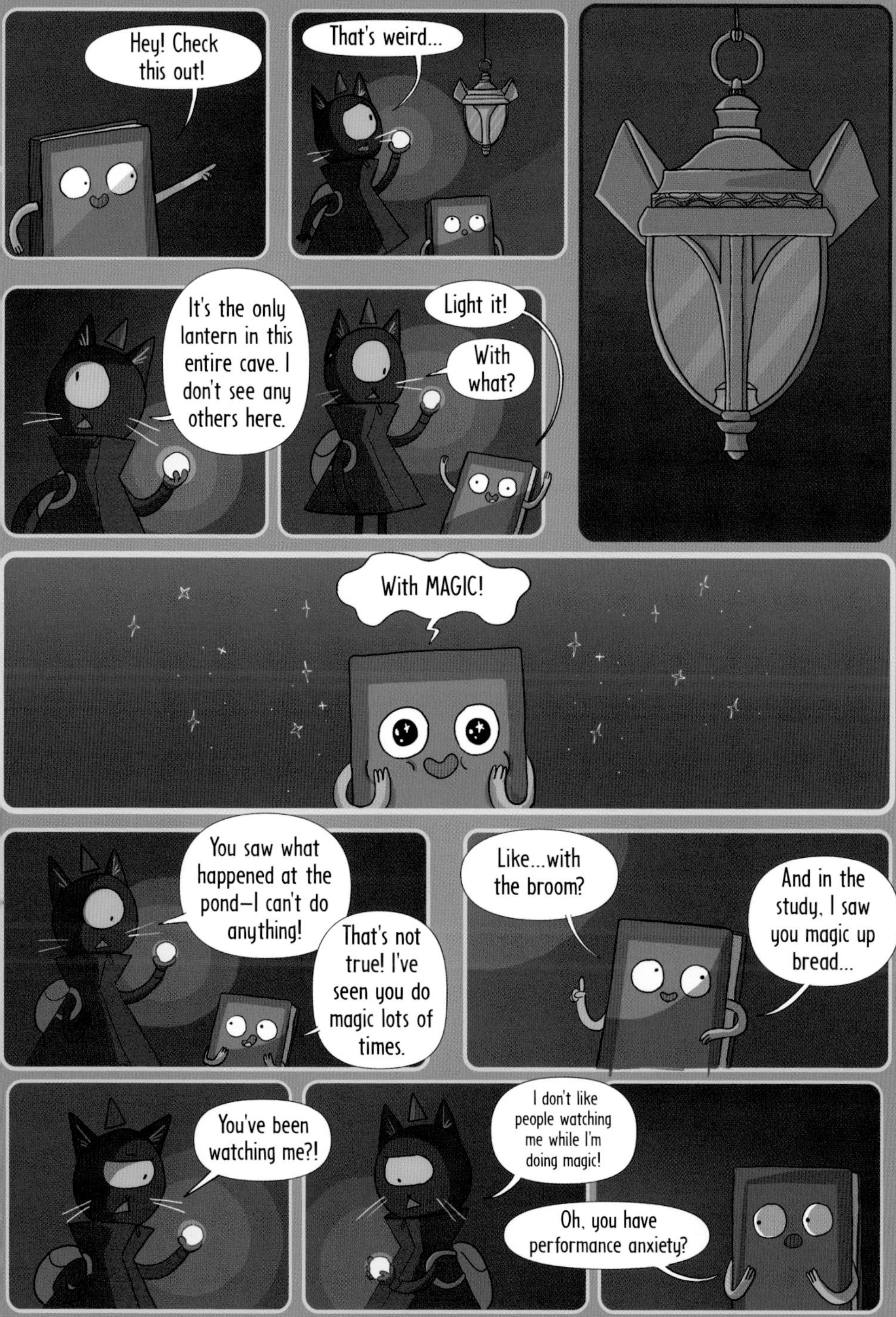

Hey! Check this out!
That's weird...
It's the only lantern in this entire cave. I don't see any others here.
Light it!
With what?
With MAGIC!
You saw what happened at the pond—I can't do anything!
That's not true! I've seen you do magic lots of times.
Like...with the broom?
And in the study, I saw you magic up bread...
You've been watching me?!
I don't like people watching me while I'm doing magic!
Oh, you have performance anxiety?

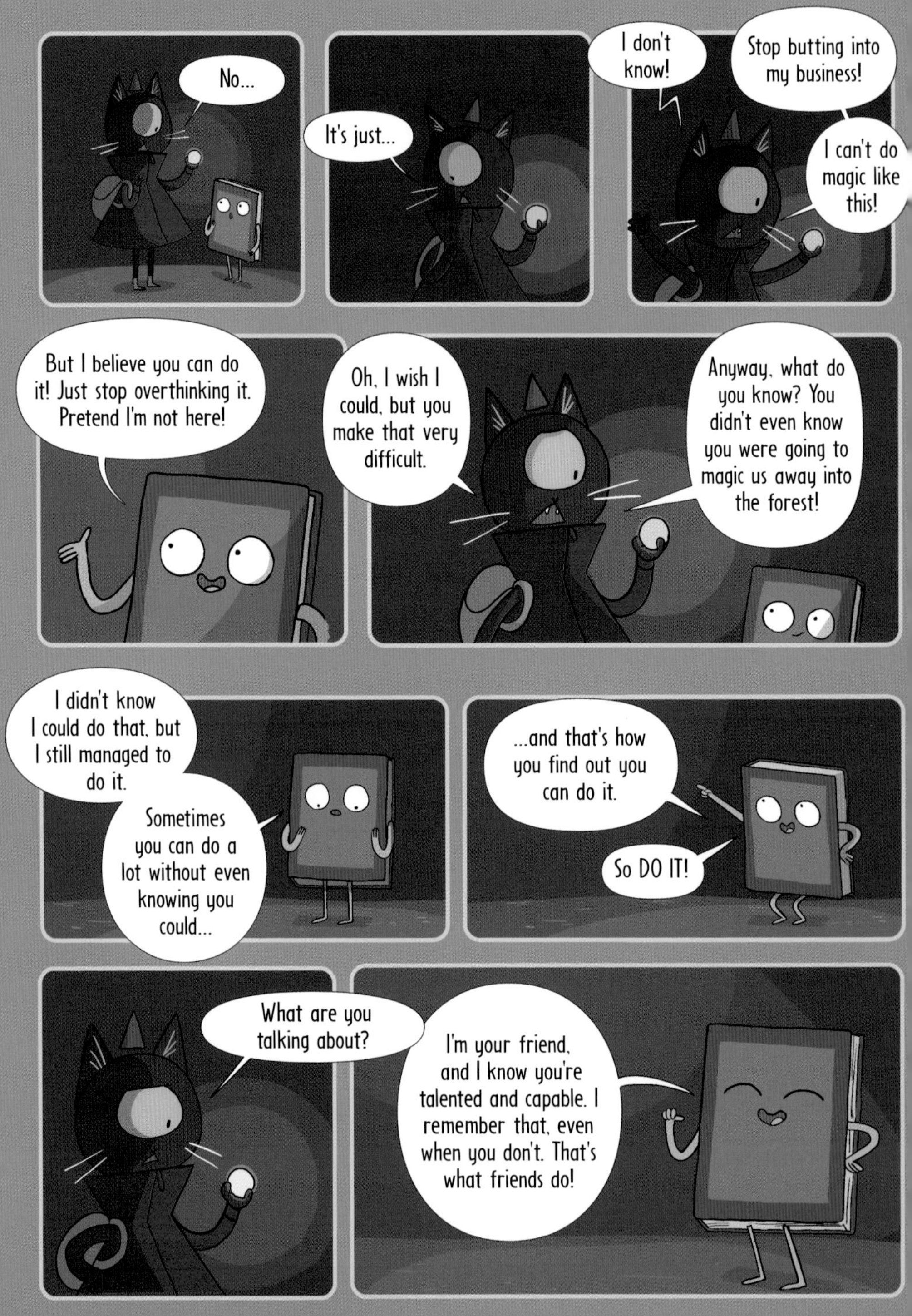
No...
It's just...
I don't know!
Stop butting into my business!
I can't do magic like this!
But I believe you can do it! Just stop overthinking it. Pretend I'm not here!
Oh, I wish I could, but you make that very difficult.
Anyway, what do you know? You didn't even know you were going to magic us away into the forest!
I didn't know I could do that, but I still managed to do it.
Sometimes you can do a lot without even knowing you could...
...and that's how you find out you can do it.
So DO IT!
What are you talking about?
I'm your friend, and I know you're talented and capable. I remember that, even when you don't. That's what friends do!

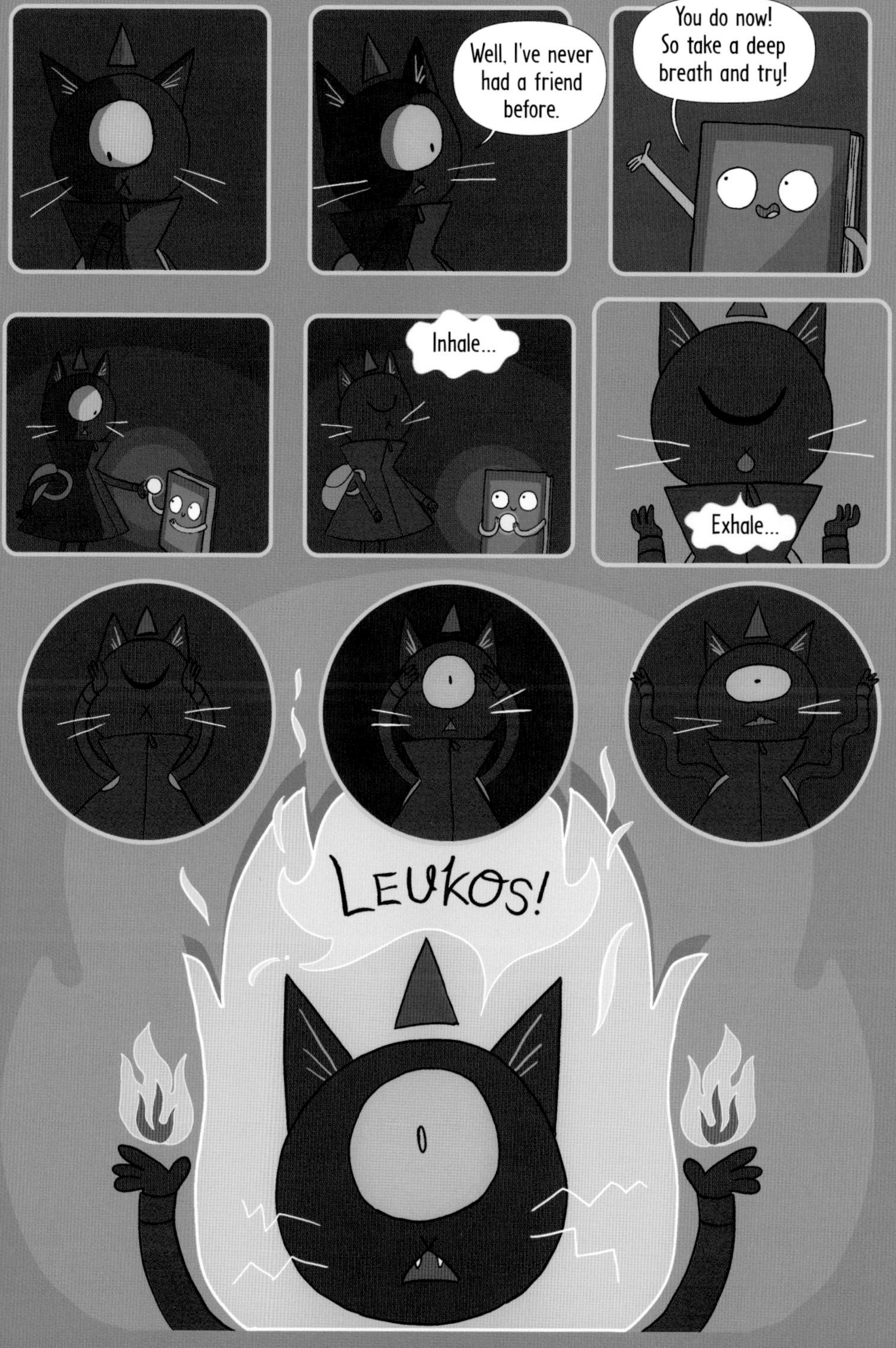
Well, I've never had a friend before.
You do now! So take a deep breath and try!
Inhale...
Exhale...
LEUKOS!

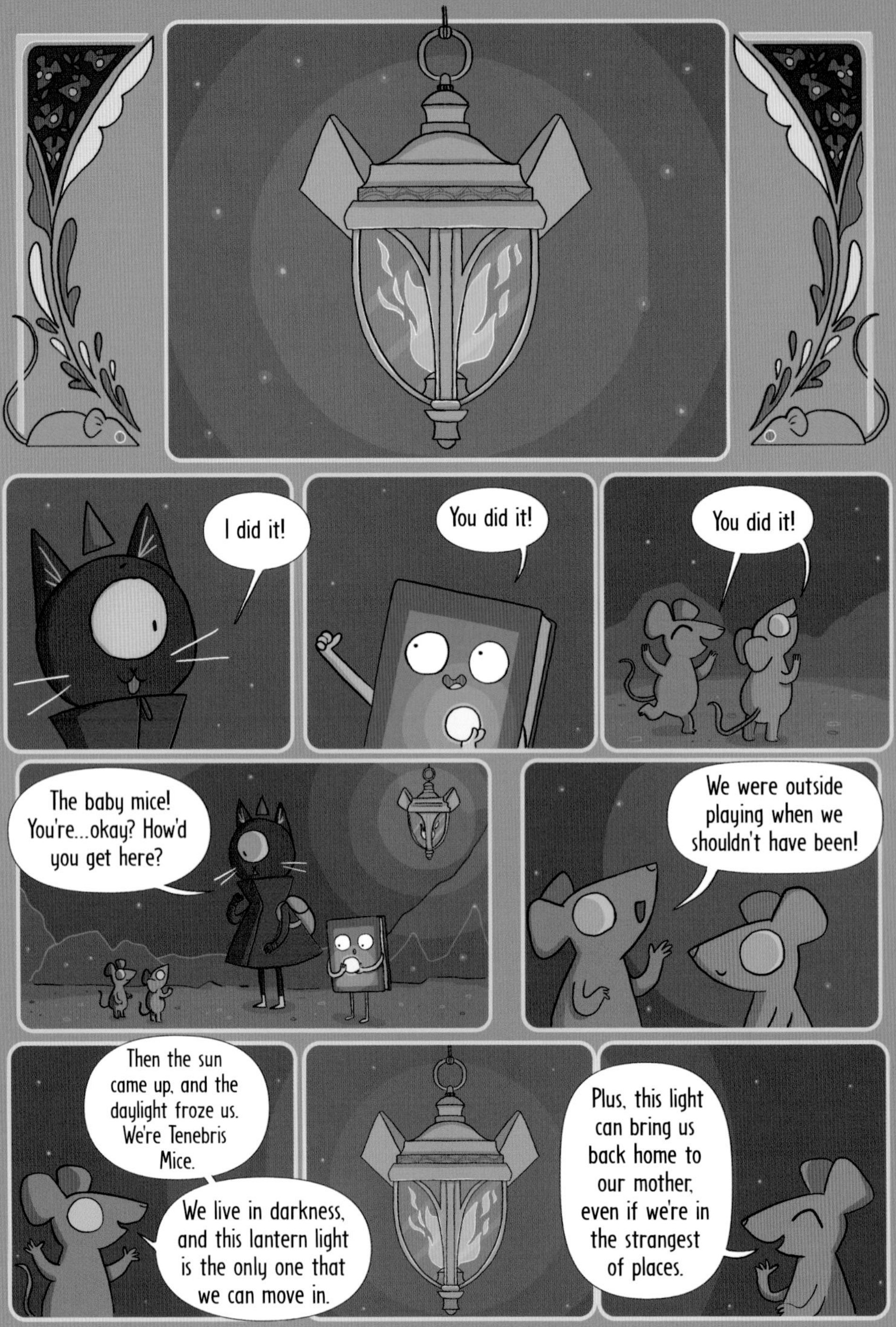
I did it!
You did it!
You did it!
The baby mice! You're...okay? How'd you get here?
We were outside playing when we shouldn't have been!
Then the sun came up, and the daylight froze us. We're Tenebris Mice.
We live in darkness, and this lantern light is the only one that we can move in.
Plus, this light can bring us back home to our mother, even if we're in the strangest of places.

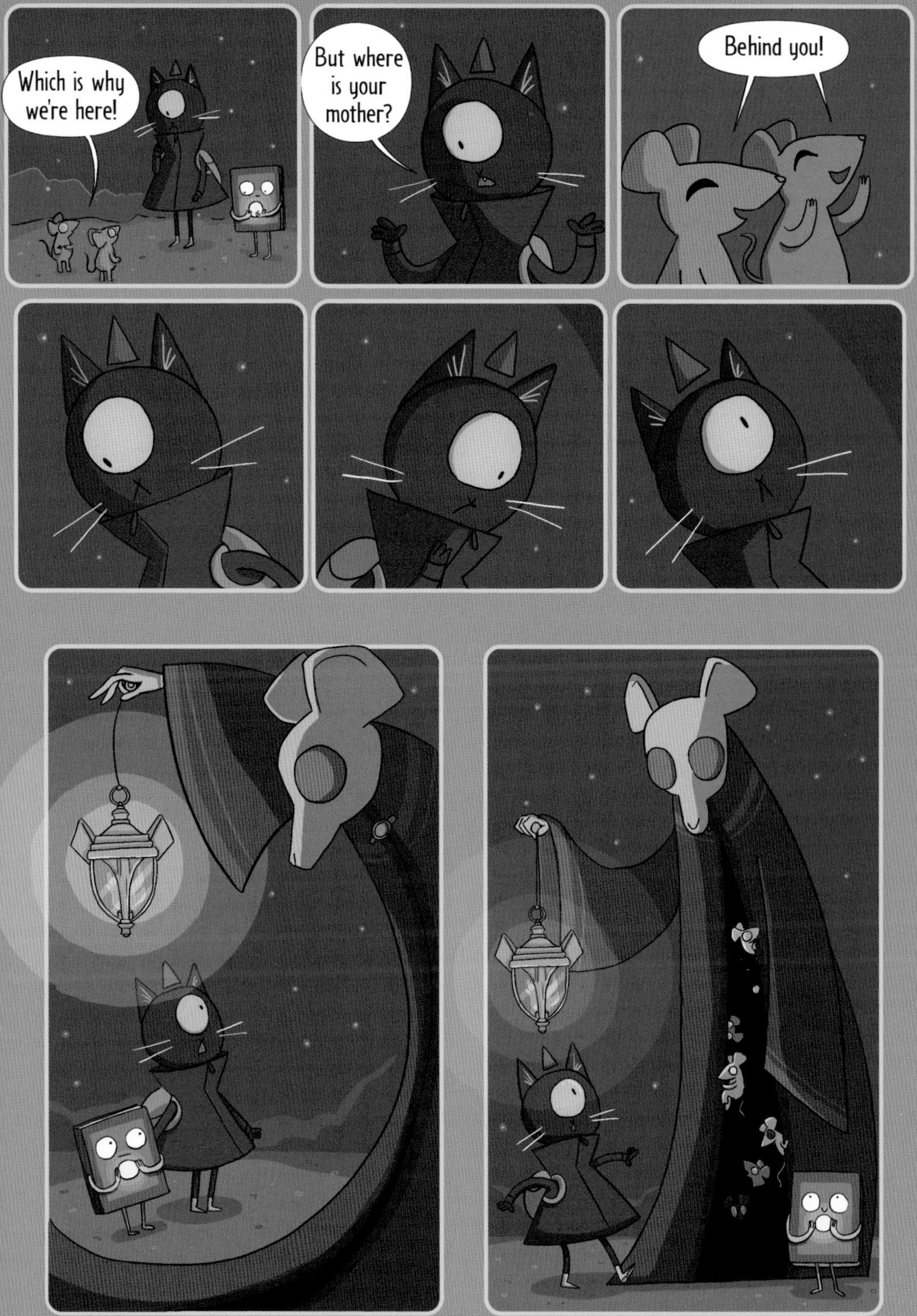
Which is why we're here!
But where is your mother?
Behind you!

Such cute little babies!
Well.
I guess we'll see ourselves out...

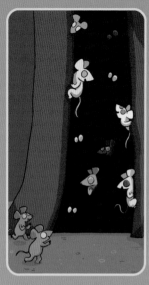

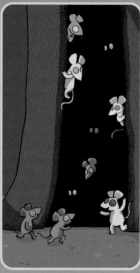

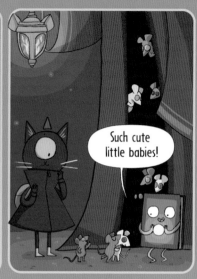

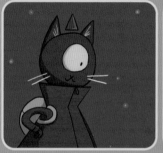

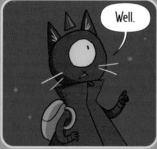

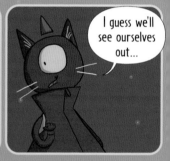

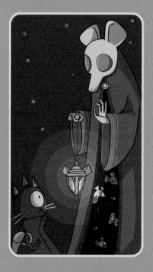

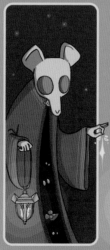

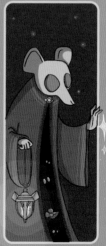

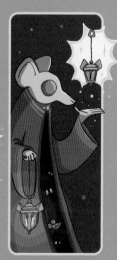

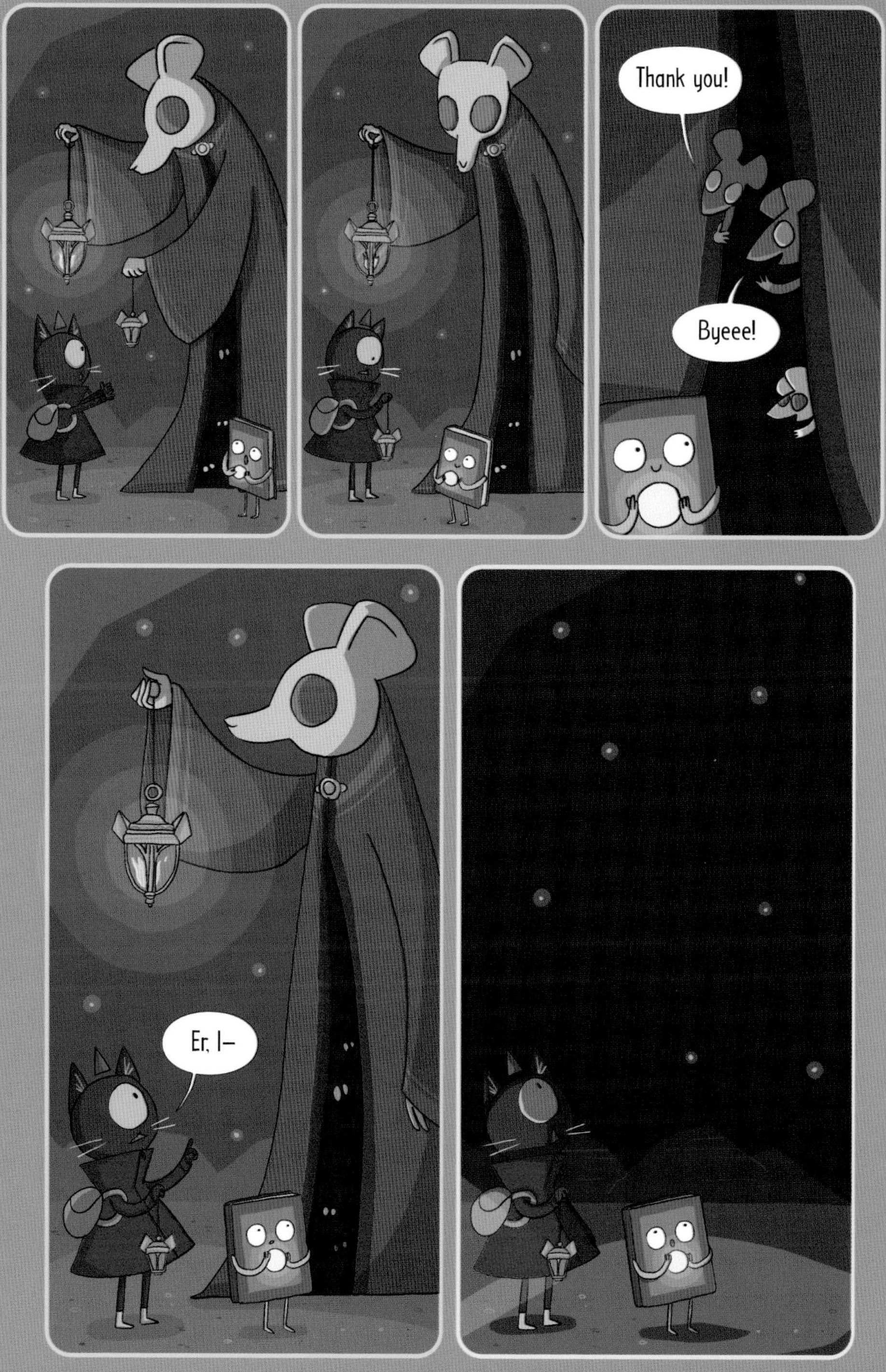
Thank you!
Byeee!
Er, I—

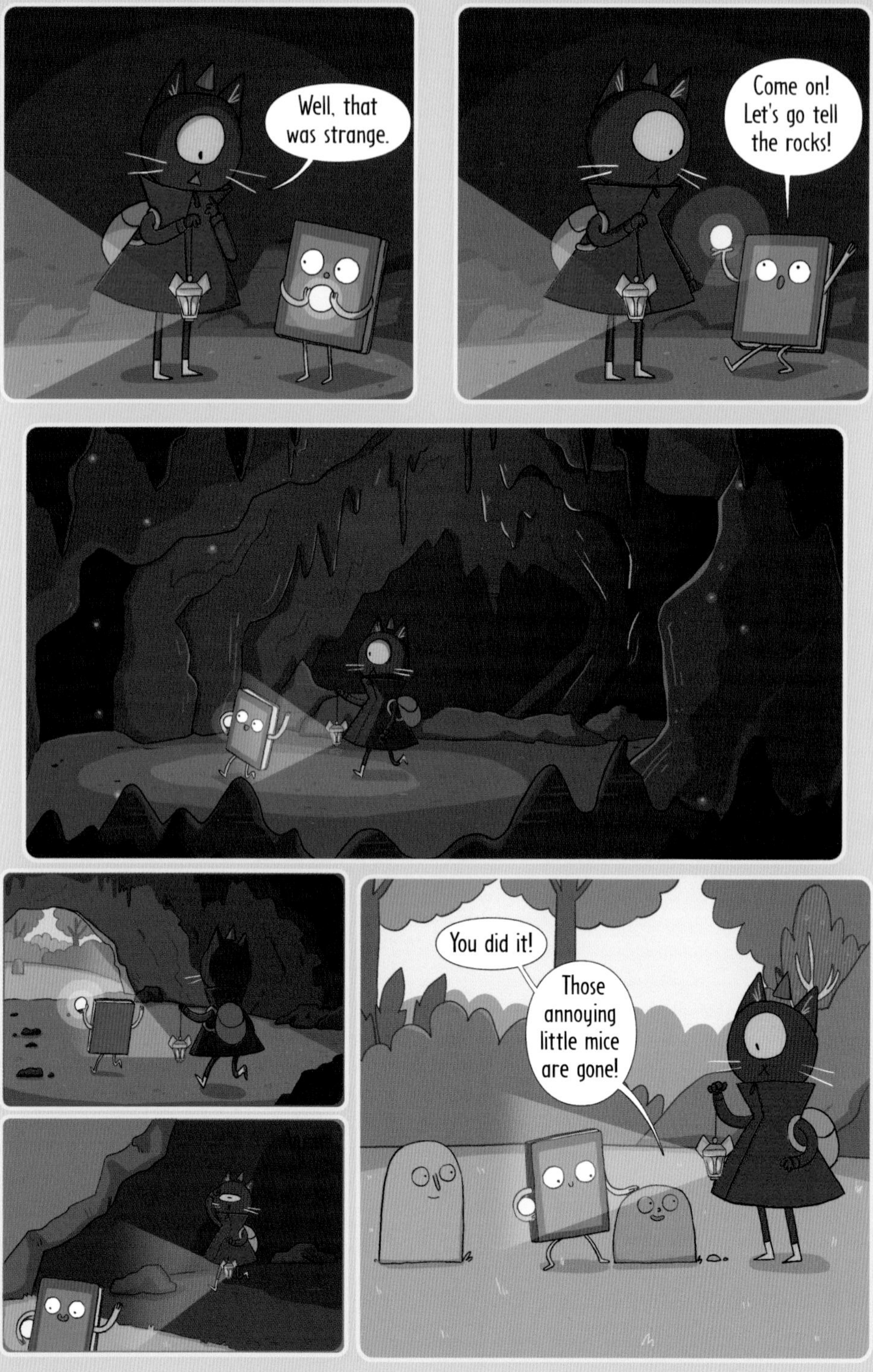
Well, that was strange.
Come on! Let's go tell the rocks!
You did it!
Those annoying little mice are gone!

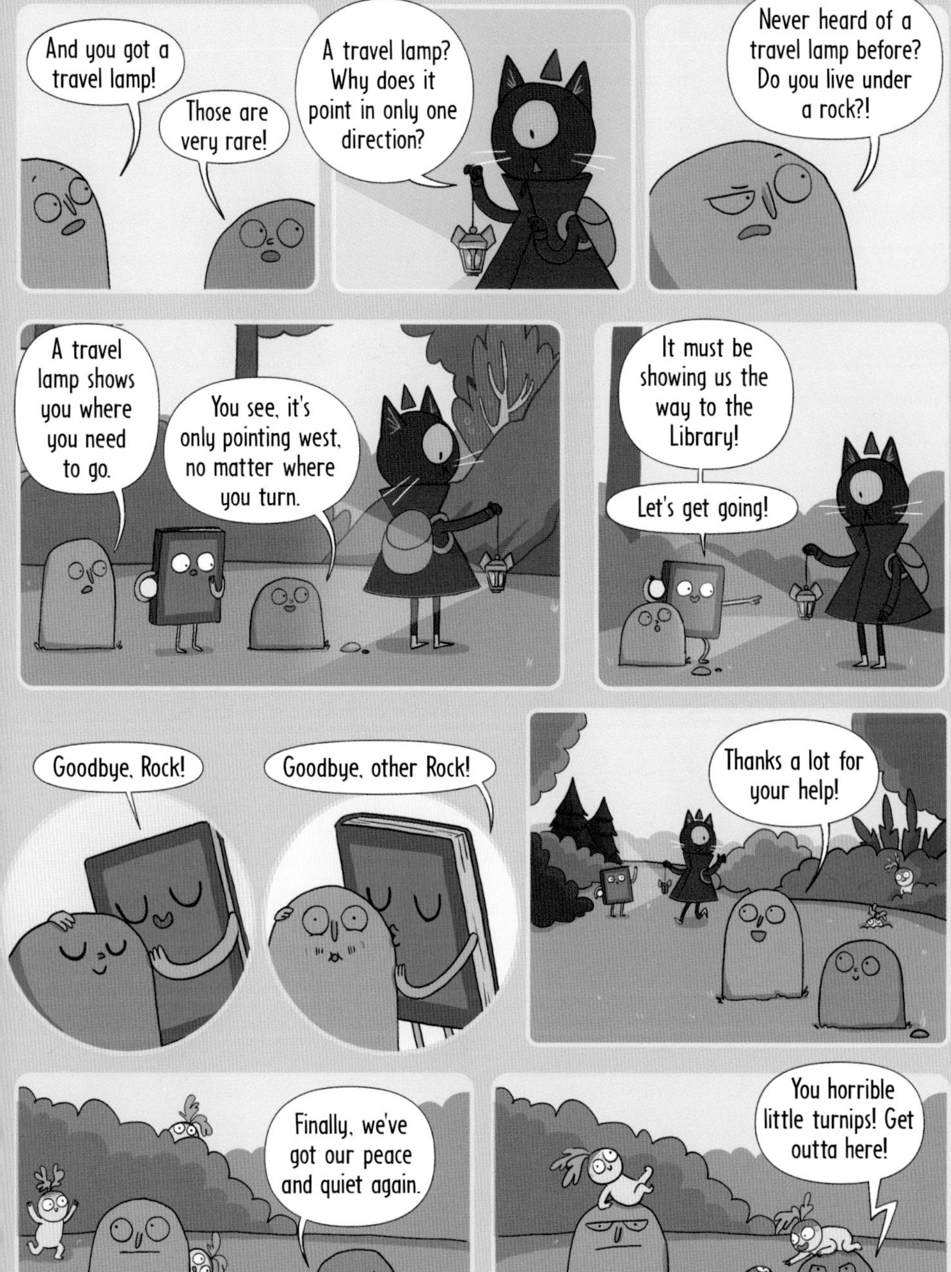
And you got a travel lamp!
Those are very rare!
A travel lamp? Why does it point in only one direction?
Never heard of a travel lamp before? Do you live under a rock?!
A travel lamp shows you where you need to go.
You see, it's only pointing west, no matter where you turn.
It must be showing us the way to the Library!
Let's get going!
Goodbye, Rock!
Goodbye, other Rock!
Thanks a lot for your help!
Finally, we've got our peace and quiet again.
You horrible little turnips! Get outta here!

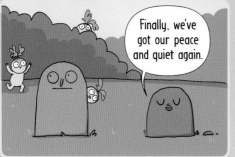

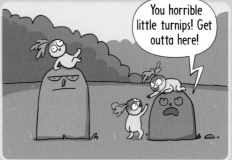

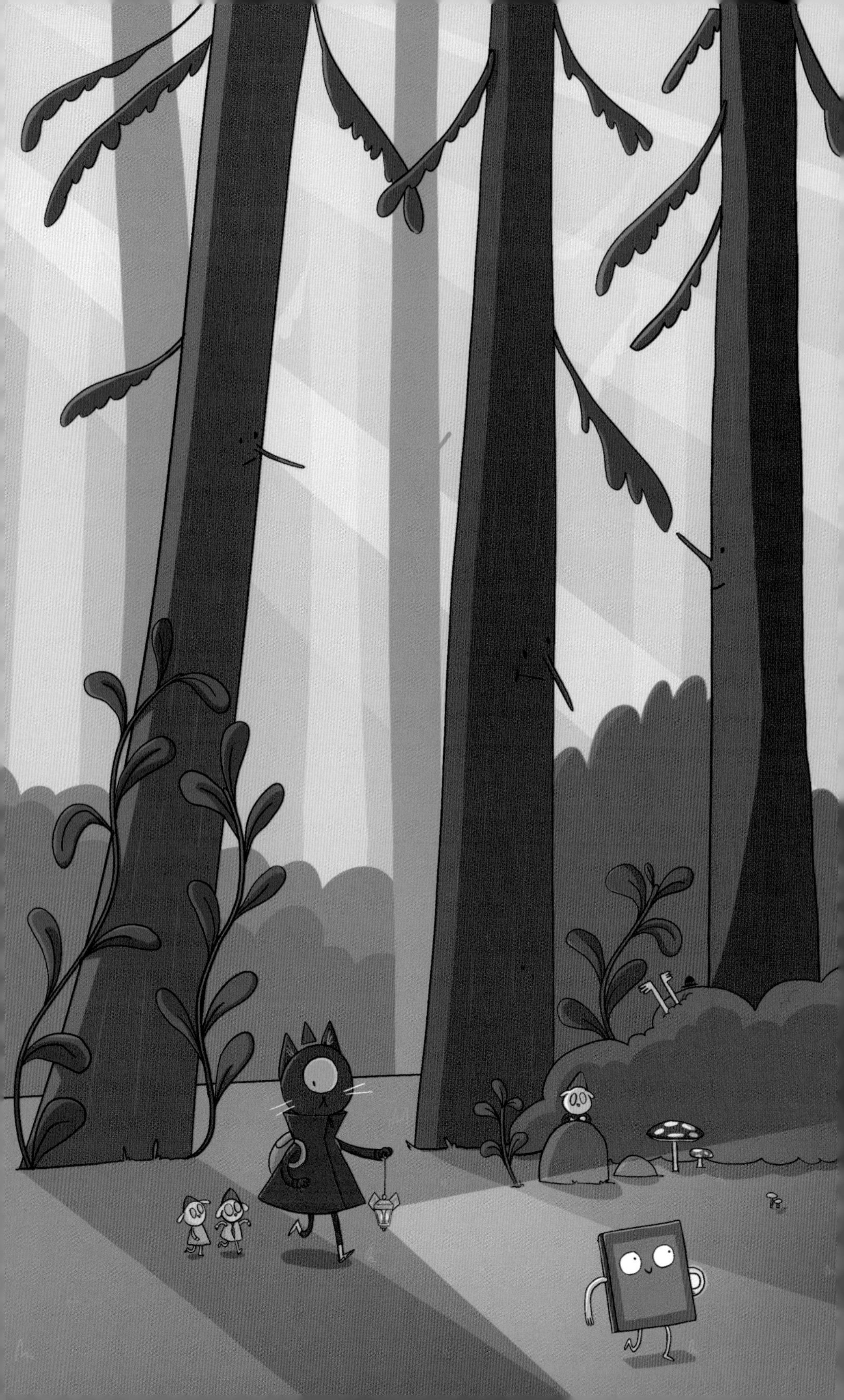

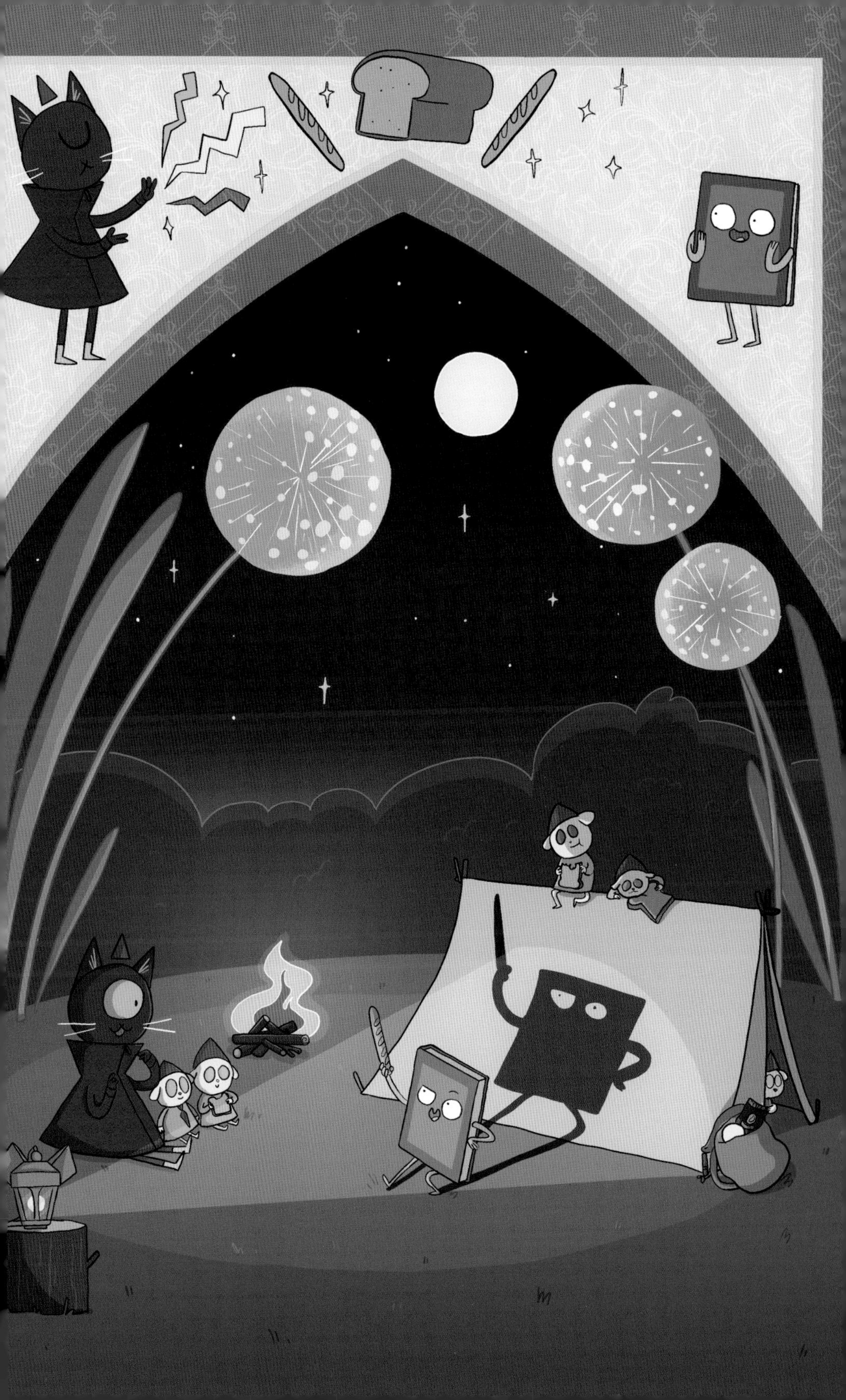

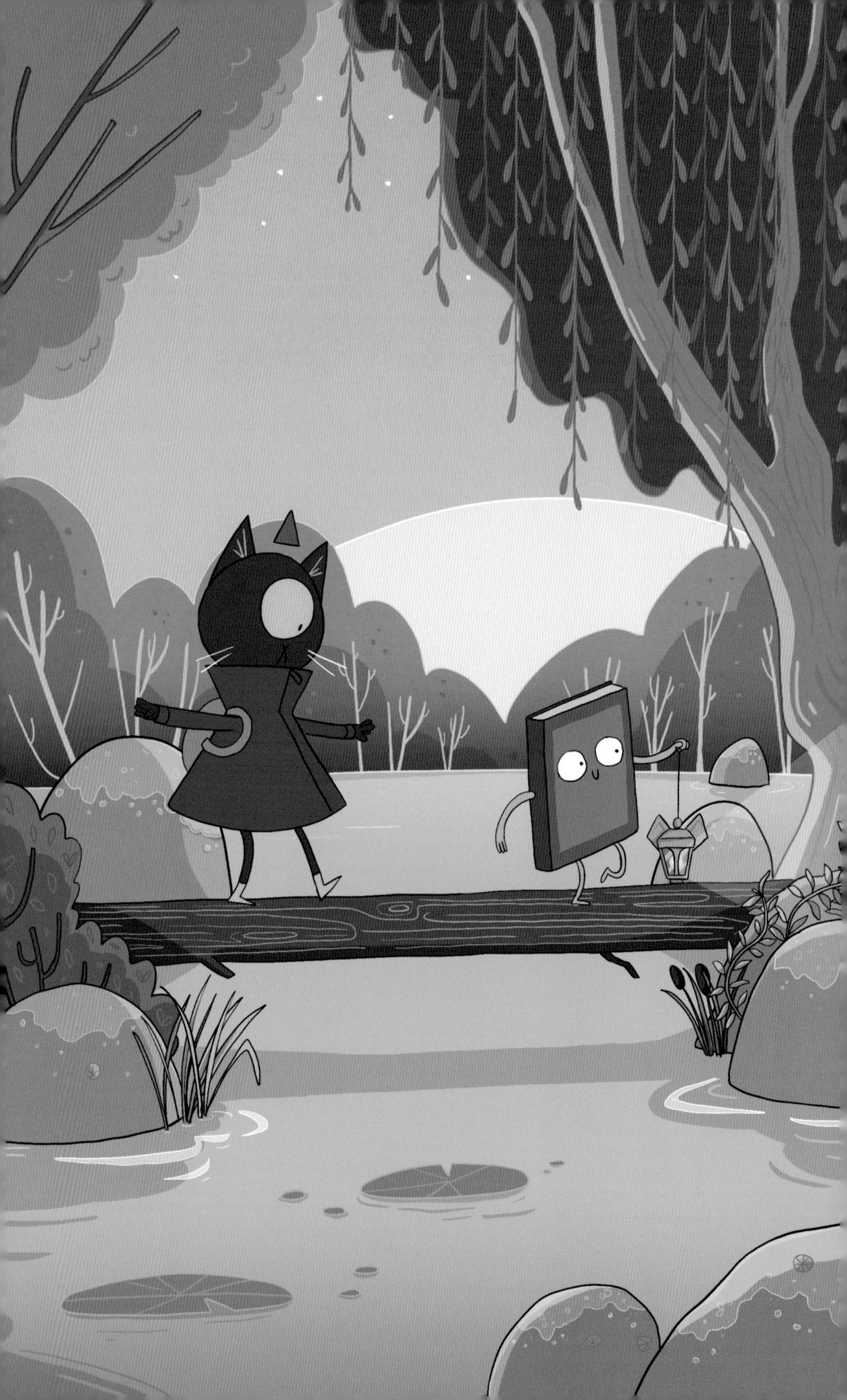

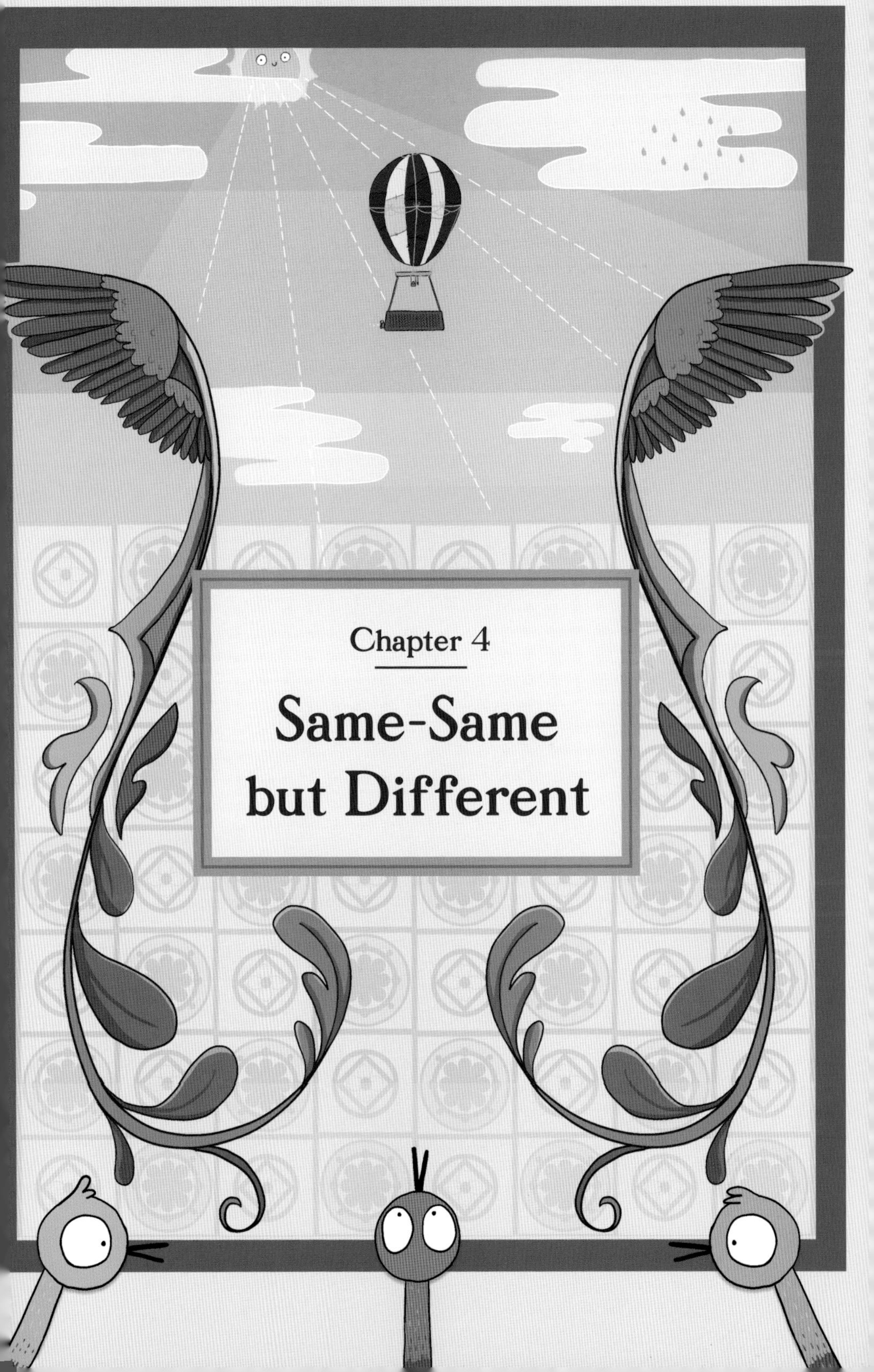

Chapter 4

Same-Same but Different

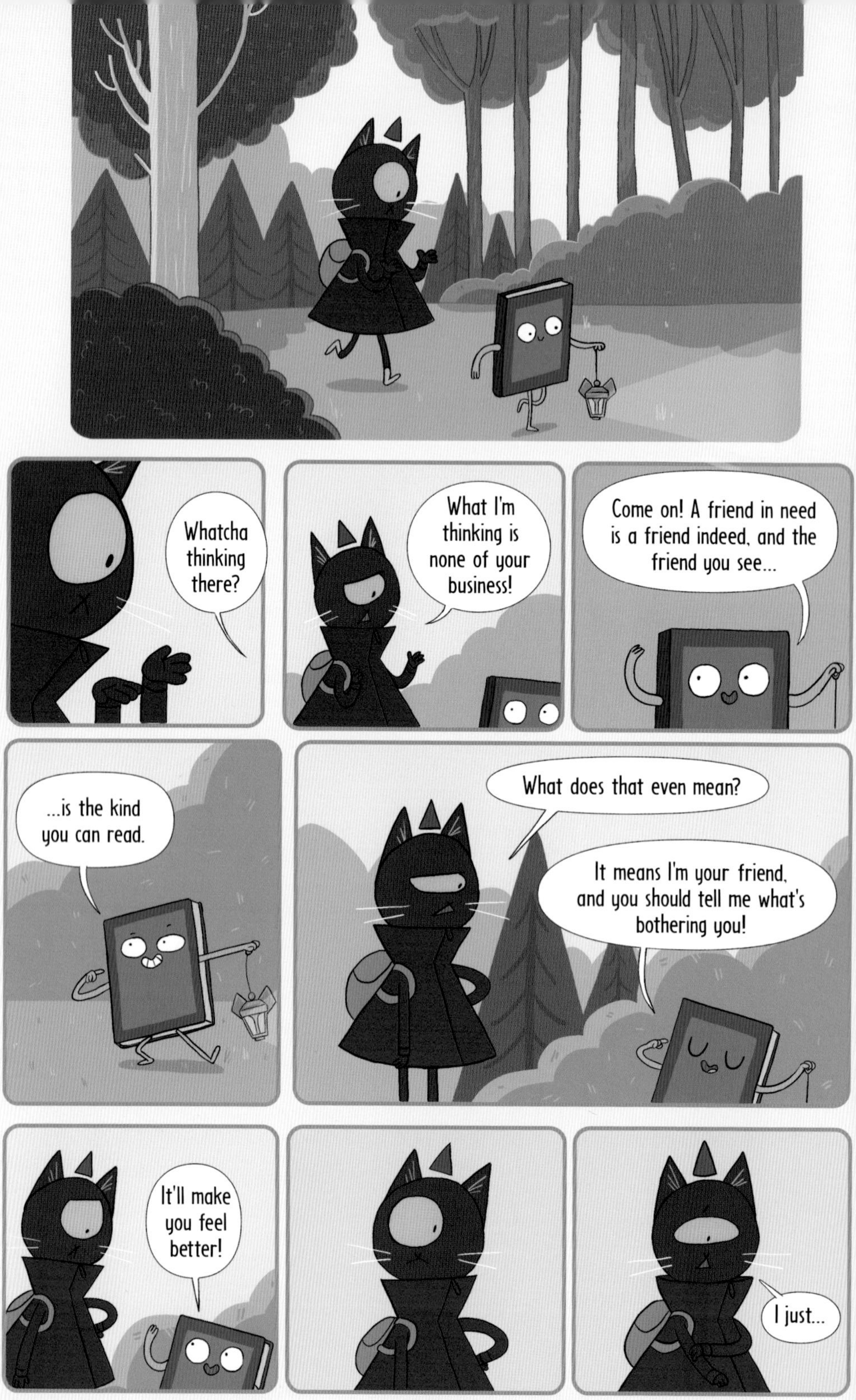
Whatcha thinking there?
What I'm thinking is none of your business!
Come on! A friend in need is a friend indeed, and the friend you see...
...is the kind you can read.
What does that even mean?
It means I'm your friend, and you should tell me what's bothering you!
It'll make you feel better!
I just...

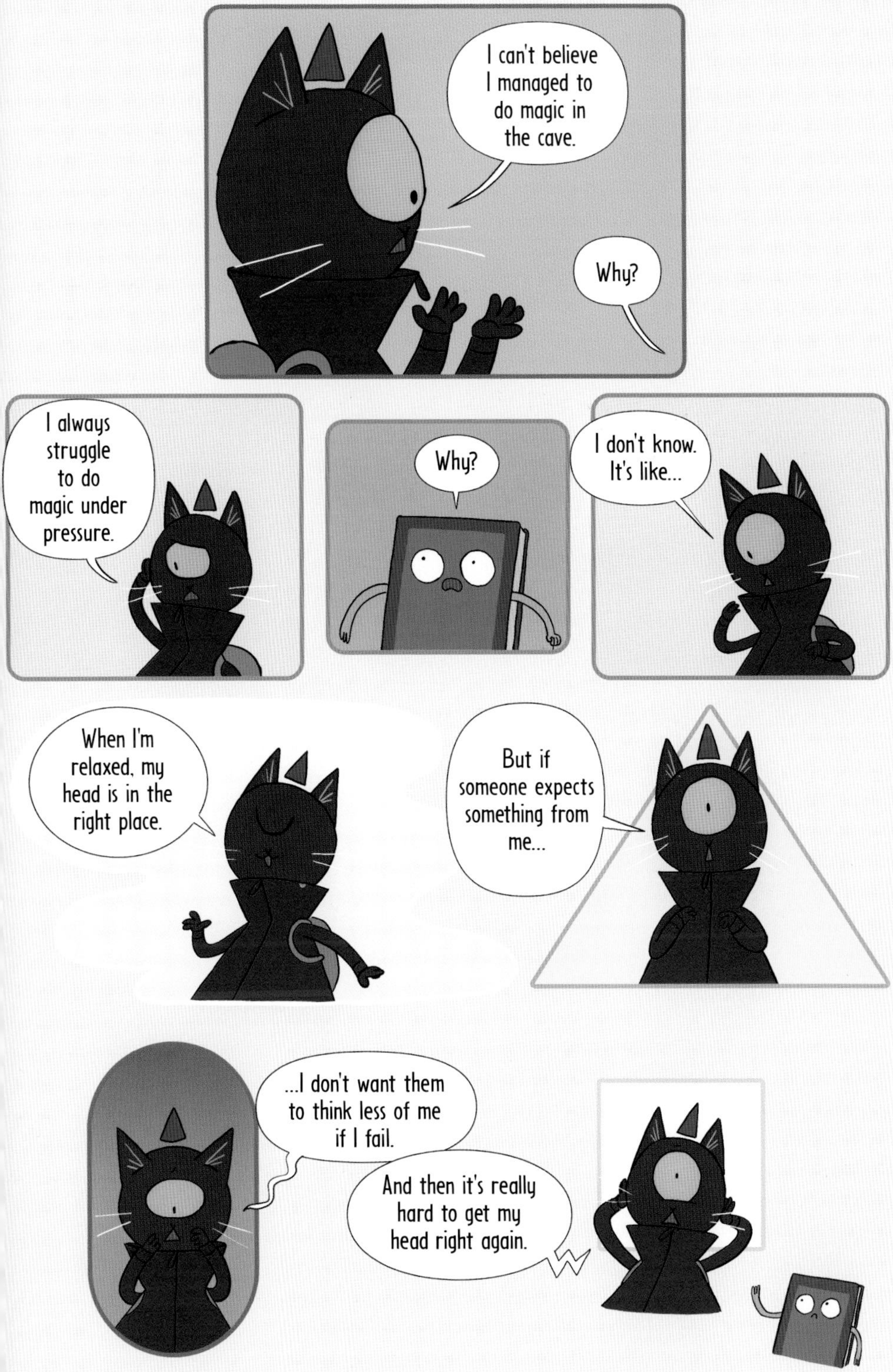

I can't believe I managed to do magic in the cave.
Why?
I always struggle to do magic under pressure.
Why?
I don't know. It's like...
When I'm relaxed, my head is in the right place.
But if someone expects something from me...
...I don't want them to think less of me if I fail.
And then it's really hard to get my head right again.

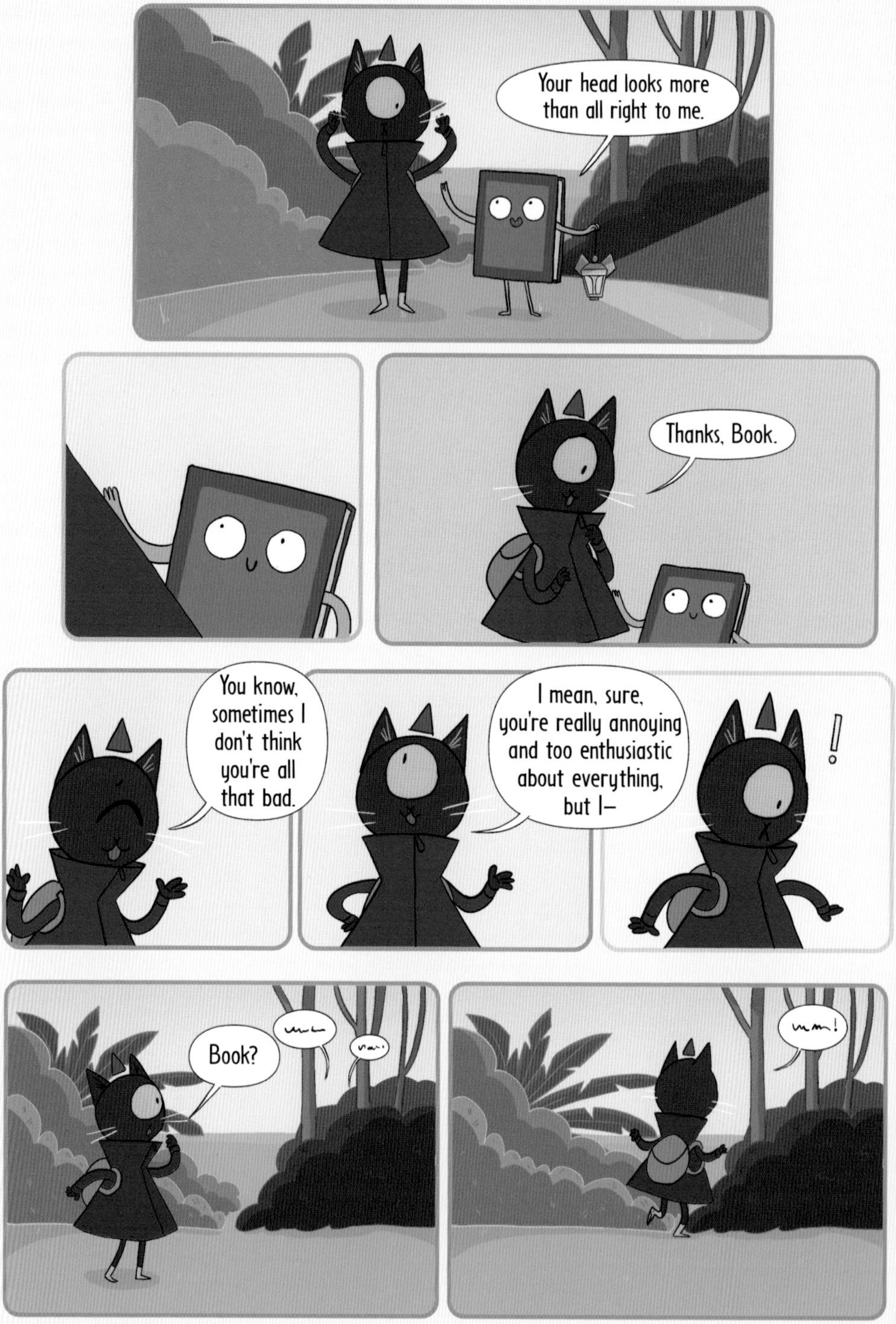
Your head looks more than all right to me.
Thanks, Book.
You know, sometimes I don't think you're all that bad.
I mean, sure, you're really annoying and too enthusiastic about everything, but I—
!
Book?

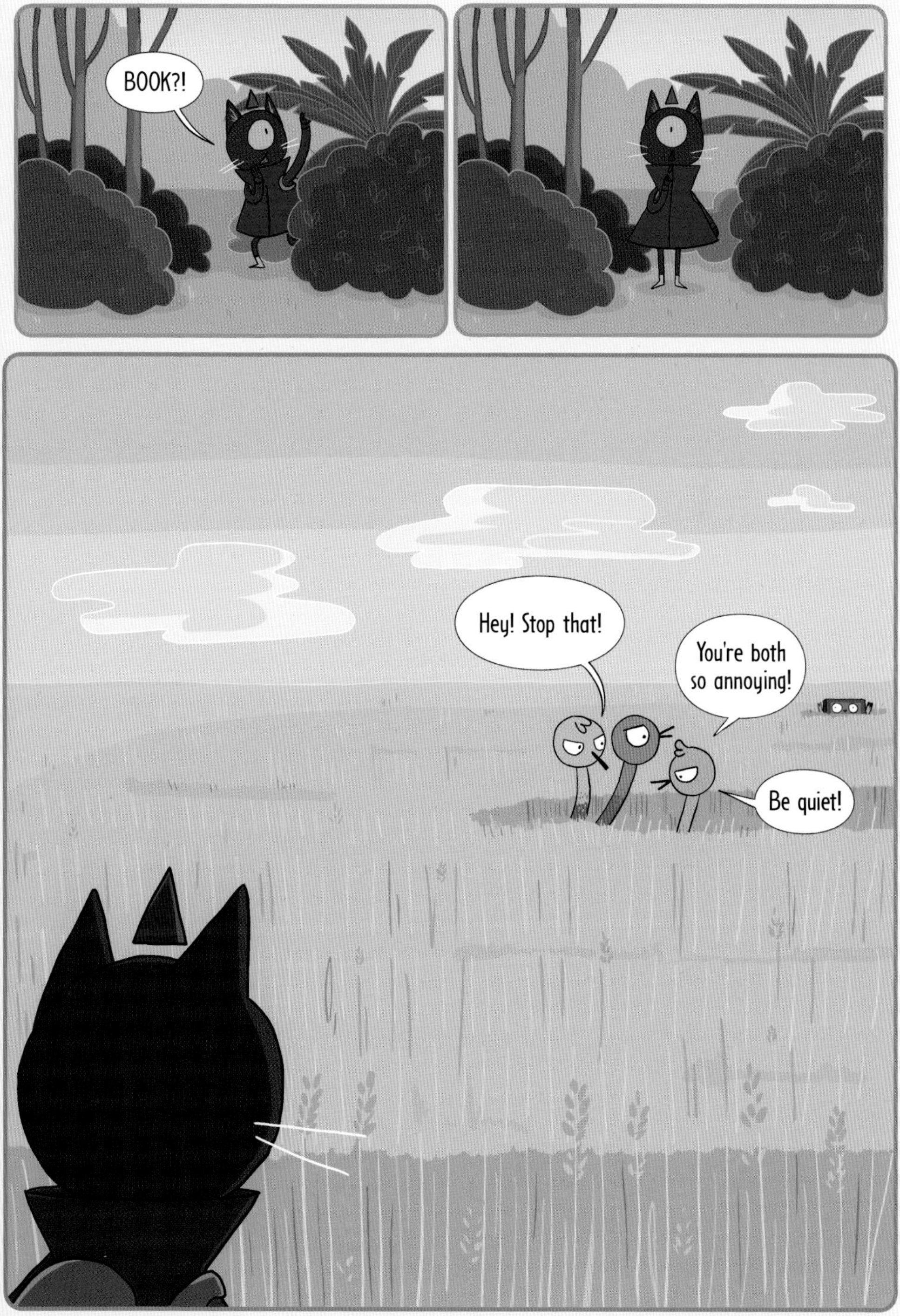
BOOK?!
Hey! Stop that!
You're both so annoying!
Be quiet!

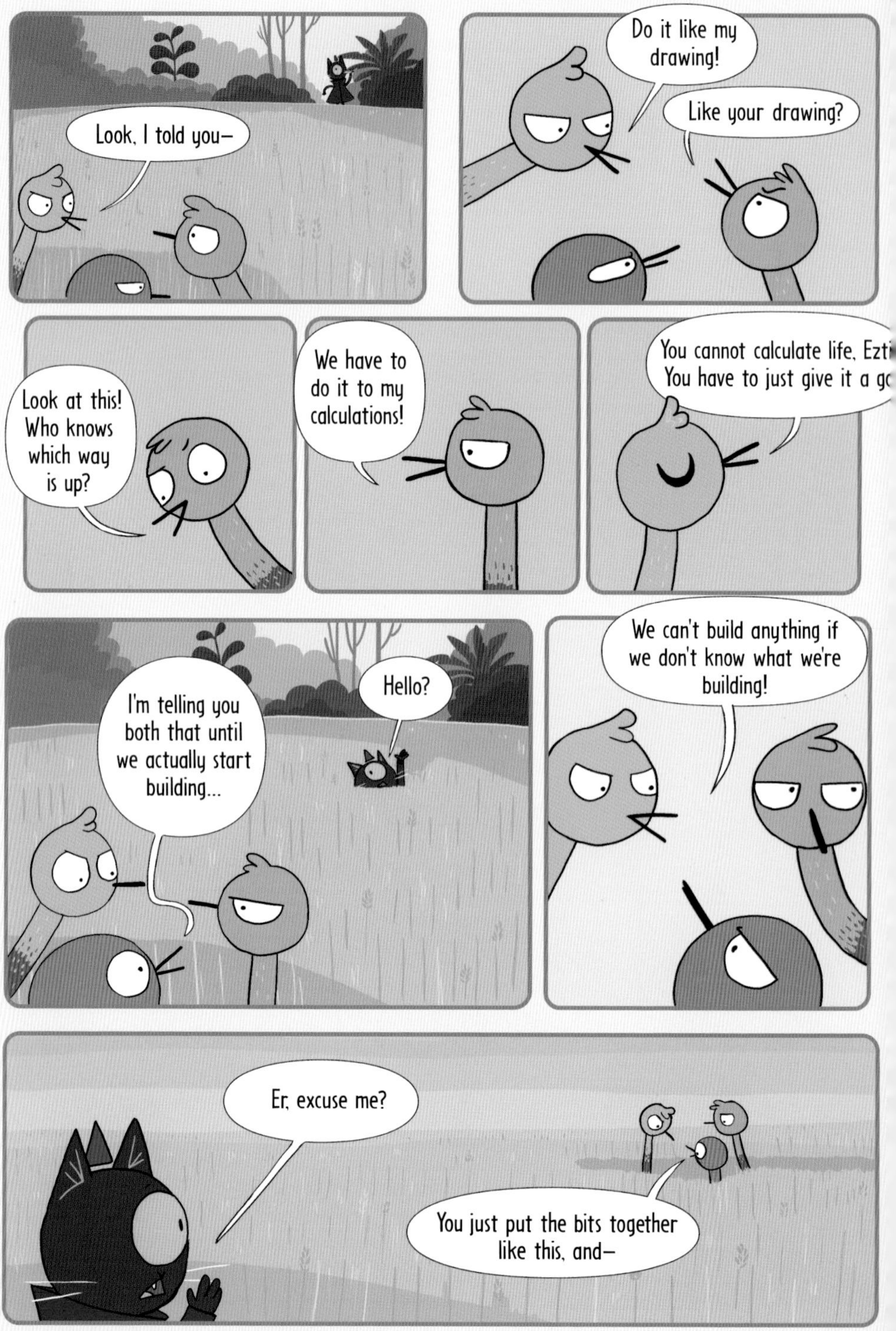
Look, I told you–
Do it like my drawing!
Like your drawing?
Look at this! Who knows which way is up?
We have to do it to my calculations!
You cannot calculate life, Ezti
You have to just give it a go
I'm telling you both that until we actually start building...
Hello?
We can't build anything if we don't know what we're building!
Er, excuse me?
You just put the bits together like this, and–

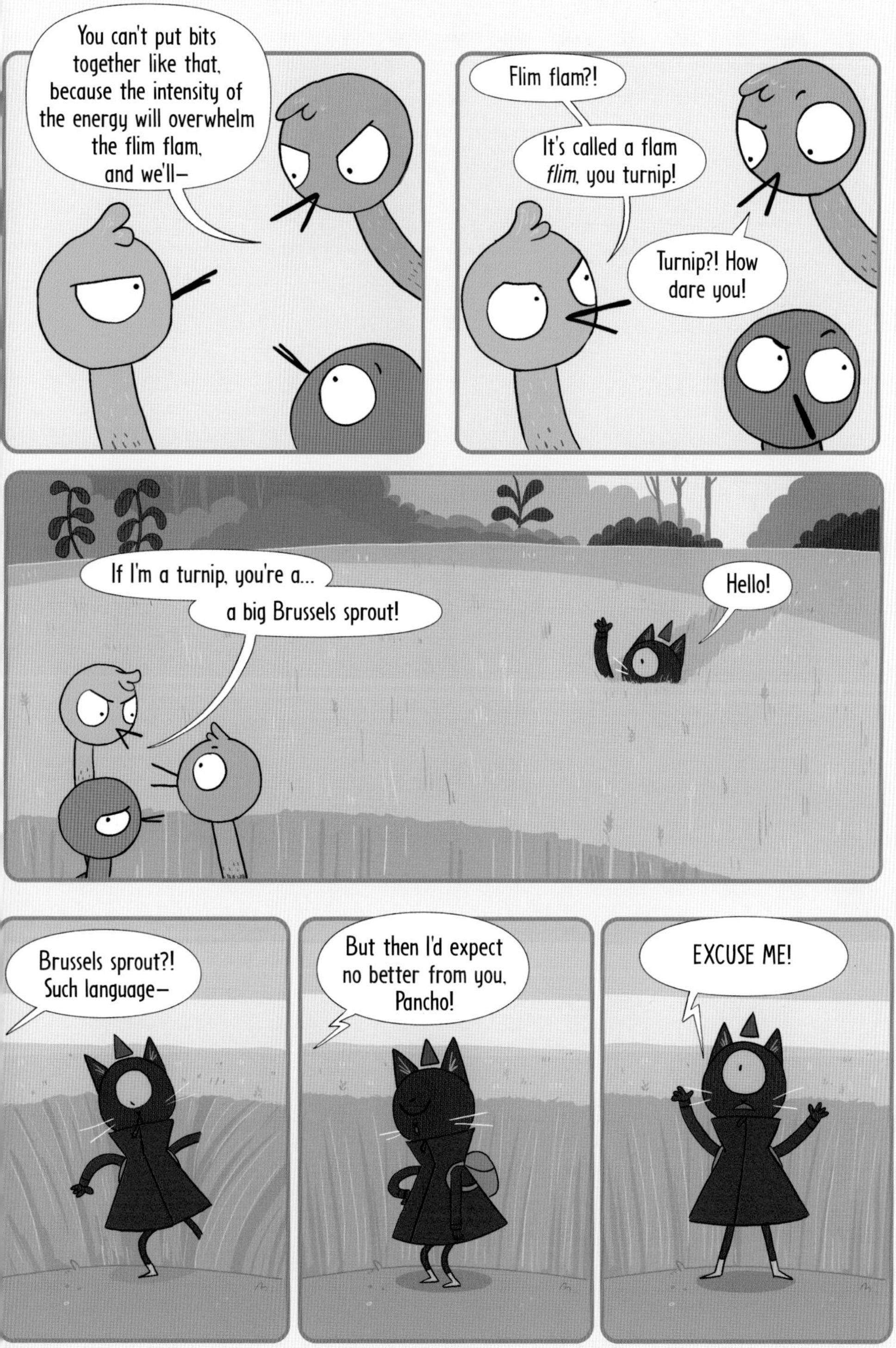
You can't put bits together like that, because the intensity of the energy will overwhelm the flim flam, and we'll–
Flim flam?!
It's called a flam *flim*, you turnip!
Turnip?! How dare you!
If I'm a turnip, you're a...
a big Brussels sprout!
Hello!
Brussels sprout?! Such language–
But then I'd expect no better from you, Pancho!
EXCUSE ME!

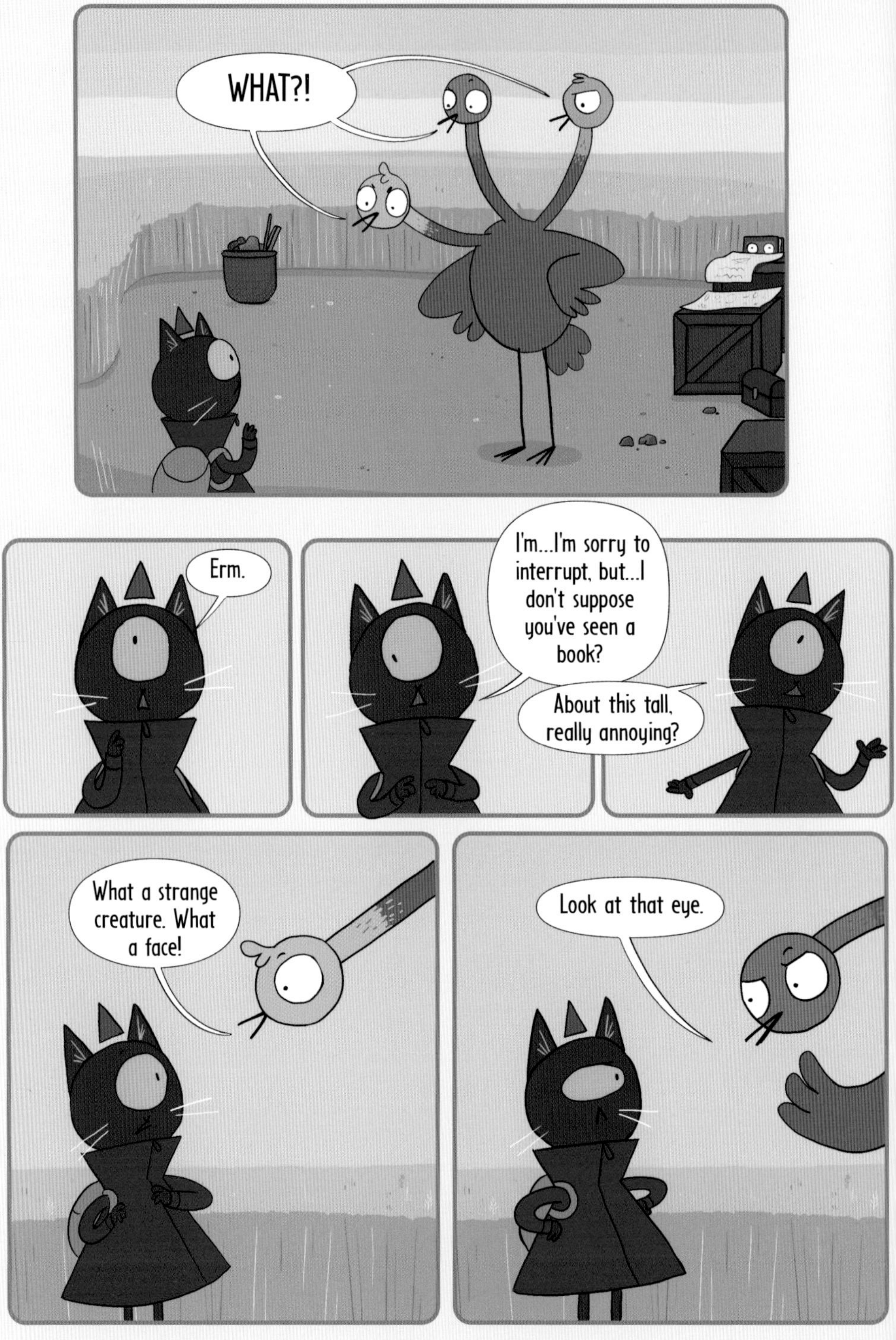
WHAT?!
Erm.
I'm...I'm sorry to interrupt, but...I don't suppose you've seen a book?
About this tall, really annoying?
What a strange creature. What a face!
Look at that eye.

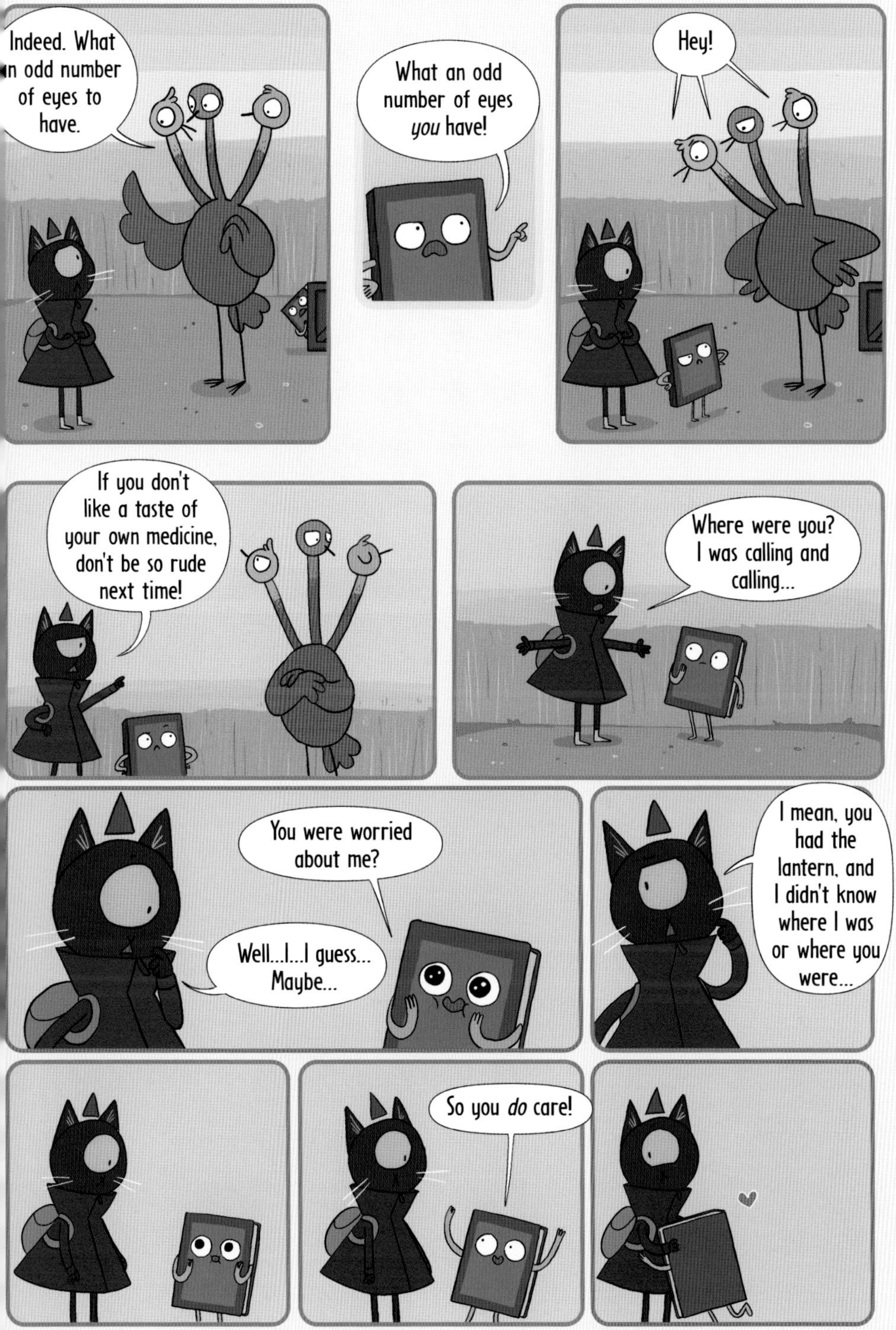
Indeed. What
n odd number
of eyes to
have.
What an odd
number of eyes
you have!
Hey!
If you don't
like a taste of
your own medicine,
don't be so rude
next time!
Where were you?
I was calling and
calling...
You were worried
about me?
Well...I...I guess...
Maybe...
I mean, you
had the
lantern, and
I didn't know
where I was
or where you
were...
So you *do* care!

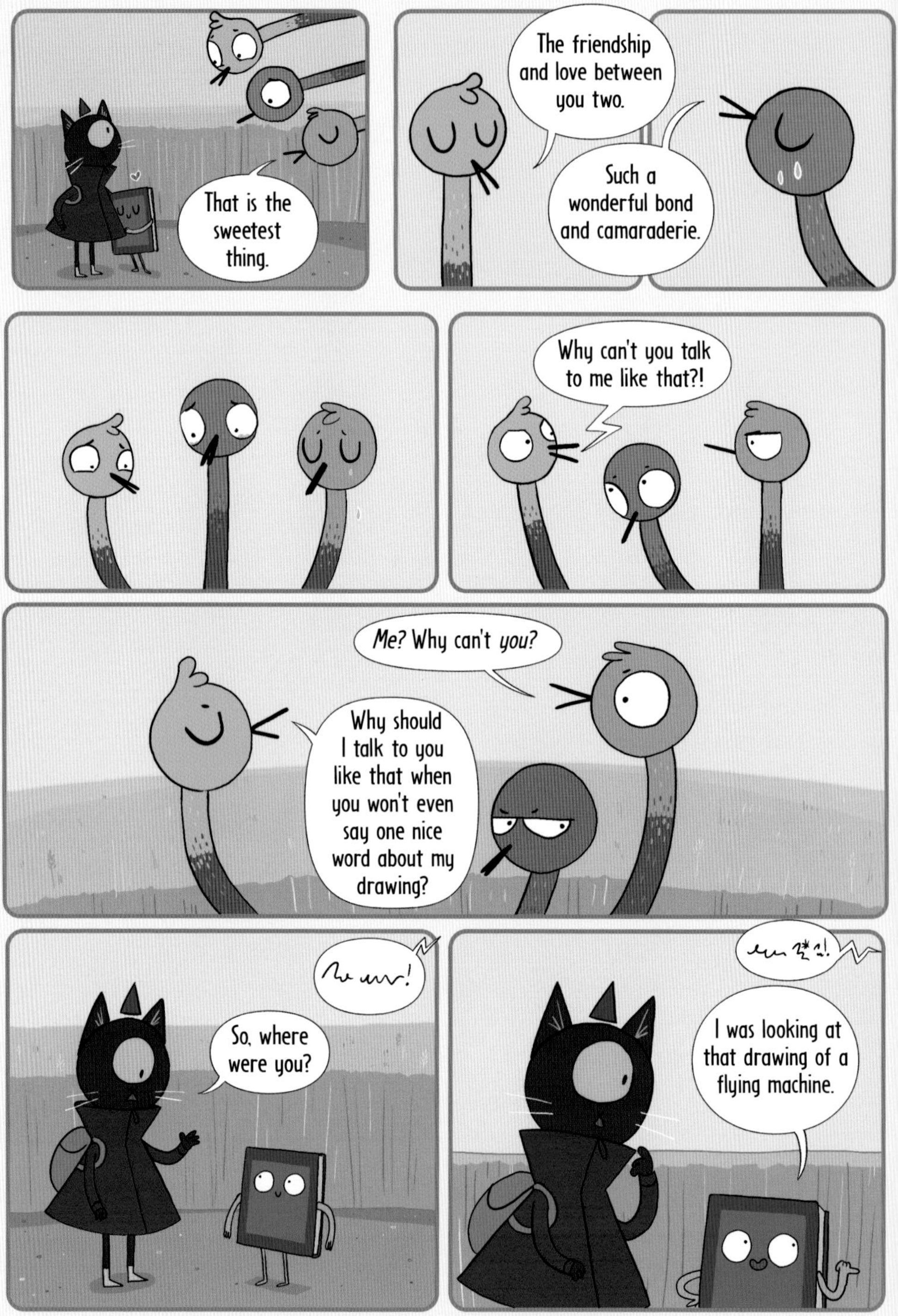
That is the sweetest thing.
The friendship and love between you two.
Such a wonderful bond and camaraderie.
Why can't you talk to me like that?!
Me? Why can't *you?*
Why should I talk to you like that when you won't even say one nice word about my drawing?
So, where were you?
I was looking at that drawing of a flying machine.

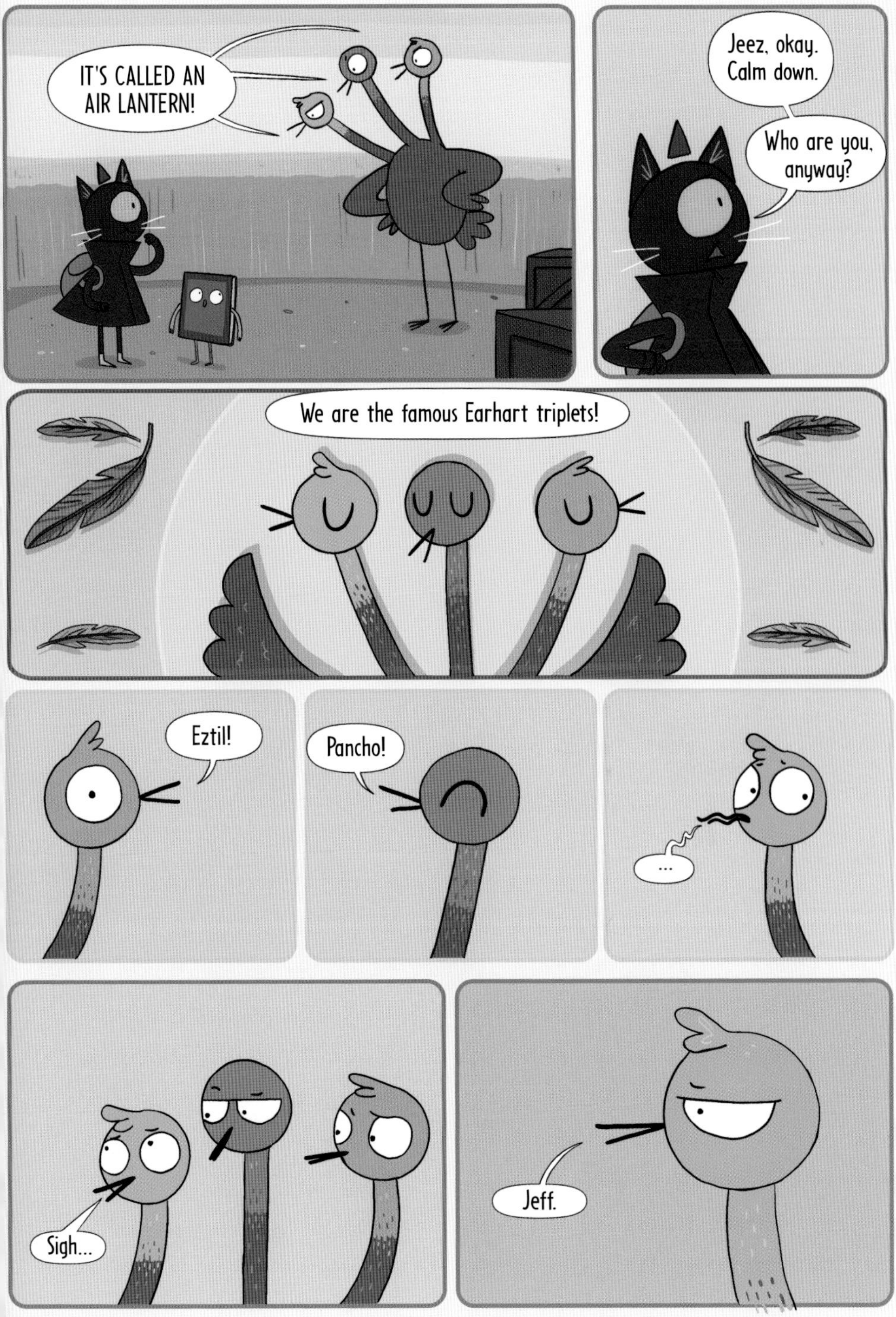
IT'S CALLED AN AIR LANTERN!
Jeez, okay. Calm down.
Who are you, anyway?
We are the famous Earhart triplets!
Eztil!
Pancho!
...
Sigh...
Jeff.

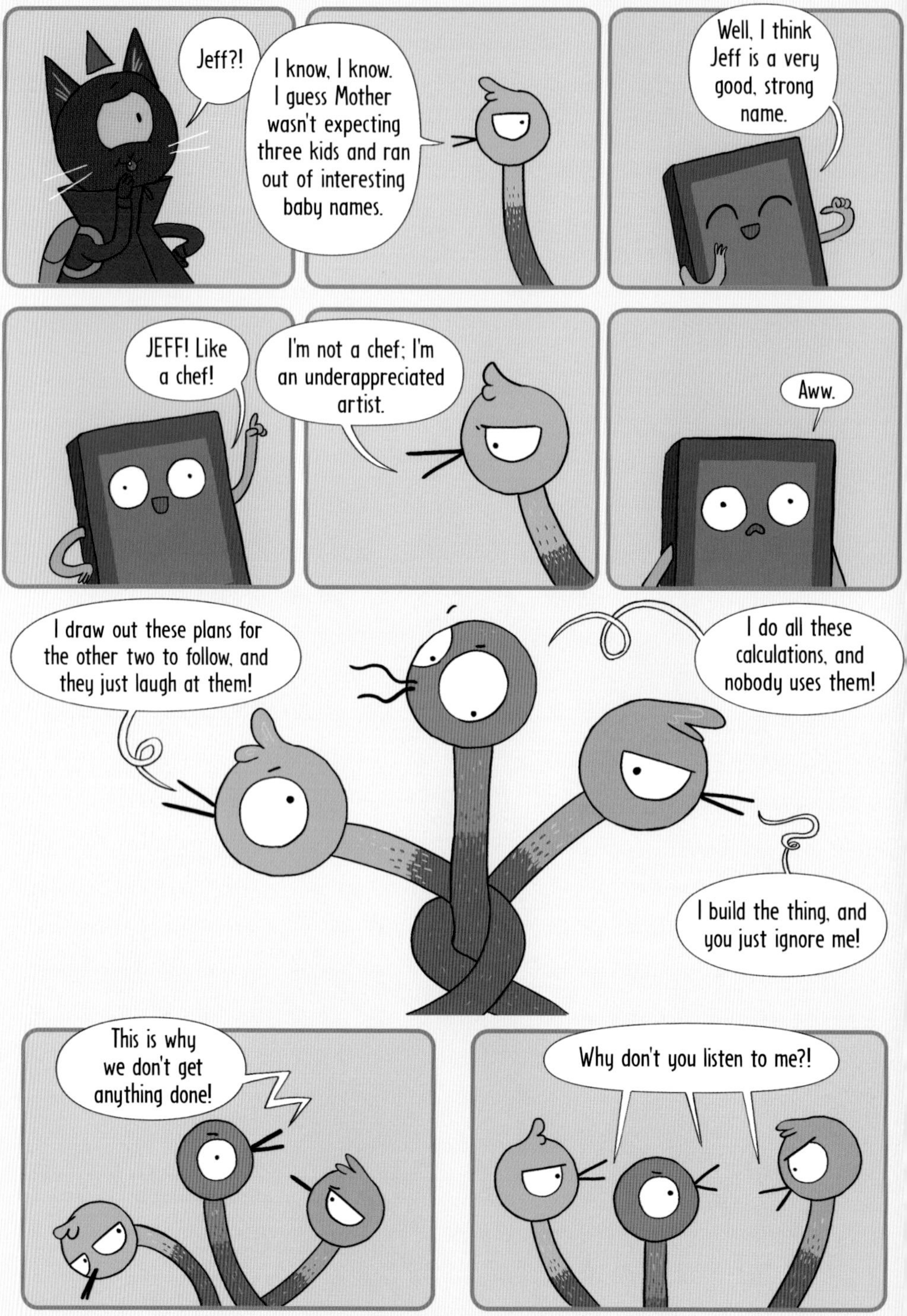
Jeff?!
I know, I know. I guess Mother wasn't expecting three kids and ran out of interesting baby names.
Well, I think Jeff is a very good, strong name.
JEFF! Like a chef!
I'm not a chef; I'm an underappreciated artist.
Aww.
I draw out these plans for the other two to follow, and they just laugh at them!
I do all these calculations, and nobody uses them!
I build the thing, and you just ignore me!
This is why we don't get anything done!
Why don't you listen to me?!

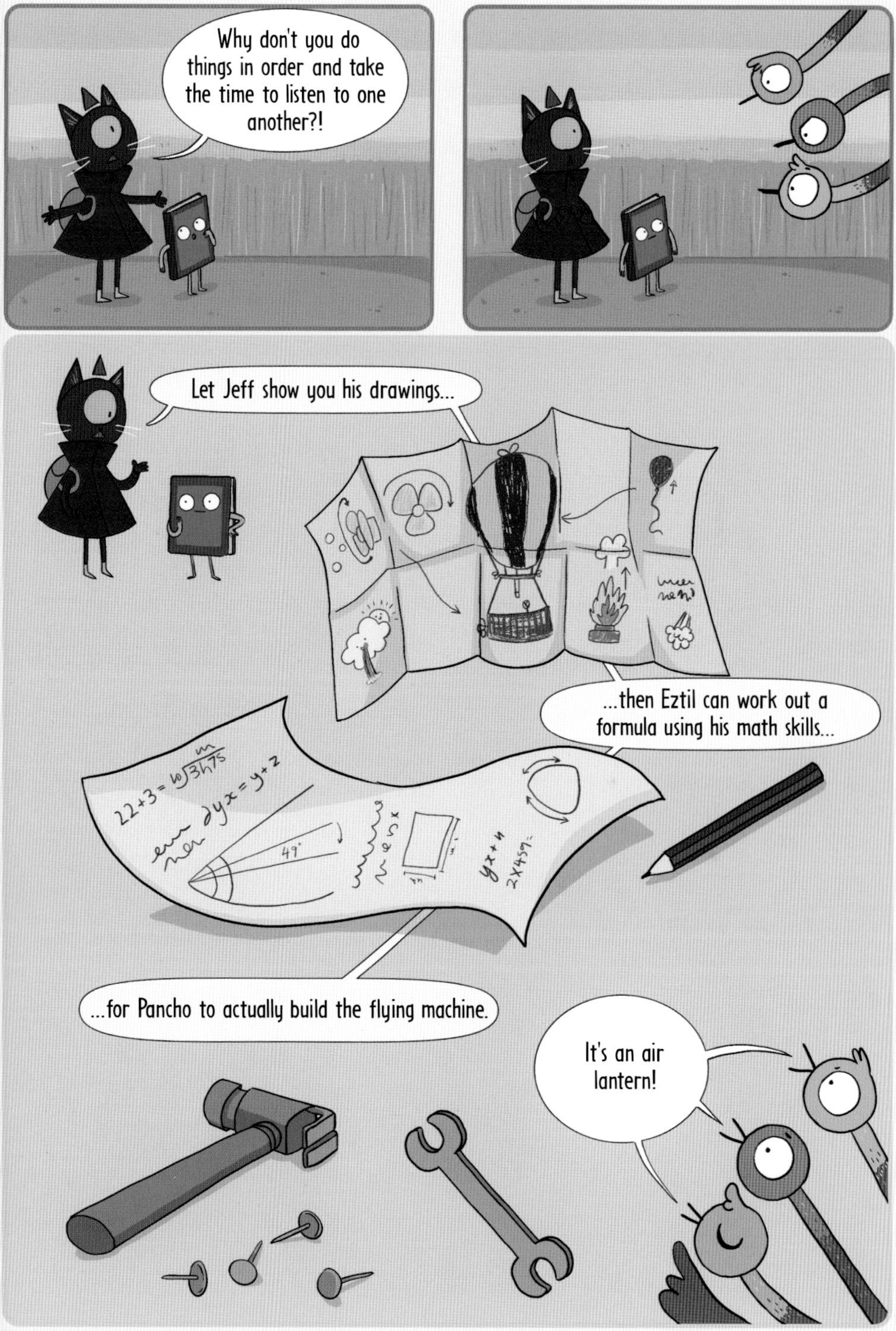
Why don't you do things in order and take the time to listen to one another?!
Let Jeff show you his drawings...
...then Eztil can work out a formula using his math skills...
...for Pancho to actually build the flying machine.
It's an air lantern!

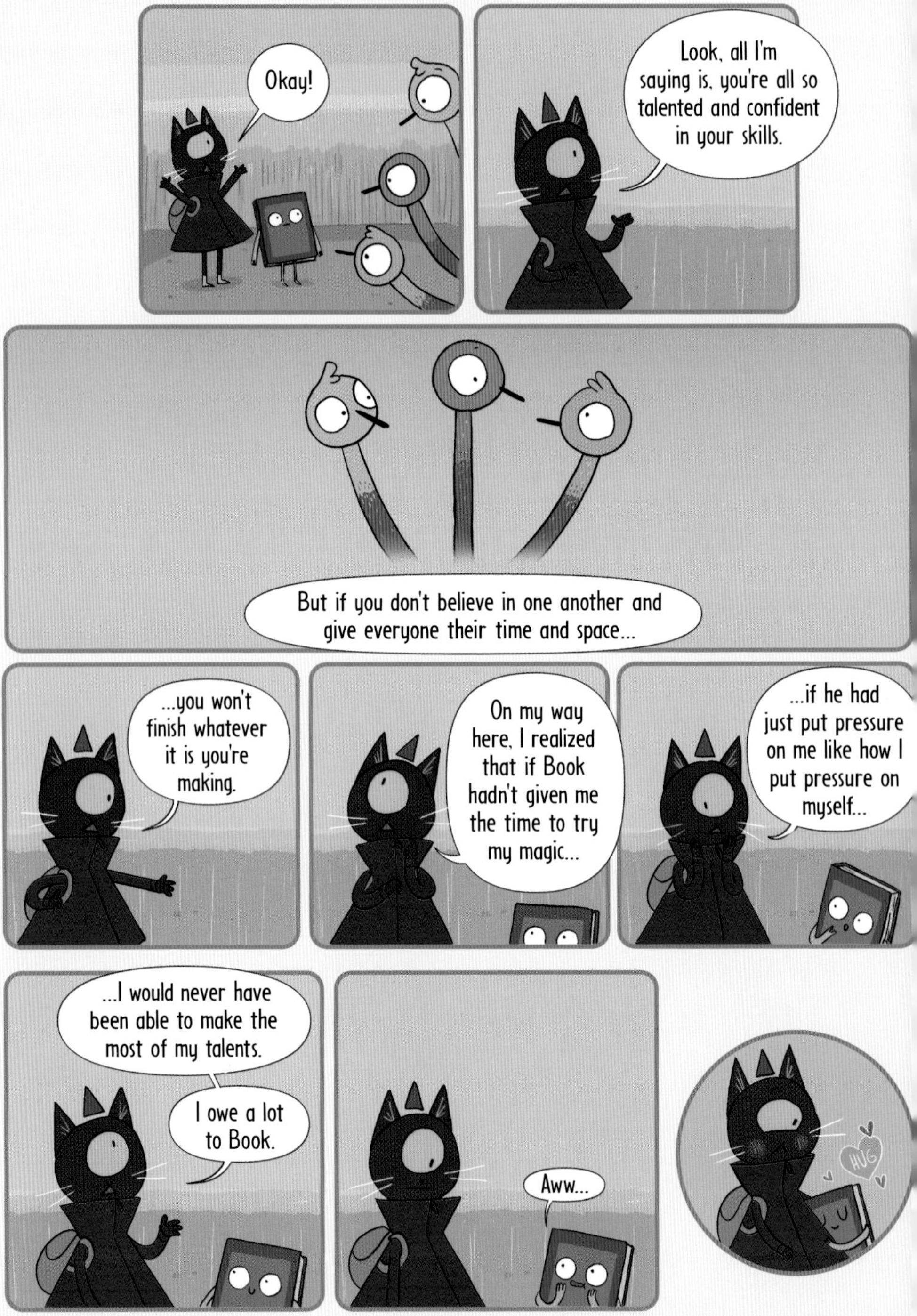
Okay!
Look, all I'm saying is, you're all so talented and confident in your skills.
But if you don't believe in one another and give everyone their time and space...
...you won't finish whatever it is you're making.
On my way here, I realized that if Book hadn't given me the time to try my magic...
...if he had just put pressure on me like how I put pressure on myself...
...I would never have been able to make the most of my talents.
I owe a lot to Book.
Aww...
HUG

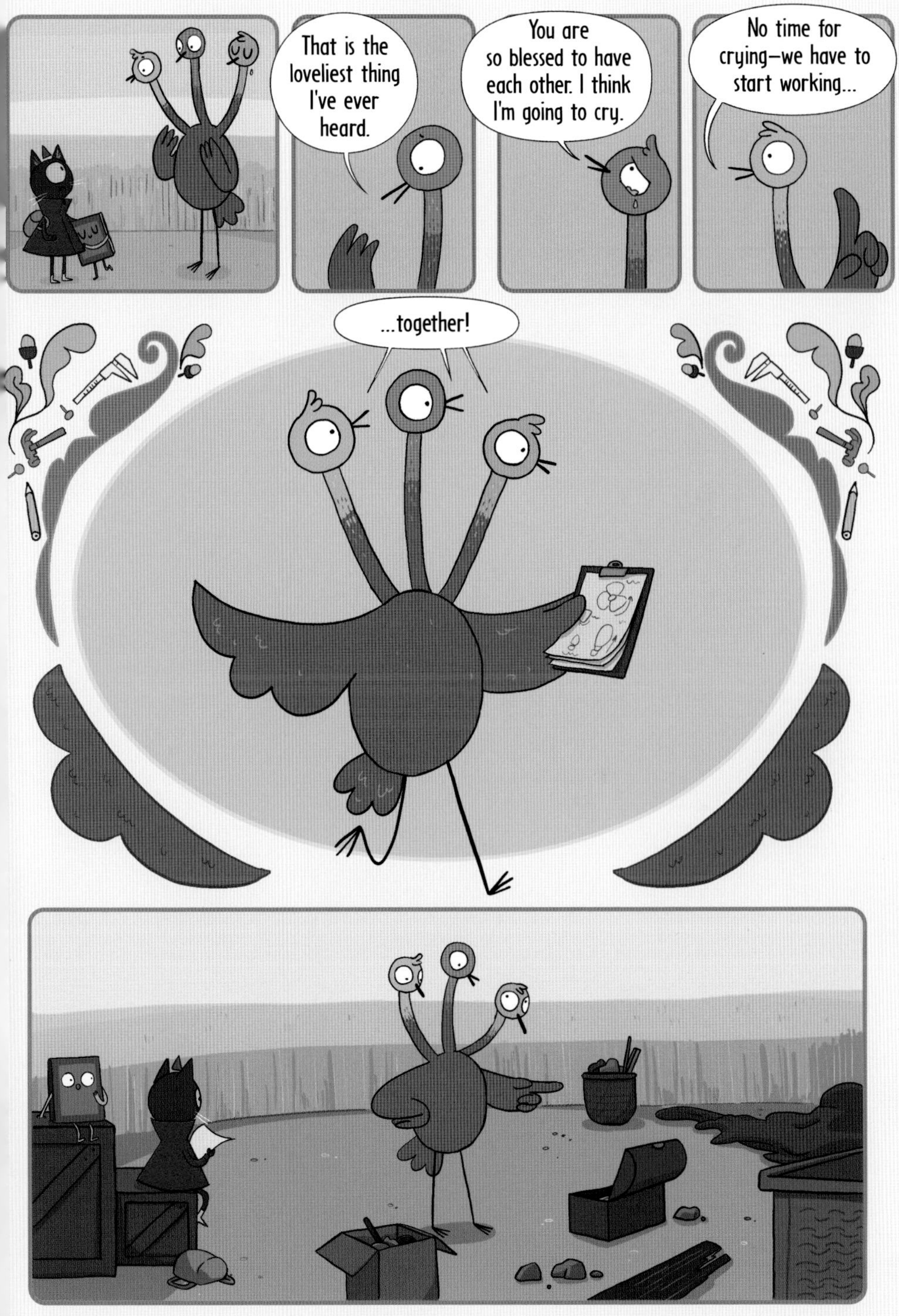
That is the loveliest thing I've ever heard.
You are so blessed to have each other. I think I'm going to cry.
No time for crying—we have to start working...
...together!

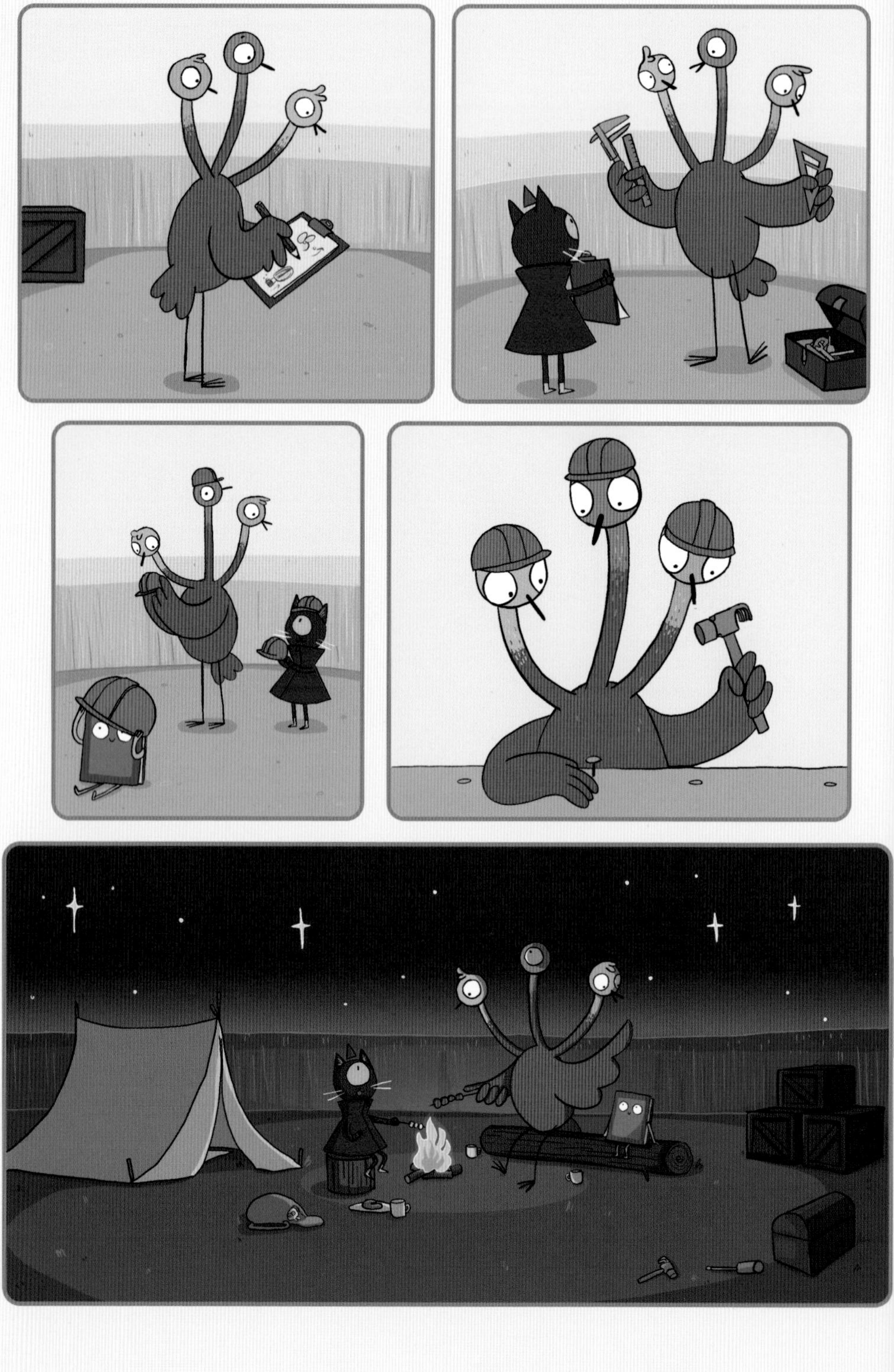

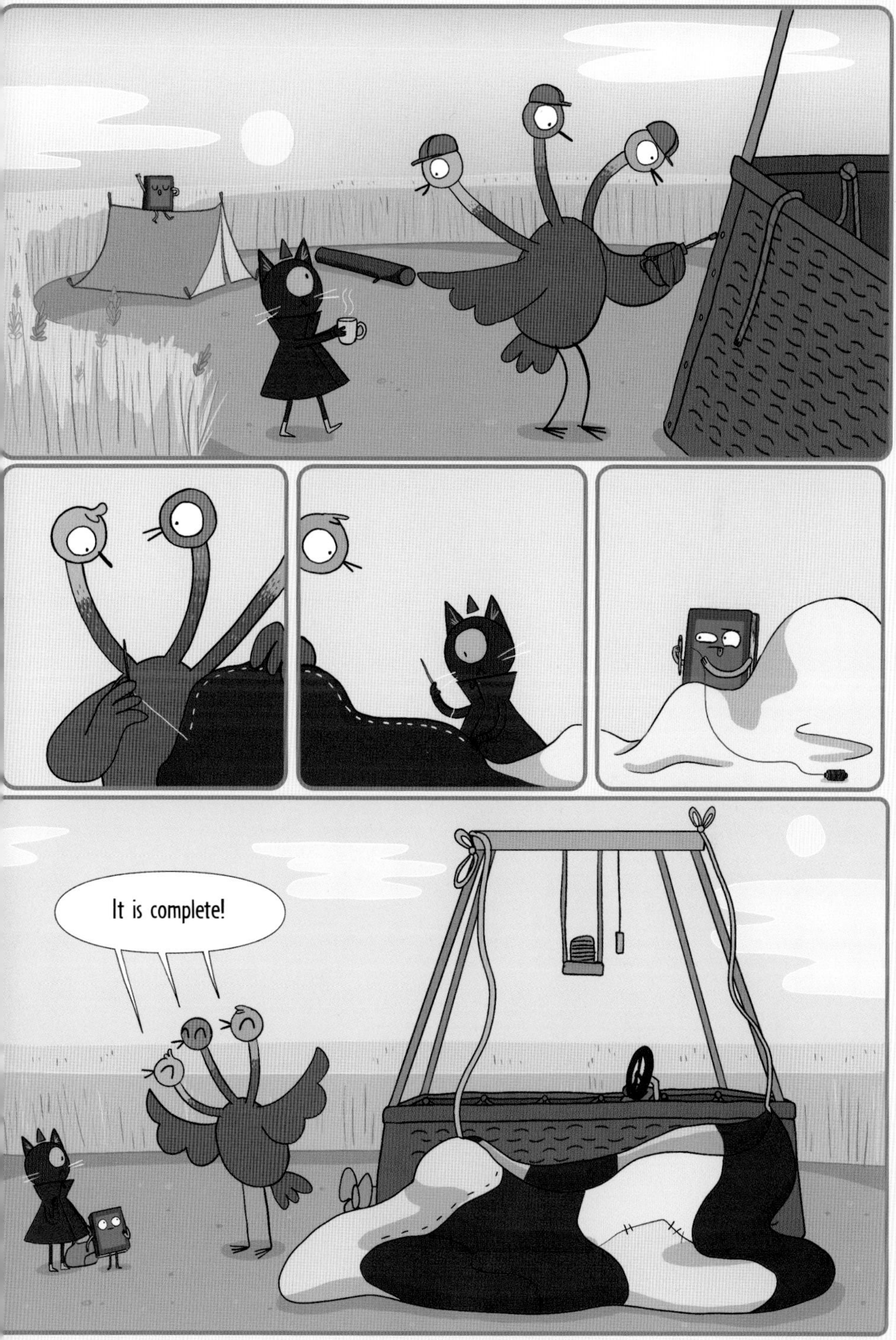
It is complete!

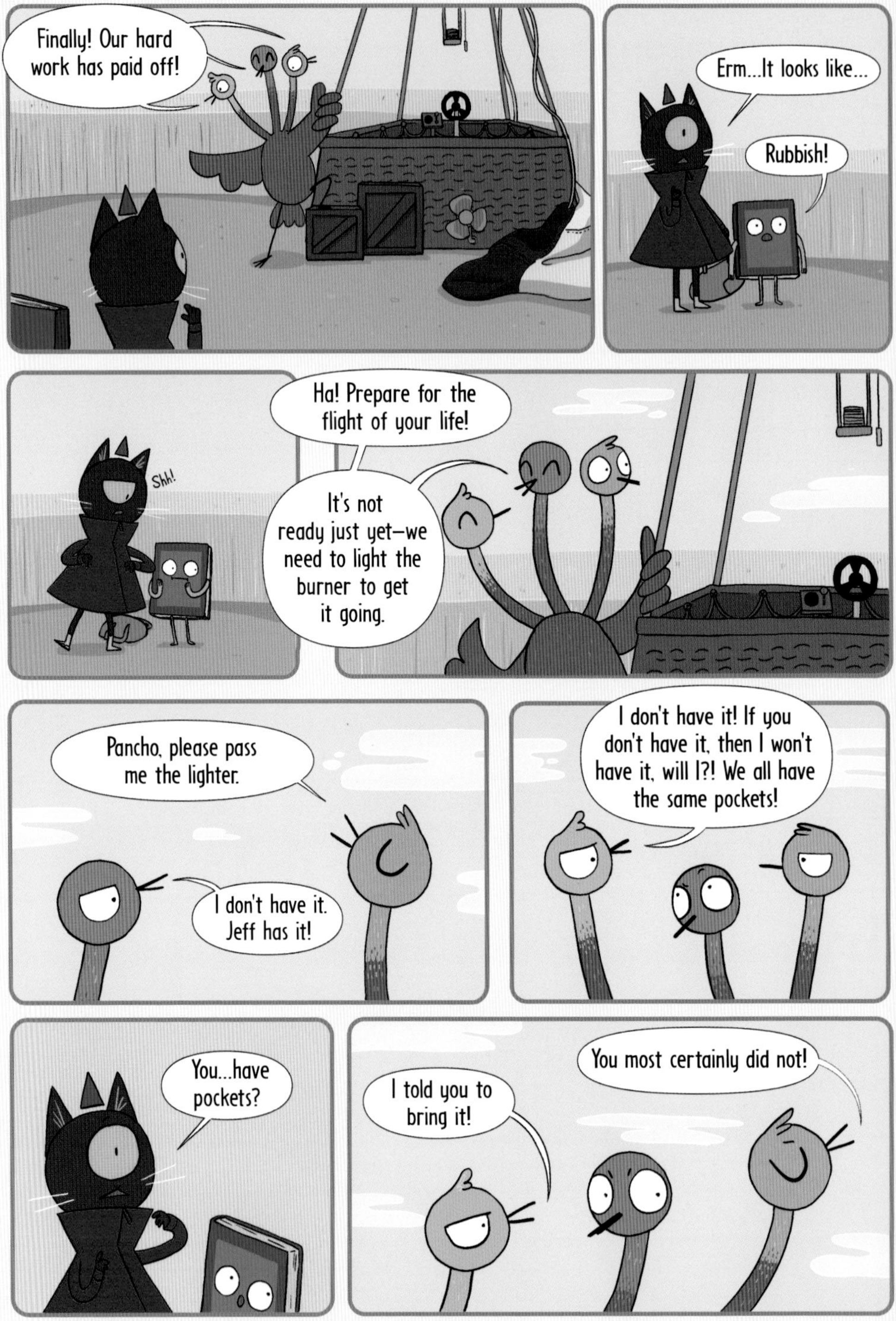

Finally! Our hard work has paid off!
Erm...It looks like...
Rubbish!
Shh!
Ha! Prepare for the flight of your life!
It's not ready just yet—we need to light the burner to get it going.
Pancho, please pass me the lighter.
I don't have it. Jeff has it!
I don't have it! If you don't have it, then I won't have it, will I?! We all have the same pockets!
You...have pockets?
I told you to bring it!
You most certainly did not!

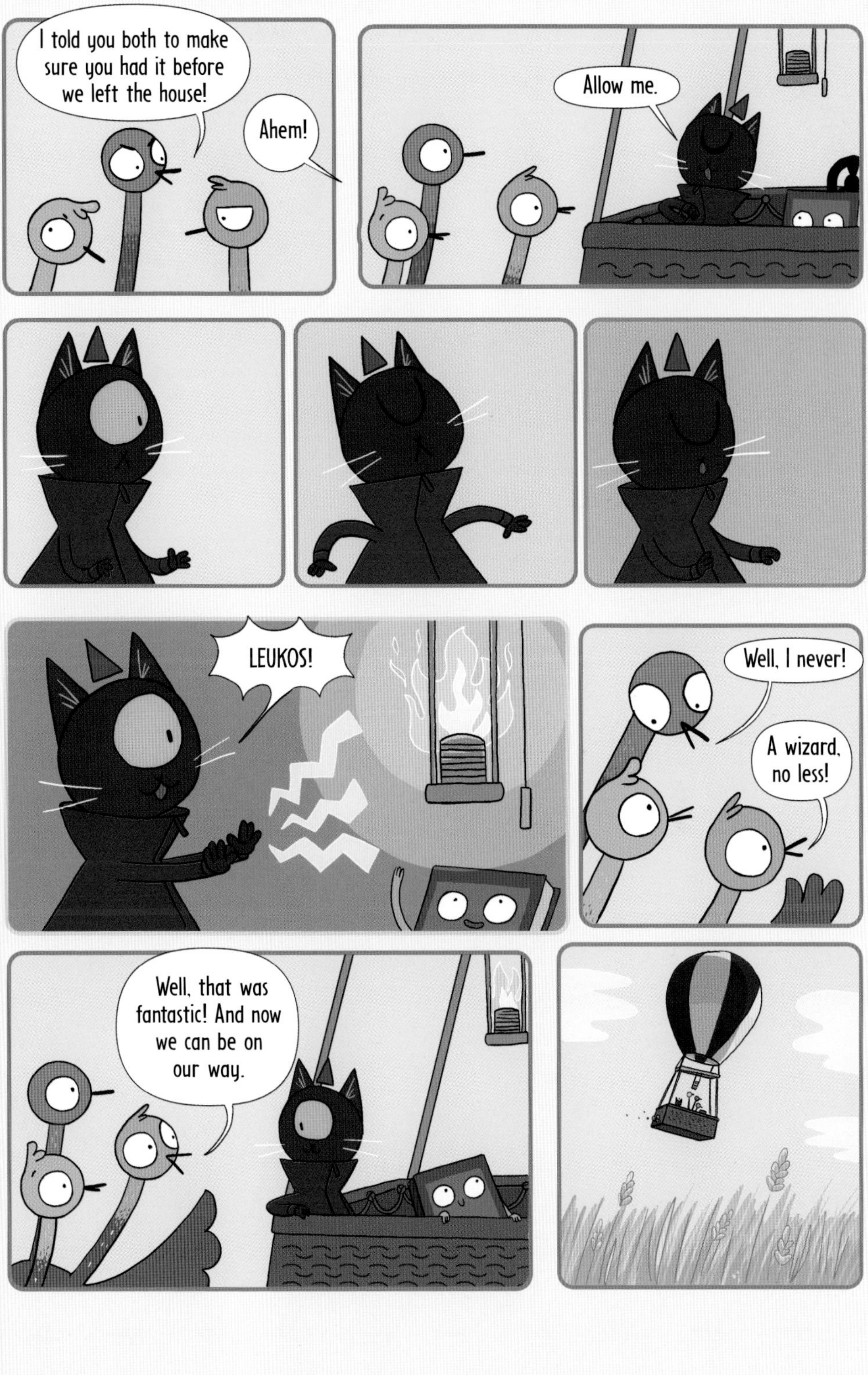
I told you both to make sure you had it before we left the house!
Ahem!
Allow me.
LEUKOS!
Well, I never!
A wizard, no less!
Well, that was fantastic! And now we can be on our way.

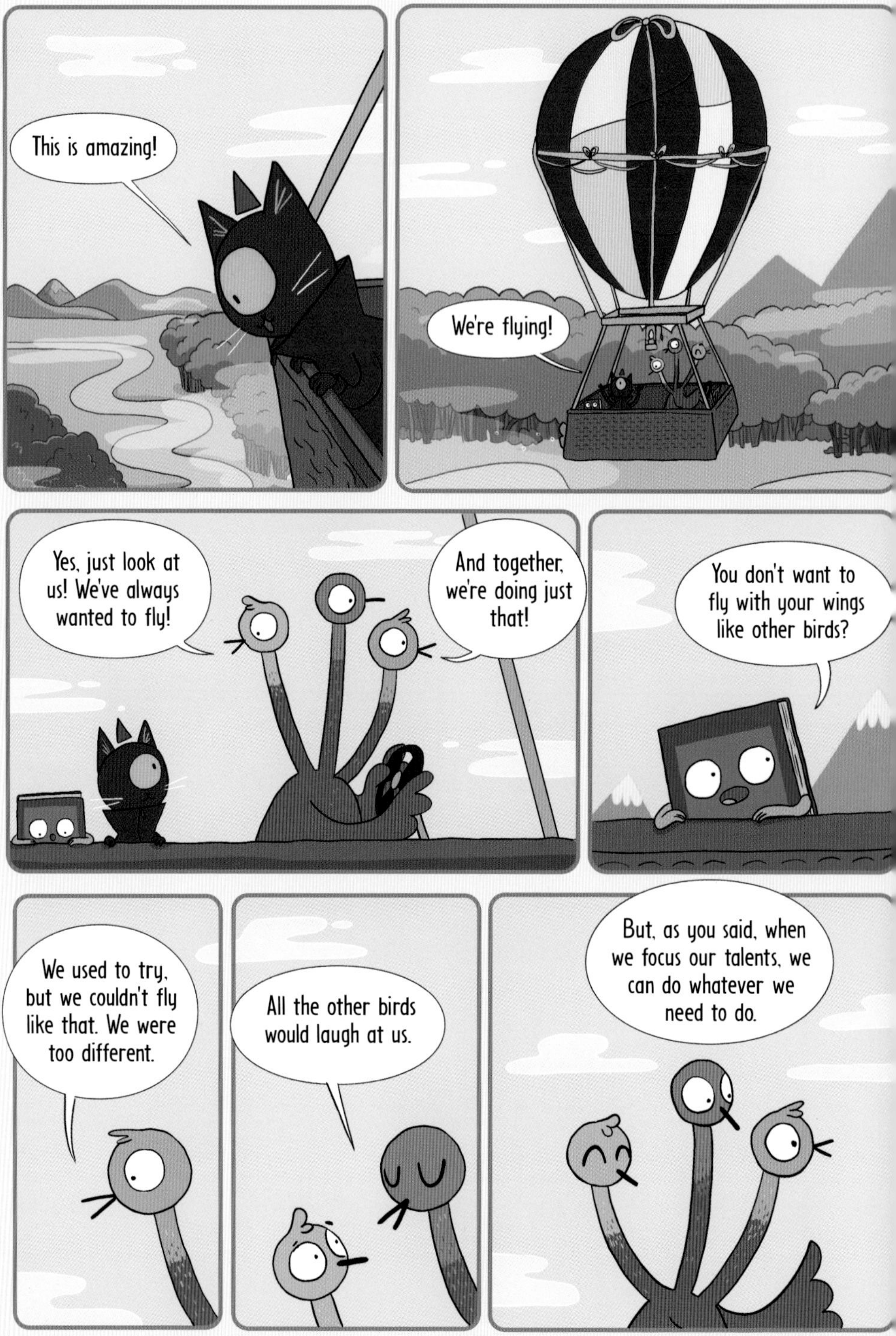
This is amazing!
We're flying!
Yes, just look at us! We've always wanted to fly!
And together, we're doing just that!
You don't want to fly with your wings like other birds?
We used to try, but we couldn't fly like that. We were too different.
All the other birds would laugh at us.
But, as you said, when we focus our talents, we can do whatever we need to do.

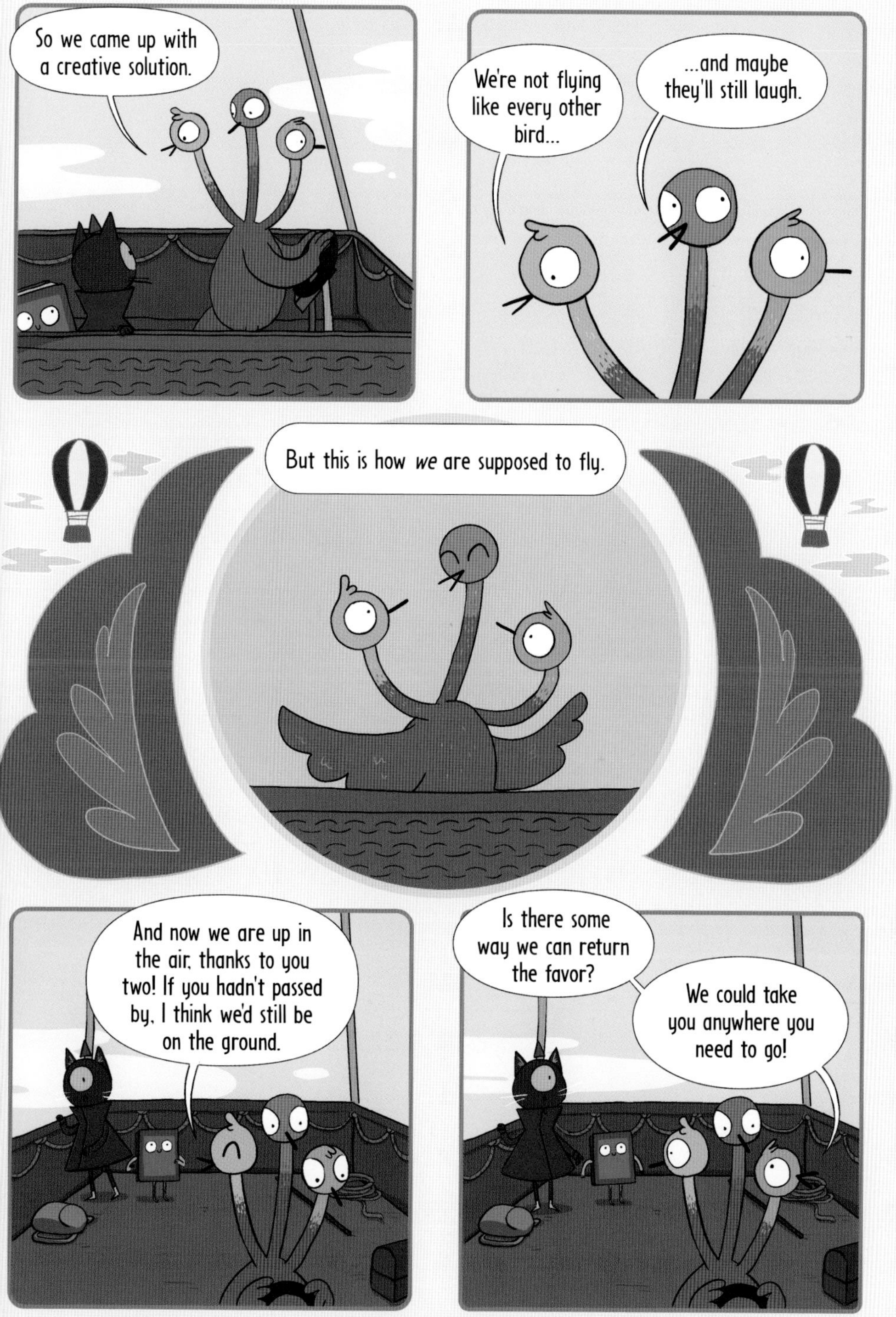
So we came up with a creative solution.
We're not flying like every other bird...
...and maybe they'll still laugh.
But this is how *we* are supposed to fly.
And now we are up in the air, thanks to you two! If you hadn't passed by, I think we'd still be on the ground.
Is there some way we can return the favor?
We could take you anywhere you need to go!

The Library!
That's right. Book needs to be returned to the Library.
Do you know where it is?
Err, no...
But we have a lamp!
Here you go!
Where were you keeping that?

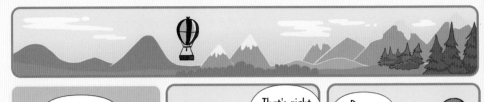

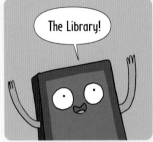

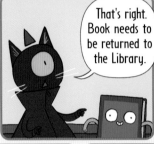

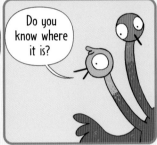

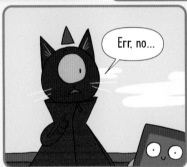

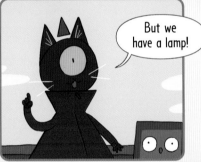

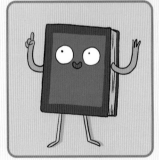

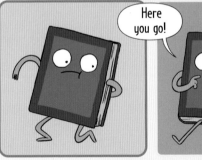

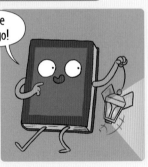

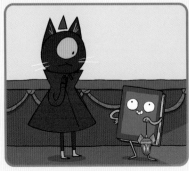

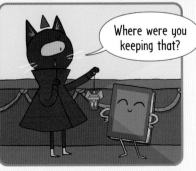

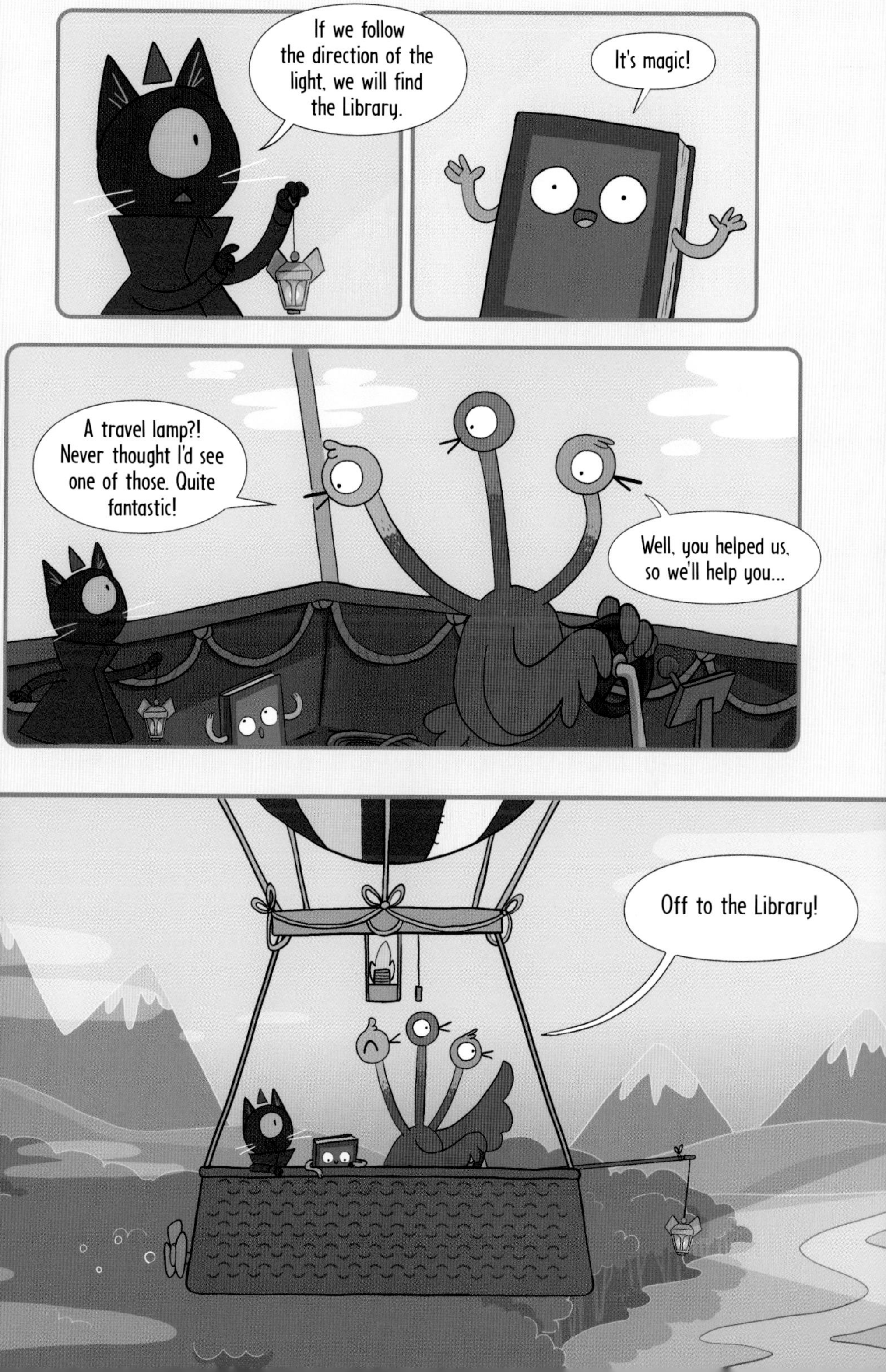
If we follow the direction of the light, we will find the Library.
It's magic!
A travel lamp?! Never thought I'd see one of those. Quite fantastic!
Well, you helped us, so we'll help you...
Off to the Library!

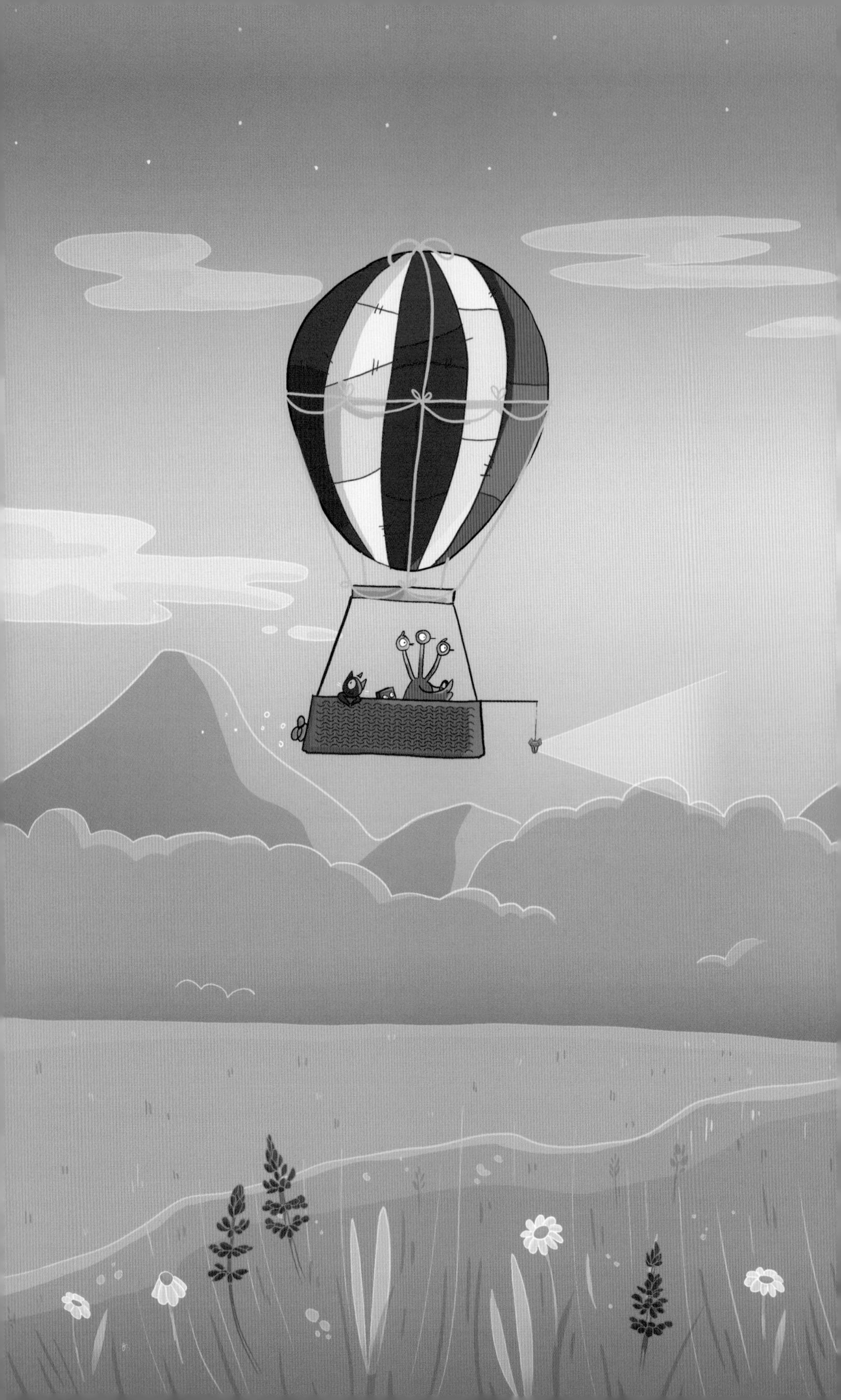

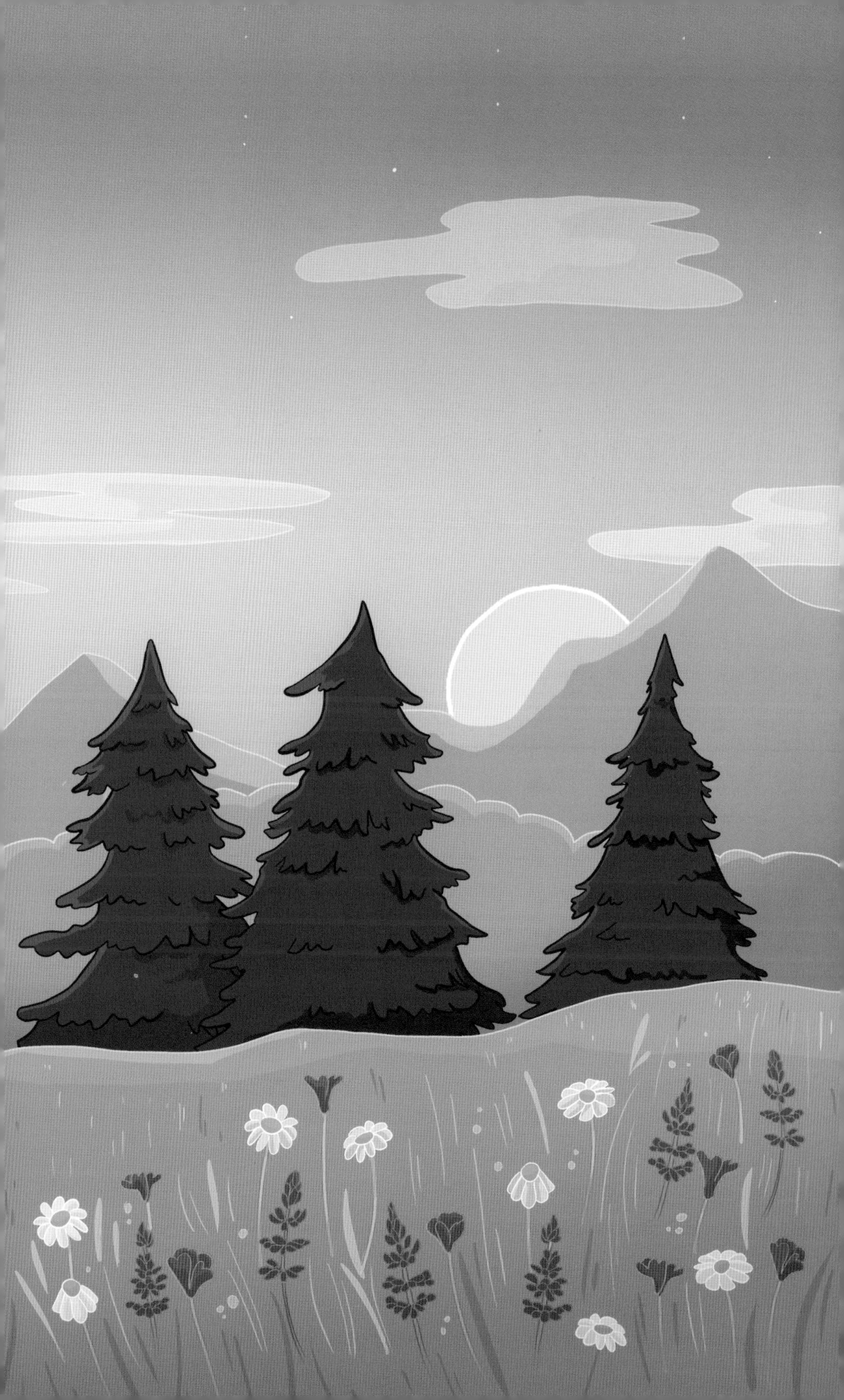

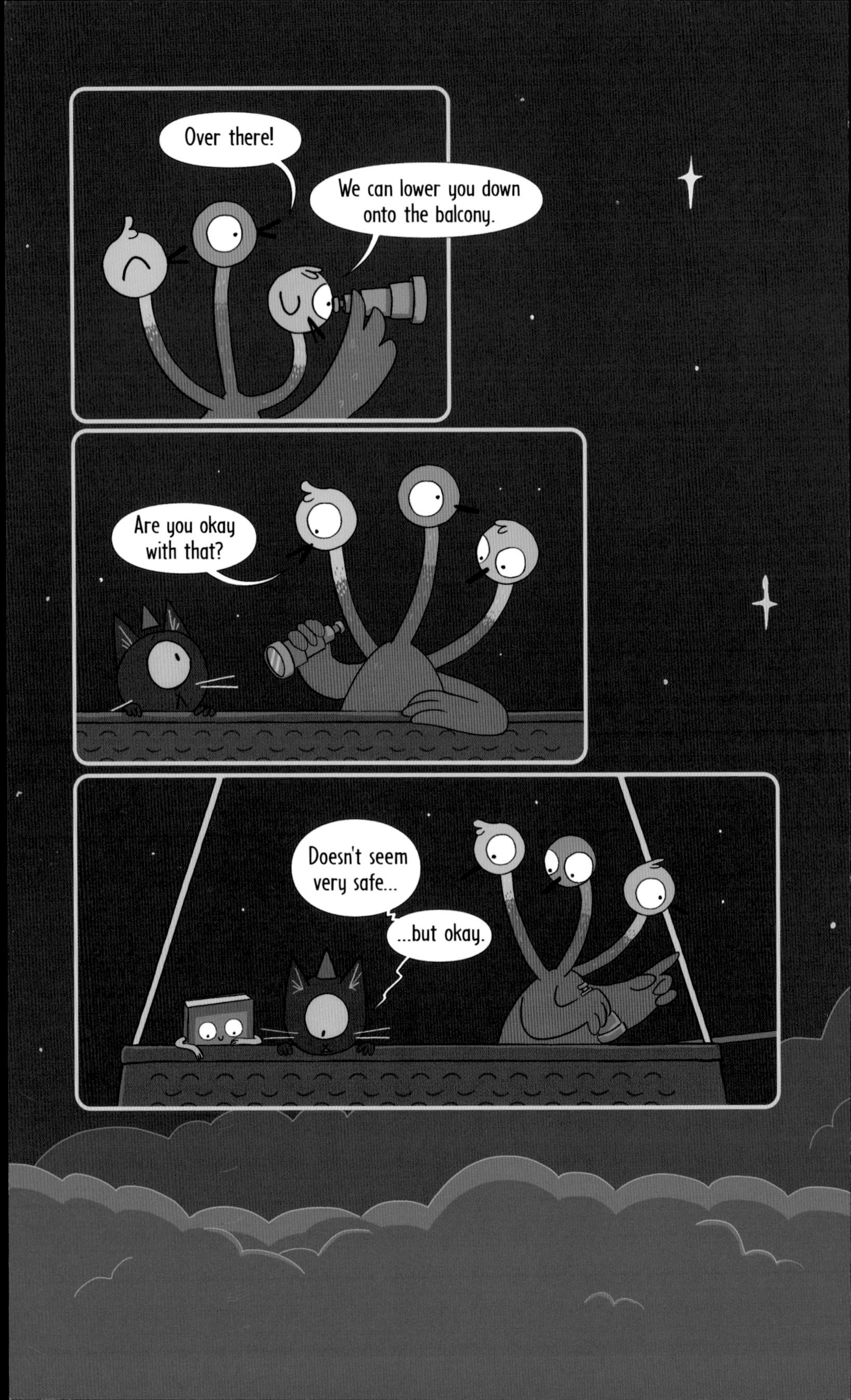
Over there!
We can lower you down onto the balcony.
Are you okay with that?
Doesn't seem very safe...
...but okay.

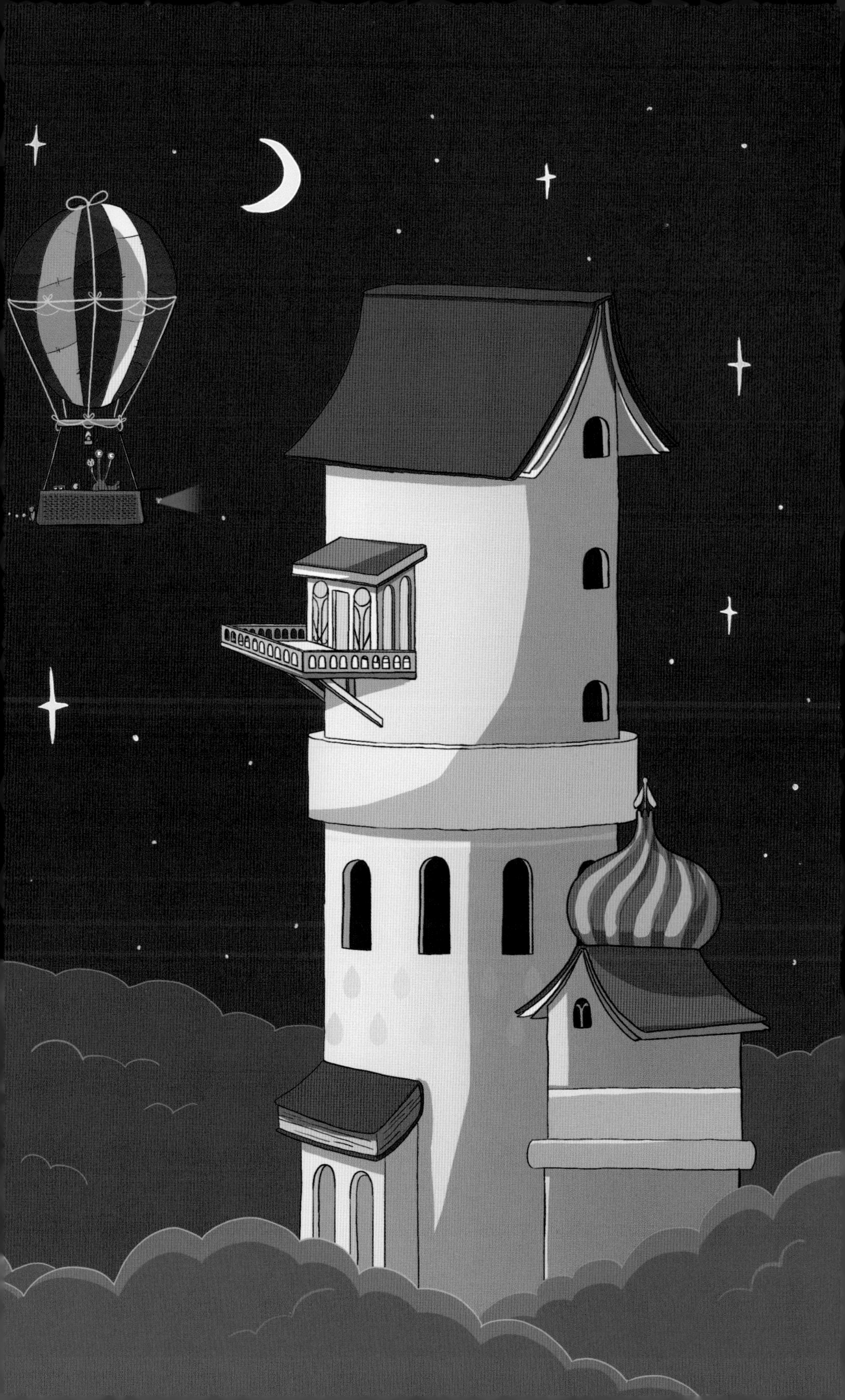

WHEEE!
What about the lamp?
Keep it as thanks!
SEE YOU LATER!
Goodbye!
THANK YOU!

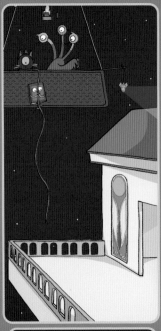

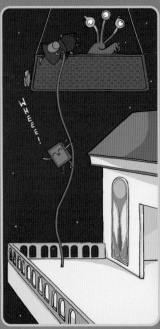

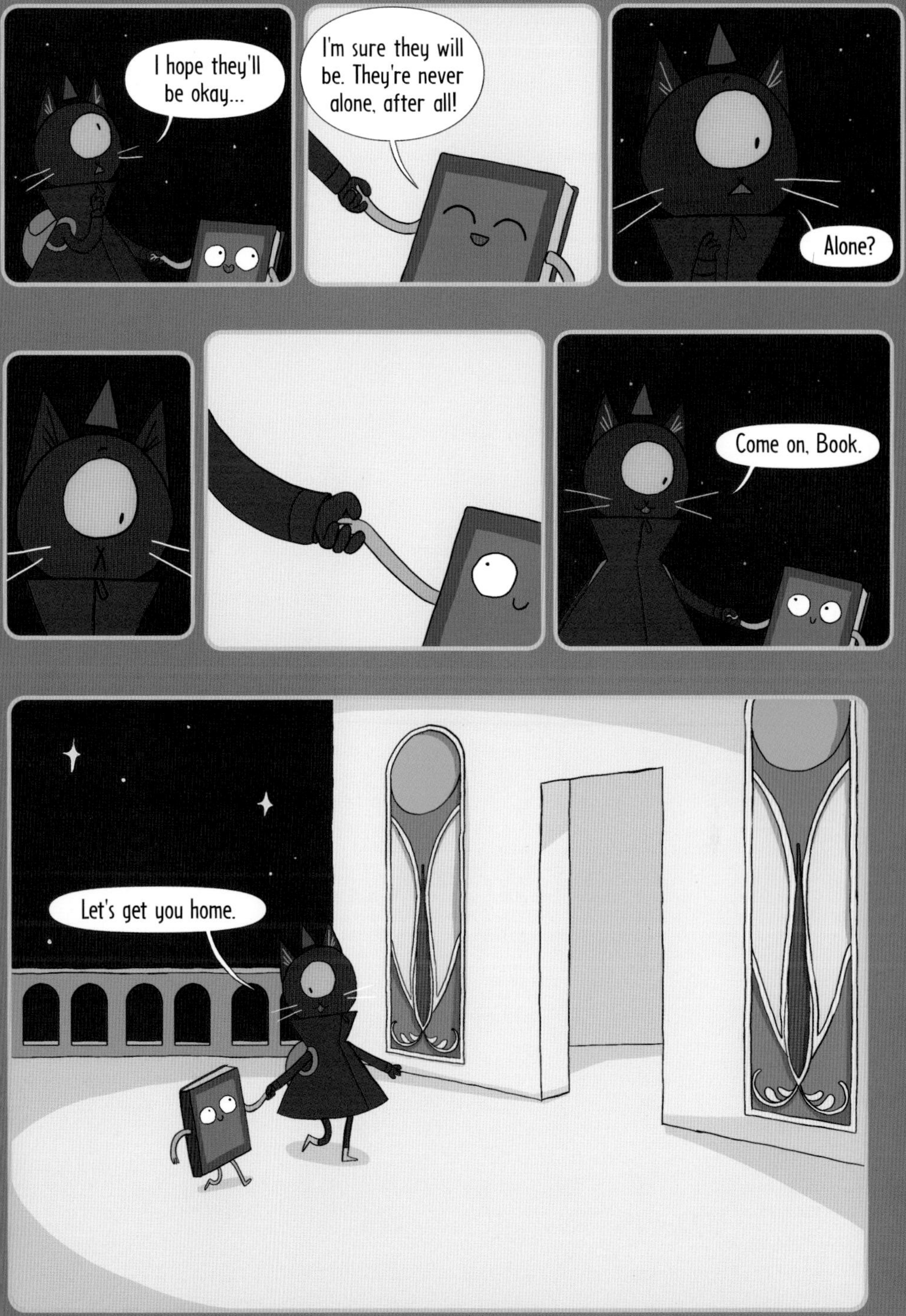
I hope they'll be okay...
I'm sure they will be. They're never alone, after all!
Alone?
Come on, Book.
Let's get you home.

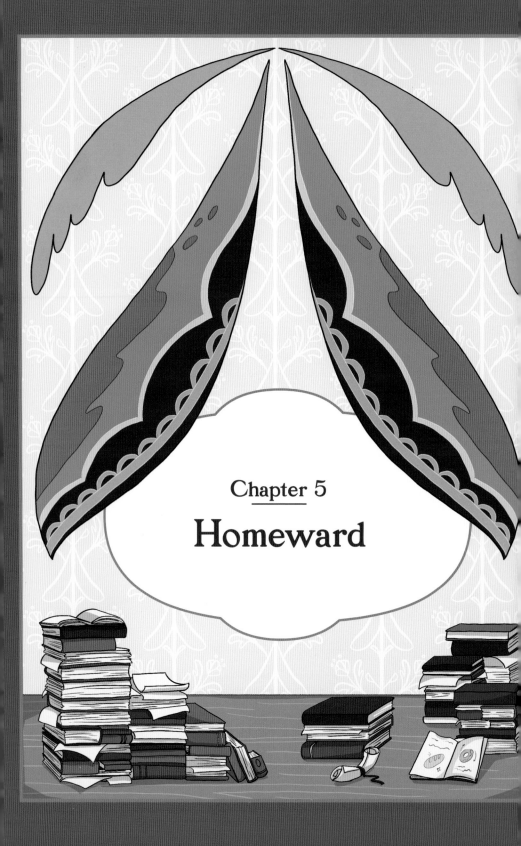

Chapter 5
Homeward

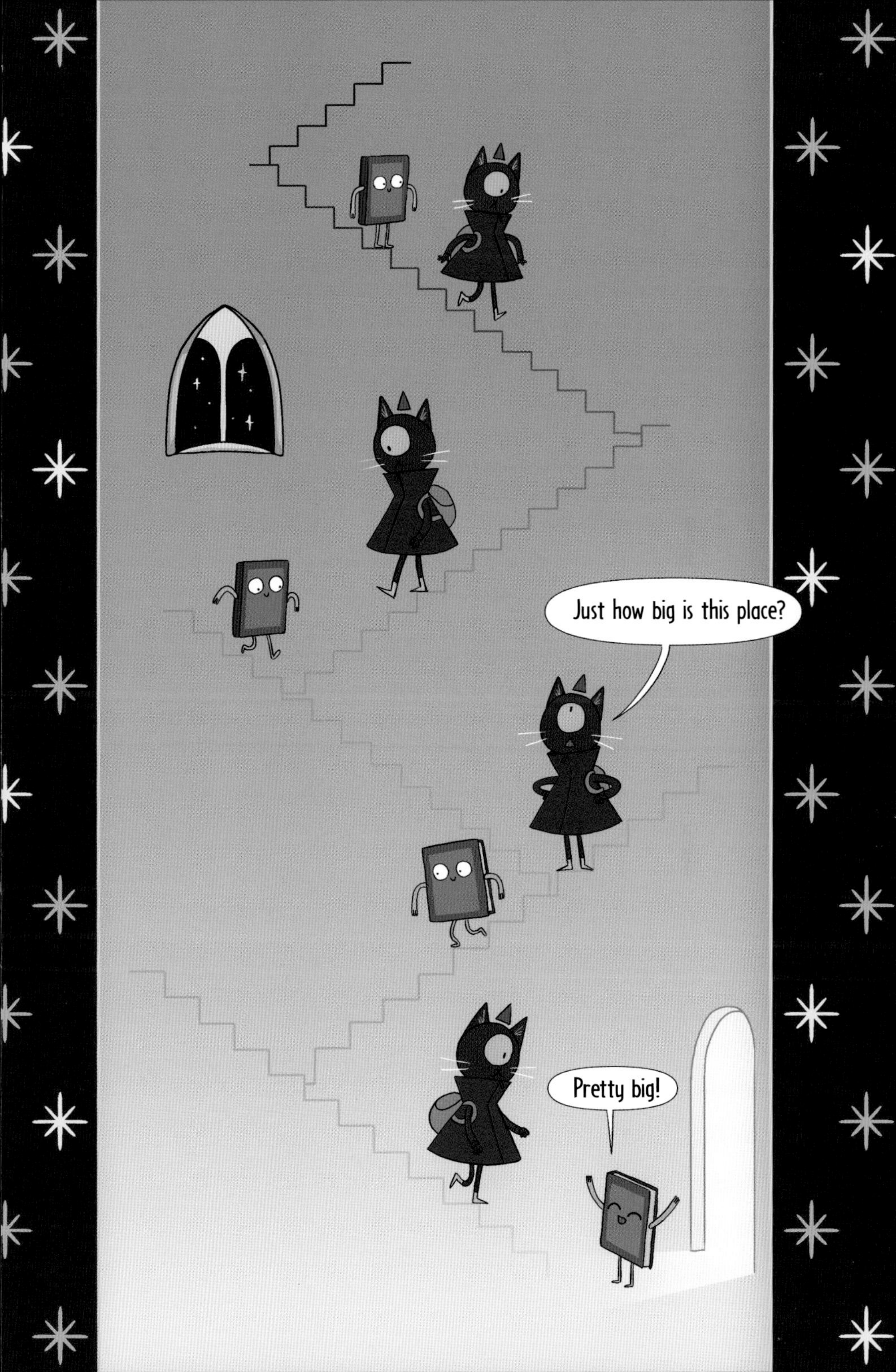
Just how big is this place?
Pretty big!

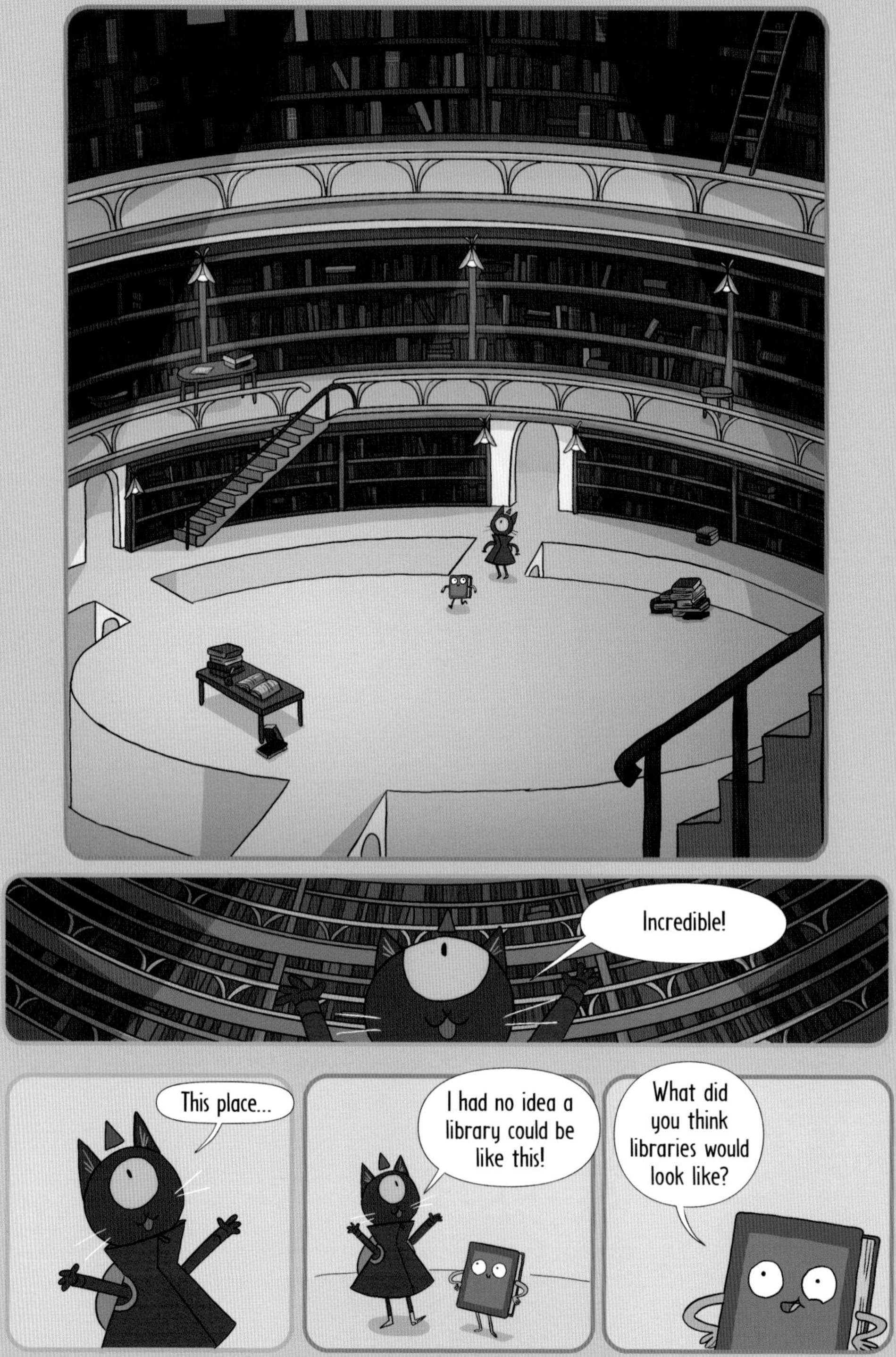
Incredible!
This place...
I had no idea a library could be like this!
What did you think libraries would look like?

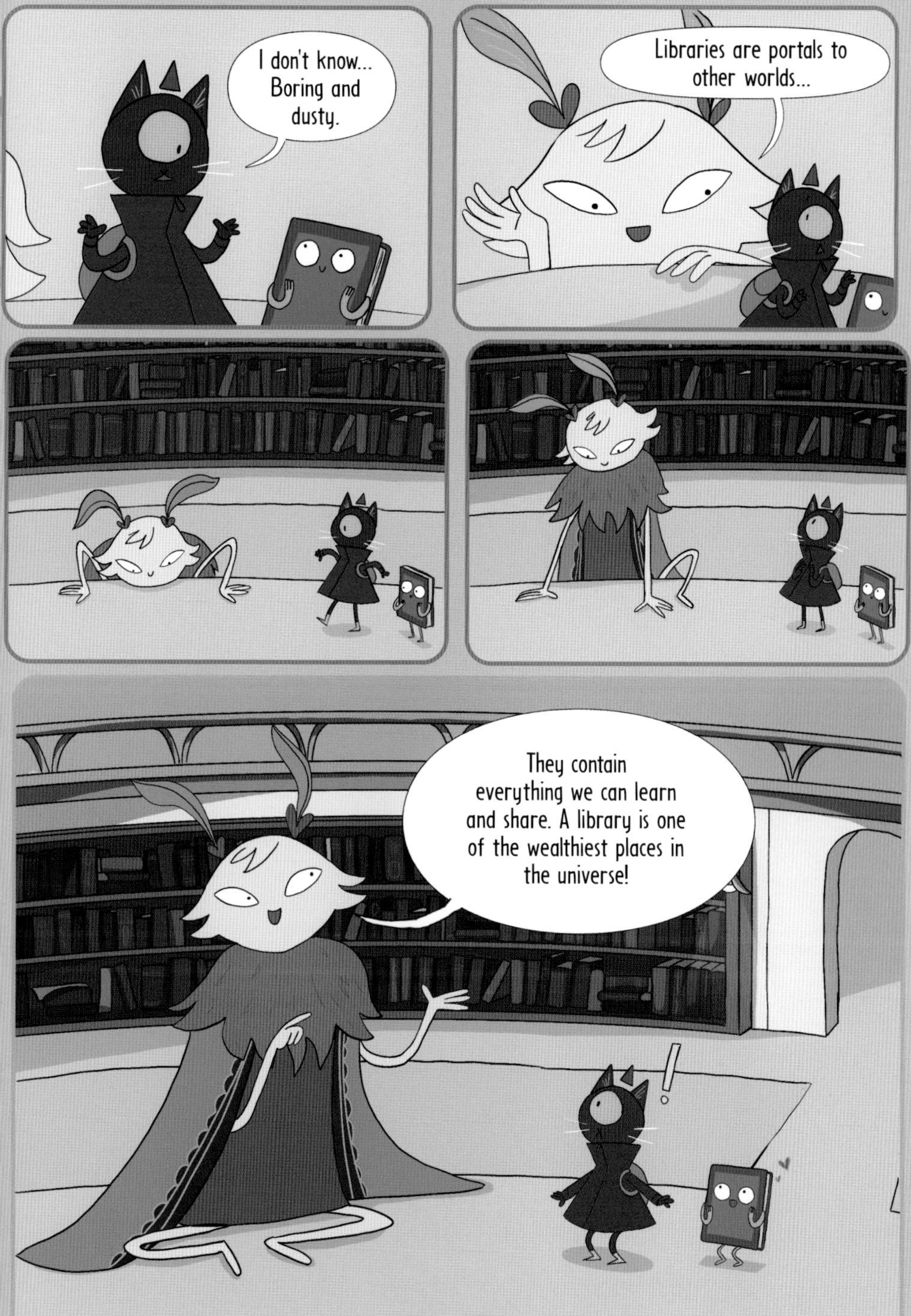
I don't know... Boring and dusty.
Libraries are portals to other worlds...
They contain everything we can learn and share. A library is one of the wealthiest places in the universe!
!

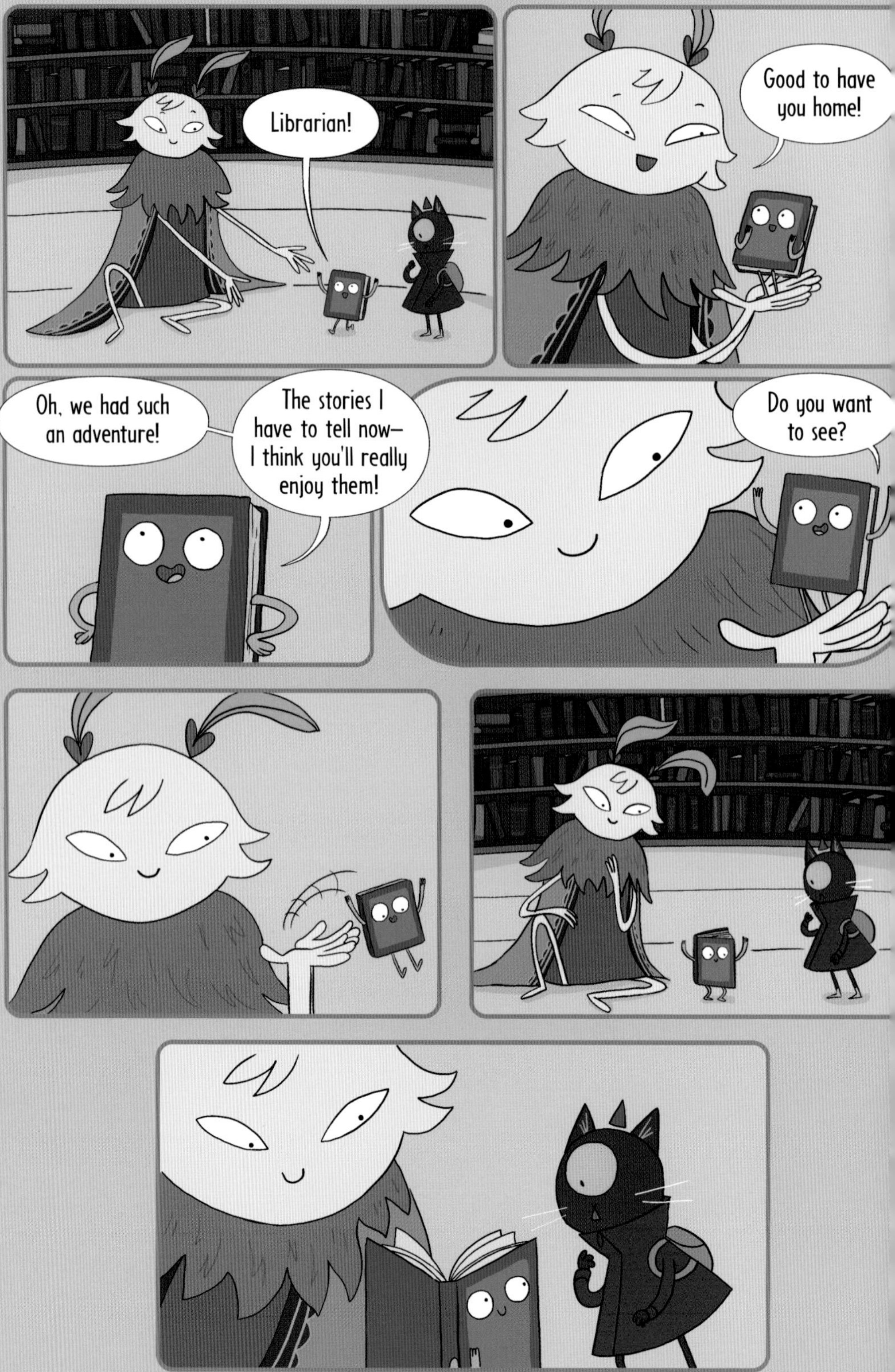
Librarian!
Good to have you home!
Oh, we had such an adventure!
The stories I have to tell now— I think you'll really enjoy them!
Do you want to see?

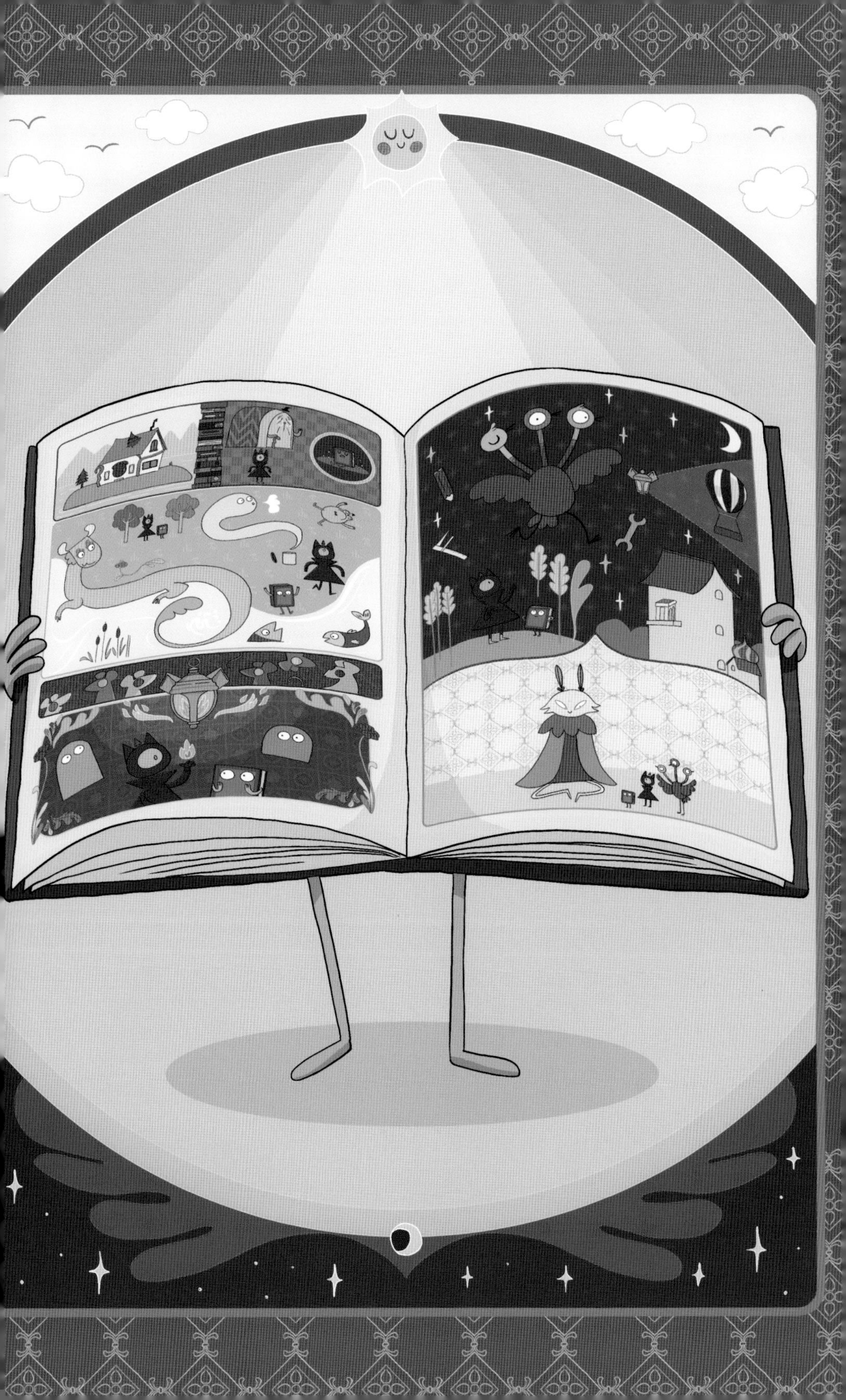

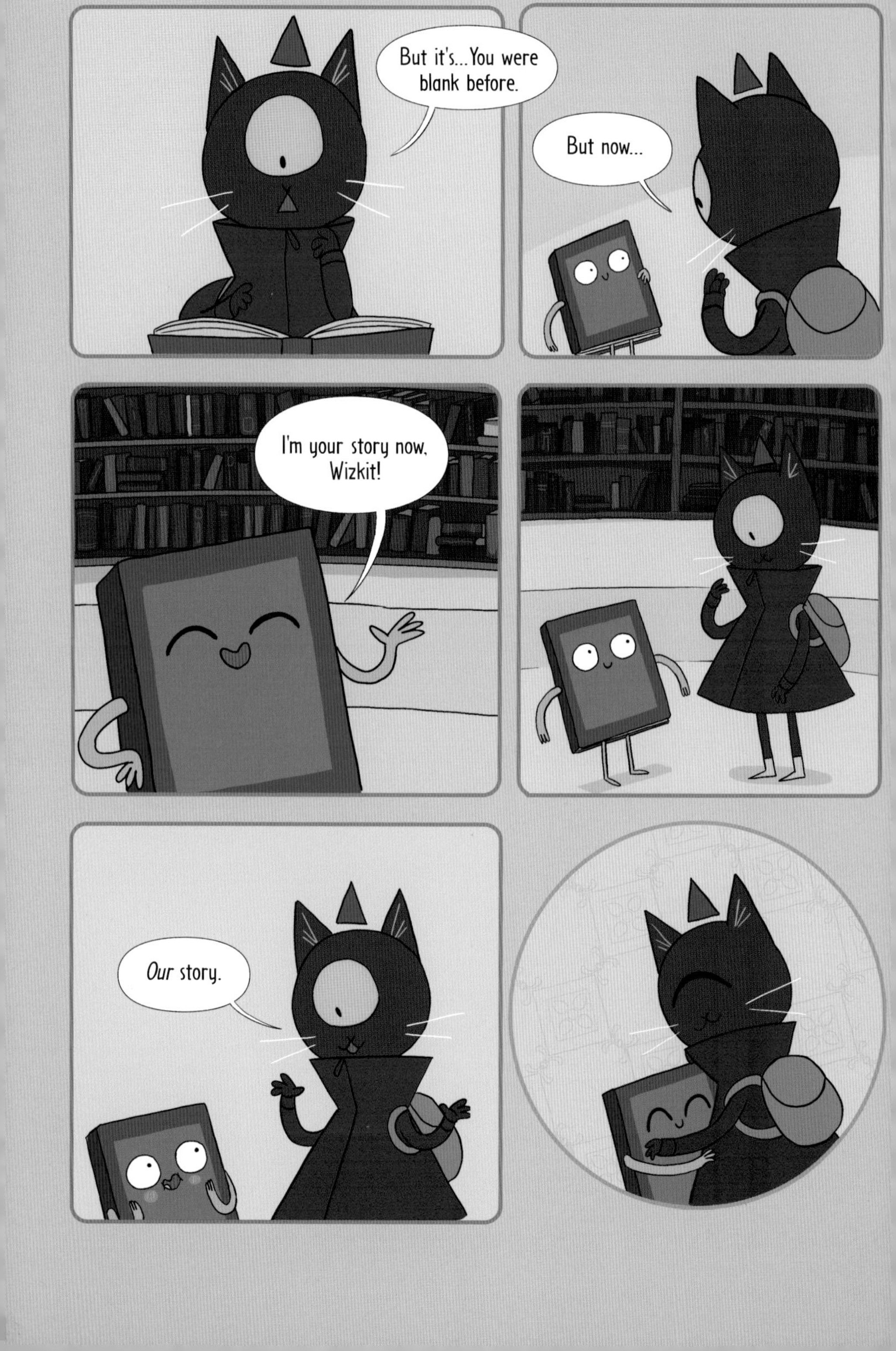
But it's...You were blank before.
But now...
I'm your story now, Wizkit!
Our story.

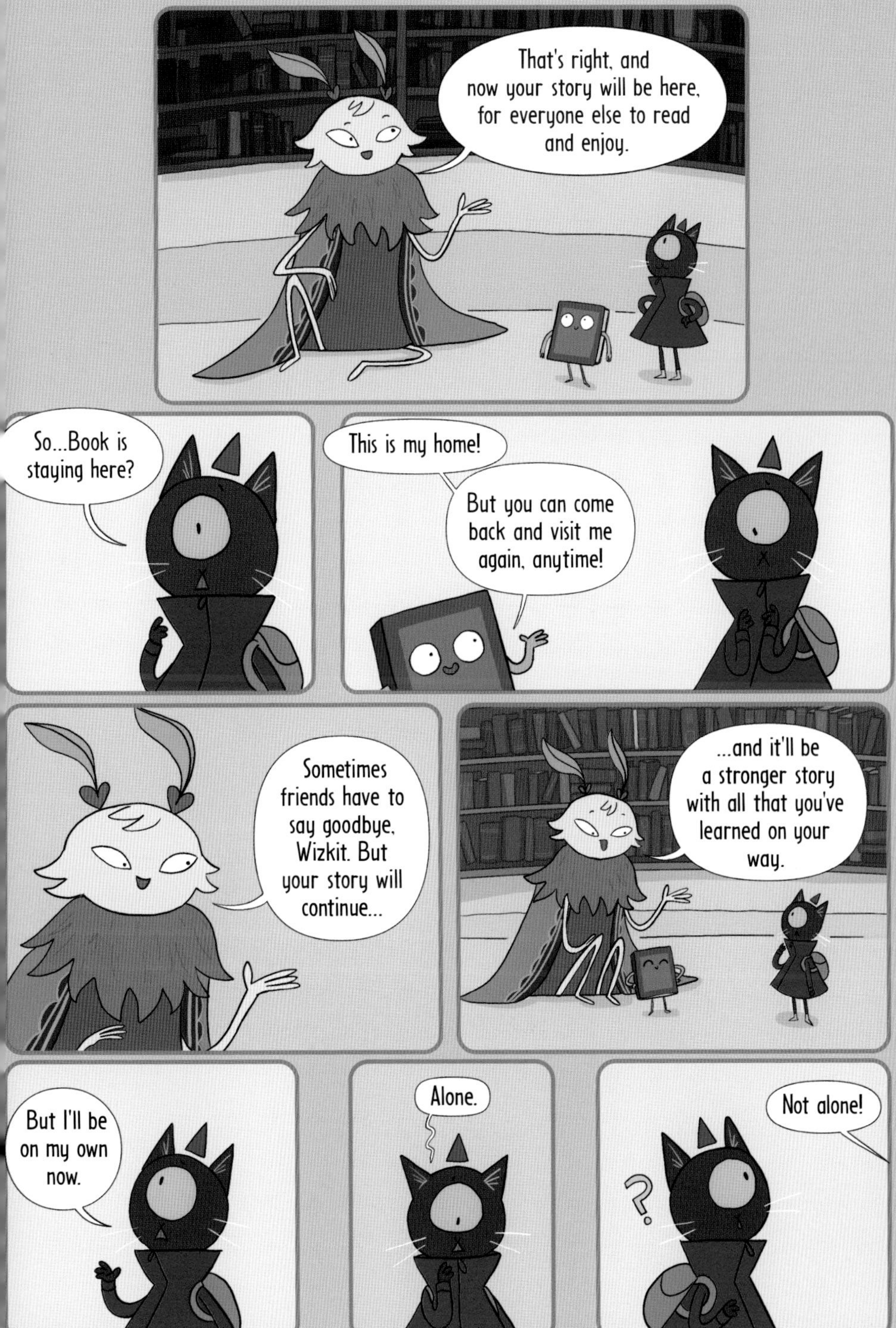
That's right, and now your story will be here, for everyone else to read and enjoy.
So...Book is staying here?
This is my home!
But you can come back and visit me again, anytime!
Sometimes friends have to say goodbye, Wizkit. But your story will continue...
...and it'll be a stronger story with all that you've learned on your way.
But I'll be on my own now.
Alone.
Not alone!

You've got us!
I thought you left!
We were just looking for parking.
Would you look at this place.
Imagine the art books in here!
Art books?! Phht! No one is looking at those until we've looked at the math and science sections!
Will you two hush!
We're here for you, Wizkit.
Now it's your turn to let someone help you home.

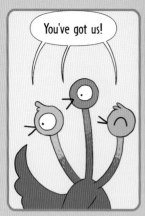

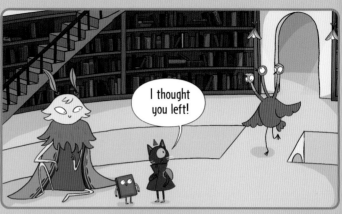

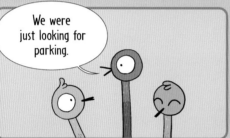

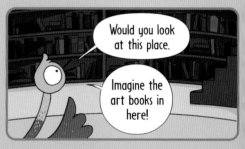

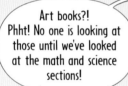

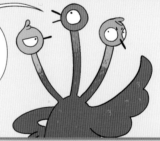

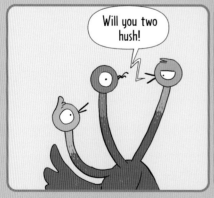

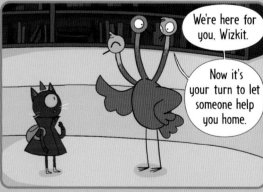

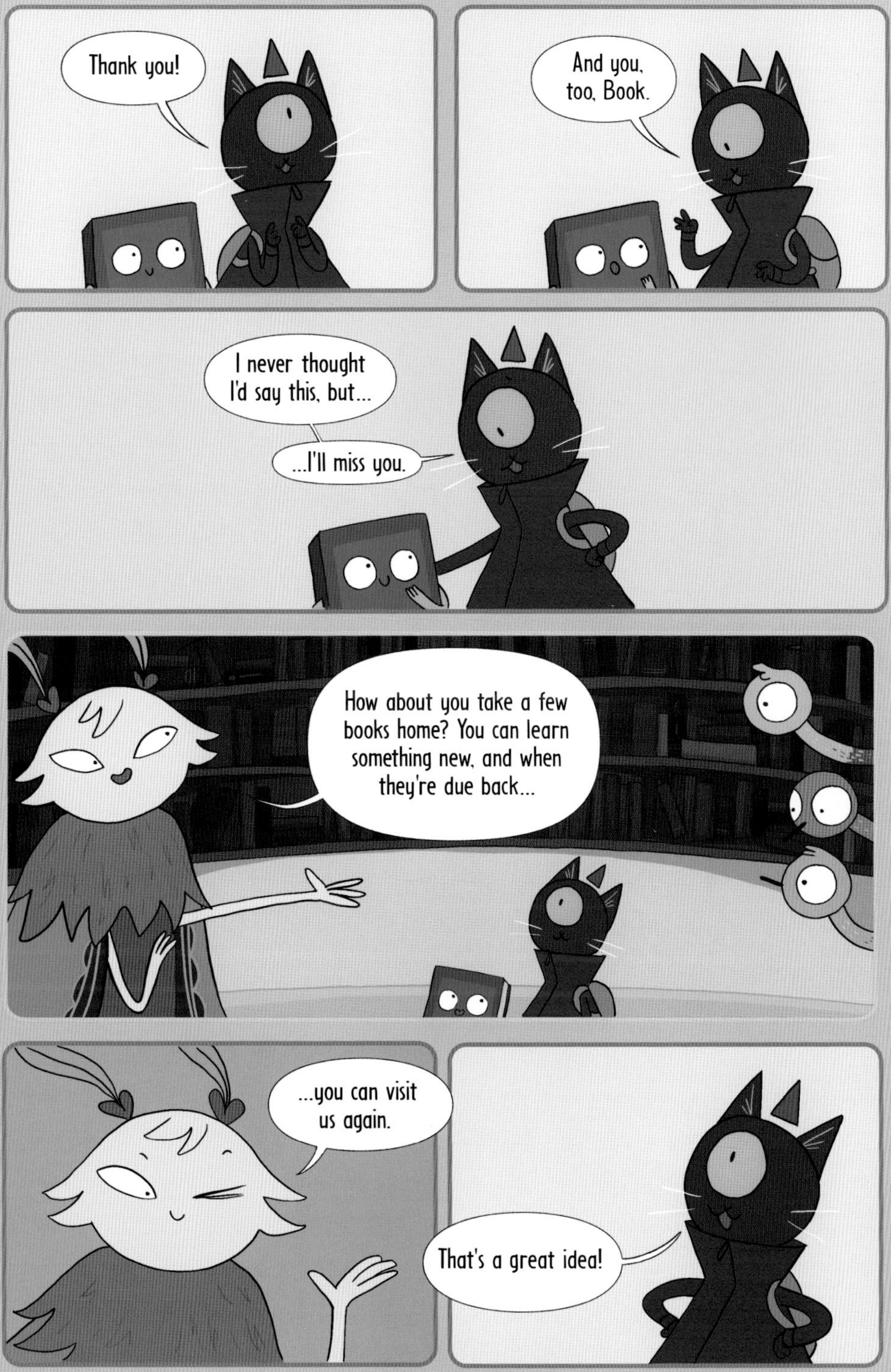
Thank you!
And you, too, Book.
I never thought I'd say this, but...
...I'll miss you.
How about you take a few books home? You can learn something new, and when they're due back...
...you can visit us again.
That's a great idea!

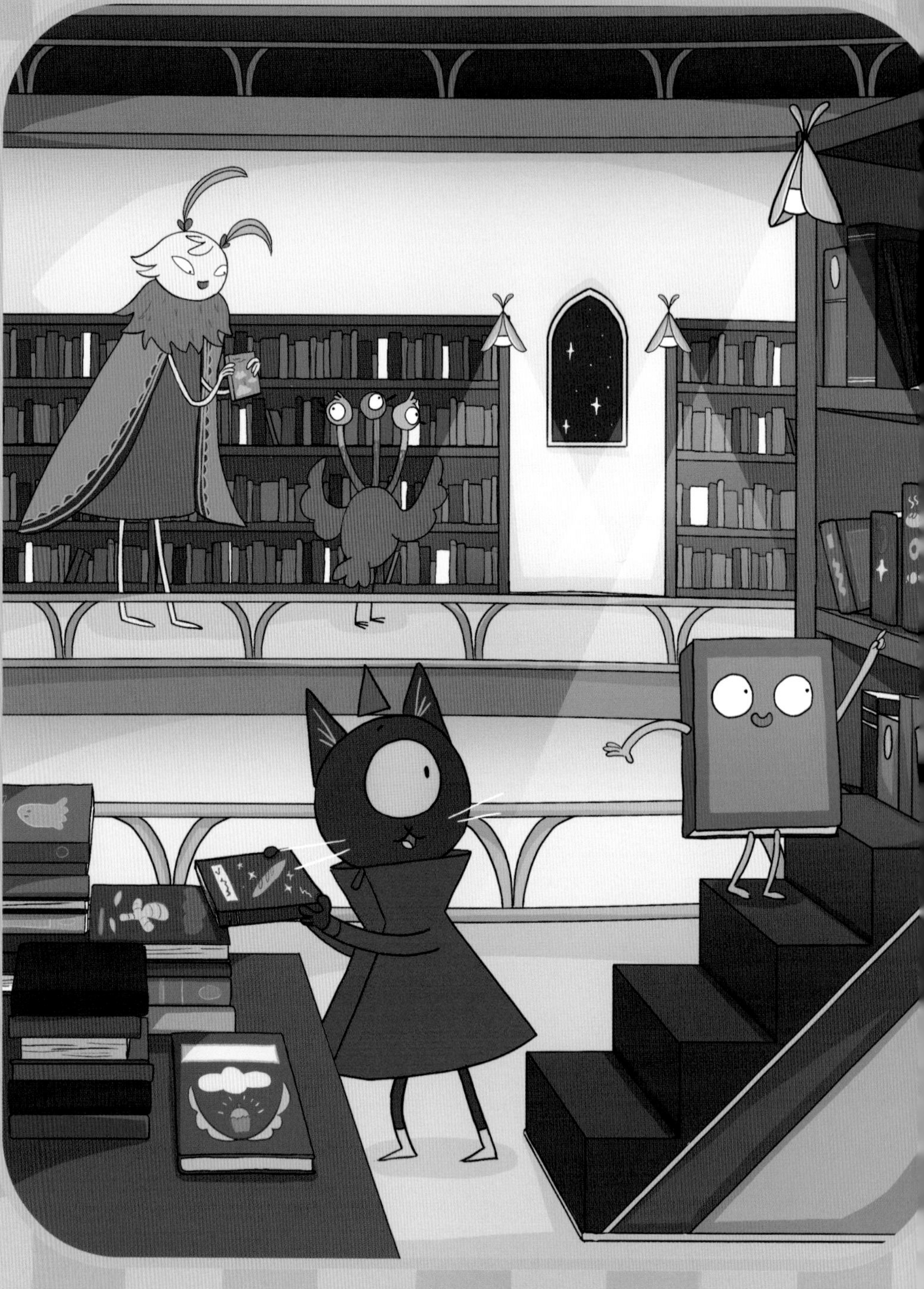

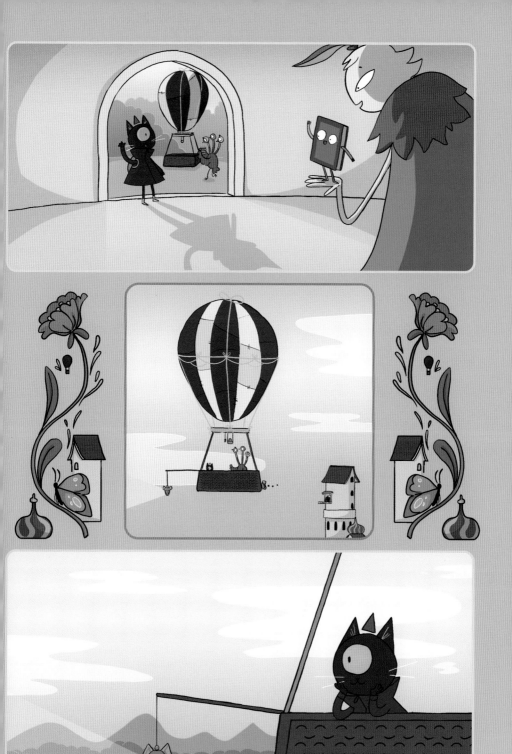

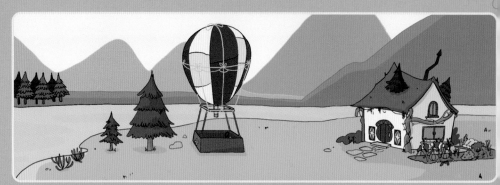

Ah, Wizkit!

OUCH!

You're home.

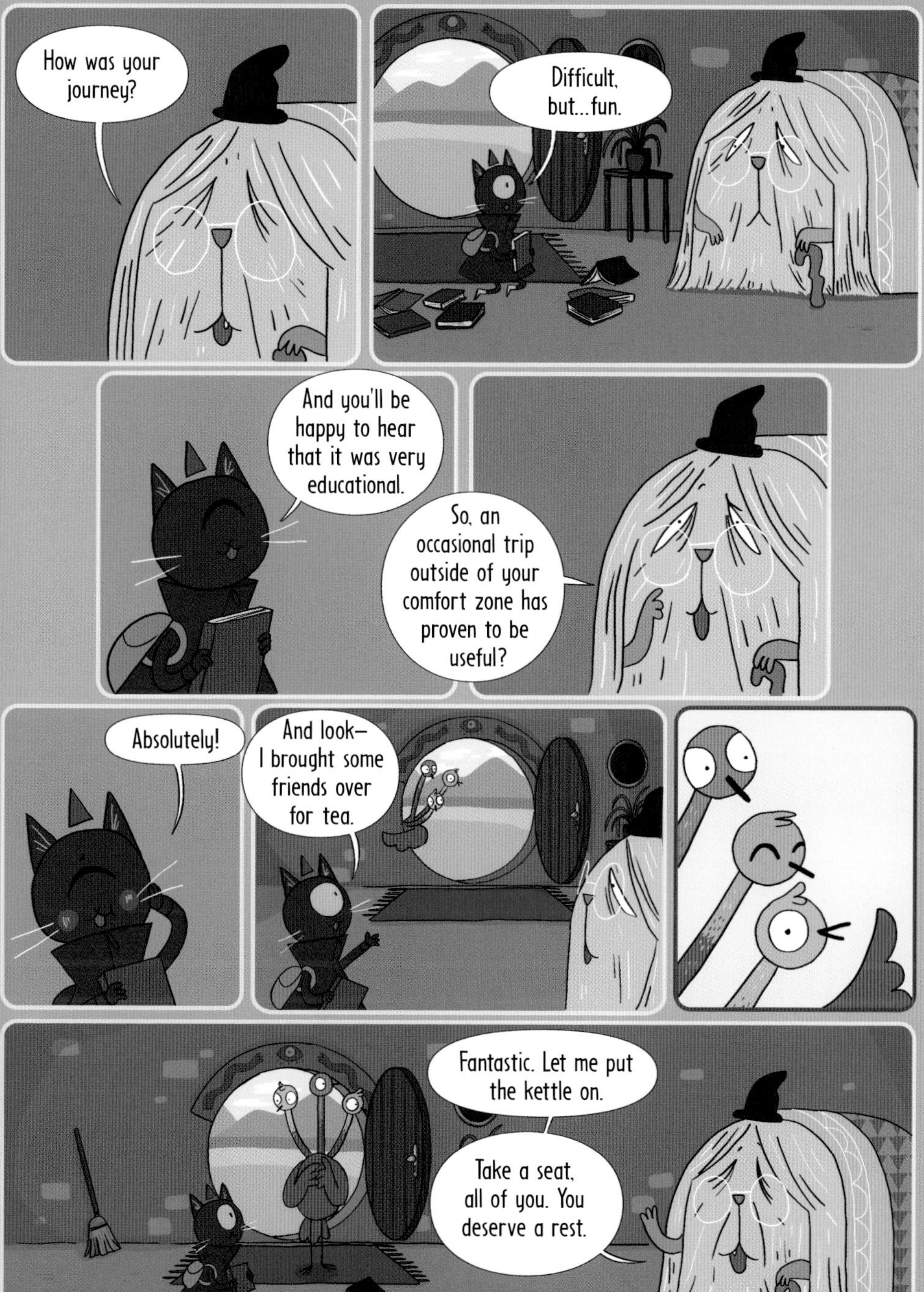
How was your journey?
Difficult, but...fun.
And you'll be happy to hear that it was very educational.
So, an occasional trip outside of your comfort zone has proven to be useful?
Absolutely!
And look— I brought some friends over for tea.
Fantastic. Let me put the kettle on.
Take a seat, all of you. You deserve a rest.

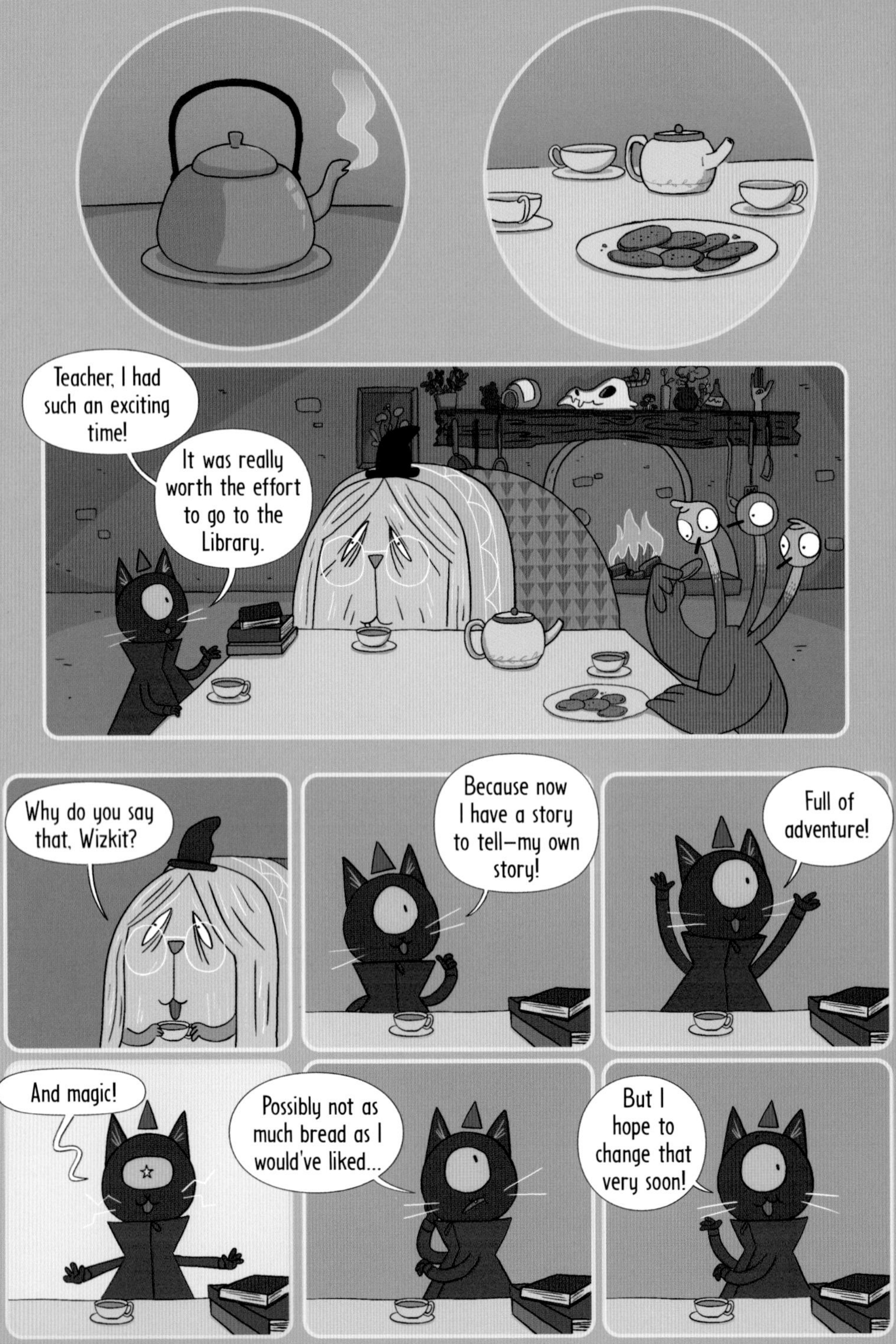
Teacher, I had such an exciting time!
It was really worth the effort to go to the Library.
Why do you say that, Wizkit?
Because now I have a story to tell—my own story!
Full of adventure!
And magic!
Possibly not as much bread as I would've liked...
But I hope to change that very soon!

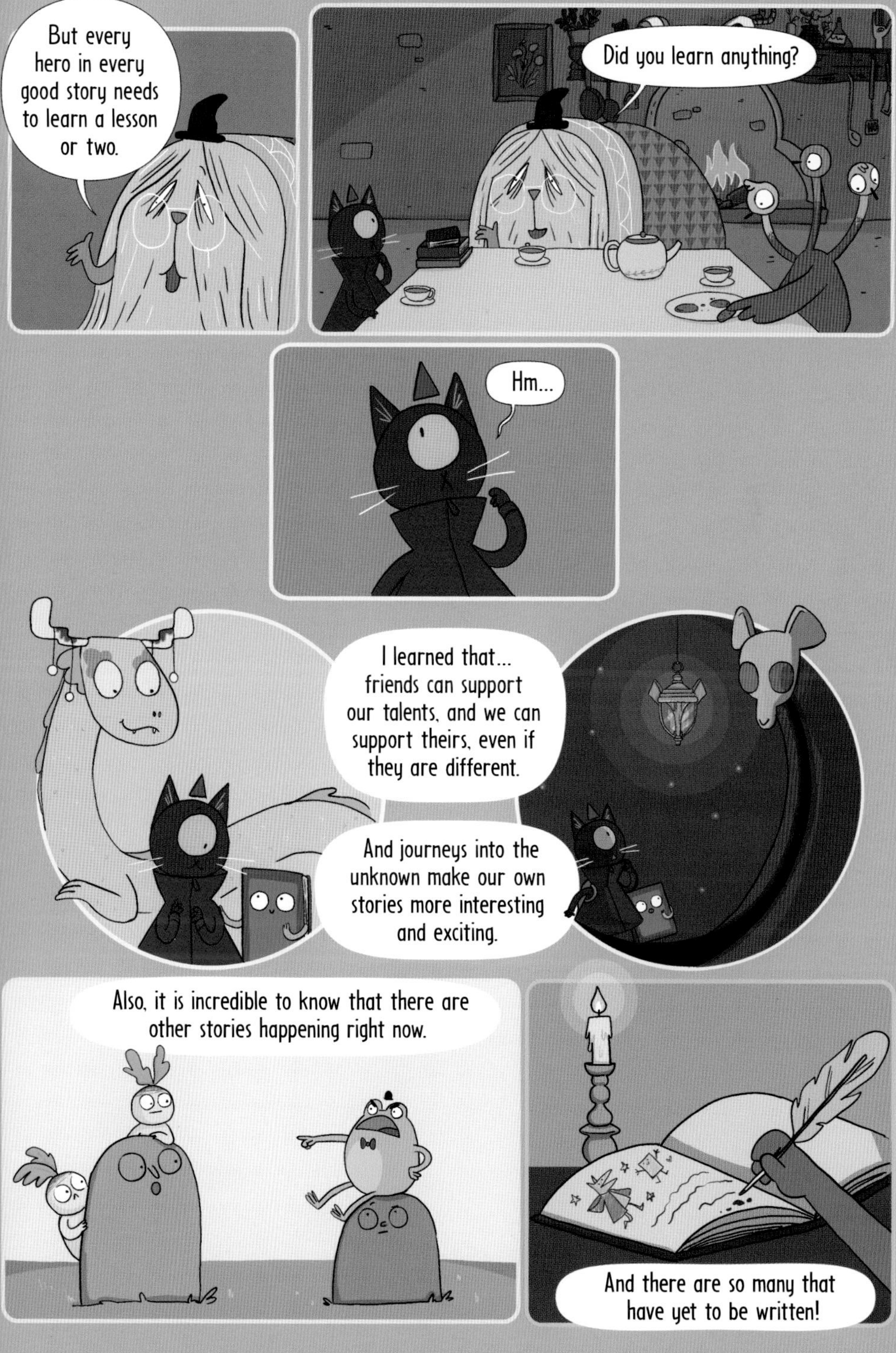
But every hero in every good story needs to learn a lesson or two.
Did you learn anything?
Hm...
I learned that... friends can support our talents, and we can support theirs, even if they are different.
And journeys into the unknown make our own stories more interesting and exciting.
Also, it is incredible to know that there are other stories happening right now.
And there are so many that have yet to be written!

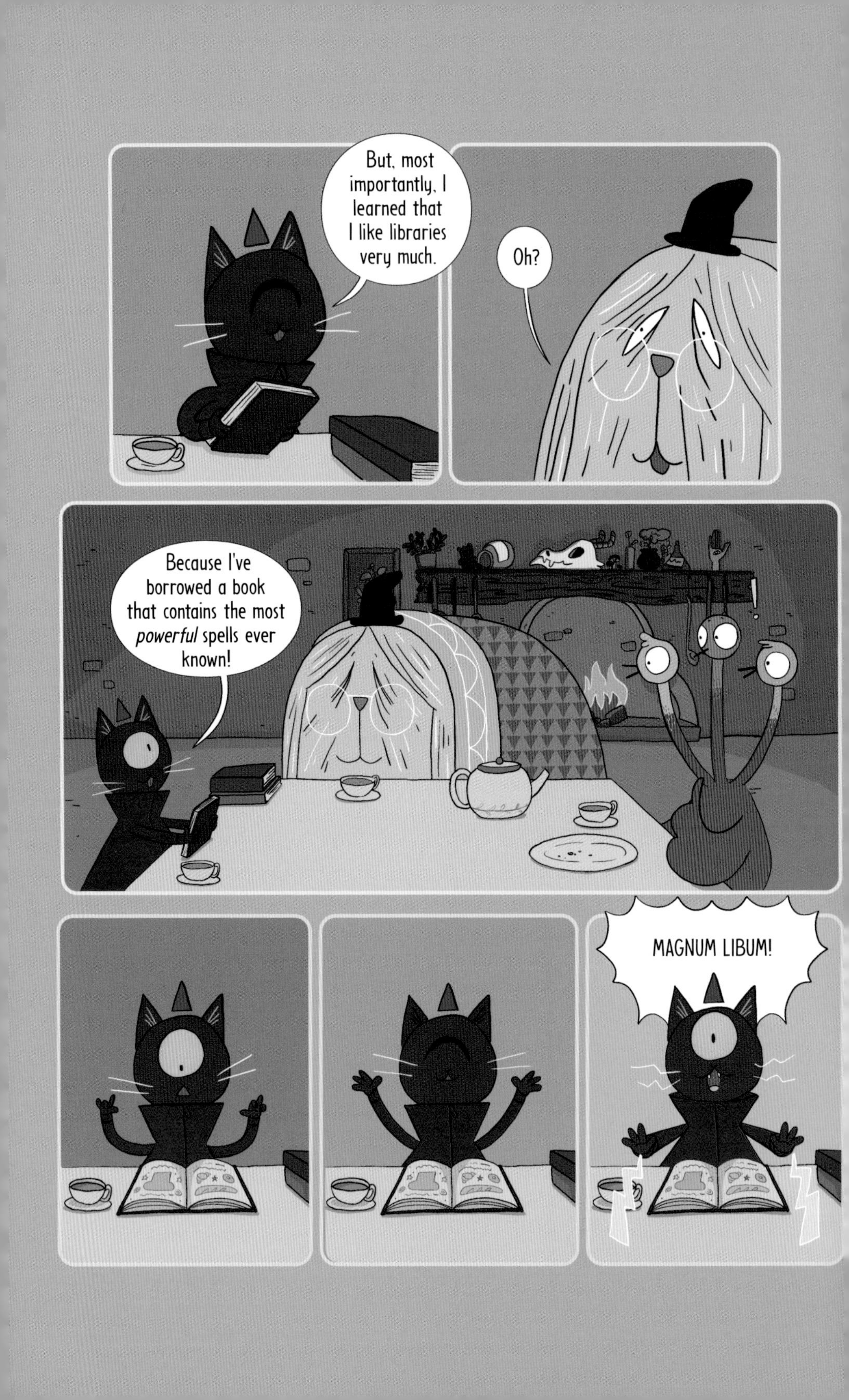
But, most importantly, I learned that I like libraries very much.
Oh?
Because I've borrowed a book that contains the most *powerful* spells ever known!
MAGNUM LIBUM!

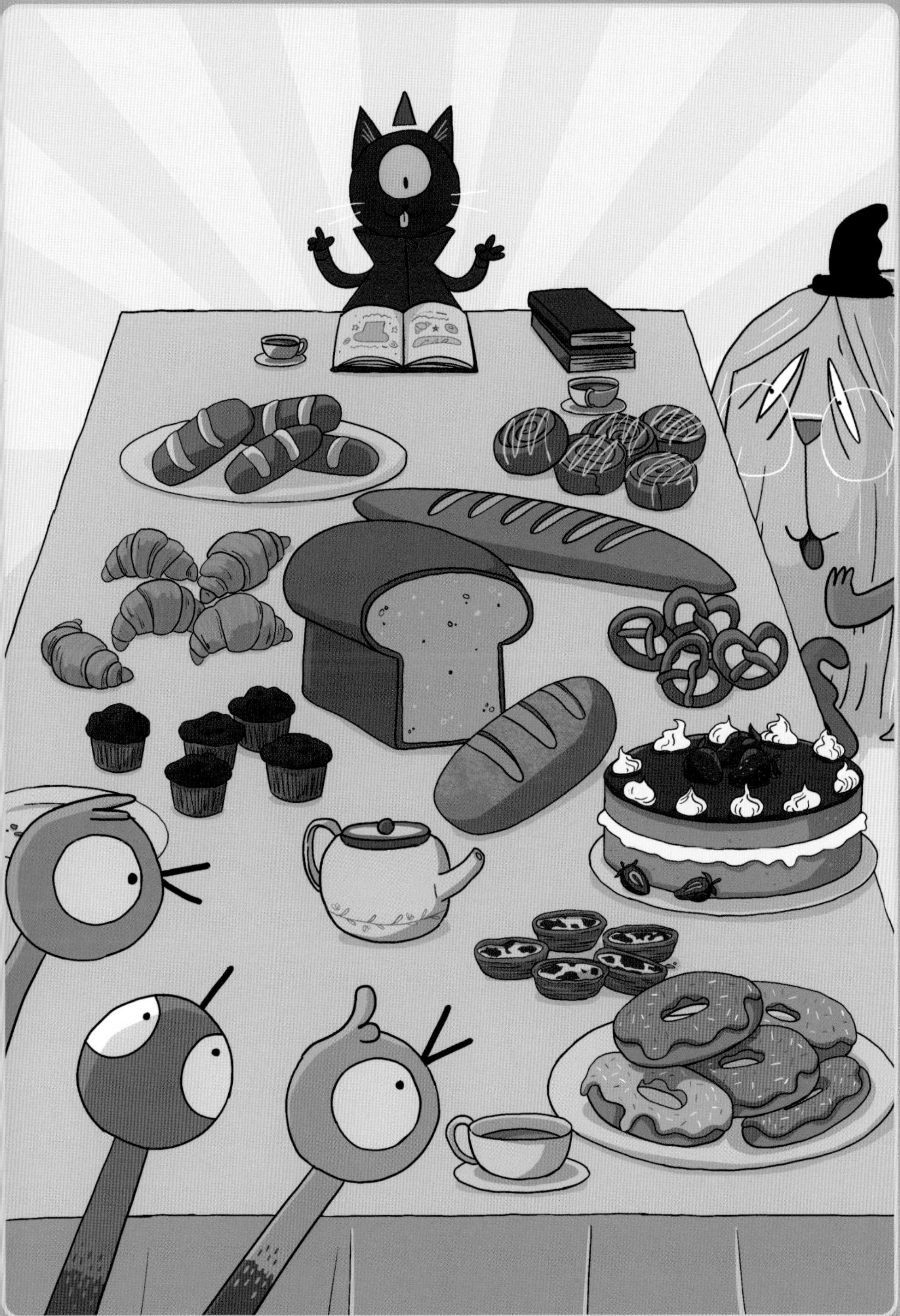

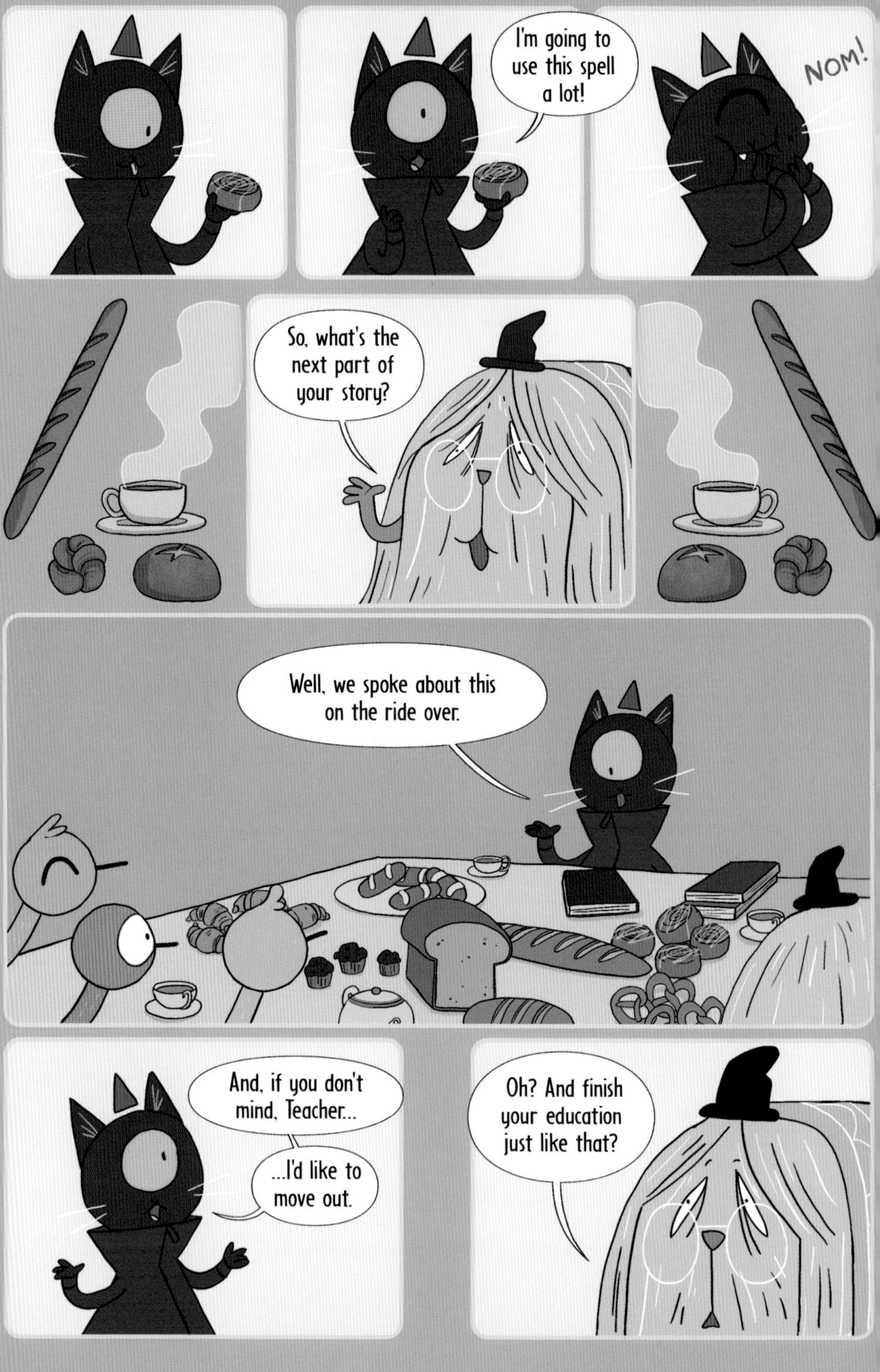
I'm going to use this spell a lot!
NOM!
So, what's the next part of your story?
Well, we spoke about this on the ride over.
And, if you don't mind, Teacher...
...I'd like to move out.
Oh? And finish your education just like that?

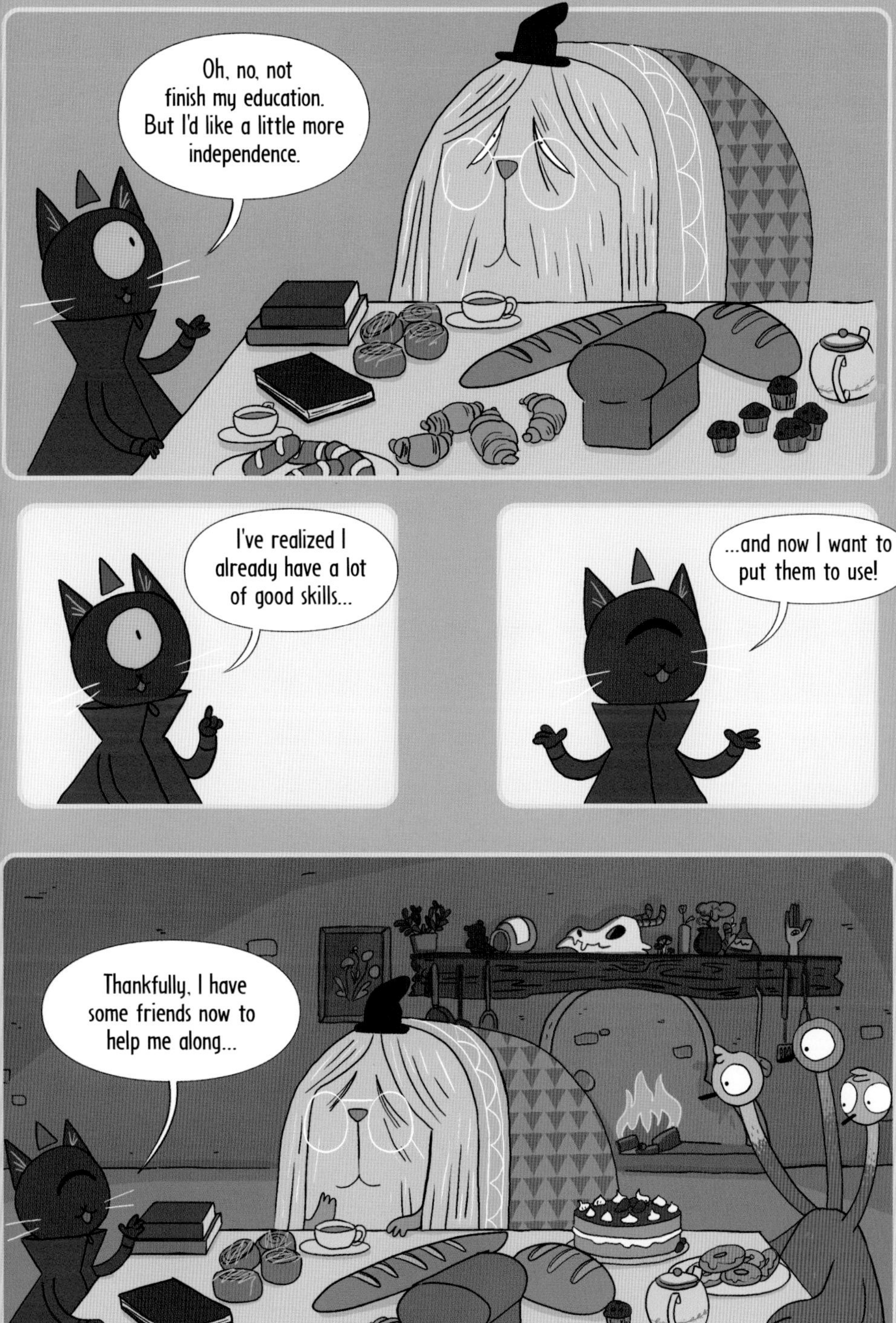
Oh, no, not finish my education. But I'd like a little more independence.
I've realized I already have a lot of good skills...
...and now I want to put them to use!
Thankfully, I have some friends now to help me along...

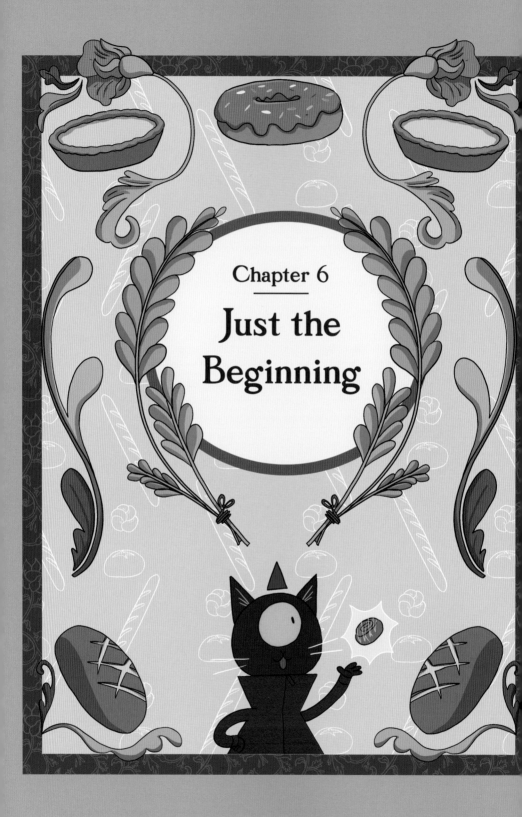

Chapter 6

Just the Beginning

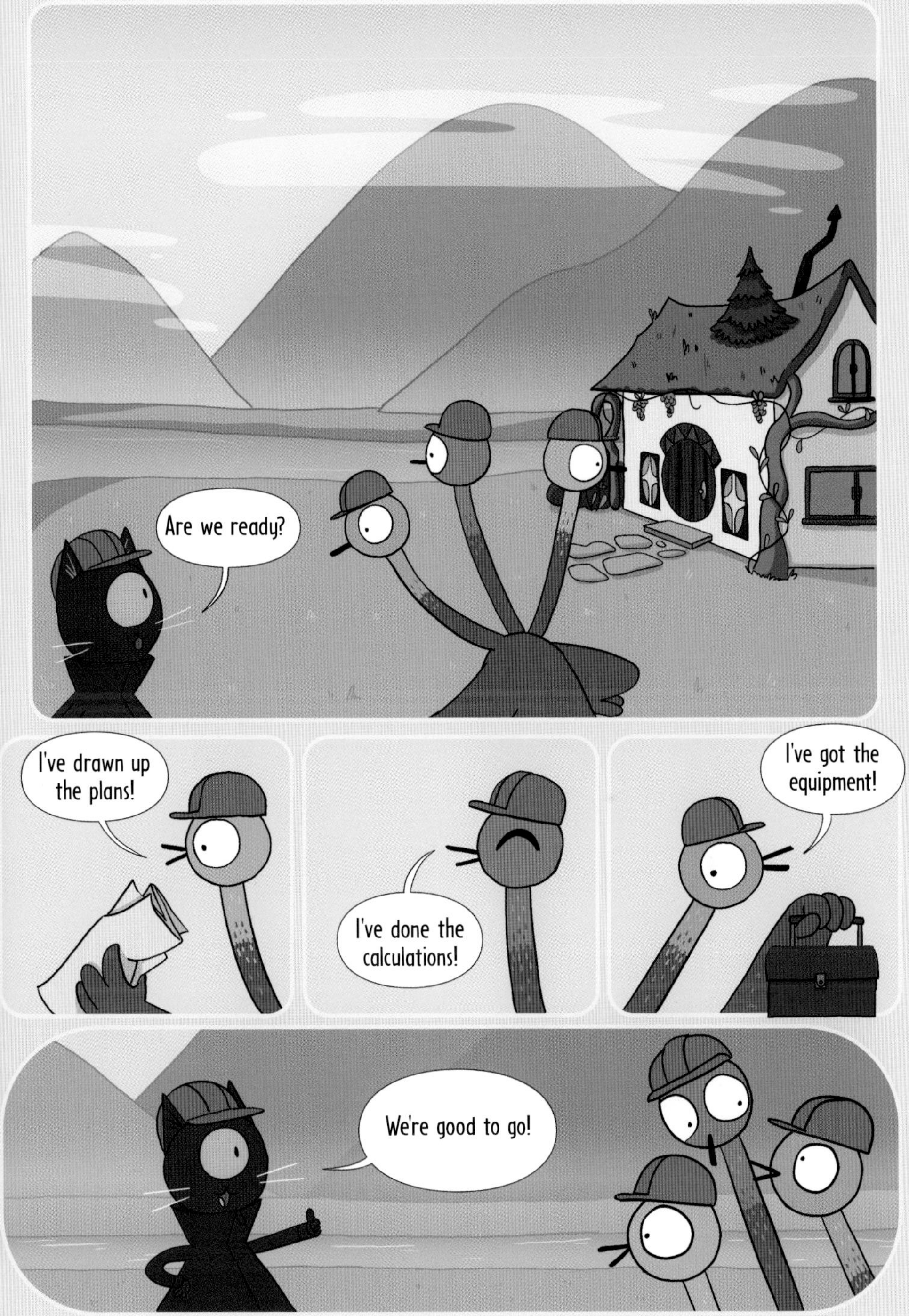
Are we ready?
I've drawn up the plans!
I've done the calculations!
I've got the equipment!
We're good to go!

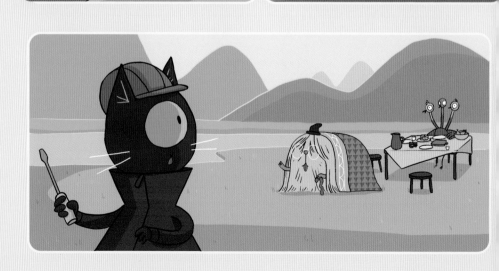

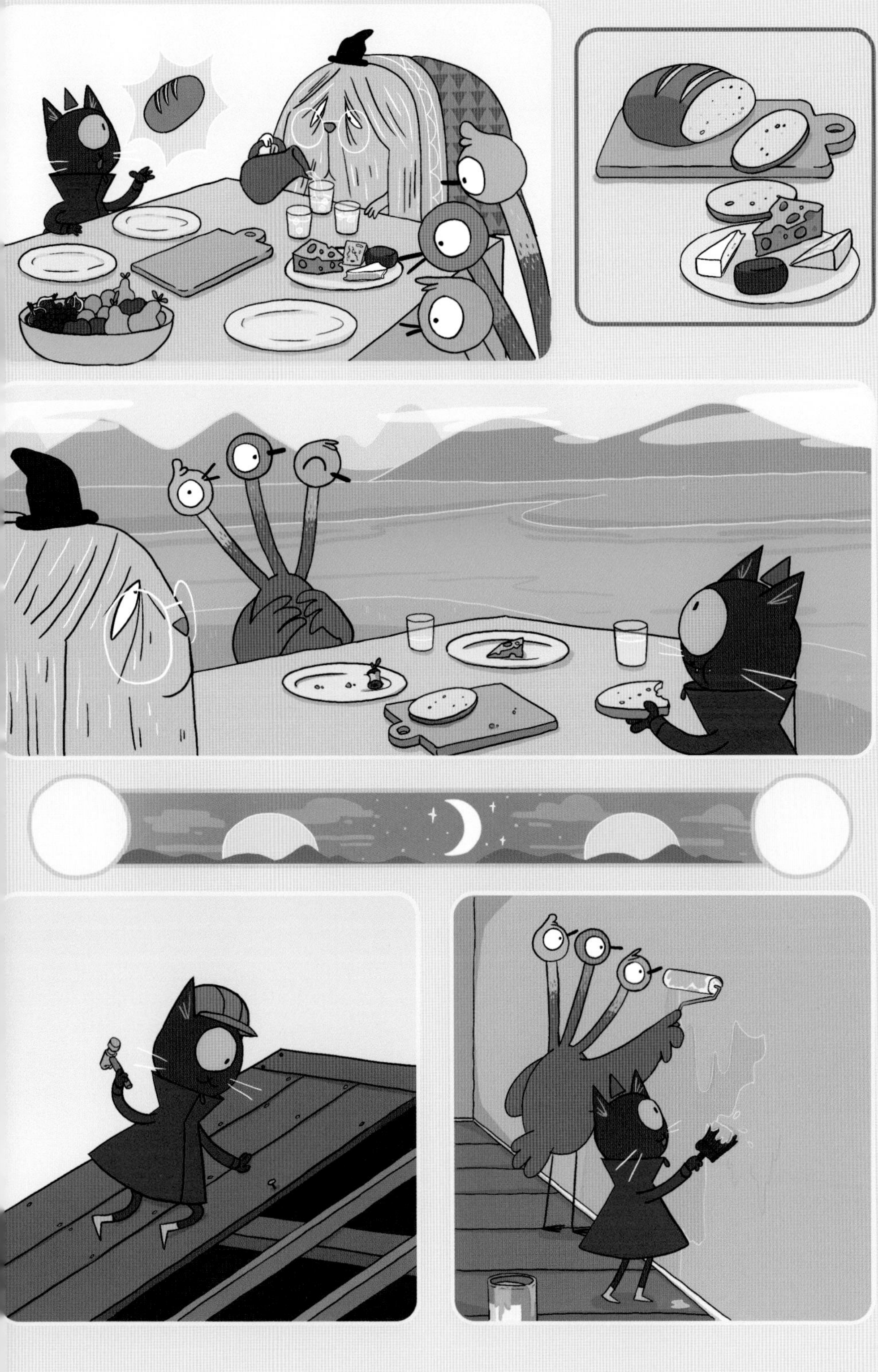

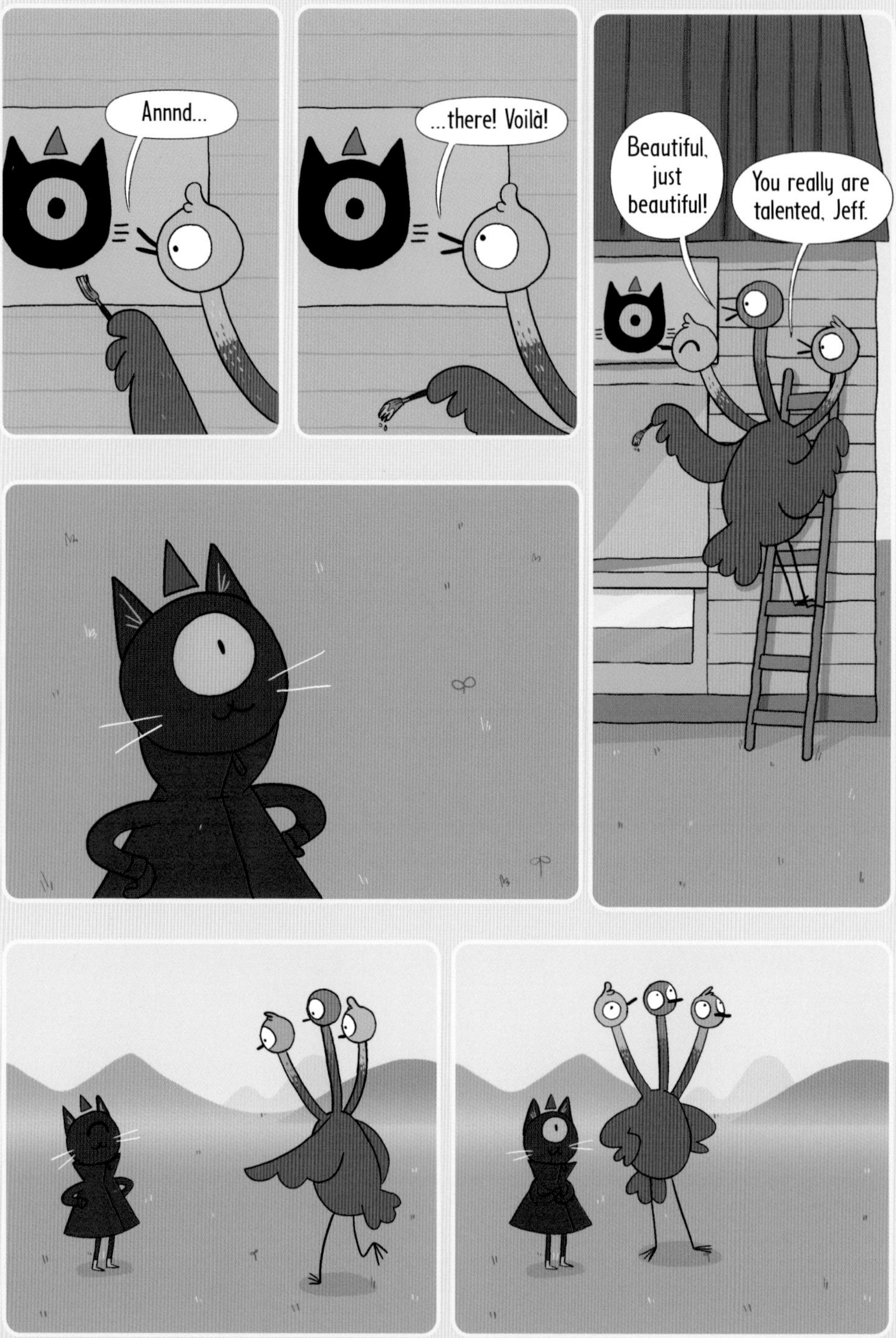
Annnd...
...there! Voilà!
Beautiful, just beautiful!
You really are talented, Jeff.

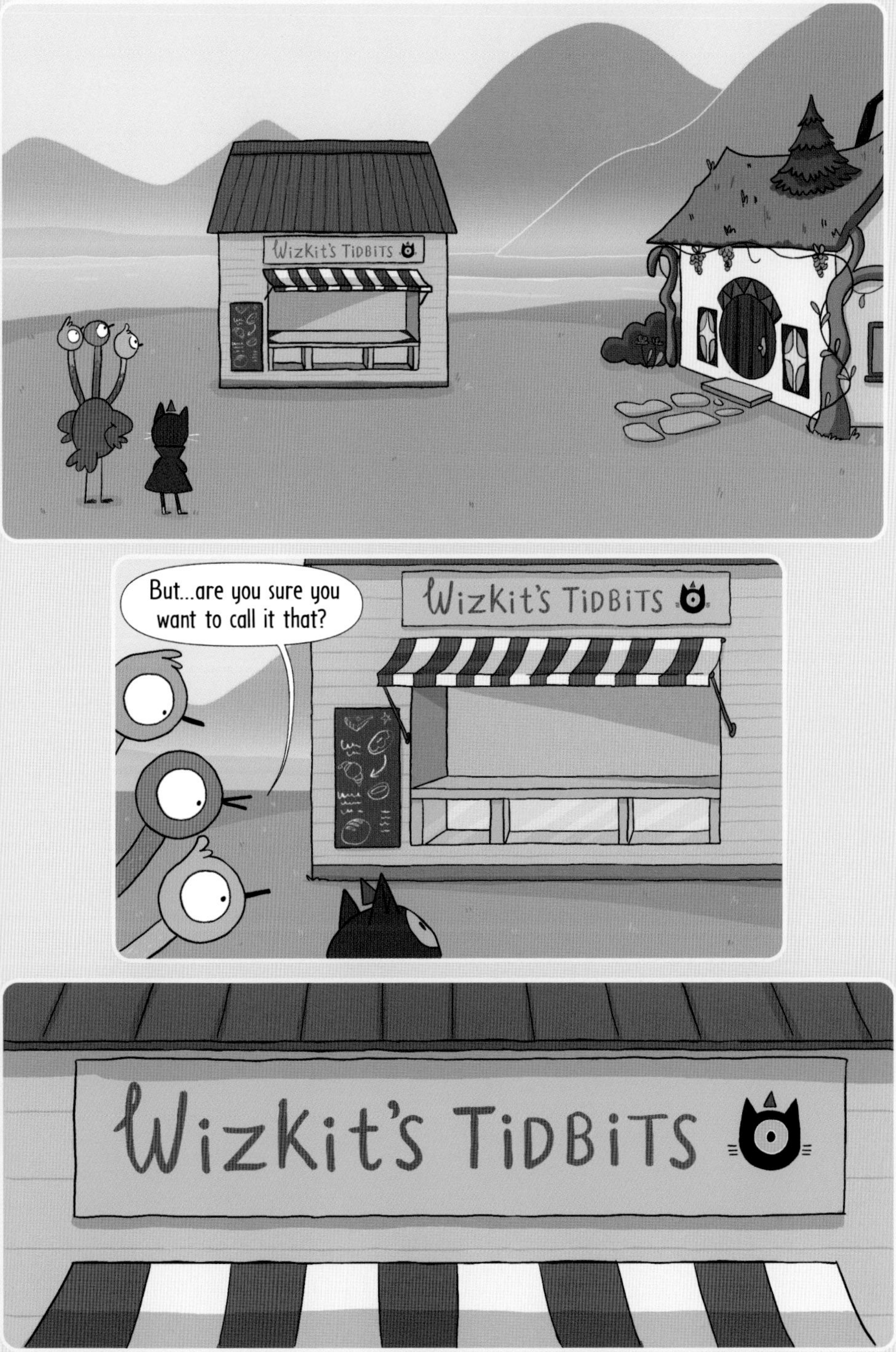
WizKit's TidBits
But...are you sure you want to call it that?
WizKit's TidBits
WizKit's TidBits

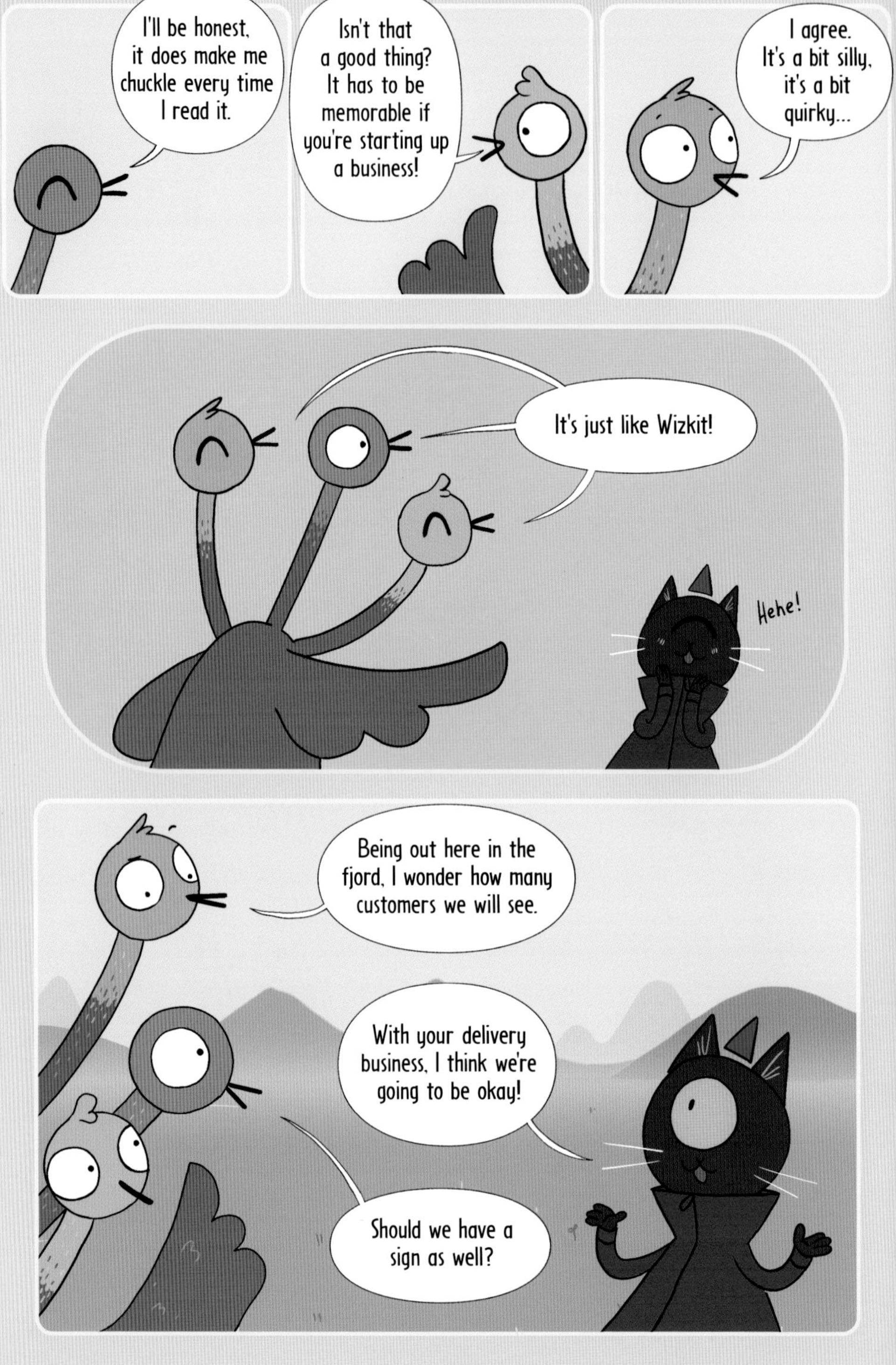
I'll be honest, it does make me chuckle every time I read it.
Isn't that a good thing? It has to be memorable if you're starting up a business!
I agree. It's a bit silly, it's a bit quirky...
It's just like Wizkit!
Hehe!
Being out here in the fjord, I wonder how many customers we will see.
With your delivery business, I think we're going to be okay!
Should we have a sign as well?

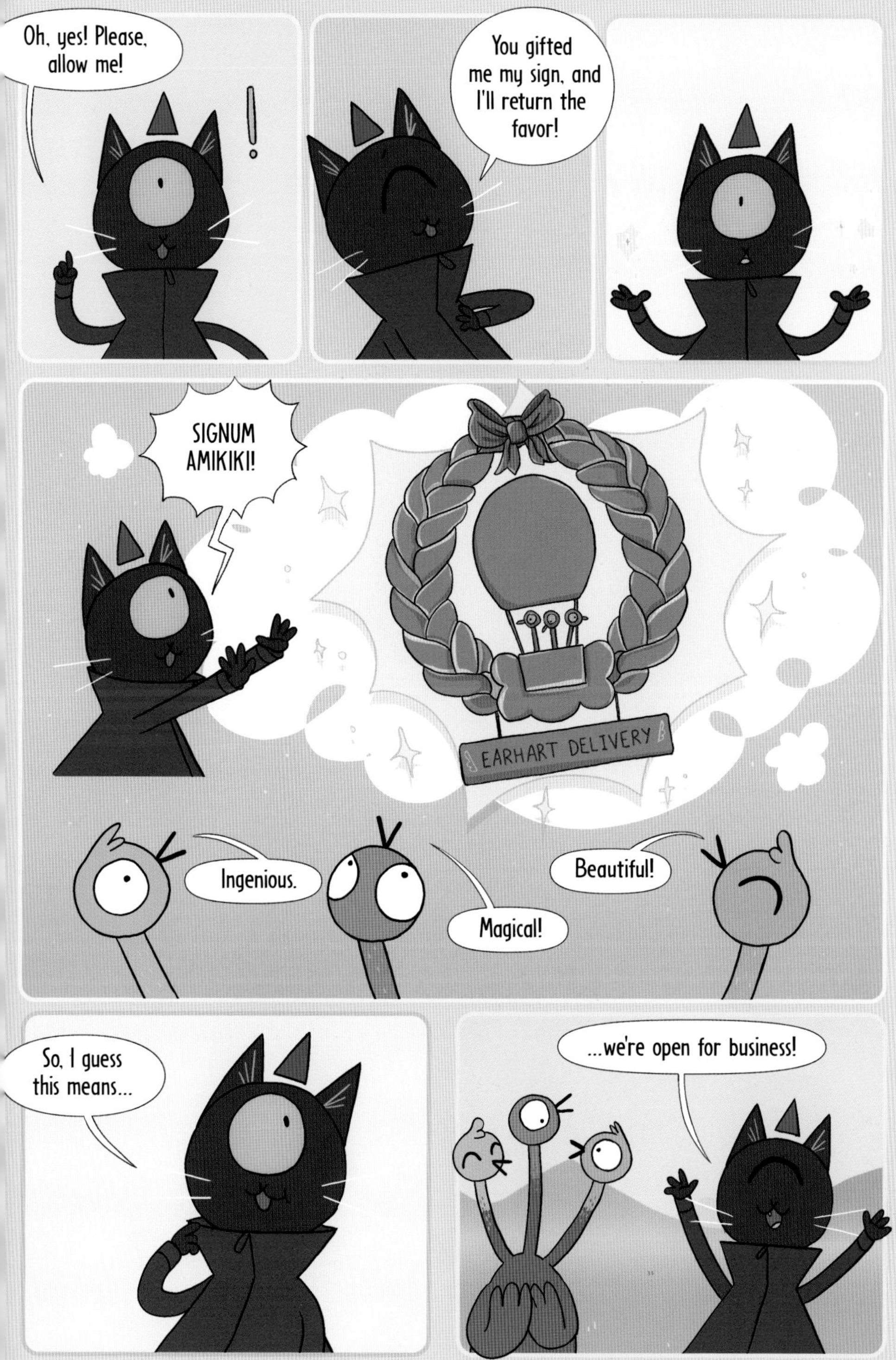
Oh, yes! Please, allow me!
!
You gifted me my sign, and I'll return the favor!
SIGNUM AMIKIKI!
EARHART DELIVERY
Ingenious.
Magical!
Beautiful!
So, I guess this means...
...we're open for business!

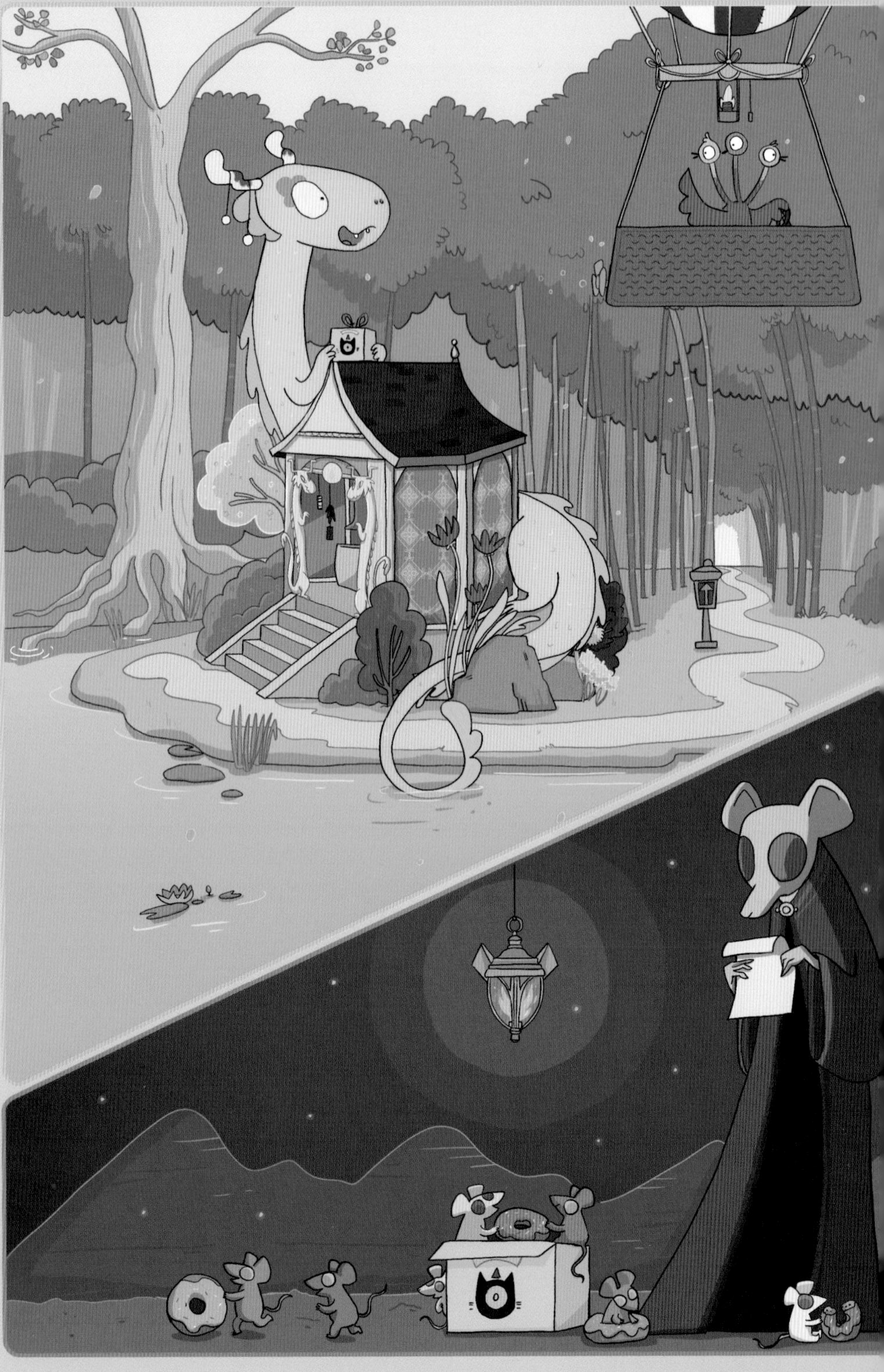

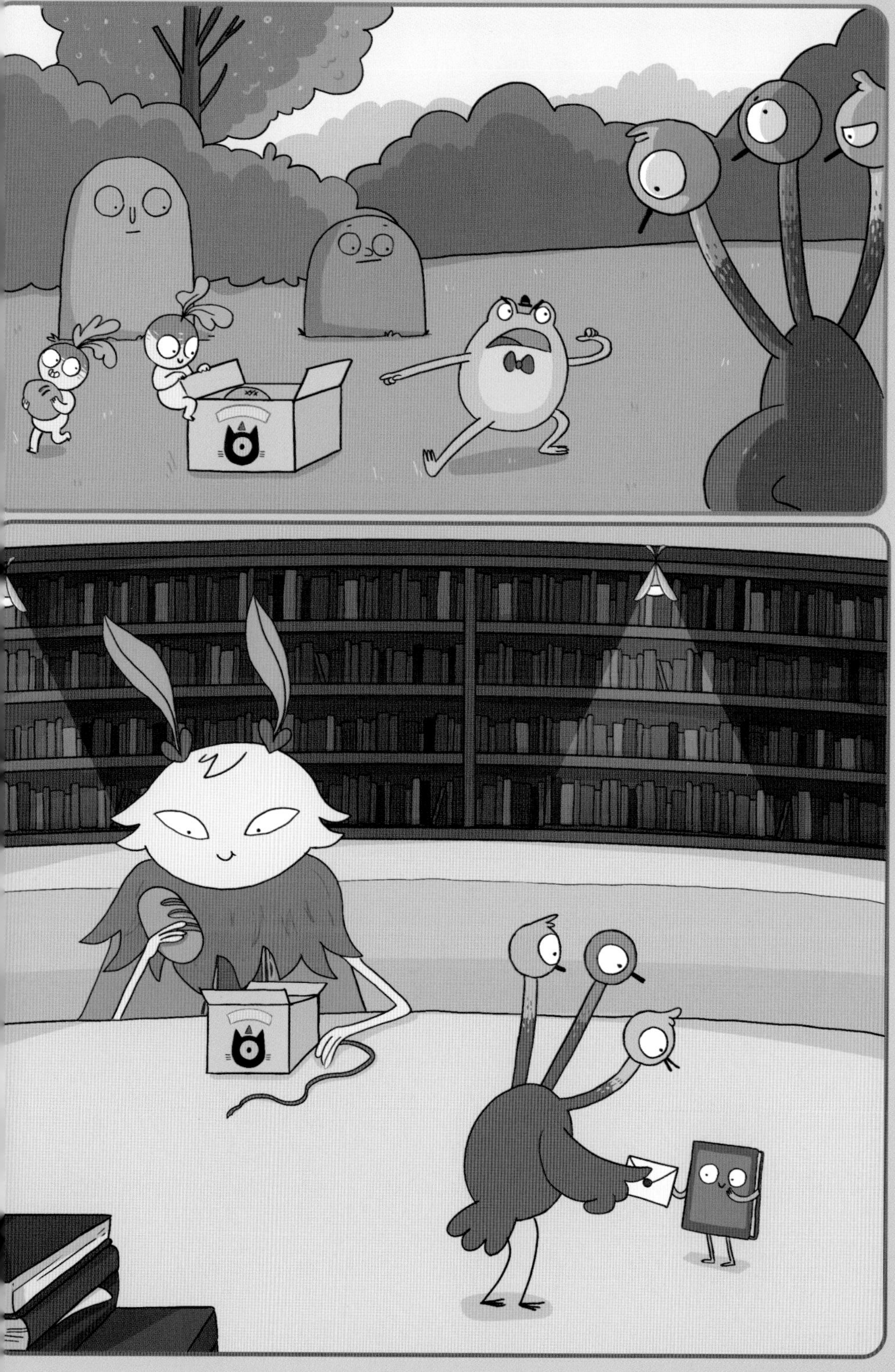

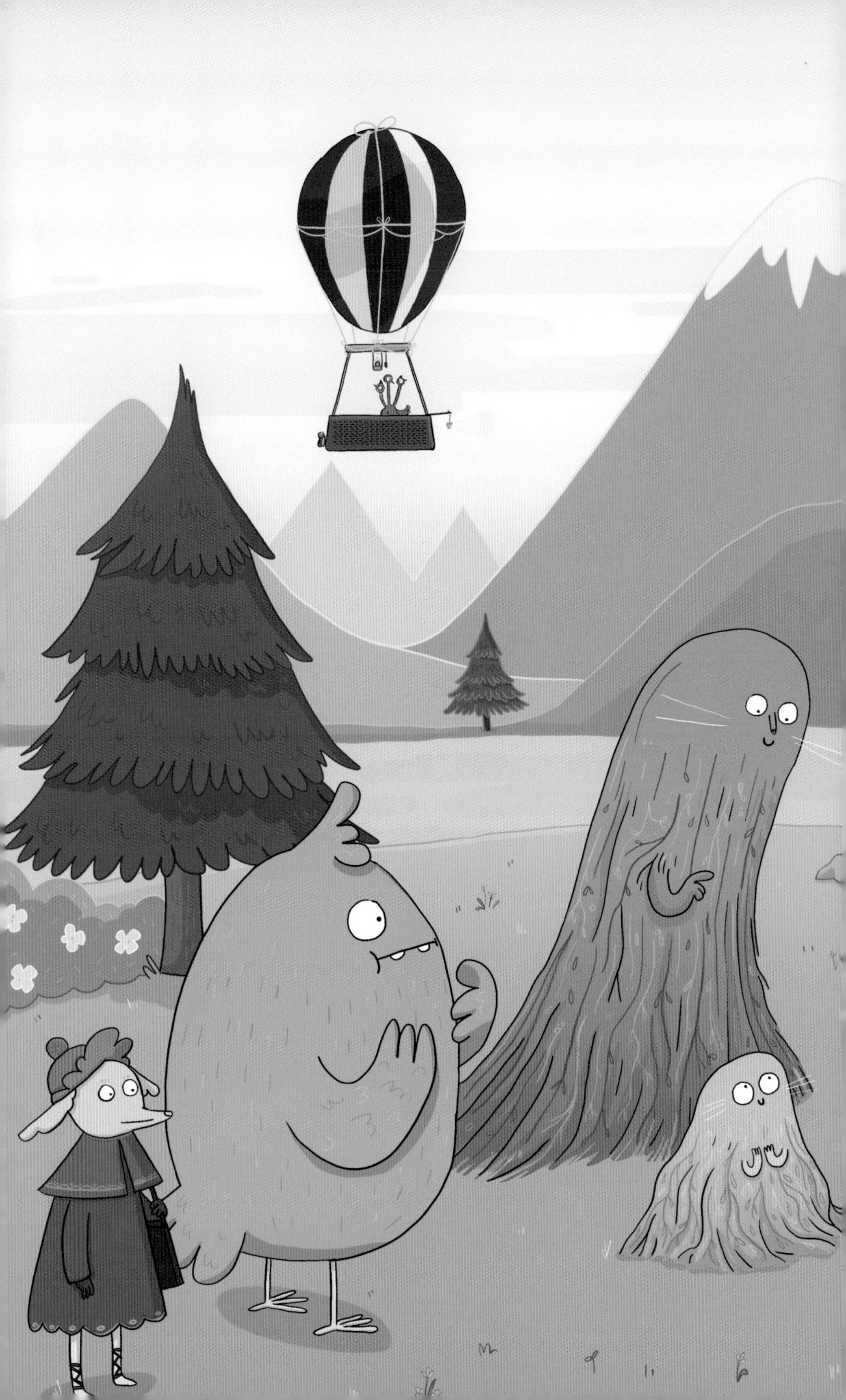

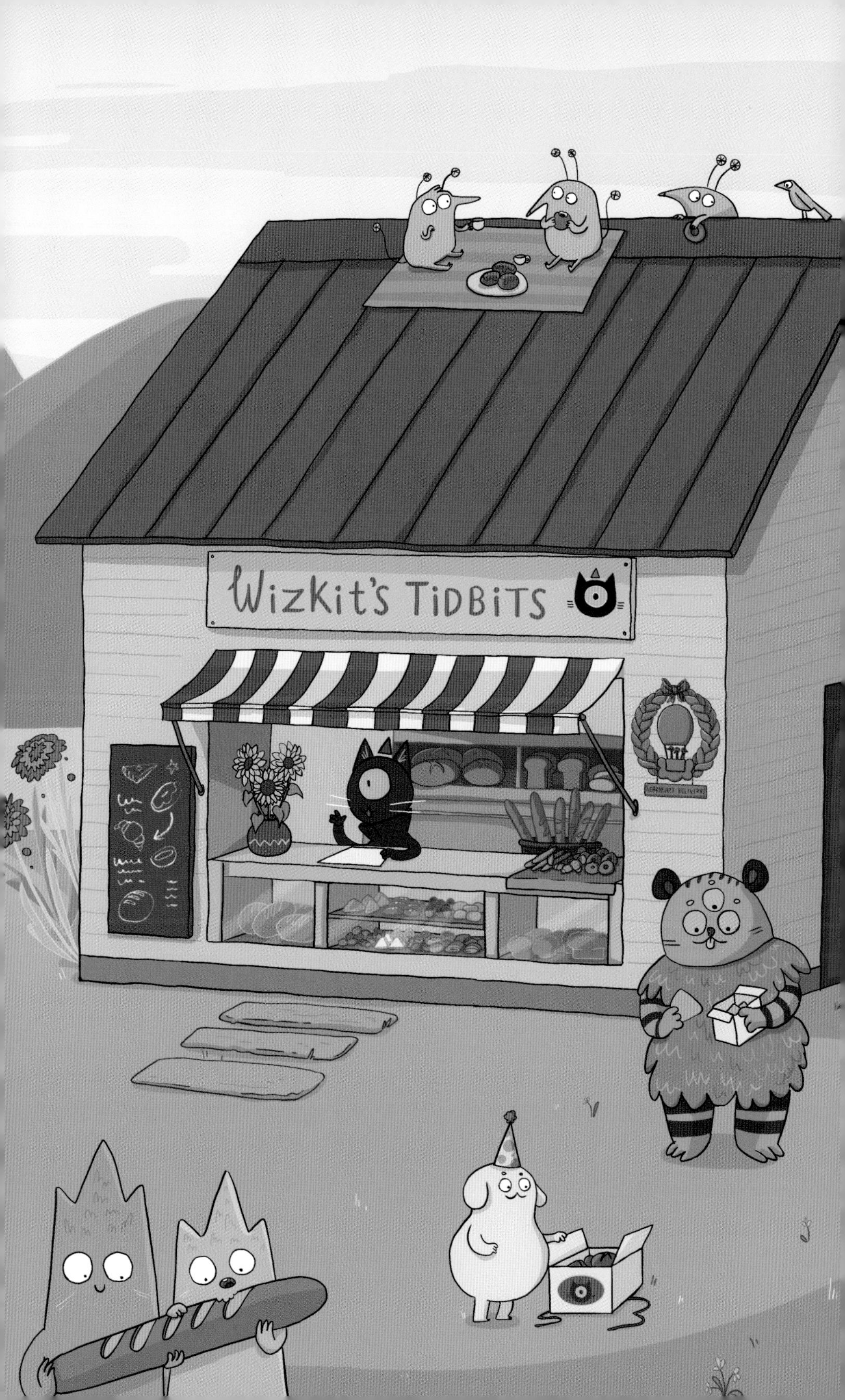
WizKit's TidBits

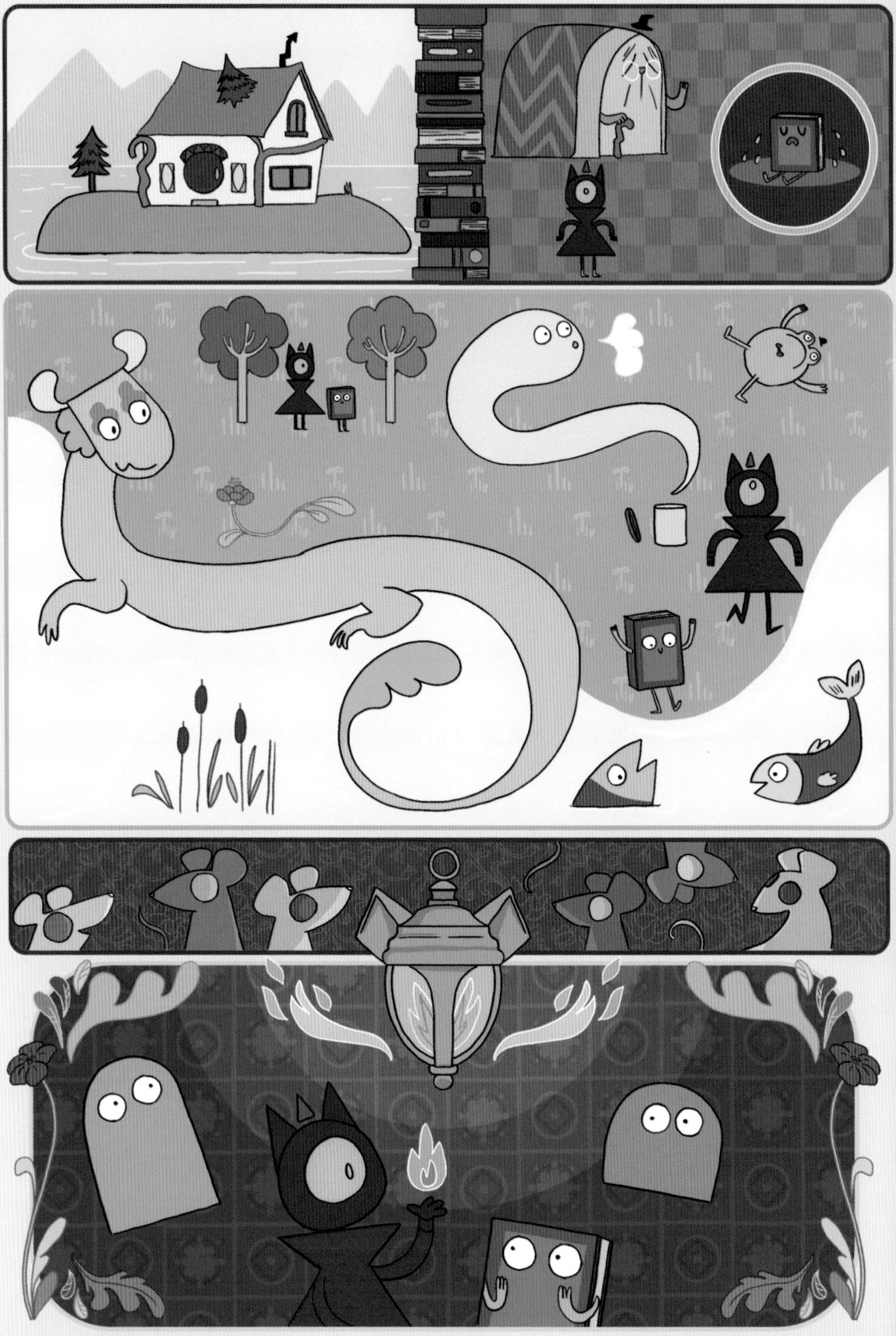

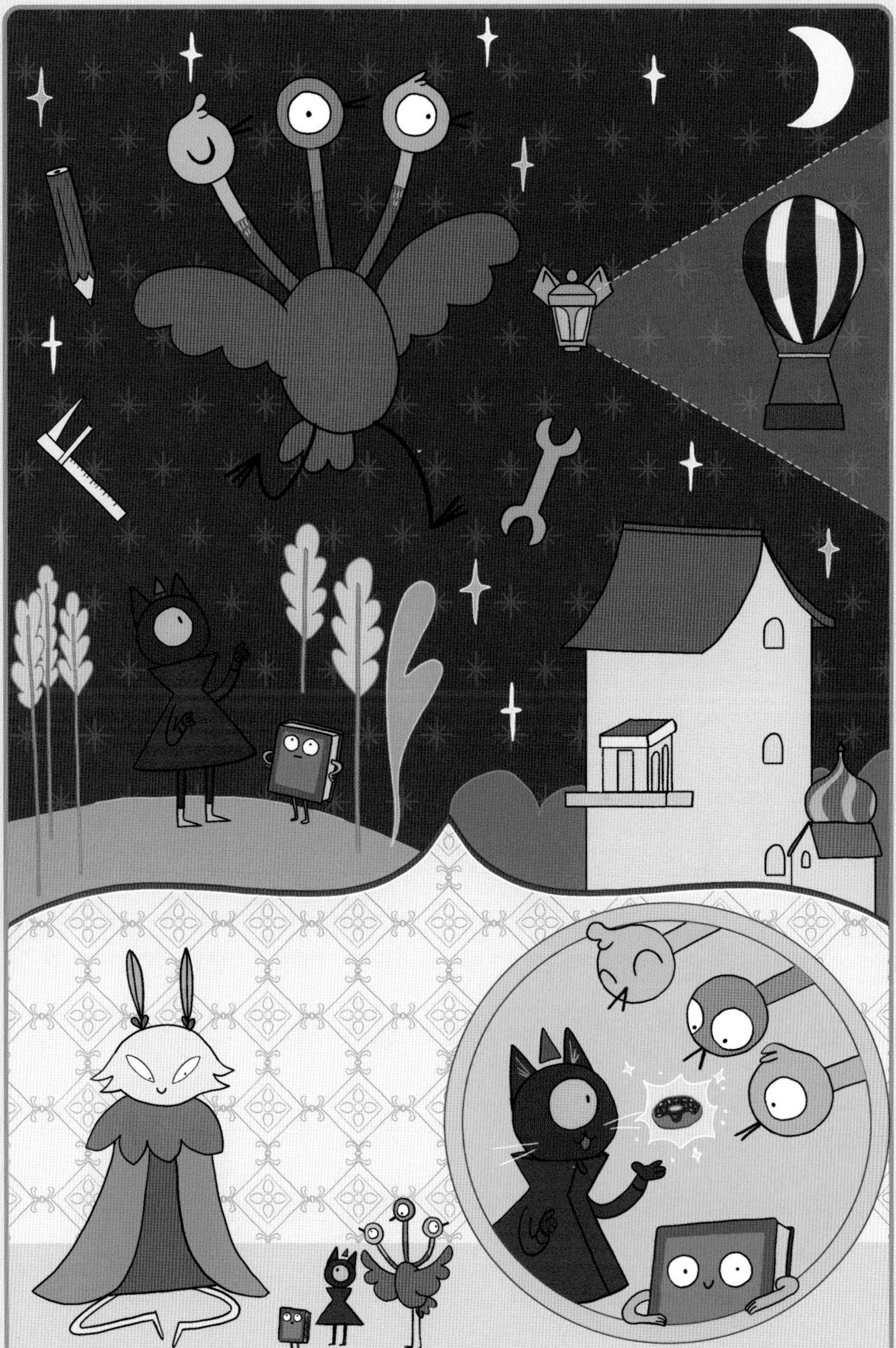

Behind the Scenes!

Some sneak peeks at early Wizkit ideas

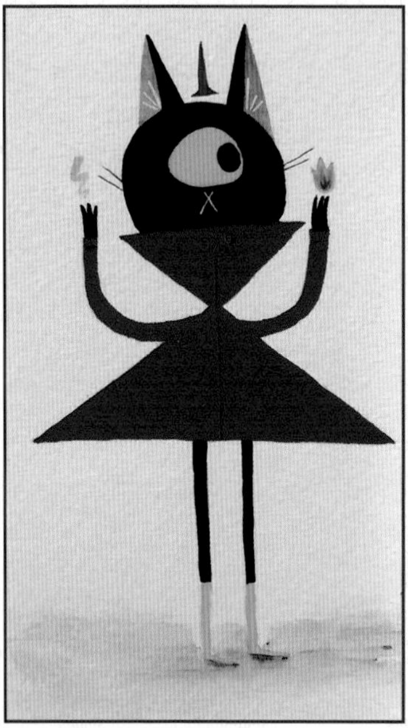

The very first Wizkit!

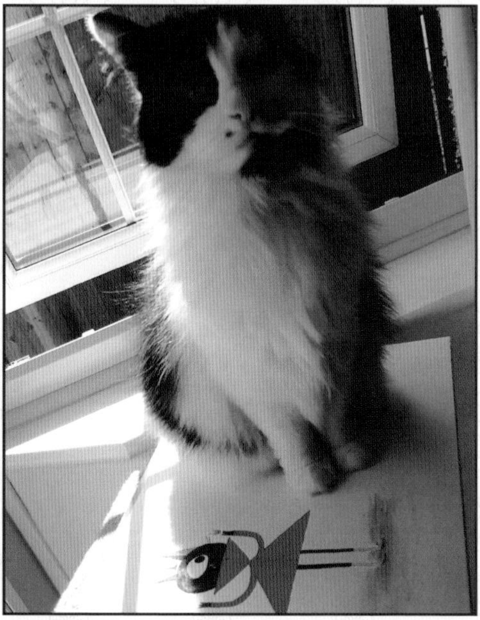

Kalia kitty-approved

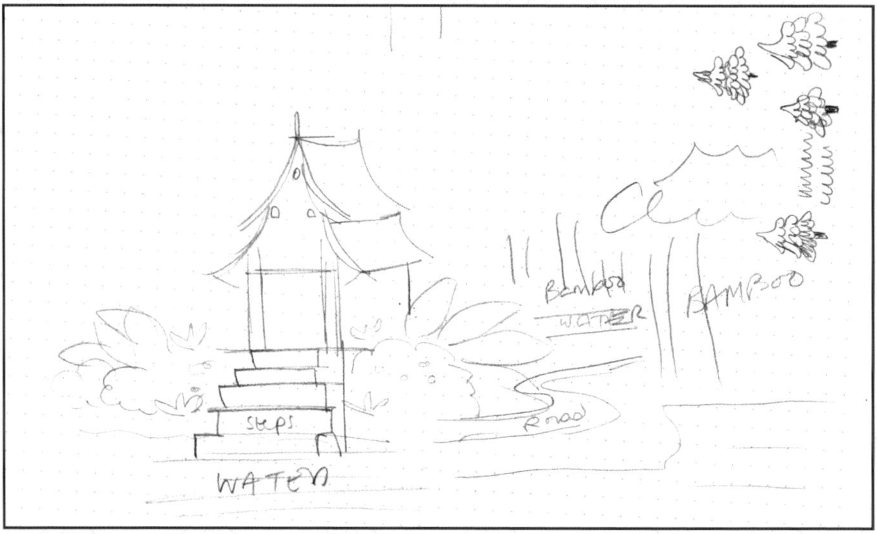
Bamboo
WATER
BAMBOO
steps
Road
WATER

Early Water Temple design

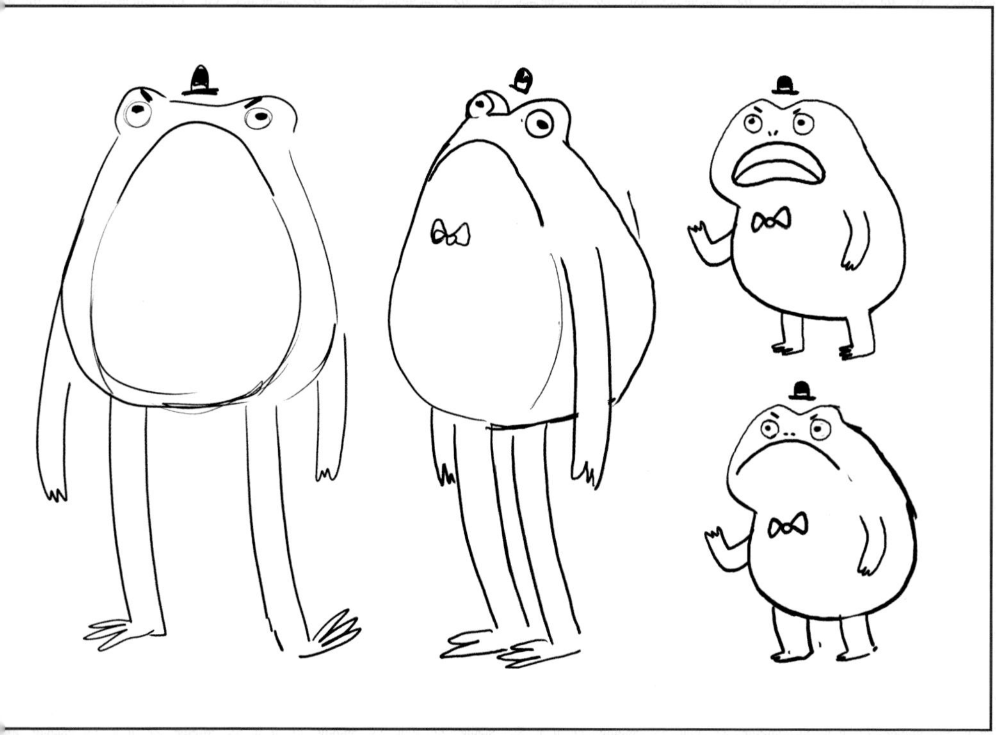

eliminary Frog designs

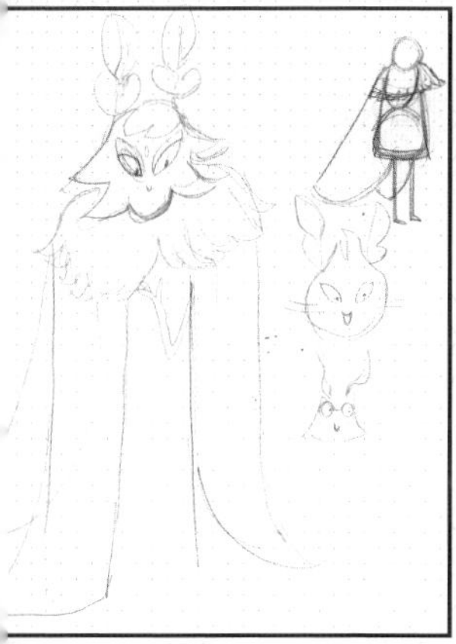

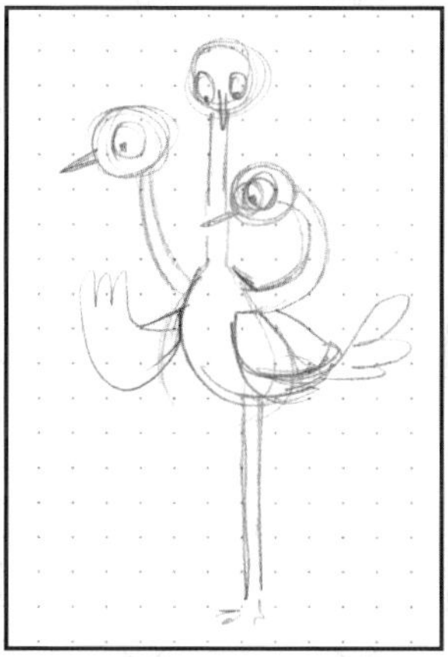

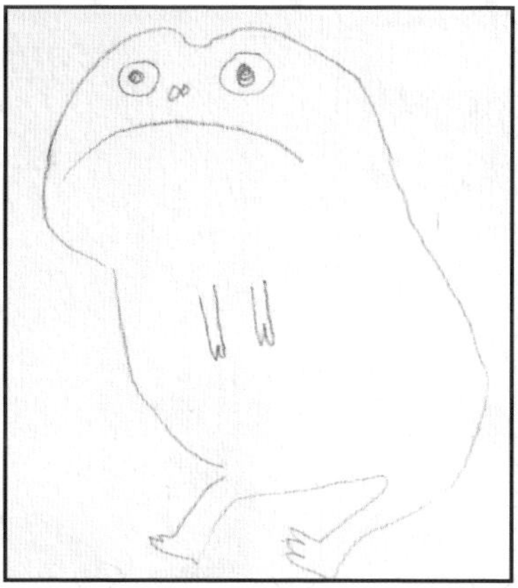

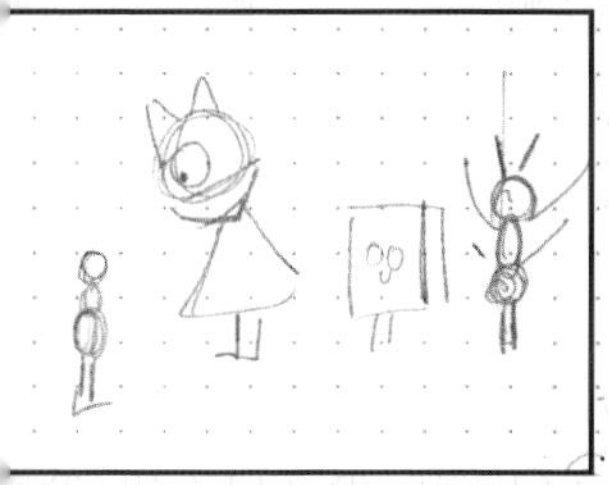

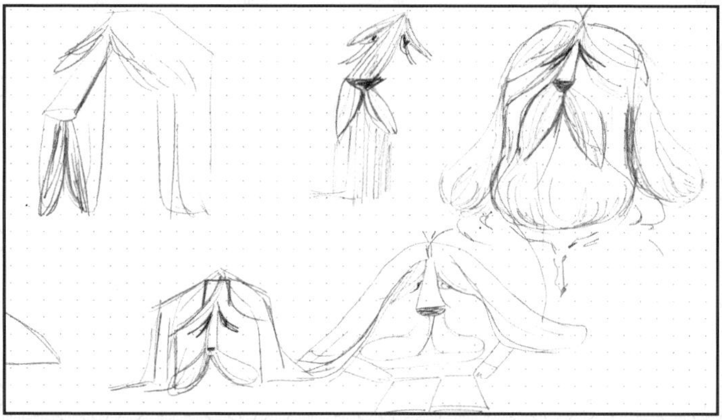

haracter studies

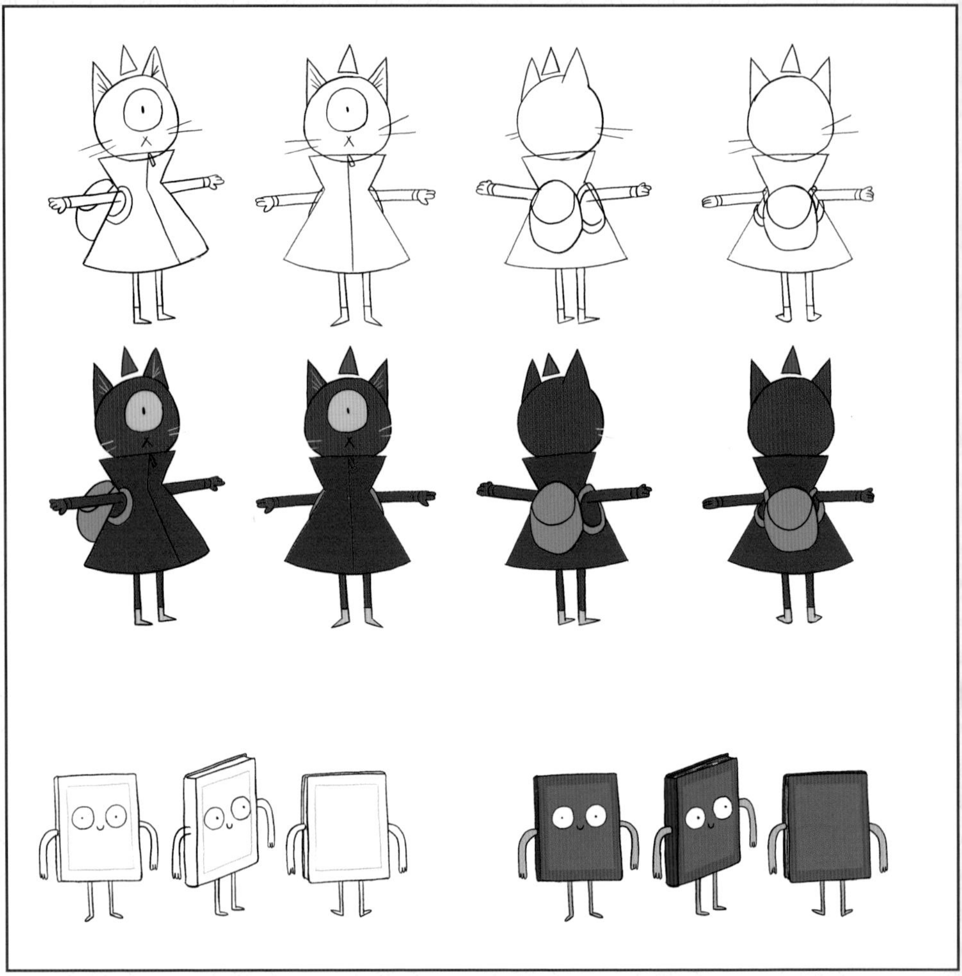

Wizkit and Book turnarounds

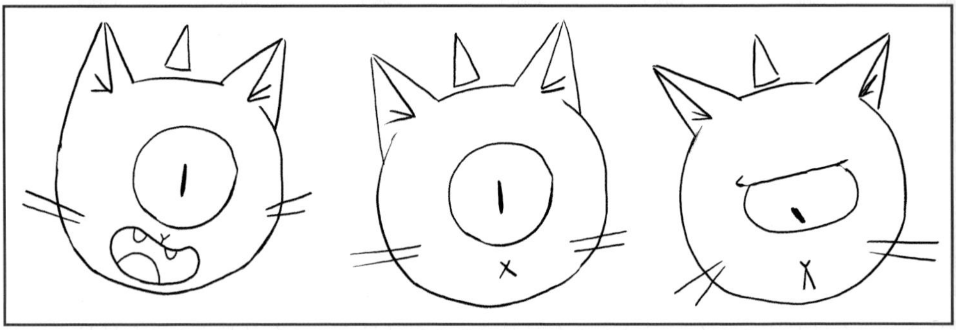

The many expressions of Wizkit

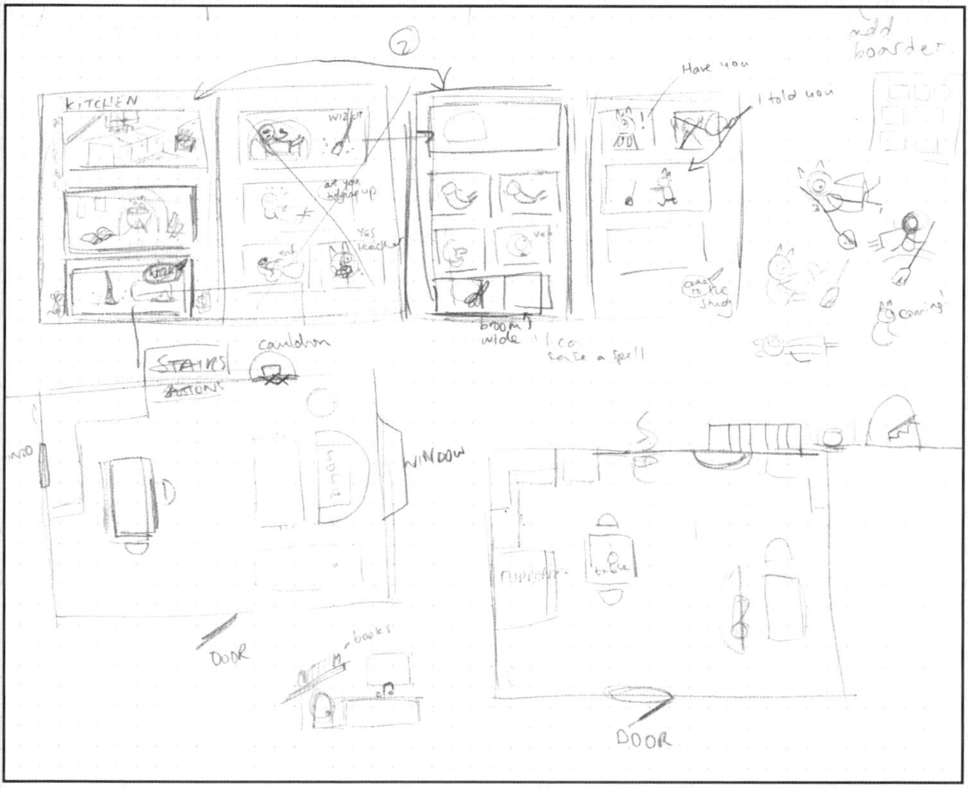
KITCHEN
Have you
I told you
cauldron
STAIRS
WINDOW
DOOR
books
DOOR

Thumbnails and cottage floor plans

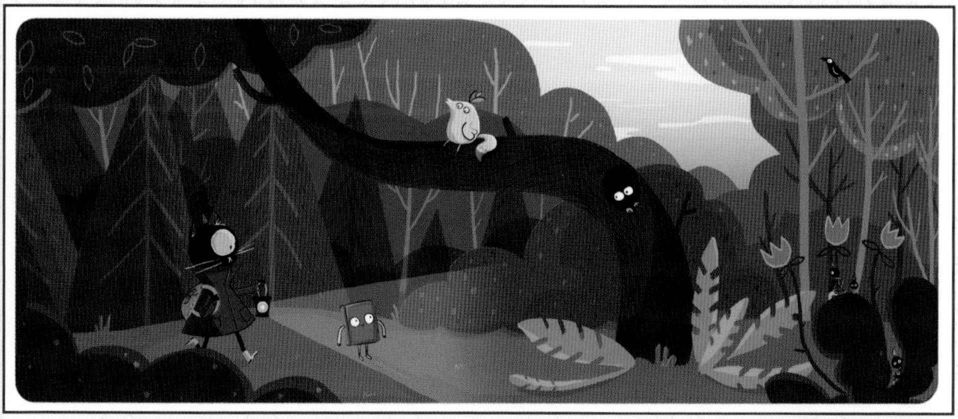

Full-color sample

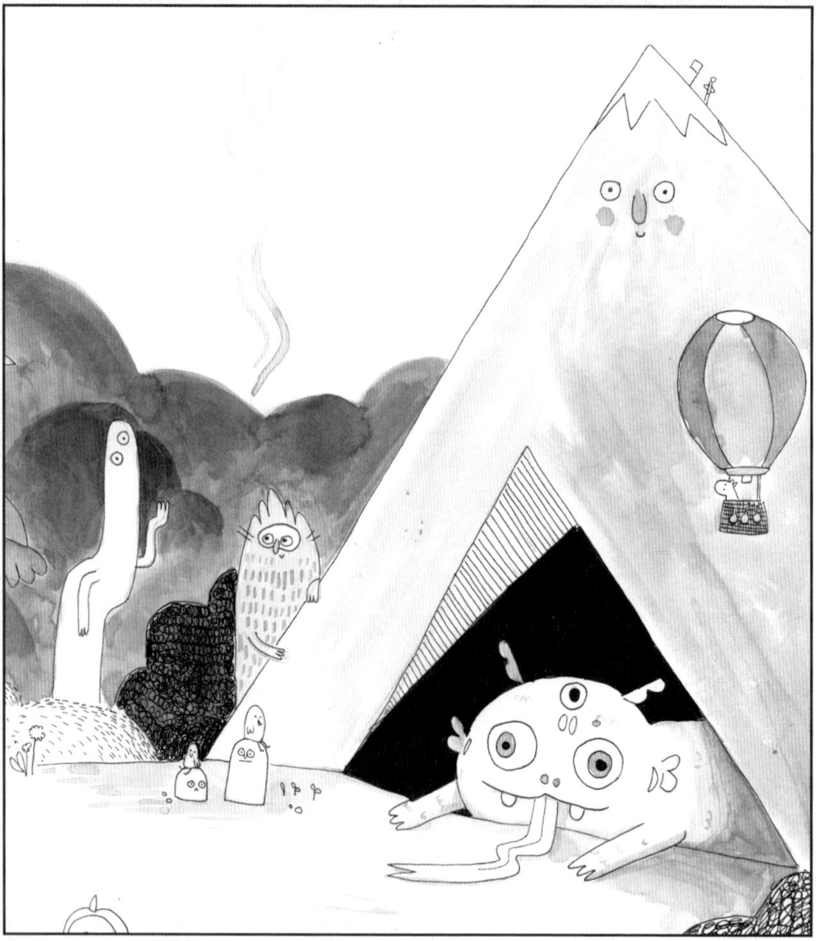

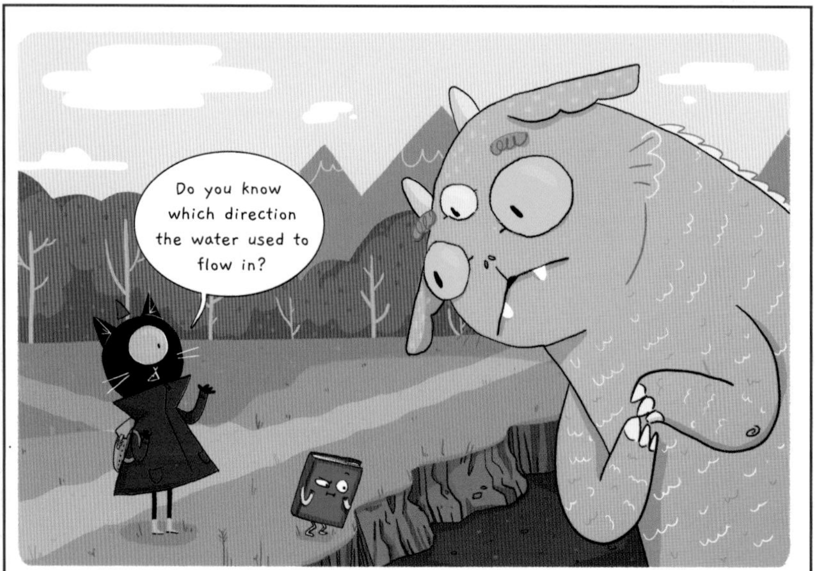
Do you know which direction the water used to flow in?

This and facing page: Character and panel evolutions

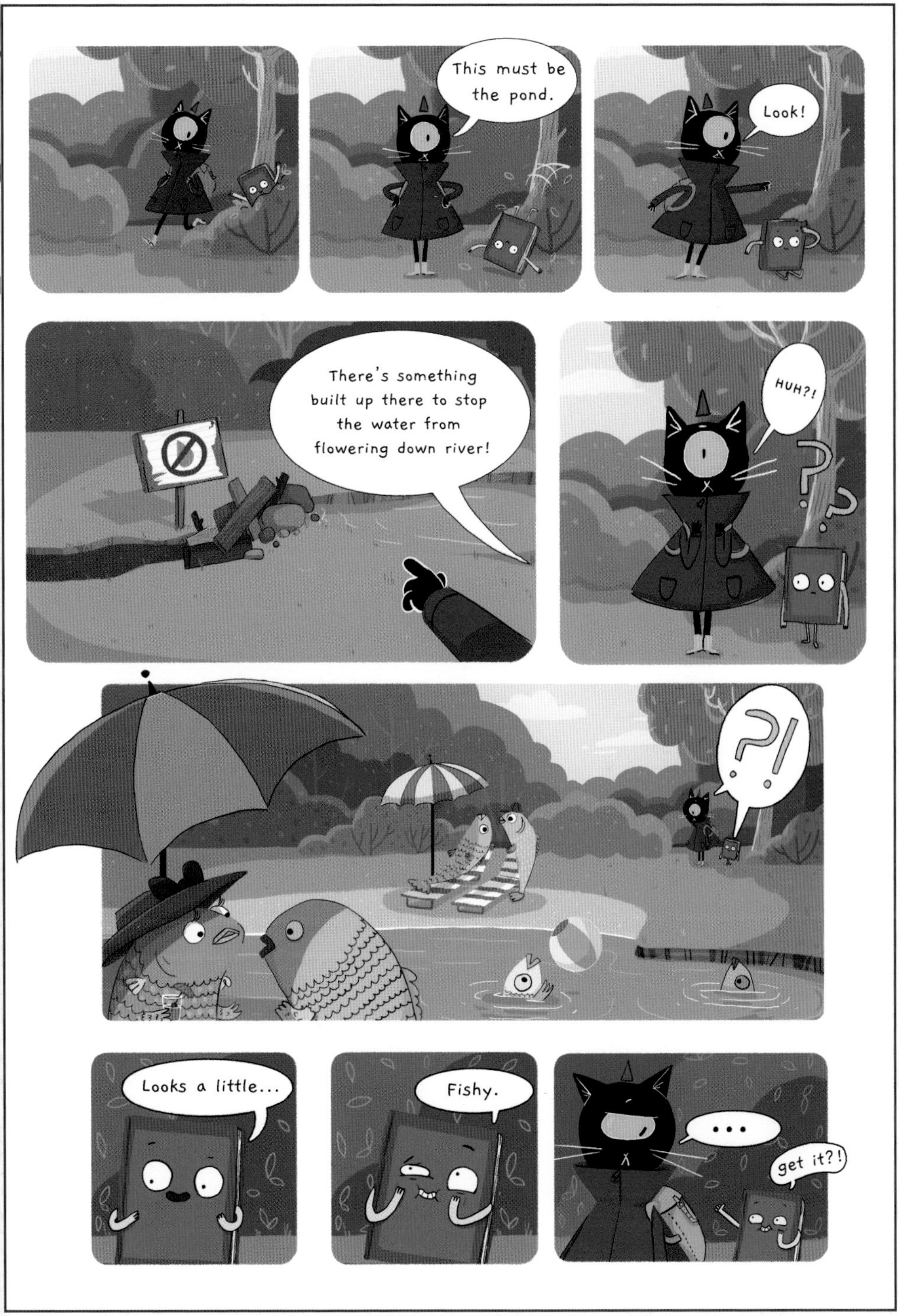
This must be the pond.
Look!
There's something built up there to stop the water from flowering down river!
HUH?!
?!
Looks a little...
Fishy.
...
get it?!